June Fires Burn

LA Robbins

ISBN: 9781805178200

Publisher: Independent Publishing Network

Editing by Tormented Author Services

Editing by Indie Editorial, LLC

Formatting by Indie Editorial, LLC

For anyone who lives for summers and spice, and everything not-so-nice.

Author's Note

Dear Readers,

This is my first attempt at putting on paper a story that's been floating around in my brain for a long time. It has been both difficult and dizzying to write and I'm so grateful you've decided to give Toni and this story a chance.

Before I go further, for my amazing family, I know you want to be supportive, but please turn back. Or I might never be able to look you in the eye again.

For everyone else, welcome to Camp Agonde. This series is set at a fictional summer camp in northern Ontario, Canada. Some places named are real, but many are not, and nothing is as it seems.

With that in mind, please remember that the trigger warnings on this book are not a suggestion. Please take care of yourselves and read responsibly.

Warning: this book contains dub-con, SA (not by any of the MMCs), minor homophobia, disordered eating and references to childhood abuse (of all kinds). If you have any questions pertaining to these warnings please contact me.

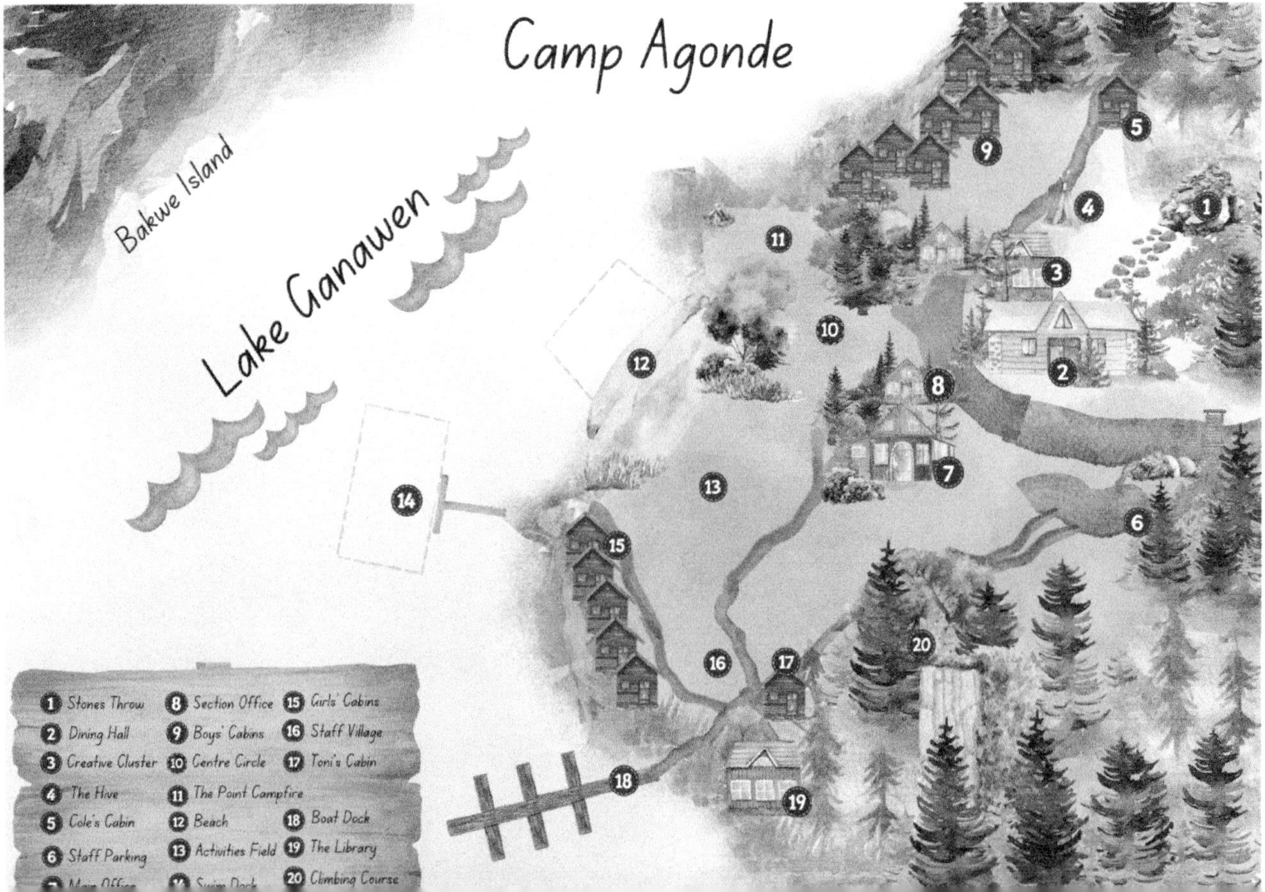

Camp Agonde
Lake Ganawen
Bakwe Island
1 Stones Throw
2 Dining Hall
3 Creative Cluster
4 The Hive
5 Cole's Cabin
6 Staff Parking
8 Section Office
9 Boys' Cabins
10 Centre Circle
11 The Point Campfire
12 Beach
13 Activities Field
15 Girls' Cabins
16 Staff Village
17 Toni's Cabin
18 Boat Dock
19 The Library
20 Climbing Course

PROLOGUE

Five years ago, four kids sat together on a beach at the edge of an icy lake and waited for the sun to rise on a still August morning. As the first rays of light made the new day a reality, they wrote their names in the sand, side by side, and waited. When the edge of the sun finally crossed the horizon, they moved together, each holding onto the other in a crush of teenage bodies, and promised each other next summer. And every summer after that.

Because when you're fifteen, you can't imagine anything different.

Chapter One

Toni

As a kid, I lived for summers. Now, those four months from May to September were just one long stretch of misery. I had been home, back in the worst part of East Barrett, for almost three weeks and things were getting desperate. I needed to find a job. And I needed it yesterday. I had spent the last two summers teaching swimming lessons at the town pool during the day and working nights at Janie's, a diner that sold cheap burgers and even cheaper beer, alongside Mum. But of course, between my luck and the reality of this shitbox town, both had closed for good in February, leaving very few opportunities for employment. Which meant that not only was I scrambling to find work for the next four months, but Mum had also been out of a job for a little while already. Rent didn't pay itself, and groceries didn't exactly leap off the shelves for free. Most summers, it took both of us working as much as humanly possible to keep the bills paid and guarantee that we could keep enough food in our cupboards for three adults to eat at least one solid meal per day. Not that Francis, my twin brother, was any help in that regard.

Antoinette and Francis Hillis. That's who we were now. Hillis as in Hills, as in the City of Barrett Hills, Canada. Between our father's affinity for the French monarchy, pre-revolution, of course, and Mum's creativity, we really were a pair. Not one I wanted to be a part of, especially since I was the only one with a high school diploma, the only one attending college, and the only one of the two of us even attempting to get a paying job. Mum always excused our differences, reminding me over and over, "He struggles." Well, didn't we all?

Most of my afternoon had been a struggle. Five hours spent pounding the pavement, as they say, down Barrett Hills' small Main Street with my resume in hand, begging anyone who'd even look my way for work. I went into every business, every single one, asking about a job. The reactions had been 50/50. Half had taken one look at my resume and sneered. Their facial expressions told me I could get fucked long before the words ever left their mouths. Silently, I told them they could get fucked right back. The other half were sympathetic, with tight eyes and even tighter smiles, as they explained how they could barely afford the staff they already had. I nodded in understanding and asked that they call me if anything changed. None of them would.

Every door that closed behind me was another reminder of how screwed we were, and now that I was finally dragging my ass through the apartment door, all I wanted to do was run into my bedroom and hide. Or maybe turn around and high-tail it to my run-down car and speed my way back to Red Range and its namesake University, better known as RRU. But that wouldn't solve anything. All I'd be doing was wasting gas money. After exams finished in April, my manager Laura had ever-so-gently told me that without the students, they couldn't afford to keep me on as a bartender, but that I "would be welcome to come back in September". So for now, hiding in my tiny bedroom was my best and only option, but that didn't work out either.

"Any luck sweetie?" My mum's voice carried down the faded walls from our kitchen diner to the front door. The false optimism in her high notes made my shoulders droop.

"I don't know, Mum, maybe though," I replied, injecting the same phoney positivity into my own.

"Mr. Granger at the pub sounded fairly optimistic, since I'm legal now and have some bartending experience."

That was a lie. Granger was a creep and had offered me a job, while running his lecherous old hand up and down my arm, on the condition that I, and I quote, "showed my gratitude." I wouldn't take him up on his offer unless things got really, and I mean really, bad. Then again, that was the best offer I'd gotten all day, so there was every chance that tomorrow I'd find myself on my knees showing "my gratitude" to his shrivelled dick for the pathetic tips I'd earn at the Barrett Arms.

Leaving those thoughts aside and my purse at the door, I headed deeper into the apartment. Mum had done her best to make it feel like a home with Walmart-printed photos hung in Dollar-store frames that lined the hallway. They looked like shit, in my opinion, but I'd never say that out loud since it would hurt Mum's feelings, and at least they hid the cigarette stains from the tenants before us.

When I cleared the corner, Mum and Francis were seated together at our secondhand dining room table. Francis had his hands dug into his hairline as he stared down at the open textbook in front of him. He grunted angrily, "I can't fucking do this. This is bullshit."

Beside him, Mum attempted to calm him down by rubbing slow circles on his back as she whispered, "I know it's hard, honey, but you're doing really well." Wrong thing to say. I knew it. She knew it, too, since she winced even as the words came out of her mouth. We both braced for impact.

"I'm not doing well. Are you fucking stupid, Mum? Can't you see this is bullshit?!" he shouted, pushing his chair hard enough that it scraped along the cheap floor. Then he pivoted toward where Mum still sat, his shoulders heaving with rage, as he stared down at her. "This is all your fucking fault. You're useless. No wonder our father wants nothing to do with us." The hitch in his left arm was enough to trigger my frozen body into action. This would end badly unless I stepped in now. The horrible words were out just as my hand reached his shoulder and he hissed, "Stupid whore." My eyes flicked to Mum's, which were already watered down with tears. Francis was the sweetest little kid, but roundabout the time our family fell apart evil replaced all that sweetness.

Knowing I was the only one who could stop this before things got worse, I turned him toward me. "Hey, Fran, you're right. This is bullshit." My voice was mostly even, with just the barest hint of agreement in my tone. His cold brown eyes connected with mine, and he smiled. The anger was still there, and the grin wasn't a happy one, but a twisted ugly thing.

"Okay, Antoinette." It was more sinister than you'd have thought a smile or your own name could be, but it meant I had a shot at controlling this now. I steered him away from Mum, toward the window where I popped the lock and let him grab my hand and drag us both out onto the fire escape. With us both gone, Mum would be able to flee to her room, where I hoped she'd stay until I paid the price of calming Francis back down. Out there on our fire escape, in the cold, spring night, I let my brother take what he needed from me, just like he had done so many times before. His angry fists were his preferred mechanism for control. His grip nearly tearing my hair from my scalp as he pushed me to my knees. The metal would leave track marks and bruises on my shins tomorrow, but those weren't even the worst part of what he'd make me endure. The worst was seeing my own twin brother look down at me and smile gleefully when, inevitably, my tears fell, catching them with the tip of his thumb and telling me, "You're so beautiful when you cry, sister."

Thirty minutes later, shivering uncontrollably, I finally crawled back through the window frame and bee-lined to our small bathroom. A choking pressure pushed at my throat, but I took the extra five seconds to flick on the fan. Its noise and stuttering whirr would be enough to drown out the sounds of what I was about to do. Dropping to my already injured shins over the toilet, I didn't even have to bring my fingers to my mouth, like I normally would, before vomiting into the porcelain bowl that Mum kept so scrupulously clean. Once the contents of my stomach were flushed away, they took the last of my energy with them, and it was with effort that I pushed myself to stand over the sink. I white-knuckled the counter's edge for a moment, before nodding to myself in the mirror.

Teeth brushed and face washed, I slipped into my mother's room and crawled into bed with her, like a little kid with a nightmare. She had been facing her lone window, but with the soft sound of my footsteps, she rolled toward me. We lay there, facing one another in silence for a few seconds, before I let the words drip out in a whisper, "We should drop him at Dad's doorstep and run."

Despite a quick dip of her chin, her sad grey eyes met mine. "No, Toni, I wouldn't do that to you, and I won't do it to your brother, either." I sighed, knowing that was a decision made long ago. It wasn't like this was the first time we'd had this conversation, so I already knew where she stood. Then again, sometimes, you know the car crash is inevitable, but you can't help screaming all the same.

"Okay, Mum. I'm just worried about you. He's dangerous, and I think it's getting worse." How could I explain that I didn't think, I knew, it was getting worse? Answer: I couldn't. Not without repeating history or offering my mother some details I knew she wasn't ready to hear. Not when she rolled away from me to face the window again. I should have just shut up, but I had to say something. I had to ask, "What happens when I'm not here to stop him?" Her silence was answer enough.

I lay there beside her for a while, until eventually, her breath smoothed out and I knew Mum was asleep. I tip-toed to the door and pressed my ear to its hollow centre, listening for any sounds of my sibling in the hall. When I was finally confident he wasn't prowling the two feet that separated my bedroom from his, I slipped out and into my room. Not bothering to turn on the lights, I stripped in the dark and pulled on a pair of ratty pjs that I'd left lying at the end of the bed that morning. They had once been a nice satin pair, but they'd seen better days now. Leaning back onto my bed, I smoothed the worn fabric of the tank top down over my belly before pulling the covers up to shield my body as much as possible. It wasn't enough. I still felt uneasy and exposed, even as I pulled the comforter closer under my chin. There was only one thing that would help me finally find sleep tonight, but even as I reached between the wall and my mattress to the corner where I kept all the things I knew needed to be hidden, I chided myself for relying on its security yet again. Tugging the faded navy sweatshirt over my head, my fingers traced the familiar lines of the embroidered Camp Agonde logo over and over again. After five years and countless washes, the fabric was thin and the smell of them was gone, but it still felt like the battle armour I needed to make it through to tomorrow.

Chapter Two

Toni

No matter how long we lived in this apartment, every morning, I woke up kicking away my scratchy sheets in a semi-panic. At least when I was away at school, I lived alone, so no one was there to hear me freak out as I tried to scramble out of bed. Here, I had to stifle the screams and remind myself of all the good and all the bad of my reality. Some time during the night, I had ripped my comforting camp sweatshirt off and shoved it back into its hiding spot. I double-checked to make sure it wasn't visible if, and when, my brother inevitably came snooping into my room and then rolled over to check the time. 5:00 a.m. on a Saturday. Most places in Barrett Hill wouldn't open for another five hours today, and the Barrett Arms, not until noon, so I had some time to kill before I sold my soul for the price of a blowjob and a paycheck.

Instead of going back to sleep, like I probably should have, I sat up and stared down at my lap. The legs of my pyjamas were wearing through, and I could practically see my pale skin beneath the fabric. It wasn't like I could afford to be picky about what I slept in, and I certainly hadn't thought about it last night, but these were haunted pjs. Very few teenagers sleep in designer, satin, feather-edged clothing, but I always had. When I was little, my father had explained to me that I was his “princess” and that ‘princesses wear pretty clothes, even to sleep.’ And so, I accepted every box, wore every soft silk nightgown, and every beautiful outfit my father bought for me—sleepwear or otherwise—including this set. Until one October morning, back in the big house, when I’d woken up—funnily enough, in this exact pair of pyjamas—to a crashing sound against my wall. In contrast to my sad single bed now, back then, my four-poster was topped with pillows and the softest pink and yellow feather duvet. When I ran out onto the upstairs landing, I looked down at my parents standing on opposite ends of our foyer. Father’s face was a snarl while Mum stood near the front door, fists clenched at her sides and a closed expression on her face. I watched in silence as Dad launched one of the laptops, I suspected the one from his office, in her direction.

“You bitch! I know what you did,” he yelled as the laptop crunched against the wall and its pieces fell to the floor.

“You can threaten me all you want, Franklin, but now I know who you are and what you’ve done, so, we. Are. Leaving.” I had been so proud of her in that moment, and even more so seconds after, when she looked up at me and said, “Toni, darling, go get your brother and please have Martina help you pack a bag. We’ll be leaving here as soon as you’re ready.” At the age of fifteen, I had no choice but to ignore my regret that my brother was coming too, and had done as she directed.

The next day, while Francis and I were at school, the news broke of our parents' split. Social media and every internet gossip blog accused my mum of having an affair. They claimed my father had kicked my mother out, and she had stolen us from him. They painted her as some sort of scarlet woman and kidnapper who'd stolen a good man's children. All that day, and hell, for the next weeks, months, and years after that, anytime I wasn't in class, girls cornered me in the halls, calling my mother ugly names and demanding that I choose my father over her because she was a - insert awful slur here -, but I could never. I was too busy counting my blessings she had taken us with her. And I stayed thankful, even when we couldn't afford the hotel suite anymore and had to move to this shitty building, even when the judge ruled in my father's favour nullifying his alimony payments on the basis that my mum had violated their prenup by cheating, and even when I got my early acceptance to RRU, there was no more Barrett money to cover my tuition payments. By then we had moved. Packed up and left our wealthy suburb in West Barrett Hills. Not that we went far. We couldn't afford to. So, in a run-down apartment in the very worst part of shitty East Barrett, Mum had dropped the Barrett last name and picked up Hillis in its place. That apartment didn't last long, and neither did the four that came after it. Although, they did get progressively worse. But no matter how deep we receded into the slums of our very much divided city, my father always managed to track us down. Until we landed here, with the worst of the worst. Surrounded by destitute widows, drug addicts, and criminals.

By all rights, we should have been fine, since the courts did exactly one thing right. The judge mandated that Franklin pay child support until we turned eighteen. But that would have meant finding us. And when you're Franklin Barrett—billionaire, town namesake, and CEO-owner of Barrett Holdings—people assume you've done everything you can do to find your children. And I fully believe he did. But somehow, by changing our names, throwing out our birth certificates and passports, and hawking every last item that our father ever bought her, Mom had managed to hide us. That meant none of that child support ever made it our way, and all the perks we'd enjoyed as children of one of the wealthiest men in the city evaporated overnight. I managed to find work and scrape by in the same way that other working people did. I got jobs through my last years of high school. I scrimped, saved, and took out crappy student loans, all so I could pay for RRU. Generally, I just worked my ass off and had exactly zero friends and zero fun. But I had the wherewithal to do it. It hadn't been the same for Mum. She married Franklin straight out of high school and had been a stay-at-home mum throughout their marriage. She had no job experience, no references and no friends to fall back on when the divorce ripped her world apart. But she was a great Mum. She never faltered and was always supportive of us, always determined we'd stick together and see it through. Some days, I envied her faith and wanted to fight beside her for it, but others, like this morning, I just wished I was somewhere—anywhere—else.

Shoving those memories to the side, I dug old leggings and a sports bra from my drawer and hoisted them on. Then I shuffled out to the door, grabbed my old running shoes on the way, and slid into the hallway without waking the rest of my family. I waited until I was in the moving elevator to slide the shoes on, breathing out a sigh of relief that I'd escaped without anyone's notice. This is East Barrett after all, so May mornings still had a bite to them, but as I eased into a run along the city streets of our run-down neighbourhood, I felt my first bit of peace in a while. Once I'd built to a steady pace, I sped down the quiet streets, past houses much smaller and much more run-down than the one I'd grown up in on the opposite end of town and made a plan. It was getting close to the end of the month. I knew we had just enough to cover May's rent, and that was it. Once that check cleared, there would be nothing left for our other bills, let alone food. So today, come noon, I would head to that awful pub and give Dale Granger the best head of his motherfucking life in exchange for a job.

When my calf muscles started to cramp, and the shaking in my legs wouldn't go away, I finally slowed to walking speed and made my way back to the apartment. I couldn't be sure, since I had left my phone in my bag last night and hadn't bothered to charge it since, but it felt like I'd been out for hours. The landline was ringing in the kitchen when the door slammed behind me. I reached into my purse, still hung by the door since last night, and grabbed my certainly dead cell phone. I would need to charge it before I went back out on the job hunt. The landline rang again, but was stopped abruptly with a crash of the receiver being hung up.

At the last echo of the bang, Mum yelled for me. “TONI?!” Her voice shrill and panicked. The good mood I’d built during my run was quickly slipping away, and the last of it completely evaporated when I hurried into the kitchen to find her sitting alone with a mug of instant coffee and tear lines on her cheeks. The squeak of my shoes against the vinyl made her look up. “Your father. He found us.” I froze at the end of the hall, scanning the bedrooms for Francis. It was bad enough he had found us, and worse still, if he talked to my brother.

“I tried to stop him, but the phone wouldn’t stop ringing. Francis got angry when I couldn’t make it stop.” Tears streamed down her cheeks. “Your brother picked up on the fifth call.” Fuck. I hustled to my mum’s side, scanning her face for any sign of injury. Francis’ memories of our childhood differed greatly from my own. He remembered the luxury, the ease, the maids and cooks and everything else. It had been nearly five years, but he still blamed Mum entirely, and she let him, content to endure his vitriol and violence. Something I knew was a natural byproduct of our father’s DNA running through his veins. As I scrutinised her face, there were no signs she was hurt beneath the tears, so I thanked God and slid into the chair beside hers. Neither of us said anything for a moment. She sipped her coffee. Its burnt smell wafted my way as she set it down. It was time to find out the damage.

“Mum...where’s—”

“He’s gone, Toni.” She pushed her mug away and let her head fall into her hands as she started to cry in earnest. “Your father sent a car twenty minutes ago.”

Fuck. *Fuckity-fuck-fuck-fuck*. I might be relieved Francis was gone, but Mum was clearly devastated. It also meant we'd be running again. It was hard to imagine somewhere worse than where we already were, but hiding from Franklin Barrett meant sacrifice. I left her sobbing alone at the kitchen table while I went to my room to plug in my cell. Mum gave everything to try to get Francis the support she could, therapy, his GED, all of it, and he did nothing but make her life—and mine—hell. She couldn't see it, wouldn't see it, and every time I raised the issue, she just said that I wasn't a parent, and I didn't get it. But I did. I was their peacekeeper, after all. I smoothed out every wrinkle, every argument, and every fit of rage for the low, low price of one piece of my soul.

The second my phone charged enough to turn on, I searched through my call logs, noting the most recent calls and the unfamiliar number that had called at least three times that morning. It was almost certainly my father. He had managed to track down a few of my cell numbers in the past, always on the hunt, but it had been at least a year since that had happened. I'm not sure what possessed me. Anger, I guess, at having to move, again, or the overflowing need to scream at someone who fucking deserved it, maybe both. Either way, I hit the call button twice, redialing the most recent incoming number. When it picked up, I launched immediately into bitch-mode.

"Hey, asshole, congratulations. You finally found me. Too bad I'm not scared of you anymore. You can hunt me 'til you're dead. I'll be sure to make an appearance at the funeral, if only so I can spit on your grave."

There was a small chuckle on the other end, and then a warm familiar voice answered, “Sorry, kiddo, I think you’ve got the wrong asshole.” It was a voice I hadn’t heard in so long, but one I would always recognize. “How are you, Toni?”

Every brain cell I had malfunctioned, so the only sound that came out was, “Uhhhhhhhhhh...” followed by a minute of silence, where I prayed he’d hang up. I had no idea why Jack Walker, Director of Camp Agonde, was calling me. He and that camp had been such a big part of my life growing up. I spent every summer there, where he’d encouraged me, supported me, and helped me find my feet each and every July when I’d shown up smaller, more defeated, than when I had left the summer before.

That place, those people, his leadership. All of it had fed a part of my soul that literally starved the other ten months of the year. From the time I was six, I feasted on those summers, knowing that famine was right around the corner when September came and I had to go back to my father’s house. But we hadn’t spoken since the divorce and since Mum couldn’t afford to send me to camp without Dad’s money, apparently there had been no reason for him, or apparently anyone else to reach out. When that first summer came around and there was no call, no contact, not even an email, that was when I had realized it was never about me; it was always about the money. It was about the contributions to a new dining hall, new cabins, a new swim dock or climbing wall—all courtesy of Barrett Holdings.

"Toni?" he repeated. "Toni, are you still there?" I don't know, was I? Why call now, after all this time? My curiosity won out, but that didn't mean I had to be nice about it.

"I'm here. Jack," I answered/ "It's been a while. How did you even get this number?" Some of my anger at my father and some of my hurt must have crept through in my voice, because silence hung between us on the line while seconds ticked by. "I'm sorry, Toni. I guess I shouldn't have called." Wrong answer, dickwad.

You should have called, you should have called a long time ago.

"K, well, great talk, then. I'm going to hang up now."

"Wait—" The urgency in his voice made me pause. "I'm in a bit of a bind, and I'm hoping you can help me out."

Oh, hell no! He might not be as big of an asshole as dear old Dad, but Jack Walker was NOT asking me for a favour right now. "Excuse me? You can't be serious?"

"Are your swim quals still up to date?"

Jesus, apparently only he was allowed to ask the questions on this call. They were up to date, though. I kept them up, even though the re-certification courses were way too damn expensive, because teaching kids swim lessons paid well. Like twenty-four bucks an hour, and I wasn't exactly in the financial position to turn that kind of cash down. Apparently, he was done with the awkward silence, though, because instead of waiting for an answer, he just kept going, "Because if they are, I have a job offer for you."

Those magic words unlocked the most practical part of my brain, the part that had been locked up while I let emotional Toni take control, and I finally answered, "They are. I re-certified in November. My quals are valid for another two years."

"Lifeguarding and teaching?"

"Yeppppppp." I let the 'p' drag out like I couldn't be bothered to cut it off.

"In that case, how would you like to be our Waterfront Director this summer?" Thankful he couldn't see my face, my eyes widened in shock. Waterfront Director. If he needed that job filled, he really was in a bind. A lakeside kids' summer camp couldn't exactly operate without someone to manage the waterfront, swim lessons and all the risks that came along with that. But it was May—how exactly did Jack let it get this close to the start of the season without one? Even thinking the question seemed to prompt an explanation.

"The girl I hired back in the fall got a better offer last week. And now I'm—"

"Ah. There it is," I said. "Why me, Jack?" I cut off. "Of all the people you could have asked, why me? Why now?"

"Well..." his reluctance to answer obvious, "you know us, Toni. You're one of us."

"Not anymore, I'm not, not for five years. Try again."

"One of our current staff members suggested your name; they thought you would be interested."

"Who?" It wasn't possible. It couldn't be. I hadn't spoken to anyone from Camp Agonde in five years. Still, the image of three young faces floated through my imagination. But why would they bring me up now?

"How about I tell you if, and when, you accept the job?" There was a slight teasing in his voice now, a confidence that he had me on the hook. How dare he? As if he knew anything about who I was anymore. Sure, five years ago, a taunt like that would have had me rising to the challenge but now… fuck, I was still fighting a fire in my belly that dared me to find out.

I was proud of myself when I managed instead to squeak out a question of my own. "What's the catch?"

"No catch. You would start in a week. The salary's nothing special, but your three meals a day are covered and you'll get forty-eight hours off every couple of weeks."

Every tiny baby bit of my body wanted to tell him to get stuffed right then and there, but again, my stupid practical brain whispered over and over that my only other option was a shitty bartending job where I was likely to be repeatedly sexually harassed by my boss. The two sides of my brain found some middle ground as I heard myself say into the phone, "Email me the job description and the salary, and I'll consider it."

It was Saturday. Two fucking days to think about putting myself through a damn timewarp. "I'll let you know by Tuesday." Ending the call, I could feel the pressure against my throat urging me on as I sprinted across the hall to the toilet.

Afterward, I lay in bed, holding that same old sweatshirt close to my chest as I read through Jack's email. This job was a blessing. It was teaching swimming lessons, and aside from the odd bit of staff training, it guaranteed a warm bed, hot meals, and freedom from my own personal hell in the four walls of this apartment. But it also meant having to come face-to-face with my past; I wasn't sure I was ready for that. The noon deadline I had given myself to get down to the Barrett Arms came and went, and it was well into the evening when I made my way out to the living room. Since we couldn't afford any of the fancy streaming services, Mum had fallen asleep on our lumpy couch to the dulcet tones of mainstream news. There were no other sounds anywhere, so I was pretty confident Francis was still gone. Knowing our father, he would stay that way until one or both of them came back for me. I was surprised it hadn't happened already. And it was yet another reason to accept Jack's offer.

I lifted Mum's knees and tucked myself down on the sofa beside her. The movement was enough to make her stir from her shallow sleep and give me a soft smile in greeting.

Not sure how to break the news to her, I simply blurted, "Jack called me today."

Confused, she answered, "Jack?"

"Jack. Jack Walker. As in Camp Agonde Jack Walker." That made her eyes open wide.

"Oh! That Jack Walker. That's been a long time." I snorted. That was a diplomatic way of putting it. "What did he want?" She asked.

"He offered me a job, Mum. A good job." The fear I had been wrestling with all day ached to be shared out loud. To be screamed, actually. I knew my mum was scared. For herself, for my brother, for all of us, and knowing all of that, a better person would have kept the next words to themselves. But not me. My fears ached to be shouted out loud, to be made real to someone who would care and comfort and take them all away. Wasn't that what parents did for their children? Soothed them? Mum would try. I knew that. If I said anything, she would put on a brave face, tell me to follow my heart and that she'd be proud of me no matter what choice I made. But, not to beat a dead horse or anything, pride doesn't pay. So all I said was, "I think I should take it, but I don't want to leave you alone. I'm worried about you."

She sat up, fully awake now. "No, sweetie, it's not your job to worry about me. If you want to take the job, do it. After all, you always loved it there."

"I'm not sure it will be the same," I replied.

"Why wouldn't it be?" I couldn't answer. I couldn't explain. "You deserve to be happy, Toni, and if you think this would make me happy, then you should do it."

"But what if—"

"No, no what-ifs." Her words cut across mine. Her warm smile and the excited flush of her cheeks said she wanted this for me and she wasn't going to let me stay now knowing this job was an option. I didn't say anything back, just nodded and took myself to bed, while Mum flicked through the channels until she found an old Friends rerun and smiled.

The next day, at 10 a.m., I called Jack's number again. "Okay. I accept."

Chapter Three

Toni

Eight hours of driving, two breaks for gas, and another three so I could pee and get some snacks had me pulling off an empty highway and onto a gravel road that Friday morning. Small pings of stones hit the undercarriage of my already struggling car and I prayed this wasn't the day Betty decided to give up the ghost. Driving head first into my past was one thing; walking into it schlepping all my shit over my shoulder was something entirely different. This drive was one I could have done with my eyes closed, each turn and dip in the road as familiar to me as my reflection in the mirror, so I let myself drift, watching the pines and rivers on either side of the wheel wells. So far away from civilization, from traffic and buildings and urban fucking sprawl; I fought the urge to roll down my windows and scream into the early summer wind. Instead, I grabbed my phone from the coffee holder; and thanks to the after-market Bluetooth stereo I had scrimped for, I turned the delightful sounds of the Preaching Pistols up even louder. I know they broke up ages ago, but ever since their Vegas residency was announced, I had been listening to their old stuff more and more.

Besides, there weren't many punk bands with female lead singers, and Rain Gamble's voice still rocked.

After screaming my lungs out for five minutes and letting all my nerves, anxiety, and fear about today slip away, I was pulled back into the moment instantly when I crested the top of a hill and a large billboard out my passenger window came into view with big bold letters that read: "Welcome to Camp Agonde," and a separate, much smaller sign beneath it read: "Staff parking in 1.2 miles," like they didn't want to draw attention to the fact that staff might have the poor taste to own their vehicles or to ever want to leave this magical paradise they'd built. Well, piss on that. I would do the job, but you could bet that the second I clocked out for my forty-eight hours off, I would be running for Betty faster than you could say 'piece of shit'. Slowing to allow my car a bit of relaxation at the end of our long drive, I took my foot off the pedal as the staff parking lot came into view. I wasn't exactly sure of the protocol, since camp hadn't officially started yet, and it was still another three weeks before kids arrived, but I figured parking out here would guarantee I wasn't doing anything wrong before I even really got started.

Veering the steering wheel to the left, I pulled into the lot as my brakes complained about the pressure I'd put on their pedal, so I took my palm and rubbed it across the dash in what I hoped was a comforting gesture.

"Thanks, old girl. You done good," I murmured to her. This car might be a giant POS, but I was still grateful for it, and for the fact that Daddy Dearest had the good sense to buy my previous vehicle, a BMW X5, outright before gifting it to me for my fifteenth birthday. Believe it or not, my ass learned to drive in that car. Since it was in my name, there was also fuck all he could do when I sold it a year after the divorce.

Despite the extreme skeez of the dealer I sold it to, I was able to get enough cash out of the deal to cover not only a couple of months' rent, but also the full resale price of my second-hand, shit-tastic, Honda Accord. Or—as I have lovingly called her for the past four years—Betty. To be fair, she's treated me alright, needing very few repairs and little more than regular oil changes, so this crappy rust bucket was easily the most reliable thing in my life. I wouldn't trade her for the world. Well, maybe for the world. Or 5,000 dollars, but you know, I was still fucking grateful.

The gravel shifted under my wheels one last time as I parked, the bumper almost touching the logs used to line the edges of the lot. My backseat was full up with cheap bedding and my ratty old suitcases, the ones I'd barely unpacked since getting back from Red Range a few weeks ago. Without a job to get dressed for and go to everyday, unpacking had seemed pointless, and now I was glad I had saved myself the effort. Parking out here meant I would have to haul this stuff to wherever I was sleeping later. For now, Jack had told me Tuesday morning to come to the office when I arrived, so I was headed there first, sans luggage.

I got out and took a minute to stretch my arms and legs, shaking out the aches that come with such a long drive. There were a handful of other cars in the lot, but mine was by far the oldest and the rustiest. The others were nice Toyotas, Fords, and practical cars that upper-middle-class parents buy their kids so they have something safe and insurable to drive around. There was also one dark red Mustang, which screamed 'I'm a jackass who feels the need to show off my muscles, car, and otherwise,' and a—holy shit—a stunning, powder-blue Porsche Cayenne. When I took a second, that actually wasn't all that shocking. There were a few other luxury cars in the lot, too, ones I didn't bother to look too closely at because this was probably as close as I would ever get to owning one. Most families who could afford to send their kids to camp for two months were at least medium-level rich, if not one-percenters. I certainly had been when Mom and Dad sent me here at age eight. And since most of the staff team was made up of former campers, the quality of vehicles made it clear nothing had changed.

More gravel pinged from behind me and had me turning around to see another car pulling in behind mine. While Betty would remain the worst one here, the dent in the front of the little silver Fiesta gave me hope that at least one other staff member was coming from more modest means. It pulled into the space beside mine, and a girl with gorgeous brown skin and two Afro space buns got out.

"Hey!" She waved. "You just got here?"

I smiled. "Yep."

She nodded, like that explained why I was standing around in the parking lot. "Have you checked in at the office yet?"

"Nope, I was just headed that way."

"Do you know where you're going?" she questioned.

"Uhhh." I bit the inside of my cheek. I was ideally hoping I could go all summer without really explaining my history with this place, but it had been all of two minutes and it was already surfacing. "Maybe?" I replied and vaguely pointed in the direction of where the office had been the last time I stepped foot on this property.

She gave me a warm chuckle. "No worries, I'll walk you there," before skipping up beside me. Old-school denim flares kicked out over her running shoes. That, combined with a flannel shirt knotted over her belly button, gave her a distinct 70s vibe. I dug it. She gestured for me to follow and headed down a wood-chipped path that swung off the far corner of the lot. I knew we had a bit of a walk before getting into the main part of camp, and this chick seemed friendly enough, or at least willing to make the effort to chat with me while we walked.

"I'm Abbi, or Abbs, as most people call me."

"Short for Abigail?" I asked.

"Yes, ugh, but only my mom calls me Abigail, and then only when I'm in real trouble. I'm not a fan." She rolled her eyes comically.

"I get it." I smirked. "I'm Antoinette, but for the love of god, please call me Toni."

She lifted her brows in surprise at hearing my full name. "Ya, I get that. Toni, it is."

While we walked and chatted, I tried to take in any changes from five years ago. Some of the pines and maples looked different, new saplings replacing old ones that had come down in storms or over the winters between then and now. And while it looked different, it felt the same. Secluded, forested, quiet except for the chirping of birds, and breezes through leaves. I found out that Abbi was my age, attending Cambria University, that remote private school out on Canada's east coast, and studying chemistry. My literature-loving ass issued an audible, "Yuck," at that, which had her laughing again. She had been a camper here, too, but only missed me by a summer, meaning she had been sixteen and an Elite camper, a.k.a. Staff-in-training, and really fucking good at something. What that was, she didn't say. Now, she was going to be in charge of Girl's Camp—a section head—meaning she got here a week ago to prep for staff pre-camp, which would start on Monday.

As we wound down the path, the red shingle roof and stained-wood walls of the office were right where they had always been and came into view right on cue as Abbi asked, "So, Toni, how did you hear about Agonde? We don't exactly get a lot of new blood. I'm pretty sure everyone else on staff right now is a former camper." I fought to hide the shiver of dread that statement elicited from me. Surely not. The universe wouldn't be so cruel.

A creaking screen door clapped shut, saving me from answering since the sound drew both of our focus. "Toni!" Jack called out from the wooden porch that fronted the office building. "Welcome back!" That earned me a raised eyebrow and puzzled face from Abbi, clearly not sure what to make of me. He then turned a megawatt smile to the girl beside me. "Hey, Abbs, welcome back to you, too. How was the time off?"

"Great, Jack!" she called back. "I mostly just filled my car with even more stuff for the summer."

"Of course, creature comforts. Thanks for being our unofficial staff greeter. Mind if I steal Toni from you now?" His eyes shifted back to mine, and his smile tightened. Probably due to the way I was scowling at him.

"Toni, care to join me in the office?" Why did that question immediately make me feel like a child going to the principal's office? I said nothing, just nodded and walked up the steps beside him.

"Nice to meet you, Toni!" Abbi called cheerfully from behind me. I turned to wave goodbye as she skidded off down a trail to the right of the office. That path used to lead to staff cabins, so I guessed it still did. Jack opened the door again and steered me by the shoulder into the fluorescent-lit office. There was the same old desk that spread across the entire front of the building, with a small lifting edge, so you could duck behind it. There were also several other unoccupied desks spread out across the timber floor. With no other interruptions, my new boss led me to his office, a walled-off room at the back with one door and windows facing out over yet another path and a tangled hedge of wildflower bushes. Everything about this office was so familiar to me. At age eight, I had sat in here and had cocoa. At nine, I had dragged friends in here so we could show off our new tie-dyed t-shirts. And I'd stood in here at fifteen and been scolded about the hazards of teenage boys. Nope, I slapped that particular door in my memory closed as quickly as possible. Not going there. Concentrating on the present, I dropped my ass down in the cheap cottage chair while Jack moved to sit behind his desk.

Ten minutes later, after a discussion about "expectations," and a brief overview of what my duties would be, he led me back out into the early evening sun.

"I think you're going to do great, Toni. I feel like this was always where you were supposed to be."

I grumbled, but didn't answer. Instead, I watched the upper branches of the large tree that had always shaded this building while the wind tangled and danced through its leaves. That was, until another movement on the left caught my eye. Two bodies moved together as one as they headed toward us. Beside me, Jack swore under his breath. "Shit."

The girl caught my eye first, mostly because she was beautiful. She was your movie star-level blonde bombshell. Think movie-star levels of gorgeous. I'm straight, but gravity-defying boobs like those deserve to be appreciated. The Director cleared his throat, making me turn away from the babe momentarily.

"One other thing. You know we always hire a good number of former campers." Translation: we only hire former campers. "So, I think you'll recognise a good number of your fellow staff."

"K, thanks, I guess." I shrugged, turning back, but the bodies were closer now. The boy had his arm draped over the girl's shoulder, their intimacy a surefire sign that they were a couple. Following the line of what was equally a very good-looking arm, I found a broad chest and even broader shoulders on a tall frame. His face was hidden under a baseball cap as he whispered sweet nothings into the girl's ear and she audibly giggled. The whole thing was giving cheerleader and quarterback vibes. Then the girl looked up.

"Hi, Jack, who's this?" she asked enthusiastically, before cracking a perfect smile and beaming it in my direction. The anxiety radiating off the Director beside me was like an alarm bell.

"Uhhhhhhhhhh... Michy, this is Toni." His voice was so flat that her smile dimmed just a fraction.

"Hillis." I cut in. "Toni Hillis." But those words, or maybe the sound of my voice, were enough to finally make the boyfriend look up from his girl's perfect tits. Across ten feet and five years, the most perfect chocolate-coloured eyes found mine.

Chapter Four

Cole

It was hard not to smile with Michele tucked under my arm, chattering away happily about pre-camp, staff training, and her plans for creative programmes. I would never understand all that artistic crap she spouted on about—drama, pottery, painting and shit—but she was super passionate about it, and I couldn't fault her for that. Just like she never laughed or teased me about anything hockey-related. We were different, but it made us a good match, at least in most ways. When we fucked, it was like two pieces of stiff cardboard rubbing against each other. It was rare that either of us finished. But she chalked it up to the pressure, while I tried not to think about it at all. I never mentioned how finishing didn't seem to be a problem when I was alone, thinking about brown hair, freckles, or dark curls, and darker nights. I didn't talk about it at all. Tuning back in, Mich jumped beneath my arm, forcing me to look up as she shouted excitedly at some girl's voice.

It couldn't be. Like it really couldn't be. Hearing that name come out of Jack Walker's mouth was a gut punch so hard, I swear to God, it sent me back in time. Then I looked up and into the face of a fucking ghost. She said her name was Hillis. But there was no fucking way. I would know that voice, that smile, and those eyes anywhere. Standing in front of me was Antoinette Barrett, my oldest friend and the girl from my dreams, or nightmares, depending on the night.

Mich pulled herself out from under my arm and jogged up the steps, extending her hand in a greeting. Meanwhile, I was frozen, looking into dark blue eyes I hadn't seen in five years. How dare she?! How dare she try to pass herself off as anything other than the Barrett princess she is?! Once a liar, always a liar, I guess. And how dare he?! How dare he bring her back here? After all this time, why would she come back?

"Hi, Toni!" I heard Michy exclaim, as she proceeded to introduce herself, before turning back and calling to me, "Cole, come say hello!" It might have been less than ten feet, but it felt like dragging myself through concrete as I stared at her the entire time. She was the same height she'd always been, tall and lean, but her clothes were faded and drooped around her body. Those jean shorts looked like they were clinging to her hip bones for dear life. There were no signs of the lightning storm that used to live behind her blue eyes. She just looked tired. Clearly, she didn't give a shit about being back here. Good. I didn't give a shit about her anymore, either.

"Toni, this is my boyfriend Cole," Mich explained as I finally closed the distance. There was static pressure in my ears this close to her that made me want to vomit. Like a bad reflex, my right hand extended, like I was about to shake this chick's hand and look her in the eyes. Let her see that she didn't have any power over me anymore. She beat me to it by cutting me off.

"Ya, I remember." Her voice was hollow, void of any feeling at all. No anger, no sadness, no nothing. The only sign of something else was the fastest flash across her eyes, but it was gone just as quickly, and in its place was the steely expression again. So, still a cutthroat bitch, then.

"Oh! You two know each other!?" There was excitement and just a hint of concern in my girl's voice as she looked my way for an explanation.

"Toni used to be a camper here. Same time as me," I snaked out, fighting to keep my rage contained. I opted for generic asshole instead. "But she had to stop coming to camp five years ago, when her dad found out she and her mom shared the same skank tendencies."

The smack came fast and hard, but not from Toni. "Cole Michaels! You apologise this instant! How dare you speak to any girl that way!" Mich turned back to Toni.

"I'm so sorry. He's a grade-A asshole sometimes. Please ignore him until he's ready to apologise." Goddamnit, Michele was too nice for her own good, I thought for the umpteenth time this year, as she glared daggers at me. I moved to wrap her up in my arm again, but she pushed me away.

"Sorry, Antoinette," I spit, relishing her flinch at the sound of her full name. "That was rude." Mich didn't catch it, though, or seem to give any thought to it. She just smiled my way as a thank you. Only for a second. Then she reached out and grabbed Toni, hooking their arms together.

"If you were here back then, you must know Xavier and Brennon, too!" my girl whispered excitedly as she dragged Toni down the steps. Jack and I made regret-filled eye contact for a second. He looked like he wanted to go for a dive right off the dock and never come back up for air. Then again, those names seemed to make Toni seize, too. Her whole body locked up, like she couldn't take another step, but she never even looked my way.

From behind, I watched her suck in breath, making her shoulders rise for a second, but her whole body seemed to crumple as she exhaled and answered, "Yeah, those names sound familiar." That filthy little liar.

True to her personality, Michele ignored every weird social cue Toni was giving and turned to our hapless Director. "What cabin is hers?"

"She's in the village, in Foxglove."

"Amazing! So close to mine! Toni, do you want us to show you where it is?"

Toni looked at me for a second, but quickly looked to the ground instead. "That's okay, Mich... ele. I think I can find it. It's in the Staff Village, right?"

Happy as ever, Michele pointed her down the path. "Yep. All the staff cabins are named after flowers, so head right past Poppy—that's mine—and Goldenrod, and you'll find it tucked away in its own little corner."

"Perfect, thanks..." She let the silence drag for a second. "I'm going to go grab my stuff and get settled."

"Great," I replied from behind them both, and then grabbed my girlfriend away from that lying bitch. The last thing I needed was for Michy to adopt her in yet another misguided attempt to rescue someone. Michele was like a target for sad, injured things, and I wasn't about to let Antoinette Barrett become one of them. Holding Mich close, we watched together as Toni walked back down the wood-chipped path, probably headed for the X5 I knew Daddy Barrett had bought her right after I had seen her last, right before any of us saw her for the last time.

Once Toni was out of sight, Mich swung my way, "Cole. You didn't have to be such an asshole to that poor girl. Can't you see she's struggling?"

"As if, Mich, you don't even know that girl," I scorned. "I do, and trust me, her struggles aren't worth your time."

Toni, age 8
13 years ago

The water swirls each time I dip my big toe into it. I like watching all the greys and blues as they mix together. It's even better, though, when the rest of the lake is totally still and makes a mirror for the sky. Then one poke from my little toes and the mirror ripples away. I'm glad today's a bit stormy. I'm a bit stormy, too. I had a fight with Jessica Alderston. She sucked. She was so mean. Just because my mum couldn't come to Parents' Day this past weekend, that doesn't mean she doesn't love me. Mum would have wanted to come, I know it. Father just didn't let her. I was sure of that, too. He always says she's not allowed to intrude on our time. My father just stuck me in the back of the car and then had the driver, Mikheal, drive us to a vacant property nearby. Then he made Mikhael get out of the car. He said we needed to have our privacy. I hated that. I was never allowed to talk about these visits. Even though they didn't just happen on Parents' Day. Even though they made my tummy feel all queasy.

On top of feeling gross, now I had to listen to girls like Jessica talk about going "into town" with their whole stupid families, all smiling mums and laughing dads. Whatever. I didn't have to be there for their teasing. But that meant I was here on the dock for this afternoon's Free Period without anyone I knew.

The camp leaders Marcy and Derek were trying to corral everyone into playing some dumb diving board guessing game. Let those other kids line up and wait to jump one time. That was stupid. I was here to swim. I liked swimming and the funny way the water rushed across my arms and back when I dived in. So instead of joining their game, I popped my butt on the far side of the dock to watch until I could swim for real. I was mostly just watching the water, though. Until a person-shaped shadow loomed from behind me.

"What are you doing?" The shadow demanded, a little angrily. When I turned around, there was a grumpy-looking boy standing there. He was wearing swim trunks that were just a little too tight, and he had a bit of a belly, but Mum says it's rude to tell people when they have a belly, so I just looked at him instead. He had dark brown hair, darker than mine, so maybe it was black because mine is definitely perfect brown, or that's what Father says. His eyes were dark, too, and he wouldn't stop staring at me.

"I dunno," I snapped back. "Watching."

"Why?"

"Because this game is stupid. And I don't want to play."

Weirdly, that makes him sit. Now his feet dangled in the water beside mine. "It is stupid. I'm not playing, either." Gone was his stony face, and now he was smiling at me. It made his chubby cheeks go wide and little dimples show up at the corners. I liked it.

I smile back. "I'm Toni."

"Tony—isn't that a boy's name?" He wasn't making fun, he was just asking. I could tell.

"It's Toni with an I. It's short for Antoinette, which is gross." I stuck my tongue out like it tasted bad. Only Father called me Antoinette, and I hated it.

"Oh, okay." He shrugged it off. "Hi Toni, I'm Cole." He reached out his hand, like he was expecting me to shake it the way grown-ups do on TV. It was silly and made me giggle, but I shook it, anyway. He smiled even more.

Chapter Five

Toni

Gone was the chubby-cheeked boy who sat with me on the dock that day. We'd spent the whole hour of that free period laughing and quietly making fun of the other kids' dives. Not very nice, I know, but we had fun. So much so that the next day Cole found me in the dining hall at lunch and asked me what I was doing for that free period, too. And the one after that, and the next one, until he didn't have to find me anymore because we'd find each other and decide what to do together. For the entire rest of that summer. The girls in my cabin all thought it was weird that I was friends with a boy. Seven-year-old girls think boys are gross, and I mostly did, too, at that age. Cole Michaels was just the exception.

But that boy seems to have vanished. Completely, now. When I'd last seen him that morning all those years ago, he'd been a lot shorter than he was now and still had some of the weight clinging to his growing frame. But his smile had been the same, all warmth and dimples. Now, he was a brick shit-house, muscles obvious under his t-shirt, and all hard lines. Even his smile seemed crueller, stiffer somehow, like it wasn't something he did for real anymore. I hadn't been expecting the warmest reception, but the anger radiating off of Cole caught me off guard. His rage was a visible thing, pushing against the boundaries of his body the way an angry animal bites and snarls at the bars of its cage.

"Well, fuck him," I grumbled to myself on my way back out to my car. As I walked, I wracked my brain for reasons he could hate me so much. I mean, yeah, I had regrets about everything that went down after I left camp that summer, and between Mom's destruction of our old lives and some choices of my own, I was caught in a shit sandwich I was still being forced to live with every day, but it wasn't like that had anything to do with him. All thoughts of Cole disappeared as I hauled my bedding out of Betty's backseat.

No way was I going to spend the next three months with just a sleeping bag on the rubber-wrapped camp mattresses, so I had my full set of sheets and comforter stuffed back there. Arms full, I waddled as best I could toward the smaller path off the dead centre of the lot, following the small wood-burned arrow that read, "Staff Village". This was a part of the property I wasn't familiar with, since it was mostly where staff or leaders who weren't directly responsible for kids lived. Typically, that meant more senior or junior staff. The ones smack in the middle held the job title, "Cabin Leaders," and lived in cabins, albeit in their own adjoining rooms, with kids. Since Waterfront Director is a fairly senior staff position, Jack had promised I'd have a cabin all to myself, so as the path wound down at a slight angle, I kept my eye out for the teeny-weeny home I'd call my own for the next fourteen weeks.

The path twisted and curved to avoid roots and glades of trees, meaning I had to squish my bedding even harder against my boobs so I could read the names posted above each of the cabins I passed. They were all fairly similar, small log buildings stained a dark brown colour. The only difference I could see from the outside, other than small variations in size, was in their name plaques. Some held names I recognized, belonging to former staff, people who'd worked here when I was just a kid, while others were named after what I assumed were other flowers. Finally, I spotted the plaque titled Foxglove, just above the door of a small cabin on my right. All by itself in a corner where the path jutted off in another direction, I felt like Goldilocks, finding the bed that fit her just right. I pushed open the solid timber door and dropped my crap. It was clean enough, and besides, it was all bound to get dusty, anyway. It was nearly dinnertime, and this far north, it would still get dark fast this time of year, so I didn't bother making the bed. That was future-Toni's problem. I still needed to get the rest of my shit from Betty's trunk, so I hustled out the door.

Halfway back to my cabin again, this time with two loaded suitcases dragging me down, I heard the sound of voices cutting across the otherwise quiet woods around the Staff Village. There was something about the depth and the grittiness of one voice that was too familiar. Not him, too. Was this for fucking real? Were they all here? Fuck. After the welcome I got from Cole, I wasn't in the mood to hold it together through yet another blast from the past. Regrettably, my desire to avoid that confrontation had me scrambling with my full luggage off the nicely groomed path through a gap between the bramble bushes and tree limbs. And there I stood on the damp forest earth, ducked down so I was hidden by the bushes, listening as two male voices got closer and closer.

"I swear, Brennon, she's such a babe," joked the voice I didn't recognize, but the name he used was enough to confirm what I already suspected. That was two outta three. Never had I ever been so happy to hide. Unprompted, I felt my body sink even lower toward my feet, desperate to stay out of sight.

"You're right, man, Abbi is a babe. Too bad she couldn't be less interested in your pathetic ass," replied the other voice, laughing, just as they came into view. The bushes hid a lot, but I could still make out two guys walking side by each along the path. And when he laughed, my heart broke. Unlike Cole, who showed no signs of the boy he used to be, Brennon's laugh was everything it had always been. Full and warm, but a bit like a bark, and I watched as he slapped his friend on the shoulder. Don't get me wrong, he wasn't the same fifteen-year-old kid. Brennon had always been a bit on the alternative side, but the lanky kid I had known looked like he had been body-snatched. The last time I'd seen him, his hair had been pink. Now it was a bright blue. There were tattoos on his arms and even creeping up his neck, and at least one piercing, that I could see, glinting from his right ear. Then, just as quickly as they'd appeared, they were gone again, beyond a bump in the path. I gave it another five minutes while I stood in shadows, just trying to breathe while visions of the past danced behind my eyes. When I was sure they were gone, and the only remaining sounds were the standard creaks and groans of a living forest, I slipped out of my hiding spot and rushed my way back to my empty cabin.

The door slamming closed behind me was a trigger, letting me know I was alone within Foxglove's four walls and could let my anxiety rip me apart. Questions bounced through my mind faster than I could come up with answers, faster than I could breathe. What if Brennon had the same reaction as Cole? What if he hated me, too? What if it was worse? I leaned back against the door and fought for breath, all while a clawing burn simmered behind my ribcage. The urge to take back control was visceral. Pulling my cell from the back pocket of my jean cut-offs, I stared into the screen, willing there to be a signal. It was a wish and nothing more. Camp Agonde was too remote, too deep in the woods for almost any cell signal to penetrate. Hell, the closest town, Trainsford, was nearly an hour away. Maybe I could race to the staff payphone and call Mum. Let her soothe my troubles away, let her tell me it was okay to come home. I knew exactly what she'd say, "Oh sweetie, come home, we'll figure something else out. You can find a job around here." As if, she'd been on the hunt for months and gotten nowhere. Giving up and going home seemed damned appealing, but what would it accomplish? Aside from maybe giving my ass a rash from too many hours spent in the car, nothing. I needed this job. So did my mum. She had waved me off this morning with such obvious relief on her face, knowing that at least one of us would have some money coming in. I couldn't just turn back up on our doorstep to dump my fears about the past on my mother's already overburdened shoulders.

I had to stomach the pressure, and there was only one surefire way I knew how to do that. It would help. There was nothing behind this cabin except trees. Nothing to stop me, no mum and no brother to overhear. Not even a need to flick the fan on for cover. I hauled ass back there and shoved two fingers down my throat without anyone being the wiser. As soon as the bile hit the ground, the tightness in my chest eased and my breathing slowed. With my emotions back under control, I went back inside and flicked on the single lightswitch, illuminating the six-by-twelve-foot space so I could officially unpack. Fuck the past. Present-day and future Toni were all that mattered.

Thirty minutes later, my cabin felt less prison-cell and more homey, with a made-up bed and my clothes folded neatly on the built-in shelves. I had managed a trip to the used bookstore on Thursday before I left, so I also had some pre-loved paperbacks stacked on the floor near my pillow, almost exactly the way I had them in my off-campus apartment all year. A knock interrupted my silent admiration of my own hard work and the door opened behind me.

"Hi, Toni. I wasn't sure if you knew the meal schedule. Thought I'd come to grab you just in case." Abbi's voice was slightly unsure, but polite. Since she'd left me with Jack, I wasn't sure what she would think of me when I saw her again. Camp is a tightly interwoven place, where news, gossip, and personal information are traded like drugs at a rave, so if she didn't know my history here yet, she would soon. Flashing her a tight grin, I decided to enjoy her friendliness while it lasted. "Thanks, girl. I knew dinner was soon, but wanted to make sure I had a place to crash afterward. It's been a long day." My weariness crept into that last sentence.

"I totally get it." She nodded sympathetically before scanning my space. "But it's looking good."

"Thanks!"

"But, uhhhh..." she trailed off. "If you're all set, want to head to the dining hall for some eats?"

My now-empty stomach had its own opinions about that, ones I decided to listen to. "Hell yeah. Lead the way."

Chapter Six

Brennon

Riley's a good kid, I thought to myself. This was his first summer on staff after being a camper for nearly a decade, but I thought he'd do great. The new staff are always nervous. It's a big transition from paying to be here to someone paying you. Lord knows I was basically one word away from shitting myself the entire first summer I was a staff member. Now, three years on, I felt a bit more at ease. But I still remembered that first summer. In some ways, it was about 86 different kinds of torture. I was eighteen, wishing for her and them. For my past and my future all at once. Now I know I'm on my own. So, if I can help Riley feel more settled, I will. Like I said, he's a good kid. I was his cabin leader a couple of years ago, and at seventeen, it doesn't seem like he's changed much, other than a few inches of height, so I listened to him fawn over how hot Abbi was and tried not to laugh. I mean, Abbi is a babe, but she would eat this kid alive.

We walked and shot the shit as we made for the dining hall, talking about college and girls and his plans for the summer. I let him lead, since I didn't exactly have a lot to share. I had been here for a week already. Prepping for the next few weeks of staff training. But most of that time had been spent alone in the office or with Jack, going through files and spreadsheets. Despite my, shall we say, artistic appearance, I was Agonde's administrative manager, and I'd been busy setting up our computer and camper registration systems, and of course, staff payroll. Honestly, I was starting to get a bit bug-eyed from all the screentime, so when Riley popped his head into the office earlier this afternoon, I took the opportunity to enjoy some spring sunshine by showing him his cabin in the Staff Village. He was sharing Clover with some of the other junior male staff, right beside my slice of paradise, so it was a no-brainer.

When we reached the dead-end of the gravel road, also known as 'Centre Circle', because it was the assumed centre of camp, there was already a crowd of other staff gathered, waiting for the Director to call us in for dinner. I recognized most of the faces in the crowd, both male and female. Even the new staff were mostly recognizable as the kids I'd taught guitar or swimming lessons to some time in the last few years before they finished their Elites training at sixteen. Mostly, everyone was standing, chatting, laughing, and catching up. Of the fifty or so total camp staff, only ten of us, the most senior, had been here since last week. The rest had arrived some time in the last forty-eight hours. Predictably, at the centre of it all was Cole-fucking-Michaels. Popular as ever and surrounded by the junior staff from Boys' Camp, who stared at him like he was some kind of hero. The whole thing made me a bit sick. Sure, Cole might be some future hockey star, but not yet. For now, he was just some kid I used to know who had turned into a stuck-up prick somewhere along the way.

The Centre Circle was full of benches and chairs made from trees and scrap bits of wood collected in the last few years. It wasn't uncommon to see staff or groups of campers hanging out there, shooting the shit. Hell, that's one of the spots we had hung out when we were kids. Right now, though, it was Cole's kingdom, where he seemed to be basking in every ounce of praise and adoration from this crowd of sycophants, content to let Michy sit on the arm of the bench beside him without actually including her in the group. What an asshole. It was hard to even look at him. What Michele saw in him, I would never know. She's great and could do a lot better than Michaels. Who knows, maybe the guy is hung like a racehorse.

Every once in a while, over the last three years, we would make eye contact and I'd catch a glimpse of the caring, overweight, kid I used to know. The one who made every effort, the one who was a good friend, who hugged Xavi after a nightmare or joked away any embarrassment I felt about being so small for my age. But then, his face would shutter closed and the current douche version would be all that was left. Despite years of former friendship, I wasn't expecting him to acknowledge me at all. Thinking back, we hadn't spoken more than a word to each other last summer. Hell, we barely spoke at all without her. Now we were just people who shared the same memories. So, his summons, "Hey, Grace—" caught me totally off guard. I let my glare answer for me, but all that got me was another call-out. "Don't be such a dickhead, Brennon. I need to talk to you."

"Whatever, Michaels," I answered, ignoring the sputters and laughs from Cole's crowd. Throwing my arm around Riley, we kept walking to the dining hall doors.

"Man, what's the deal with you and Michaels?" he asked. "Even as a camper, the vibe between you was fucking weird, but that was outright hostile."

"It's not worth getting into. Ancient history." More fool me. I should have known better. In this place, nothing is ever history. The past gets dredged up and gossiped about just as much as the present. With the three of us still on staff, our history was always going to be a point of interest. And Michaels' shitty attitude didn't exactly help. But I had no reason to think about that at that moment. The dining hall doors were stained this deep maroon colour that only just stood out against the brown that covered most of the buildings across the camp. I sorta loved it. There was an everyday anticipation of opening these doors and knowing that this was the space where everyone in camp came together. Right now, it was just staff, but soon enough we would add kids of all ages from seven to sixteen into the mix, and it would create this chaotic maelstrom of energy during every meal. That energy fed parts of my soul I still didn't fully understand, although my shrink would say that my upbringing had something to do with it. But Dr. Talia hadn't experienced the magic of 300 people singing along to the same bad pop song, so her opinion didn't exactly hold water with me.

Inside, some of the junior staff were setting tables for dinner. Once campers arrived, each cabin group would be responsible for its table, but right now, we worked on a three-day rotation. Junior staff first, then Cabin Leaders, and then Senior staff last, and we'd keep that schedule up until staff training ended in two weeks. Riley waved me off and headed to join some of his friends as they laid plates and cutlery on the long oak tables. Since I had no responsibilities tonight, I headed toward the kitchen. The staff who worked the camp kitchens generally kept themselves apart, but I made a point of getting to know them every year. A growing boy needs extra bacon to make him feel at home. So no one said anything as I tucked through the swinging door and snatched up one of the pre-prepped serving dishes waiting under the heat light. We'd be having fajitas for dinner since the tray in front of me was a chili and cumin-spiced mix of peppers, onions, and chicken. I reached under the counter to the trays of spare utensils, and, finding a fork, started mindlessly picking away at the dish.

"Brennon!" Crap, there was Chef Brad. I was about to get my ass scolded. "Get outta here!" he shouted, but the laughter in his voice was clear as he followed that up. "How are you still hungry after the extra brownies at lunch? I swear to god, kid, you're a bottomless pit." He used the metal tongs in his hand to gesture toward the door.

"I'm a hungry boy, Chef. Can't fault me for that." He laughed but pointed me out yet again. I sighed, "Alright, I'm leaving, but only because you pointed so nicely."

We shared a chuckle as I headed back the way I came, planning to grab my fourth coffee of the day before sitting down at a table. But when the door swung out in front of me, I froze. A tiny set of jean shorts on lean legs paraded in front of me. My eyes traced the line of those perfect limbs, up to a too-narrow waist, a too-visible rib cage, and shoulders that showed all the bones that were supposed to be tucked away under a layer of life. With every inch my eyes took in, the alarm bells in my brain screamed louder and louder until I reached the girl's face.

Shoulder-length brown hair, blue eyes that matched mine, and seventeen perfect freckles danced across the nose of a god-damned ghost. There was no way it was her. She couldn't be here. But even as I stared, I knew it was. I'm not sure when it happened; maybe the first time she smiled that sunbeam-smile my way. Maybe it was the first time she laughed in that wild girl style of hers. Not sure, but either way, my brain had memorised the placement of every single one of those freckles. I could have been blind, deaf and dumb, and still, her heart would have called out to mine, screaming at me to fly toward her. My lost little bird. Maybe she was back because she was finally ready to come home. But obviously, that wasn't what she wanted, that had never been what she wanted. If it were, she never would have disappeared. It was that reminder that had me glued to the doorframe, acting like a fucking creep, staring at the girl of my dreams as she laughed and chatted with Abbs.

Fuck—this was definitely what Michaels wanted to talk about. With that realisation, I wanted to drag his ass away from his acolytes and grill him about Toni, but I knew I'd never get the chance as Jack made his way onto the small stage at the centre of the hall. “Welcome, Staff, to the first dinner of the summer!” Welcome indeed.

Brennon, age 8
13 years ago

Dad bought me this guitar, so, of course, I love it. I don't know how to play it or anything, but I know I'm going to be great. Because Dad is. So I drag the heavy case along the road with me as I head toward The Creative Cluster, the home base for all of camp's creative programmes. This will be my first guitar lesson ever, mostly because Dad said he didn't have time to teach me and Mum always explained, "Oh angel, you don't need lessons. Music is in your soul." I wasn't sure she was right about that. She was always so sleepy that I wasn't sure she was right about much. She didn't even seem to know that I had just passed my eighth birthday. But I would impress them both when they came for parents' day. I would know at least one song, and probably about a million chords by then.

An hour later, I stomped out of the lesson early. Tears burned in my eyes, and I stared at my fingertips, wishing they were different. Why wouldn't they cooperate? I was supposed to be great at this, the kid of a famous musician. I expected to wow the programme leader, and instead, I'd stumbled over every string and every chord. It was so embarrassing, especially after they'd taken attendance and

I'd heard some of the older kids in the class whisper to each other, "Grace... as is Blue Grace's kid."

Dad was going to hate me. He would hear about how bad I was, and then I would see him even less than I already did. The guitar case felt even heavier now than it had on my way here, and jealousy boiled under my skin as two other kids ran screaming past me with glee. The boy fought to hold his sweatpants up as he ran and laughed, while the girl turned and ran backward with the hugest grin ever decorating her face. She teased, "Nice try, Cole! You'll have to run faster than that!"

"Not fair, Ton, you had a head start!" the boy yelled after her. But he kept running, even though she stopped. She stood still in the centre of the path and turned to look at me instead of her friend. I couldn't understand why, but it made me stop all the same.

She looked at my guitar case, and with wide blue eyes, asked quietly, "What's in the case?"

I stopped moving, and the two of us stared each other down, until her friend caught her by the shoulder. "That's a guitar, Toni. Duh!" he explained, like she should have known better.

"Oh," she answered, like his explanation was obvious. But it clearly wasn't, since her lips pinched together in a question and she asked, "What's a guitar?"

I smiled, and the boy laughed, which made her pale cheeks go pink. And I felt bad. It's not nice to laugh at people. People laugh at my mum all the time and I don't like it. "It's an instrument," I explain, as I drop my case to the ground and pop open the clips to show her. Both she and the boy creep closer until they're standing over me and my case. When I lift the lid she, "Oooohs," audibly. "It's pretty!" she says, smiling my way. I'm a bit embarrassed, but I also want to show off. Only, I can't bear to have her hear how bad I am. So instead, I answer, "Ya, it was a gift from my dad."

"Do you know how to play it?" asks the boy.

"Not really..." I admit quietly. "But I'm going to learn this summer."

"Cool!" he answers.

The girl watches us both silently for a minute, and I feel a bit nervous, so I lower the lid again to protect my guitar, just in case. I'm sure they'll both be gone as soon as I clip it closed. The only cool thing about me now out of sight, but as I do, they are both still there.

"I'm Toni and this is Cole. We're playing hidden soldiers. Want to play?"

I'm embarrassed since I don't know that game, but Cole explains, "One of us takes a turn hiding, and then the other hunts them down. If they find you, you have to run until they catch you. It's kinda dumb."

Now he seems embarrassed, so I say, "That sounds fun." But my guitar case is heavy, and I can't just leave it.

"I want to play, but I can't leave my guitar."

The girl, Toni, gets even closer. "You don't have to." She walks to the narrow end of the case, "What if we help you take it back to your cabin?"

"Ya! And then we can all play together!" Cole shouts excitedly.

"Okay, " I say as I lift the bottom handle and Toni holds the top of the case. "Let's go!" she shouts. "Cole, lead the way!"

Chapter Seven

Xavier

I made a point of being late for the first dinner of pre-camp, making sure to arrive after Jack's usual pandering welcome speech. With everybody already busy eating and nattering on, it was easy to sneak in the back doors, slide through the kitchen where the chefs' team was busy, and inch out into the dining hall unnoticed. From my vantage point, I could look out across the faux wood, but actually linoleum, floors and the simple rectangular tables laid out in their neat lines separated just enough so you could slip an equally simple pine bench on either side. Watching the new staff eat was like watching baby birds crack their way out of their eggshells. First, it was slow and tentative, all of them nervous and awkward, and then much quicker as senior staff worked to put them at ease, cracking jokes or asking questions that reminded them they weren't strangers here.

Since all of them were former campers barely a year ago, you would think they would be a lot more comfortable. They're not the ones I was focused on, at least not really. I was on the hunt for a spot where I could eat in peace, which meant scanning each table for two particular faces and then doing everything in my power to avoid them both. It wasn't always like that, though. Once upon a time, as they say, the three of us would have walked in here together and sat down at one of the centre tables, like we were taking dominion over everything that happened in this hall. We would sit together, laughing, joking, and eating, while other kids and even our cabin leaders tried to push themselves into our orbit, trying to make us see them. It sounds harsh, but their jokes, their stories, anything they had to say really, none of it penetrated the walls we'd built around our friendship. It was only after the three of us took a flamethrower to those walls ourselves, leaving our little fortress and friendships in tatters, that others were able to pull our attention.

Spotting Brennon was easy. That awful blue hair he seemed so proud of, stood out as he sat chatting with one of the new staff, Riley. I knew only because all senior staff were part of the hiring process and I recognized him from the photo in his new staff file. Almost as if he could sense me watching, Brennon looked up from his plate, his blue eyes softening for a second before he schooled his expression and looked away again. Well, that corner was out. Shit, so was the opposite one, I realised, as I heard that asshole Mitchell Greer ask, "So, Michaels, what do you make of the new talent?" He even wiggled his eyebrows suggestively, as if his question had been in any way subtle and as if Cole's girlfriend wasn't sitting right there.

Cole's not winning boyfriend of the year, but at least he had the good sense to reply, "I don't give a shit, Greer. I've got the only talent I need right here," swinging his arm around Michele's shoulder at the same time. The action made me grind my teeth.

Classic Michele, not content with that response, jabbed her fork in Greer's direction. "Mitchell Greer, don't be such a sleaze, or I will warn every girl on this staff team that your dick is shrivelled with gonorrhoea." That shuts the asshole up, and in the vacuum of silence that followed, Cole's face found mine. Or I guess I shouldn't say 'found'. He was watching the crowd, too, which was unusual. Cole was usually too wrapped up in himself to pay attention to anything outside his immediate sphere of Michele and the other hockey bros he hung out with. For him to do otherwise meant he was looking for something or someone. I knew it wasn't me since, as always, his eyes skated over me like I wasn't even there. It was always the same. He didn't acknowledge me, didn't speak to me, didn't even react to hearing my name. The only times I'd gotten anything else from him in the last four years weren't worth mentioning.

Whatever or whoever he was searching for, he didn't give up, so as I finally managed to find a seat at the table closest to me, I ignored the bland faces around me and continued to watch him. When his focus finally landed on something, a grim scowl descended over his face. Following his line of sight, I landed on the table smack in the middle of the dining hall and Abbi. Strange. Abbs was popular with just about everyone. She was fun, kind, and didn't take herself or anything too seriously. She was also a beautiful girl, so that helped, too. Abbi said something I couldn't overhear from back by the kitchen, but it must have been funny because the whole table laughed. But I didn't care about the whole table, hell, they barely even registered anymore. There was a buzzing in my head, and the only sound that penetrated were the notes of a laugh I was certain I would never hear again. The laugh was quieter, more subdued than the last time I had heard it. My entire field of vision narrowed to the brown-haired girl beside Abbi. To her freckles, to the crinkle in her forehead as she laughed. To the way her eyes, too, scanned the room. Antoinette Barrett. Our long-lost best friend. My wild girl. The buzzing in my head became worse. Seeing her was like a shot of adrenaline in my veins and sent a current of anger through my fucking soul. She was here, but she couldn't stay. Not now. Not after everything.

Five years later and all it took was the sound of her laugh to draw me right back under her spell. The effort involved in pulling my eyes away from Antoinette Barrett, from my Nettie, frightened me. Now that I knew why he was scowling, I looked back to Cole. And for the first time in—God—what has to be at least a year, his eyes met mine. There was no smile, no joy at seeing her again, just rage and something a little like disgust. The thing about knowing someone for over a decade is that even when they change, age, and evolve, there are bits and pieces of them that stay the same, that you can continue to read and understand. You become a sort of translator, an interpreter of their experience. That's how I knew the small lift in Cole's chin was a directive, an instruction, to follow him to the one place where the three of us could have a conversation that needed to be had. After a quick whisper of god-knew-what bullshit into Michele's ear, he stood and walked with his typical swagger down the centre aisle between tables.

The moment he made eye contact with Brennon, I felt it. Our old connections still hung between us, much as we might each hate it, and there were times over the last few years when I swore it was a physical thing. Like a current travelling down very frayed wires, but still ultimately connecting the entire circuit. Cole's exit out the double doors drew a few looks, but otherwise went unnoticed. Thirty seconds later, Brennon followed suit. I didn't bother watching his retreat; I'd find them both soon enough. What I lingered on instead was the way Nettie's back straightened, the way her shoulders pushed back and the tiny glances she threw toward the door after both Brennon and Cole. Although she still hadn't noticed me, and wouldn't unless she made a point of turning all the way around, her reactions signalled that regardless of recent history, ours had always been a four-pointed circuit, anyway.

Rather than follow directly after the other two, I snuck out the same way I'd snuck in. Exiting the building through the door by the walk-in fridge, tucked away at the back of the kitchen. From there, it was easy enough to edge behind the building down the path that the kitchen staff used whenever they needed a smoke break. Nobody but them, and me I guess, ever really came back here. Other than the chef's team, staff weren't allowed to smoke on camp property and honestly, most kids are oblivious to a lot of shit. Not me, though. And not my wild girl, either. I kicked the plastic bucket of sand the chefs used as a makeshift ashtray and thought about my first cigarette ever, smoked at age fourteen on a

July night right in this spot. To this day, I had no idea where she got them from, but Toni had snuck this crumpled pack of cigarettes in her camp bags and she'd told me it would be our secret.

"Xav, don't you want to try it, just once?" she'd asked, even though she knew I'd already decided. I would try anything given the opportunity, and summers were my only opportunities. Add to that my favourite girl in the entire world was, and of course, I was going to say yes. So we'd stood here in the dark, using matches Nettie had swiped during a candle-making activity to light a single cigarette. We didn't even finish the whole thing; we were too busy laughing and trying not to cough too loudly, the burn in our lungs and the head rush from the tobacco both terrible and delightful all at once. Nettie had insisted we smoke it back here so that we had somewhere safe to put it out. She'd been so careful about shoving the butt deep into the sand of the then-ashtray. But the only reason she'd found this spot existed in the first place was because she was so goddamned skinny, even then. She'd been able to tuck herself through a tiny gap between tall blackberry bushes one day when she had been sneaking back to the girls' side of camp after hanging out with us in our usual spot.

It was that same gap I was about to leverage. It was a bit overgrown now since Nettie hadn't been around to use it, but I could still find it. I pushed through, letting the twigs and thorns drag lightly over my bare arms and tug momentarily on the fabric of my t-shirt. On the other side, was a wider dirt trail that led further away from the now muffled sounds of the dining hall. The forest around ate up the sounds of people and gave back its own symphony instead. Everything about what was to come would be unpleasant, so I took my time even though they'd be waiting for me. Cole, impatient dick that he is, was probably growing increasingly frustrated by my delay.

Sure enough, I rounded the last corner of the trail as I heard him. "What the fuck is taking him so long?"

"Calm down, Cole. Here I am," I replied as I stepped into the small clearing. Brennon was half perched on one of the big stones, his palms pressed against it for support. He looked casual, almost relaxed, if you didn't know any better. Cole, on the other hand, had been pacing.

"What took you so long, asshole?"

Ignoring his question, I pushed one hand into my curls, scraping them away from where they'd dropped over my face, so I could look directly at him. Rage and something darker simmered in his stare, demanding an answer. "Ugh, fine. She noticed you two leave, okay?"

Brennon's eyebrows rose, but he said nothing. "I thought I'd take a more subtle approach. Unless, of course, you'd like me to go back and get her, too." I pointed to the dining hall, my voice dripping with disdain. "I'm sure she would love to hear what we're all about to discuss."

"Fuck off, Rothberg." He'd used my last name just to piss me off, and fuck if it didn't work, my lip rising to an involuntary snarl.

Always cool, calm, and not-giving-a-fuck, Brennon cut us off, "Can we get on with it, please? I'd like to get some dessert."

His logic was sound, so I stepped within the bounds of Stones' Throw. This random circle of stones was ours, even if there wasn't an us anymore. Five stones of varying sizes lay in an almost perfect circle, two of them large enough to call boulders, two in the middle, and one so small it looked child-sized compared to the rest. This spot was buried deep in the woods, far enough away from any of the other buildings or activity centres of camp to feel isolated. To feel sacred. I might have discovered it first, but the Throw as we'd named it, was as much a part of our friendship as any of us. This was where we hung out, where all important conversations were had. And where eventually, everything fell apart.

Now that we were being forced to relive the past, we had to start somewhere. "Do either of you know why she's here?" I threw out.

Brennon answered first. "I've got nothing."

"Me either, but I ran into her coming out of Jack's office before dinner," Cole explained.

"Okay, but that seems normal, right?" I asked. "I mean, they were always close. Isn't he like friends with her dad or something?"

"Or something." Cole glowered.

"Not anymore, I don't think." Both Cole and I stared at Bren. "I work in that office, the walls are thin. I've heard him call the guy a few times." He shook his head at our expectant looks. "No specifics, but none of those calls ended well. The last one ended with him slamming the phone down."

"It has been a while since there have been any Barrett Holdings-sponsored upgrades around here," I pondered out loud. "Maybe that's why she's back."

"Who gives a fuck about the reason. I want her gone."

"Okay, Cole, so how do you propose we do that, then?" Brennon asked, his pierced eyebrow lifting at the question.

"I don't know. Fuck!" He ripped his cap from his head and ground it into the dirt. Then he looked up at me, at us, again, the anger not completely gone, but instead, channelled into a wolfish grin.

"I do know one thing, though, she's still a little liar. She introduced herself to Michele as Toni... Hillis."

Across from me, Brennon's eyebrows lift even more. "Do you think she's trying to hide who she is?"

"If she is, we can work with that," I replied. "Because it's not about us wanting her gone, it's about us needing it. Or did you idiots forget what could come out if she stays?" My words loom over all three of us, acting like invisible storm clouds over an otherwise clear evening. Two solemn faces looked back at me, and in their darkness, amongst the shadows of my former best friends, I felt a plan take shape. "I think I have an idea, a way to remind her that we haven't forgotten what she did—what she made us do..."

After I'd walked them through my plan, there was some back and forth, some squabbling over what I'd call 'logistics', but eventually we settled on a series of events we were confident would work to send my wild girl back to whatever hole she'd crawled out of. By the time we were done, we all stood together at the centre of the circle staring at each other. As we prepared ourselves to leave this space, to put our plan into action, Cole made one more demand.

"So, we agree," his attention flickering between Brennon's face and my own, then down to where he'd extended a fist. We hadn't done this in forever, or in five years, to be exact, but something about it felt right. Clearly for all of us, since both Brennon and I bumped our fists out, too. The soft knock of three sets of knuckles connecting sent one final bolt of life through our dying connection.

COLE, AGE 8

13 years ago

"Toni?!" I called out into the woods. Where did she go?

On my right, I heard Brennon call out, "Toni?!" He sounded so unsure. He obviously couldn't find her either, since he called out again, "Birdie?! Where are you?" Brennon had started joining in on our games over the last couple of weeks. I liked him. Unlike the other boys in my cabin, he never said mean things about my weight or laughed at the lines my swim trunks left on my stomach. Just like I wouldn't ever tease him for his long arms or big feet. I wasn't sure why he'd started calling Toni 'birdie', but she liked the name, and when I had asked her, she said it was because she's 'a free bird.' I still have no idea what that means, but Toni was like that sometimes. I'd never tell her, but I secretly thought it was because she's a girl.

We'd been playing Hidden Soldiers since the last activity period ended early, but this round has gone on forever. Too long, I think. We're all supposed to be back at our cabins before dinner, and I'm pretty sure that's soon. I called out again, "Toni?! It's almost dinnertime! Come out!"

The sounds of branches breaking got closer. Good, Toni heard me and she's coming out of her hiding spot. But it's Brennon, who crashed through the bushes instead.

"Did you find her?" he asked, and he looked a little scared. We were in the forest behind the Creative Cluster, and there was nothing out here, at least I didn't think there was. But what if she was hurt? What if she fell or something?

My chest became tight, and I blinked lots, so Brennon wouldn't see me tearing up. "No. I don't know where she went."

The two of us moved closer to each other and started to talk about what we should do. Should we go find someone? Would that mean we would get in trouble? Would they ban our game? We didn't want that, so we agreed to keep looking for another five minutes. Brennon's dad got him this really cool watch with a timer on it, so he set the alarm. If we still hadn't found her when it went off, we'd have to go get a Cabin Leader for help. Instead of splitting up again, Brennon and I decided to stick together as we continued looking, even though that wasn't the game. But the game was over now.

We each took turns calling for her. "Birdie!" "Toni!" But there was still no answer.

There were only two minutes left on our timer when Brennon slapped his hand against my chest. "Shhhhh, I think I hear someone!" he shushes.

"What if it's Toni?" I whispered back.

"What if it's a camp leader?" he countered, and I shut up. Once I did, I heard the voices, too. Silently, Brennon pointed us in their direction, and we creeped forward, one pace at a time, so we didn't

break any twigs or branches under our feet. The closer we got, the more I was sure one of the voices wasToni's. I didn't recognize the other one, but it sounded like a kid's voice, too. After a few more steps, the voices became clearer, when the bushes gave way to a small dirt path. There was a bend in it, but I could just see around it to a small clearing. There were no trees or anything, just dirt and a bunch of rocks. And there was Toni. Sitting on one of the smallest stones, her back to us. The scared feeling in my chest went away, and beside me, Brennon whooshed out a, "Phew."

She wasn't alone, though. I knew I had heard another voice, and since she couldn't see us yet, I could tell she was talking to whoever it was. Her voice was quieter than normal, and it sounded weird.

"Thank you for helping me." And then she sniffled. She'd been crying. I knew Brennon caught it, too, because his eyes got really big. We ran forward toward her.

"Toni, are you okay?" I asked, as I skid to a stop and caught myself on the bigger rock beside the one she was sitting on.

Brennon was on her other side. "Birdie, we were calling! Didn't you hear us?"

"No," she muffled, and she swiped her arm across her eyes, not looking at either of us.

"She's okay. But she was running too fast and she tripped over that rock." I finally noticed the boy sitting in the dirt in front of Toni. "She skinned her knee is all." I looked down. One of Toni's legs was extended in front of her, and there were dirt marks all over her knee.

Brennon knelt close to the boy to look. "Where did you get the band-aids, Birdie?" I didn't notice that, but now I can see she has six or seven band-aids lined up across her shin.

She wiped her fingers under her eyes, leaving more dirt smudges on her face, but she smiled at Bren. It wasn't her big smile. Just a little one. "Xavi gave them to me." She pointed at the boy. "He fixed my cuts. But it still hurts a bit." Then she pointed at us. "That's Cole and that's Brennon, they're my friends."

The boy, Xavi, smiled at her now, and he held out his hand to help them both stand. "It's fixed for now. But you need to go see the nurse. I didn't have anything to clean it up." Now that he was standing, I could see more than just his hair. He was small, skinny. Skinny like Toni was, but it was hard to tell because he was wearing long pants and sleeves, even though it was really hot today. His eyes matched mine, but he was much paler. And when Brennon and I stepped a bit closer to them both, he looked scared.

"Thank you for helping our friend, Xavi." I said his name slowly. I didn't want to be rude, but I really wanted to get Toni out of here and take her to the nurse. Silly Brennon stopped us, though.

"What is this place?" he questioned, looking around. "How did you find it?"

"It was an accident. I was looking for somewhere quiet. I meant to go back to my cabin, but I found this place instead."

"Out here?" I asked, maybe a bit harshly, since he looked away shrugging. "I needed a break from all the noise."

Toni reached out and touched his shoulder. "That's okay. Sometimes I like the quiet, too."

"You do?" I questioned.

"Ya, Cole!" she snarked. "Sometimes, I like to be loud, and sometimes..." she dragged the word out, "I like quiet. That's allowed."

"Of course it is. Sorry." I was embarrassed now. I didn't mean to make Toni or Xavi feel bad. Toni grabbed me, too, now and squeezed my hand twice to tell me it was okay.

"I like it out here." Brennon piped up, jumping onto one of the taller rocks. "These stones are cool! Did you notice how they make a perfect circle?" he said, looking down from where he was now standing over us.

"What? Cool!" Toni replied, and she ignored her hurt leg as she climbed up onto the slightly smaller rock beside Brennon's. Not to be left out, I climbed up, too, onto the biggest rock in the circle, and because I still felt bad, I reached down to help Xavi up beside me. This rock was big enough that he and I could stand shoulder-to-shoulder on it with no problem. Brennon was right. It was almost a perfect circle when you looked down.

I smiled at Xavi. "This is a cool spot."

His cheeks turned a little pink when he mumbled, "Thanks," but he was grinning, too. So were Toni and Brennon when we looked over at them on the other side of the circle.

Toni scrunched her face up just a little. It was her thinking face, I'd learned, so I knew she was going to say something. "I'm a free bird, right, Brennon?" she asked.

"Sure are, Toni."

"Well, birds fly!"

Xavi looked at her like she was crazy. And she was a bit.

"Toni," I scolded. "You're not really a bird, and you can't fly. Besides, you're already hurt."

She ignored my worry. "Cole, we can all fly. At least here. The circle is magic, duh." Oh, this was her game. Toni did make up good games, so I went along with it.

"Okay, so how do we fly, Toni?"

"We're going to jump! All together!" She reached across the gap between the rocks to Brennon. She didn't even have to ask, he just reached back and grabbed her hand. She looked to me. "Cole, grab Xavi's hand, and on the count of three, we all jump into the middle, and maybe we'll fly."

It was silly. I knew we wouldn't fly, but I still looked at Xavi, and I hadn't really noticed, but our hands were still together from when I had helped him up. I guess we just never let go. Before I could say anything, Brennon started the countdown.

"Three... Two... One... Jump!"

And we all did. Then we almost crashed together in the dirt. Our four sets of arms and legs got a bit tangled, but we stayed standing. Xavi pulled his hand away, and I thought maybe he was still upset with me. I didn't know what else to say. I always did this. Maybe I ruined things. Dad said that sometimes.

"We should go. We're all going to be late for dinner." I wanted to run away. Maybe that was what Xavi meant about finding somewhere quiet.

"Wait!" It was Xavi. He looked almost startled by his own voice. Like he'd called out by accident. He stuttered over his next words. "Can I... umm, what I mean is..."

"You're going to come with us right, Xav?" Brennon asked. "We're friends now, right? Since you helped Toni?"

He nodded excitedly. And I got an idea. My dad watched boxing on Saturday nights, and sometimes I was allowed to watch with him.

"Let's touch gloves!" I exclaimed, but they all just looked confused. "It's a thing boxers do, like to agree to the start of a fight. Only we're agreeing to be friends."

"I like that!" Toni's smile was huge, and when the other two saw it, they agreed too. I made a single fist and held it out toward the middle of our little huddle. Toni's was next, and her knuckles touched mine, then Brennon and Xavi last, until all four of our hands connected.

Chapter Eight

Toni

It was like someone lit a match. Three matches actually, and then blew them out one after the other. First Cole's, then Brennon's, and Xavi's last, of course. I saw the first two leave, not that they weren't careful, leaving just enough time between their exits that people wouldn't notice or connect them. Xavi's departure, on the other hand, was more of a feeling. He might think I didn't notice him behind me or feel the second his eyes connected with the back of my head, but he would be wrong. Xavier Rothberg, the boy who knew everything, saw everything, had forgotten that I was the girl who did, too. So, when he left the room, it wasn't so much that I saw it, but that I felt him go, like the last warm embers of a fire flickering to ash.

I'd bet Betty's rusty old ass that those three were sitting together at Stones' Throw talking about me right now. Trying to solve the problem of Antoinette, Barrett to them, Hillis to everyone else. Part of me wanted to storm out after them. The other part of me was too tired and too focused on filling my belly with fajitas. Besides, Abbi had been nice enough to include me, to invite me to sit with her amongst all these other staff, when she could have left me to fend for myself. She was popular, judging by the way she held the rest of our table rapt with her stories about exploits from last summer. So I stayed put, introducing myself, fake name only, of course, to the other staff around our table, and tried to smile for real when they greeted me excitedly.

The meal carried on, and the three of them never came back, not even as dessert was passed around. God, it'd been a long time since I last ate dessert. Maybe since January, when I'd let this guy Kyle from my Intro to Literary Theory class take me on a dud of a date. Trying to hide my eagerness, I grabbed a single brownie as the tray was passed around our table and nibbled at it slowly, letting the chocolate sit on my tongue. Even if I decided to quit this job tomorrow, the long drive in each direction would have been worth it for this meal alone. The end of which also brought announcements, with Jack heading back to the stage.

"Alright, folks, I know lots of you have travelled a long way to be here today, and I'm sure you're all just as excited as I am for the start of our staff training sessions tomorrow." A few people around the dining hall whooped out their excitement, including Abbi and Cole's girlfriend, Michele from her table in the far corner. The Director laughed along.

"Like I said, I know we don't start sessions until tomorrow, but our executive staff team has prepared something special for us all, so please join us at The Point for our Welcome Campfire at 8 p.m."

The brownie-induced bliss I had going on faded with that statement. It might have sounded like an invitation, but I knew a demand when I heard one, even if it's coded. And the way Jack's stare found me in this crowd left no doubts at all. What I wanted was to head back to my little solo cabin, curl up in bed, and sleep a dreamless sleep. Instead, I'd have to try and be a nice person for at least another few hours. My social battery was going to be at zero by the time this night was over. I used to be a social butterfly, but years of keeping my head down and staying as inconspicuous as possible to hide from my father, meant I was out of practice having friends, and even being around people. There were more announcements, including a run-through of tomorrow's schedule, which I didn't bother listening to because Jack had already shoved a copy in my hands in his office earlier. Right after we had discussed the need to keep my full name and phone number to himself.

A creaking sound over my shoulder had his and everyone else's eyes drifting that direction. All except for me. I kept my focus straight ahead and desperately willed myself not to look. That sound meant one, or more, of them was finally back. A grim displeasure passed across the Director's face as Brennon sauntered through the room. He bypassed his earlier table, strolling right up to stand behind me so he could stage-whisper, loud enough for the whole table to hear, "Move over, Little Bird."

The use of his old nickname made my skin prickle and had heat dancing over my face. I couldn't look at him. I couldn't do anything, except follow his directions and push closer to Abbi. The gap I left on the bench was barely big enough for this new man-sized version of Bren, but he sat down, anyway, ignoring the stares from the rest of our table and the rumble his actions elicited from Jack, who was still on stage. Brennon grabbed the last brownie from our tray and stared directly at the boss. Under his icy blue gaze, the Director visibly gulped and sped through the rest of his announcements. Less than a minute later, he wrapped things up with a, "We'll see you all in an hour," before he retreated from the stage.

From what I remembered, the end of camp meals always brought an eruption of chaos with staff and kids flurrying to clean off tables and stack benches. And there was still some of that, but it was subdued compared to normal. Instead of the laughter and noise that had been omnipresent during the meal, Brennon's return had ripple effects, so even as staff cleared tables and headed off in all directions, their voices were quieter, their whispers and gossiping obvious. Particularly as they passed where both Brennon and I still sat glued to the bench. Mentally clutching the last bit of my courage, I managed to keep myself from running out onto the deck that lined the whole building and throwing up right over the railing. In a move of solidarity I didn't deserve, Abbi stayed, too. I was even more grateful when she started speaking, clearly deciding to ignore Brennon.

"Yikes, I gapped that opening campfire thing was tonight." The way she said it had me doubting she had actually forgotten, and was just attempting to give me an out from the nervous chokehold I was in. "I need to prepare my song for tonight, want to help me out?"

Normally, I'd have laughed and explained to my new friend that I had the singing voice of a stray cat trying to claw its way out of the shower, except his continued presence on my other side was a weight made of panic and fear that sat on my chest.

"You don't want her help, Abbs," Brennon spoke for me, his deep gravelled voice full of derision. I didn't want to risk looking at him, terrified of what I'd find, but I couldn't resist. I could never resist. The smirk on his face was cruel and mocking as he looked down at me. I'm not petite by female standards at five-foot-ten, but Brennon had to be at least six-three or six-four, so he was looking down. "I've known Toni here a long time, and believe me, her singing voice will have you slitting your wrists."

"Brennon!" Abbi reacted sternly on my behalf. "That's not funny."

"Maybe not, but it's true," he replied, tossing his palms into the air like he hadn't been purposely malicious, and slipping off the bench. Strutting toward the doors, he grabbed an apple from the fruit bowl that lived permanently on the serving counter, tossing it into the air playfully before catching it again and taking a bite. Brennon could always do that, act like he didn't have care in the world. He didn't look back once letting the doors slam behind him. That made two out of three, and now I knew I couldn't expect a warm welcome back from Xav, either.

"Girl, what the fuck was that?" Abbi looked horrified.

Without the heat of him pressing against me, the pressure eased and I swear to god, my jaw finally unlocked, "That was the past coming back to bite me in the ass." Classic Toni luck, I'd made it less than six hours in this place without my history rearing its ugly head. It would be a miracle if news of my presence here didn't get back to my father. Fuck, it probably already had.

"Um, after that, I think you're going to need to explain." Abbi hooked her arm through mine just like she'd done earlier tonight and dragged me from my seat, "You can tell me all about it on our way back to the Village, and as payback, you can listen to me practise the cover song I'm supposed to be singing tonight."

How do you explain a decades' worth of friendship? How could I explain that I'd met my soulmates at eight years old? How did I tell her why things fell apart? How did I tell her any of that without revealing who I was? She'd only end up hating me, too. So, I did the only thing I could think of: I lied, or more accurately, I lied by omission.

"We were best friends," I explained, as we started down the road back to the offshoot path and the Village. "I met them my first summer here. We were eight years old, and even though I thought boys were mostly gross, and still do, they were different."

"Hold up. You keep saying 'them'. 'Them', who?"

"Cole, Brennon, and Xavier, obviously." Those three were a package deal, always had been.

"Come again?" Her shock gave me pause. "Not to doubt you or anything, but are you sure, Toni?"

"We were best friends, Abbi, for years. Of course, I'm sure."

"Holy shit!" Her reactions weren't making any sense, so I carried on. "Well, ya, so we were best friends until right after the summer we turned fifteen. After I left camp that summer, my parent's marriage sorta fell apart, and my mum couldn't afford to send me to camp anymore." What a crock of shit. More like I planted a stick of dynamite in their marriage and watched it blow, and everyone close to me felt the collateral damage of that explosion. "I'm not sure why they hate me," Lie, my brain screamed. I knew exactly why they hated me. "I tried to protect them. It didn't work." Lie again. They were still breathing, so it worked. "So, now they hate me, I guess."

"Protect them from what?" Abbi asked.

"It's ancient history now." One last lie for good measure. I doubted we could ever really escape what had happened. I shrugged, unsure of what else to say. There wasn't a single part of this story I could tell without bringing even more shit down on myself or my former friends, not that they seemed to care. Thankfully, Abbi let it drop without any more probing as we got to her cabin, just a few down from my own. We spent the next forty minutes there, me sitting on her bed, her burnt orange bedding and brown knitted blanket matching her whole aesthetic, while Abbs rehearsed on her guitar and sang her song for me a handful of times.

We made it down to the campfire with only a few minutes to spare. Since it was still only May, the sun had already set, so we relied on the lights from across camp and the small paper lanterns that lined the descending path into The Point Campfire to avoid tripping and falling. The Point was one of the main gathering points in camp. It was probably tied with the Dining Hall for the most used space. Once the kids arrived in a few weeks, we would all gather here twice a day, before breakfast and before bed, to share news and updates about everything and anything. But there had always been something more reverential about this place to me. Like it was holy ground. Maybe because it was where we hosted all the important camp ceremonies, openings and closing campfires, greetings and goodbyes, and somehow, even as an adult, I still felt that same sanctity here.

The benches were new, clearly updated recently, made of half-cut logs affixed in neat lines, row over row, to create an outdoor amphitheatre. And since we were amongst the last to arrive, most of them were filled. We were saved the search for a seat by Michele, who waved us over to the bench she was currently sharing with a bunch of other female staff. I quickly looked for Cole, expecting he would be somewhere near his girlfriend, but with no sign of his muscular frame, it felt like a safe enough bet. After all, Michele had been super sweet when we met earlier.

"Hi, Toni, hey, Abbs, grab a seat with us!" she said as she scooted over. I sat beside her, admiring how the firelight from the already raging campfire illuminated her tanned skin and blond hair. Honestly, Michele looked like an amalgamation of every popular mean girl you saw in teen movies, but so far, she'd been nothing but nice. I made a mental note to ask Abbi later if it was all for real. I suspected it was, though, because my usually hyperactive bullshit detector wasn't going off, and as if cementing it, she turned to me, and as quietly as she could, murmured, "Toni, I'm so sorry about Cole earlier today. I don't know what got into him."

"It's okay, Michele."

"He's normally really friendly, I swear." Was he? Because the Cole Michaels I knew was kind of a jerk to everyone but three specific people. But I kept those thoughts to myself. "And please, call me Michy. Everybody does."

She smiled at me with so much hope that I couldn't help but smile back. "Okay, Mich-y."

The sounds of movement from behind us made me turn, and the Director swept slowly down the centre aisle until he reached the bottom, moving to stand behind the campfire. Where seconds ago there had been whispers and murmurings of conversations, little bits of chatter between all the staff gathered in this space, there was only a weighted silence and the sparks of the fire. Campfires hold their own bit of magic, and this one was no exception. The crackles and pops were a warm-up act for the music, entertainment, and mirth that was to come. Opening campfires, in my experience, were joyful affairs, and even from our seats at the back, it felt like the warmth of the flames was reaching out to embrace me.

I let that heat and the feeling of being close to other people envelop me. After so long, the feeling of other people this close was quasi-claustrophobic. But neither Abbs nor Michele seemed to need anything more from me than a settled silence, and that helped me relax into the wooden bench beneath my ass. Instead, they seemed to be listening intently as Jack opened the campfire with yet another welcome. I didn't bother paying attention. Instead, I gave in to the urge I had been fighting against all evening, the urge to find their familiar faces in the crowd. And my search forced long-buried memories to the surface, from the last campfire I was at. One where I had cried, and the three most important people in my life had held me like I was some precious, breakable thing.

As the Director called the names of the night's first performers, I finally got a glimpse of one of them.

"Please give a warm Agonde welcome to our resident office manager and guitar virtuoso, Brennon Grace."

I was mesmerised by him as he hauled that same old guitar case on stage with him. He was beautiful. Tall, lean, and with the firelight, I could see the eyebrow and lip piercings I had missed earlier. The dark of the fire lit up the edges of his tattoos, poking out under the ratty cardigan he was wearing. But, after all of that, it was the guitar case that I zeroed in on. The last time I saw it, stickers from his dad's most recent tours covered the exterior. He'd been so proud of Blue Grace. Now it was like it had been stripped completely, all those markers of his dad's fame gone. Minus one sticker, near the head, that made my blood rush. A small sparrow in flight. And I think I gasped out loud.

Thankfully, my shock was covered by the man himself opening his mouth, and the voice that came out was more than I could have ever anticipated. Fifteen-year-old Brennon had a good voice, but now it was something else. The song he sang was meant to be happy, welcoming, a celebration of the start of something new.

And it was, if you stayed at the surface. But for those willing to listen just a little closer, there was a depth to his voice that added nuance, shading all that happiness with a tinge of something sadder. When he finished, everyone clapped, including all the girls around me, and some people cheered. I did nothing, and when Brennon looked directly at me, all I wanted to do was cry.

He nodded a quick thanks to the crowd and retreated into the shadows at the edges of the campfire. My eyes followed him into the dark until I couldn't see even the outline of him anymore. God, what next, I wondered to myself, and I resumed searching the crowd for signs of Xavi and Cole. Neither of them were big performers, but I didn't know if I'd survive if they took the stage. When I finally spotted Xav, he was on the other side of the campfire. He wasn't even sitting on a bench. He was alone, leaning against one of the huge Red Pines that bordered this space, with his arms crossed. Everything about his posture, his face, said, "No, you're not welcome." And I didn't think it was just about me. It was a universal message. Where was the kid who used to carry extra band-aids around just in case someone hurt themselves?

"Oh, yay!" I heard Michele clap, pulling my attention away from the brooding boy. "Here they come!" She was excited about whoever was up next, and a glance at the crowd told me she wasn't alone. Everyone around us was smiling and had their eyes glued to the small platform stage and campfire. One at a time, four guys traipsed up there. Two had guitars, one a harmonica, and holy shit, Cole was there with a guitar of his own.

From the side, the Director shouted, "Back by popular demand, the Back-Hill Band!" The name made a great send-up and the acoustic cover of a pop song they proceeded to play was great. Cole's voice was surprisingly rich, not quite as strong as Brennon's, but lighter and clearer somehow. Everything about this was so opposite to the Cole I knew. That kid would never have put himself on display like this. The song itself was upbeat and fun, everything an opening campfire song should be. I didn't pay much attention to the other guys he was performing with, although they played well together. What I couldn't understand was why Brennon and Xavi weren't a part of this group. How did Cole end up in a pseudo-band without them?

When this song ended, the cheers were next level. Michele wolf-whistled for Cole and shouted, "Way to go, babe!" These guys were a hit. The crowd ate that up.

I ignored it and instead cheered for Abbi as she was called down to the stage. After listening to her rehearse earlier, I knew her voice was killer—sultry, but powerful. She was pop star meets gospel choir, so while everyone was still cheering for Cole and his friends, I stood and screamed over them, "Get it, Abbs!"

She seemed unfazed for the most part, but when she heard my shout, she turned back to me and chuckled before making her way up front. She was also not lacking in popularity, and most of the girls in the crowd were hollering and shouting her name excitedly by the time she was up there. Her song was beautiful and the perfect way to close this night out. It was an invitation to embrace everything the future held, the excitement of the things to come, and even my jaded ass felt a bit swept up in it.

When she finished, the Director finally climbed back up in front of the now-dying fire. "Thank you all for being a part of tonight. I am so excited for what this summer has in store for all of us, and I thank each and every one of you for being a part of it." He paused for dramatic effect. "Now, off the bed!"

We had been dismissed, and all of us knew it. The whole crowd started to head back up the slight hill that led to the main road and the dining hall. Half the staff split off to head toward the Boy's Section or the Girl's, while those of us living in the village travelled as a crowd in that direction. Still sandwiched between Abbi and Michele, I let them chatter harmlessly about the next few days, while questions swirled around my head. Well, one question. Five years ago, Xavi, Cole, and Brennon were everything to each other. To me. Tonight, they hadn't come within five feet of one another. At least not that I could see. It felt like they couldn't stand to breathe the same air. I swallowed a lump of fear and interrupted Abb's breakdown of tomorrow's schedule.

"Um, girls, I realise I might be missing something, but the last time I attended an Agonde campfire, Cole Michaels, Brennon Grace, and Xavier Rothberg were inseparable. Clearly, that's not the case anymore. What happened?"

You'd have thought I killed someone right then and there. I swear to God the actual temperature dropped when those words came out of my mouth.

Abbi grimaced. “Uh, Toni, remember how I said there was ‘some fucked up shit’ in your story earlier?” She used air quotes.

“Yeah?”

“Well, this is what I was referring to. Those three are not friends.” She shrugged. “I don’t think they can even stand to look at each other.”

Michele piped in, “I started coming here when I was fifteen. I’m a year younger than Cole, and I remember what they used to be like.” She sucked in a breath as if bracing for her next words. “I’ve asked Cole about it.” She sounded so sad.

“He refuses to tell me what happened, and by the time we got together, it had already been a couple of years. He got so mad when I asked that I never brought it up again.” She visibly shivered. Was she afraid of Cole? I hoped not. Nobody deserved to live in that kind of fear.

“Ya, girl, I don’t know what to tell you. All three of them are on the exec team with us, and honestly, the vibe they give off in meetings is hostile… at best.”

We were well into the village, and Michele waved us both goodbye with a small, “This is me,” and she stepped into one of the smaller cabins. I could see my own just up ahead and Abbi’s just a bit beyond it. Once we got to my door, I was more than ready to swap my joggers and sweatshirt for pjs, but I still needed to brush my teeth and wash my face, which meant another short trek back to the girls’ bathroom.

I was about to say goodnight to Abbi, but her ever-present smile was gone. “Listen, I know you say you used to be friends with those guys, but you've been gone a while, and trust me, I've seen them in some major dust-ups over the last few years, so just be careful, yeah?"

"I appreciate it." I was being sincere. "After today, I'm just avoiding that whole mess." I twisted open my door and stepped inside. It wasn't a lie. I was going to make it my mission to avoid them. Every glimpse of them hurt, and I wasn't a complete masochist. Thank you very much.

Before I closed the door behind me, I stuck my head back out and hollered at Abbi's receding back, "Hey, Abbs! Thank you for today."

She smiled back at me over her shoulder, "No problem, that's what friends are for. Welcome back to Camp Agonde, Toni."

Chapter Nine

Toni

"Toni." The voice is stern, firm, demanding. Xavi.

I spit the last of my toothpaste in the sink before I answered, "Yes, Xavier?" I didn't look up, and I think that might have made it worse. After waving goodbye to Abbi, I grabbed my toiletries and booked it to the girls' bathroom. The building itself was one long cabin with stalls lined up on the left and sinks on the right, shower cubicles at the back. After a whole day in the car, and then what felt like another whole day of blasts from my past, I was ready to army crawl my head onto my pillow, so I peed and washed my face as quickly as I could, but not quickly enough.

"Toni..." he practically growled. "What are you doing here?"

For those that didn't know him, which to be fair was basically everyone, everything about his appearance was perfect. For those few of us who did know, we could recognize it like some cosmic sleight of hand. Everything about his face, from the soft curls sweeping over softer brown eyes dotted with flecks of green, to the delicate lines of his cheeks and jaw, was designed to draw you in, and make you see him as this sensitive soul. And I was well aware he could be that, but that was not who was here right now. Standing in this doorway, like it wasn't the girls' fucking bathroom, was cunning Xavi, cutting Xavi, the one primed to say something that would bruise me completely. Brennon's barbs and Cole's jabs were one thing—they were surface-level, designed to wound you instantly. When Xavi used his words to inflict pain, they were the kind to burrow, to dig in and make a home inside your brain so you heard them over and over again.

I responded with the only truth I knew. "I'm getting ready for bed." Wrong answer, I guess. He didn't move or bother looking away, and I could feel the heaviness of his eyes, even without looking up. "No, Nettie, what are you doing back here?"

First of all, fuck him and fuck this. After five years of wishing for them every damn day and knowing I could never have them. After doing what I did to my mum and my life, just to keep them out of Franklin Barrett's firing lines, I didn't need to take any shit from them. "I'm here to work, Xav. To do a job. That's it."

"Bullshit."

I finally summoned the courage to look at him, and his eyes were narrowed at me in disbelief.

"Lying about your name. Lying about why you're here. Lie after lie after lie." His words were spat at me. There was so much venom in them. Foolishly, I had held out hope that maybe Xavi would still be the boy I had desperately missed. After all, his relationship with his family was just as fraught as my own. If anyone could understand the fucking disaster that had become my life, I had thought it would be him. But I was wrong. He was still just as beautiful as he'd been at fifteen when he'd aimed his cruelty at anyone who dared to come between the four of us. Now it was aimed at me.

"Once a liar, always a liar, it seems."

"I don't know what to tell you. I don't know what you think I'm lying about" I shrugged my shoulders as I tried to push past him, out the door. All I wanted was to crawl under my covers and pretend for a few hours that this day had turned out differently. Xavi had other ideas. Instead of letting me pass, his hands shot up and gripped my upper arms bruisingly.

"Are you going to hurt me, Xavier?" A dangerous cocktail of hatred and something else flashed across his face.

"Stop calling me that."

He started it. I could be cruel, too. "Why? You don't like it?" I taunted. "It's your name, isn't it? Xavier Rothberg?"

His fists closed a little tighter around my arms. "Shut. Up. Antoinette. Hillis, is it?" He smirked at the mention of my phoney last name.

"That's what it says on my passport, or would if I still had one," I fawned, jostling my shoulder to loosen his grip. "Now, let me go."

"No." I tried to keep up the semblance of bravado I'd managed so far, but I couldn't. I was desperate to look away as the anger on his face made me feel nothing but sadness. And a desire to give up the fight. I was tired. I needed to sleep. So I broke our eye contact to stare at the floor.

"What do you want from me, Xavi?" On his name, my voice cracked ever so quietly.

"I want the truth. But I'll settle for giving you a warning, Nettie. You need to go. Go home. Go back to wherever you've been hiding and never show your face here again."

I practically choked, "I can't." I didn't know if it was the cracks in my voice or just the admission itself, but he finally released his punishing hold.

"Last warning. If you stay, Nettie, I promise we'll make you regret it." And with one last solemn look, he turned and left me clinging to the door frame for support.

I'm not sure why—why I couldn't just eat the words, especially since he was already gone—but like a secret that just had to get out, I mumbled, "I have nowhere else to go."

Morning came faster than I could have ever expected. Despite the dread I felt after my little toilet chat with Xav, I couldn't help but crash. My sleep was deep, but plagued with nightmares all the same. Scenes from the past and the present mingled into a terrifying cocktail that left me feeling distinctly unrested when my cheap battery-powered alarm went off at 7:30. So while I still lay in bed, I resolved to do everything in my power to avoid them, to put my head down and be the best Waterfront Director I could.

Cheesy, yes. Necessary for me, also yes. I wasn't lying when I said I had nowhere else to go. How could I explain to Mum that her July rent check would bounce? That my bank account now held a balance of forty-six cents? I couldn't, and I couldn't leave, at least not until I'd gotten my first paycheck.

It was a relief when Abbi knocked on my door before breakfast. I was still in my pyjamas and wasn't sure what to do. Surprisingly, she wasn't alone, and Michele's bright smile also met me at the door. The two of them didn't wait for an invitation, instead barging into my space.

"Ready for the first day of training, Toni?" Michele asked.

"Ugh... not really. I'd prefer to sleep for another eight hours."

Abbi winced. "Not a great sleep on the camp cot, then? I know, they're uncomfortable."

"Compared to what I'm used to, that mattress was divine. It wasn't that." Both of them looked at me like I had two heads. "I had some nightmares, I guess. I think I'm nervous about today." I couldn't bring myself to explain that my nerves were down to three men whose anger I couldn't bear. Or that I'd already forced myself to vomit bile behind my little refuge this morning. Honestly, I'm not even sure why I told them I was scared in the first place. Maybe because neither of them asked, and something about their undemanding presence gave me space to speak. I braced for their pity, anyway.

I didn't get any, although I did get sympathy. "Nerves are normal. Believe me, I get it," Abbi said warily. I think I knew what she meant, and that maybe she knew the meaning of real anxiety even more than I did. I was afraid of a couple of guys from my past. But she was so beautiful, and so Black, in a place and space where that's not exactly the norm. And sure, people embraced her, her popularity obvious last night. But whatever fear was feeling must have been amplified for her a thousandfold the first day she stepped foot onto Agonde property. She was one of only a handful of non-white staff members. It was a stark reminder that this was a privileged space. Unbidden, Michele reached for Abbi's hand and squeezed it twice. None of us said anything for a moment. Then Mich was up and moving.

"Okay, if you're nervous, then let's fix that. Clothes maketh the man, or woman in this case." And she dove for my suitcase.

"Ughhhh, I don't know what you're going to find in there."

She giggled, and it was a cheerleader-like noise. "Trust me, girl. Clothes are armour, and I'm about to make you invincible." She ripped through my suitcase and held up item after item of my clothes, asking how each one made me feel. With Abbi's help, we eventually settled on an old pair of branded jeans and a creamy knit sweater, and I couldn't help feeling grateful that my size hadn't changed much since I was fifteen. That's normal, right? I didn't ask, but grabbed the outfit, and turning my back to them, changed into it. When the sweater slipped over my head, I had to admit Michele had done something. I felt comfortable and confident all at once. Yesterday, I had pinned a small plastic mirror to a nail I found in the wall, and I used it to run a lick of mascara through my lashes and then the three of us headed out.

During breakfast, I sat between the two of them. Their popularity was a shield. Not a single guy approached the table, not even Cole. But almost the entire female staff team did. I met a mix of the new junior staff, who would be running programmes all summer, and the female cabin leaders. I learned so many names, I found myself struggling to remember them all, but it felt like I was being embraced and welcomed. Until one last girl approached our table and instead of a friendly greeting there was an excited screech. "Toni?! Holy shit girl!"

"Isabella?" I sputtered. It was her. Her Latina skin was already darker in May than mine would be come August, and her white smile stood out against it. Unlike all the other girls I'd met this morning, she dodged around Michele and Abbi and bent in to hug me where I sat. It was a hug I didn't deserve. Isabella had been a fellow camper back when we were kids. Hell, we had even been in the same cabin that final, cursed summer, but we had never been that close. Not close enough for the comforting hug I was getting now.

Not that it was her fault. It was mine. I'd been too wrapped up in the boys to seek anything or anyone outside of their friendship. Sometimes girls had tried to latch on to me, but mostly because they thought I could help them get in with Cole or Bren. It was never about being my friend. Isabella had been different. She never gave a fuck about the guys, making time to hang out with me instead. When they weren't around, or couldn't be, during swim lessons or craft sessions, she had been the only reason I didn't sit alone. At the time, I hadn't considered what that meant, but now I knew. Women needed other women. We needed each other.

The rest of the meal was surprisingly peaceful. The twelve girls sat around our table, laughed and joked, while we all inhaled breakfast burritos. I didn't even bother to look around the hall for them, and when the Director called an end to the meal and directed us to our first training sessions, I was emboldened. I could do this.

Chapter Ten

Cole

Watching her at breakfast was like watching a queen holding court, and all I wanted to do was go over to that table and destroy it. I wanted to fist her ponytail and drag her away from Michele. She might not know it, but the way Abbi and Mich had embraced her told all the other girls on staff everything they needed to know. Those two were going out of their way to make her popular, and I fucking hated it.

Last night, after the campfire, Mich had stormed into my cabin and given me shit for a solid thirty minutes. She asked all sorts of questions about the past.

"What is your problem with Toni?"

"Why were you being so mean? Didn't you used to be friends?"

"Toni said you all used to be best friends! Did you two used to date or something?"

"What's going on?"

Goddamn Antoinette Barrett, making me keep things from my girlfriend. I'm not that guy, at least I haven't been with Michele. But now, I didn't have a choice. Our history was something locked in a box and buried out in the woods past the library. Hopefully, by now, there was nothing left of it. When I didn't offer any answers, or any justification, except to ask, "What did Toni tell you?" I knew any hope I had of getting laid last night had died a quick death. Michele just snapped her tongue angrily, sighed, and left. She didn't even kiss me goodbye, just slammed the cabin door behind her. Now here she was with Toni this morning, smiling and laughing like they were best fucking friends. This couldn't stand. How dare that bitch crawl back into my universe and ruin my perfectly constructed relationship? I was going to fucking kill her.

I couldn't help it. I spent the entire meal staring at her from my spot by the coffee machines. I didn't sit. I didn't eat. I just sucked back cup after cup of shitty camp coffee, willing her to turn around, look into my eyes, and run away in fear at what she saw. It never happened. When the Director sent us off to the first sessions of the day, I didn't move as I watched my girlfriend and that bitch leave together over the edge of my cup. I had to resist the urge to slam the mug to the floor. The yellow ceramic dishware we used was basically indestructible, though, so there wouldn't even be a point.

A warm body slid against the table's edge beside me and another cup clapped against mine, spilling a few drops over the rim. "I did warn her." Xavier's voice was calm and steady.

"Watch it," I grumbled, pulling my cup back and shifting so there was space between our hips. "For all the good it did. She doesn't seem to have listened."

"No." I felt him shake his head, and I'm not sure why, but I wanted to pull on those brown tangles that now hung across his face. "She clearly didn't listen." We each nursed our coffees in silence. Only when the rest of the staff had left the building did Brennon approach us.

"So, our Birdie's still here."

I nodded. "She is."

"So?"

It was Xavi who confirmed, his typically drawling voice harsher than normal, "So, now we make her leave."

We agreed to let today pass without too much disruption. Toni was going to be in sessions with other staff for the rest of the day. It was a mix of soft skills training, things like 'what to do about bed-wetting, homesickness, and other fears campers have' and hard skills, how to teach this, that, or the other. Because my focus was entirely on Boys' Camp, plans for section games, campfires, and other boys-only activities for the summer, I spent most of the day in the Sections' office muttering to myself. Only emerging for dinner once all of July's themed activities were planned and the supplies I needed had been ordered. Both Brennon and Xavi had been similarly occupied. Camper registrations and details came in fast this time of year, and I could hear the clacking of Bren's keyboard as he took camper information and assigned kids to their skill programmes for the month of July.

Xavi, on the other hand, might have actually seen her today. As 'Lands' Head', he oversaw most of the staff training when it came to land-based activities. Although, as she was our new Waterfront Director, I doubted there was much overlap. Things worked a bit differently right now, and would do for the next couple of weeks, as staff went through training, but once campers arrived in the first week of July, those kids would become everyone's first priority. Things would get infinitely busier, and it would be about a million times harder to just get rid of Toni, so we needed to make sure she was long gone before that. None of us wanted to compromise any kids' camp experience. I mean, after all, there was a reason I worked here. It's not like summer camp was the best-paying gig. But I also knew that Toni was basically a ticking time bomb. Eventually, her shit had a tendency to explode everywhere and take out anyone it touched. I knew from personal experience. Dealing with the fallout of that shit last time almost killed me. My dad's career was just collateral damage. Not to mention, she almost ruined my hockey season. Fuck, my whole hockey career. That could never happen again, not now, not when I was so close. I was heading back to Michigan State in September for my Junior year, with hopes of being drafted before the season was through. That was everything. And I wouldn't let her crush that dream for me.

Every night during the next couple of weeks, there would be a series of activities, mostly hosted by members of the senior staff team, which thankfully included Xav, Bren, and I. They were meant to help us bond as a staff team, build friendships, all that wholesome crap. And while staff weren't required to attend, most would, and it made for a perfect opportunity to expose Toni so badly she would scurry back to Daddy Barrett. He was clearly the one who pulled the strings to get her here, anyway.

Dinner passed much the same as breakfast and lunch, with my girlfriend ignoring me in favour of the girl who couldn't be trusted, who turned me into something I never wanted to be, made me do things that still haunted my nightmares all to save her undeserving skin. I stood alone, wishing I could have a beer, or eight, but settling for coffee instead. There was zero tolerance for alcohol on camp property, so beer was never an option, anyway. Greer came over while I was leaning against the serving counter.

"Hey, man, looks like the new girl stole your girlfriend." He chuckled, and all I wanted to do was clock him.

I didn't, opting instead to hint at what was coming. "Not for long, bro. Trust me, that's going to change tonight."

"Oh, yeah?" Greer smiled, obviously picking up on my displeasure. He and I played Junior A together, and he'd always loved a bit of drama. He'd always been happy to help me teach someone a lesson, whether on the ice or off. Michele was not a fan of Mitchell. She always said he gave her 'the wig', but I think that's just because she doesn't have a mean bone in her body, so she doesn't get it.

"Toni Hillis," I replied to Mitch, "is not the nice girl she seems. Everyone needs to know that, and I'm going to make sure they do."

"Fucking right." He put out his hand like he was expecting a fist bump. I didn't move at all, and eventually, his fist fell again, just a hint of disappointment on his face. "She's a bitch. I tried to talk to her today, just being friendly or whatever, and she completely ignored me."

Something about Greer calling Toni a bitch made me want to punch him all over again, but still, I didn't. He walked away and let me go back to my new favourite hobby—staring daggers into my former best friend's back.

Chapter Eleven

Toni

As far as first days go, today wasn't bad. Particularly in light of Xavi's dour warning last night. Maybe it was the combined effect of his toned frame leaning over me against the backdrop of the late-night sky, but something in his words had me expecting an ambush at breakfast. One that never materialised, and as the day went on, and I went to session after session, each time expecting the worst, only to end up having a good time, I slowly started to relax. I ate lunch with Abbs, Isabella, and Michele, and just like at breakfast, we went unbothered before returning to sessions through the rest of the afternoon. I couldn't remember the last time I'd made it more than twelve hours without the urge or pressure driving me to throw up. But today I had.

The lone dark spot on the day had been that asshat Mitchell Greer, who'd approached me during the session this afternoon called "Recognising Children's Red Flags," where Michele, who was working on a psych degree, talked about key indicators that something was wrong in the life of a child or teen. The session was held in The Library, a small building, out past the Village and tucked away in the furthest corner of the property, used mainly for training with the Elites. Because I was never an Elite, I'd never really spent much time in this building, but it was full of comfortable old sofas and shelves of reference books. It had that comfortable cosiness of a library. That was probably the only reason I made it through the session at all. When I had first arrived, I grabbed a seat on one of the last empty sofas in the corner of the room. Other staff were already filling the other seats, while most were scattered across the open floor, sitting on pillows or beanbag chairs stolen from around the room. I didn't have the seat to myself for long. Mitchell sat down only a minute later. I didn't mind him sitting; I could share the sofa. What did bother me was the fact that instead of taking up the other arm, he sidled right up against me, so his sweaty thigh was pressed against mine and his breath was way too close for comfort as he breathed hot against my ear.

"Hi there, Toni, is it?"

I nodded.

"I'm Mitchell. It's nice to meet you," he continued.

"Hi."

I didn't think it was possible, but somehow he nudged even closer. "Are you enjoying staff training so far?" he asked, in an attempt to be smooth, but I was distracted by the smell of lunch clinging to his breath.

"Yep," I answered, again keeping my responses short. Not that that discouraged him. He continued to pester me, asking question after question about what school I went to and if I had a boyfriend. I finally had to ask him to be quiet so I could pay attention. His eyes pinched for a second before he grimaced and turned to the whiteboard and Michele, but he never moved. And I could feel his clammy thigh against my own for the rest of the session.

Meanwhile, the hour went by, and Michele handled these topics with such grace and sensitivity but it was a struggle all the same because honestly, her key talking points read like my own autobiography, and I couldn't help but wonder if this had been part of the training when I was a kid. If it was, well fuck me, not a single staff member had listened. Symptom after symptom she listed, I displayed them all, and no one had ever asked me about any of it. By the time the hour-long session was up, I was emotionally strung out and desperate to get away from people, so I made the mad dash back to my personal oasis, which is how I'd come to think of my cabin in the Staff Village. There, I spent the next hour diving into a book about fairies, dragons, and secret forbidden love. That break was a little bit of bliss, and by the time dinner rolled around, I had managed to recapture the peace I'd felt earlier that day.

But like all things in my life, of course, that feeling couldn't last. After dinner, which was every night at 6:30, we had an hour of unscheduled time, followed by an evening activity. According to Michele, these activities were planned by the senior staff team and if it wasn't for the fact that I'd just joined last minute, I would have been part of planning them. Since that wasn't the case, I got to participate along with all the junior staff. The game tonight was going to be a version of Family Feud, female staff against male staff. To make the game work, Xavi had handed every single person a printed quiz when we entered the dining hall. When he'd passed mine over, he managed to grip my fingertips, too, and squeezed them to the point of pain as he sneered, "Oh, Nettie. Should have run when you had the chance." The triumphant smile he shot me when he finally let go was such a fucking double-whammy. Did it give me shivers? Yes. Did it also make me blush? Yes, again.

The questions themselves were pretty innocent—my favourite camp activities, best thing about being on staff, worst camp meal. Like I said, all innocent, and I filled in my answers over barbecued chicken and rice, before dropping my answer sheet in the little bucket the Director had placed on the stage during the pre-meal announcements.

I didn't think any more about it until a few hours later, when I was walking with my newfound friends back to the dining hall. As we stepped onto the wide pine deck overlooking the Centre Circle and the beach, we'd mostly been chatting about school stuff, classes, uni parties, that sort of shit, until Isabella brought up the game.

"Those were some weird questions, huh?"

"Seriously," Michele replied.

Abbi agreed, "Yeah, so weird."

Their responses set off alarm bells, and those bells got louder as I said, "I don't know. I thought all the questions were pretty innocent?"

All three of them looked at me with concerned eyes, but it was Isabella who spoke up. "Uh… no judgement, but our definitions of 'innocent' are pretty different."

Abbs laughed, albeit a bit nervously. "Yeah, I mean, from those questions, it seems like Xavi planned to make tonight's game a bit on the spicy side, if you know what I mean." She wiggled her brows suggestively.

Now it was my turn to look a bit stunned. "Um, girls, I'm not sure what you consider spicy, but the hardest-hitting question on that quiz was 'Who's the best-looking staff member?' That's not exactly what I'd call spicy."

Michele stared back at me and swallowed hard. "Toni." Her voice was riddled with uncertainty. "What other questions were on your quiz?" I rattled off a list of the different questions, but before I'd gotten through more than a couple, Abbi held up her hand to stop me. "Toni, stop… those were NOT the questions on my quiz sheet." She looked around to the other two girls for confirmation, both of whom nodded their heads aggressively.

"Yep."

"Definitely not, chica."

"Oh." I felt my face colour a little. "What kind of questions did you guys have?" My stomach turned over, and a lick of anxiety crawled up my throat at my question. Maybe I didn't want to know.

"The dirty kind, Toni."

"Oh," I said again, fucking stuck on a loop caused by the fear now pumping through me. "Maybe Xavi gave me the wrong quiz sheet?"

"Hmmmm, maybe," Abbi answered, but she couldn't say much more, as other staff began to fill the deck, waiting for the doors to open and the game to start. The four of us leaned against the railing, all sporting grim faces, and when doors swung open to the Family Feud theme song blasting from the speaker system, I don't think any of us felt particularly confident about playing this game. It was hard to concentrate on anything going on around me as we headed inside, and I let myself be shepherded to one of the benches angled toward the stage. The tables we had eaten at not that long ago had been moved to the sides of the building, leaving an open space at the centre of the room where benches were set up to face both the stage and some makeshift cardboard podiums arranged into two distinct teams.

For a second, nothing happened, and as the fifty or so other staff gathered around us, I let their chatter wash over and ground me. Once everyone was seated, the fluorescent overhead lights that usually made the dining hall feel almost too bright at night went dark and left a single spotlight aimed directly at centre stage. The music dimmed a touch, and from the kitchen behind us came a deep voice over a mic, raspy enough that it could only belong to Brennon.

"Ladies and gentlemen," he boomed. "Welcome to the Camp Agonde edition of the Faaaaaammmily Feud!" He paused for dramatic effect, and most of the people around me clapped and cheered in response. When they quieted again, he resumed, "Please put your hands together for your host, the one, the only, Cole 'The Most' Michaels!" More clapping and cheers, even louder than before, erupted as Cole slowly jogged from out of nowhere to the stage. He looked ridiculous, sporting a ruffled dress shirt that wouldn't have looked out of place on a pirate and a faded orange sports coat. And someone, maybe Cole himself, had drawn a comically large moustache on him in dark eyebrow pencil. The whole look was finished by a pair of too-tight, powder-blue dress pants that barely contained his boxers, let alone the pipe he was working with. I couldn't believe Michele had let him go on stage like that. I'd murder anyone who got that good of a look at my boyfriend's dick. Not that I'd ever had a boyfriend, so what the fuck did I know?

But I couldn't help but stare, my eyes roaming over Cole. Unprompted, a flash of Cole minus the ridiculous outfit popped into my mind. What would it be like to watch him? When he held himself, would it be a firm grip? Would he stroke himself hard and fast, or go slow and take his time?

Jesus. I cut myself off, scrubbing that image away and returning to reality. My thoughts rarely ran that way. I didn't fantasise, I tried not to think about guys. And I'd never pictured someone that way. I'd never even had an orgasm, as far as I knew. Based on the sounds my first-year roommate made with her boyfriend, I definitely hadn't. Sex was an emotional minefield for me and not one I wanted to tackle, ever.

Chapter Twelve

Xavi

Watching again. Always watching. That was where I felt the most comfortable. Once Cole was on stage, reading the lines I wrote for him earlier today, I was happy enough to stand in the shadows and watch. The serving windows from the kitchen were open, but the lights were off, so from where I stood leaning against the counter, looking out into the bright space, I could stare at Nettie to my heart's content. I watched her when she came in, chewing her bottom lip in worry. There was always a risk one of the girls, maybe Michele or Abbi, would comment on the questions I handed out at dinner, but it was a gamble worth taking. Besides, even if she suspected something, she was still here and wouldn't have anywhere to hide once my plan picked up speed.

To my left, the door separating the main dining space from the kitchen swung, and I knew it was Brennon because I caught a glimpse of dyed hair and piercings in the little bit of light back here. He stepped up beside me, and in a hushed frustration raged, "You better be sure about this, man. Look at her." He gestured aggressively to Nettie, and I did look at her. I couldn't see her face back here, but since her hair was up in a ponytail, I could see the pale skin at the back of her neck when it turned pink under the lights. It was also clear as day what part of Cole she was staring at. "That little slut's eyes are practically glued to Cole."

"You sound jealous, Brennon."

"Fuck off, Xav." I rolled my eyes because yeah, fucking right. "I just thought tonight was about getting her the hell out of here. Not watching her drool over Michaels."

"It is," I snapped. "Just because you have no mind for strategy doesn't mean my plan isn't a good one. How about I call you when we need someone to take notes, since you're basically the Director's secretary at this point." Then I turned back to the crowd, effectively dismissing him. Or so I thought.

Quickly and quietly, Brennon was on me. His right fist snapped to my hair, and he used that grip to turn me back toward him, twisting and pulling painfully. His other hand pushed into the counter, caging me in. In the shadows back here, we were invisible to the crowd and the volume of Cole's mic meant that no one could hear us, either. "Don't make me ruin that pretty face, Xav. Trust me, I'll enjoy it." A wolf's grin cut across his face, turning him from college punk-rocker to something much more predatory. But as quickly as we had gotten here, he backed off and headed out the back door, leaving me alone in the kitchen, very confused. I was used to that shit from Cole, but with Brennon, it was different.

To re-centre myself, I focused back on Nettie and the game. Cole had made it through the explanation and the teams had taken their spots behind those ridiculous podiums he made. This game was Cole's idea, and while it's not one I would choose, it certainly worked in our favour. There were now four female staff and four male staff lined up to face off at the front of the stage. Over the mic, Cole called out the start of the game:

"Each team must send up one contestant for the face-off!" He was still using his falsely deep game show voice. A girl, whose name might be something like Susanna, I honestly couldn't give a fuck, approached the stage alone with Brennon's little protégé, Riley. A thin prickle of anticipation licked across my skin. After looking at everyone's answers, I'd set up the questions so we started innocently enough, but by the end of tonight, Nettie would run screaming, and everyone else would be happy about it. There was already a hum of tension in the crowd thanks to my questions from earlier. Apprehension and excitement mixing in a heady cocktail. It was absolutely intoxicating.

The first few questions truly were innocent, designed to lull the herd of nobodies into a false sense of comfort. After all, most of these white-bread kids liked their games the way they liked to fuck. Vanilla to the end. Pushing them out of their comfort zone was a perverse kind of thrill, one that made my blood rush. Cole asked the first two players to buzz in on, "What is the best camp activity?"

The girls won, and from that point on, the game flowed easily. Three rounds later, things started to heat up. The anticipation was giving me a head rush and stirring a fire elsewhere inside me, too. Cole had already run through a bunch of different questions. "Who's the sexiest staff member?" Michele won, and so did Cole.

The fucking prom king and his queen. They were all wrong, of course. It was obviously my wild girl. There were questions about sex, drugs, drinking, and all the fun naughty bits. And unsurprisingly, the answers were as routine as I expected. But it was the next question that had me inching forward to watch Toni's reaction.

Cole smirked behind the mic and dropped his voice an octave he asked, "Which staff member is most likely to be charged with a crime?"

The feeling in the entire room changed. A chill took over, and honestly, if the Director were here, he would probably have put a stop to this long before now. But he wasn't here. He usually left senior staff to run these events, or at least he did last year. He'd been increasingly missing in action the last couple of years. Not that I was complaining, since it meant he couldn't derail our plans tonight. Both teams were chatting nervously, and even the staff who weren't playing were rife with embarrassment, casting their eyes around the room like they were going to spot the criminal just by looking at them. Fat fucking chance. Others were practically pink with fear. Most of them came from homes where their idea of a violent crime was forgetting to put the cover back on the hot tub. I only had eyes for Toni. She was sitting stiffly straight, her posture full of an edge it didn't have before. It's the guys' turn to go first, and the kid who answers buzzed in, "Uhhhh... Brennon?"

The man in question cackled out loud, before asking sarcastically, "Is it the tattoos?"

Every member of the guys' team immediately blushed or stared at their shoes. No one said a word, which was perfect because the answer didn't matter. And the silence just ensured the recording I was about to play would be heard perfectly. We were always going to play the recording, but something about it felt extra special, extra punishing, after such a reasonable guess. If Brennon didn't want people to think he was a criminal, he shouldn't have put all that ink on his body. I couldn't help but stare at Toni's back as Cole said, "Great guess, Boys' Section! That was the most popular guess... but was it the right one?" His host smile morphed before my eyes into something much more sinister. "Not quite."

And then the recording started, playing through the sound system's secondary audio. We had all been in the room, all given testimony as minors, during Franklin and Diane Barrett's divorce hearings. Not surprising, given we were Toni's closest friends at the time, and the kind of accusations that had come out. To this day, I wasn't sure why I had even made these recordings or kept them. I was sure if the judge or any of the bailiffs had seen me do it, my phone would have been taken, but no one ever caught on, my wild girl included. She would know now.

The voice broadcast over the speakers belonged to a man, her father's lawyer. "Did you know your wife was having an affair?"

The solemn, media-friendly version of Franklin Barrett's voice answered, "No. At the time, I was not aware of my wife's infidelity."

"And how did you discover the affair?"

"It was with a staff member at my daughter's sleepaway camp. The camp office called me when she arrived at the property unannounced."

"So, your wife goes to your daughter's camp to meet her lover and gets caught by the administration?"

"It seems that way, yes," Franklin confirmed. There were a few seconds of silence on the recording, during which, no one in the dining hall moved to stop it. It was like the entire staff team was frozen in place.

The lawyer's voice picked up again, louder now, "Let the record show that the defence's legal team has submitted photographic evidence of the plaintiff on the summer camp property with the alleged staff member in question, one Nicholas Patterson."

"Your honour," he continued, "we have tried to contact Mr. Patterson several times, but have been unsuccessful."

"In fact, both his boss at Camp Agonde and his family have reported that he disappeared shortly after these photos were taken. Why do you think that is?"

Hearing the camp name over the speaker kicked off a round of wide eyes and whispers through the crowd of staff. There was genuine fear belying some of the chatter now.

I heard the accusation and remembered the touch of smugness that Franklin Barrett couldn't keep at bay as he said the words, "I cannot say for sure, of course, but I think my wife may have had something to do with his disappearance."

"Do you think your wife killed her lover?"

Franklin never got a chance to answer, because a small voice screamed across the audio. "No!" Her cry was lighter and higher than her voice now, but it was still recognizably Toni. "My mum didn't hurt him! I did!"

That was enough to finally make the crowd erupt. Michele, in particular, shouted, “Cole! Turn it off! Now!”

“Oh, fuck! I’m so sorry, everyone.” I had to give it to Cole. He was normally a hothead, but his acting at that moment was top-tier. He fumbled with the mic, pretended to fiddle with the speakers, and did everything he could to make it look like he was shutting that shit down all while mumbling into the mic, “I’m sorry... I have no idea what... I’m not sure what’s happening.” Credit where it was due; he did a good job of feigning awkwardness once I shut the recording off.

“Ummmm, again, I’m so sorry about the interruption. How about another question folks? Maybe something a little tamer?” It was my turn to smirk. The questions needed to ebb and flow, or the whole thing would be too obvious and over too early. It took a few rounds, but eventually, everyone settled back into the pattern of the game. Everyone except Toni. Hearing her voice had clearly had an impact. Her shoulders curved in on her body, and her head dropped, so she was staring at the floor. Meanwhile, Cole put on a show, reverting to his friendly game show host persona. Then he let question after question fly, drawing on only the safe ones from the version of the question sheet I’d given Toni, the one without any suspicious questions.

We were more than halfway through the game, and I was ready to rattle my wild girl’s cage yet again. Obviously, so was Cole, when his eyes caught mine over top of the crowd. Of course, he and Brennon knew I was back here, controlling our plan from a safe distance. No one had seen me come in earlier. And no one else knew to look for me now. "Alright, gents, now that you've stolen the last round from the ladies, it's time for your question." There was a small drumroll from the audience, everyone slapping their thighs or the benches. To silence them, Cole swept his hand out in a wide, cutting motion. "What is the most common thing parents say to their kids on drop-off day?" It was a perfect question. There was nothing suspicious about it, not a hint or even the slightest suggestion that this was part of our private game. Until the first kid buzzed in. Cole moved toward him, pointing the mic at this poor kid, who barely got his mouth open to answer when I hit play on another recording.

I knew what came next. After her outburst in the courtroom, the judge dismissed Franklin and called Toni to the stand instead. Audible sniffles could be heard through the speakers, and I remembered how Toni had looked that day, sitting in the box beside the judge. Her face had been blank; every bit of the brave girl I knew drained away. It felt like looking at a stranger. That was the first time I wondered if it was all an act. Caught between the lure of the past and the sounds of the recording, I was drawn back to the present as Toni's young voice was barely audible over my phone's audio, but the silence of the dining hall was enough for everyone to hear her explain.

"He tried t-t-to-touch me."

"Touch you how, Antoinette?" The lawyer's use of her full name only confirmed what everyone in the dining hall should have already guessed. Around her, Michele, Abbi, and Isabella drew closer, trying to comfort Toni, but she never even looked up, and the recording just kept playing.

Toni had tried to respond, but her tears just ramped up and her answer had come out in a fit of sobs. "He... he..." And then the whole story came out.

Back then, Toni told us everything. She'd told us about the first day Nick had approached her during a sailing lesson. He was a staff member already—older, good-looking. And she was a sucker for his attention. For a month after that, all we heard about was how great Nick was. How he helped her dock her boat every day, how he taught her knots, how he saved her the best-fitting life jackets. Until, finally, one day after lunch, when we'd been together at the Throw, she'd asked, "Guys... have any of you been kissed before?" Her question had stunned us all into silence, and while I couldn't remember now what we'd been talking about, I could remember the way our conversations ground to a halt in that moment. I thought Cole was going to crack a tooth, he gritted his jaw so tight. "Because somebody tried to kiss me today." She didn't look at any of us when she said, "And I think maybe I'm bad at it." She put her face in her hands, hiding from us. She was sitting on the smallest rock in our circle, using a stick to dig into the dirt, and her cheeks bloomed a bright pink as thin tears ran down either side of her fingers.

It was Cole who got there first, kneeling in front of her. "No way, Ton..."

"How would you know, Coley?" She always called him Coley when she was nervous. Brennon and I crowded in on either side of her then, so when Cole reached out his palms and lifted her face, she saw each of us in turn.

"Not possible, Birdie."

"But Bren, he kissed me and then he ran away."

I had stifled the growl that had been threatening to come out and looked her dead in the eye. "Nobody should be kissing you in the first place," I fumed, rife with jealousy at the time.

Her anger flared instantly. "Why? Just because none of you want to kiss me, Xavier?!" she shouted, and then, for the first time in our long friendship, she ran away from all of us. Back then, I had cursed myself for upsetting her, for making her think she wasn't kissable. Twenty-four hours later, my idiotic words wouldn't be more than a vague memory, lost in other, stronger regrets when it came to Antoinette Barrett.

The next day, the three of us waited at the Throw as usual, expecting Toni to join us. We waited nearly thirty minutes, as long as we could before the next programmes were due to start, and just as we were about to leave, she burst through the forest behind us. One look at her was all it took to know something bad had happened. Her brown hair was a rat's nest, there was blood running from her eyebrow, and her clothes were a mess, torn and smeared in dirt. She staggered toward us and croaked desperately, "Guys... help."

We had crowded around her, each talking over the other, demanding to know what happened. "H-h-h-he fell," she sobbed. "It was an accident. Help!" She was our best friend, so of course, we were going to help. The four of us retraced her steps through the woods. Eventually, lost amongst the pines so far from the main property, we couldn't make out a single sound beyond the rustle of animals in the undergrowth or breeze through the trees. That's where we found Nick. Or the body that used to be Nick. There was blood still running from an open wound on his head, but his eyes were open and empty. Cole bent down to feel for a pulse before looking up at me and shaking his head. I immediately turned and threw up. Pretty sure Brennon did, too. Cole seemed to handle it better. Later, he would chalk it up to watching too many horror movies. Nettie, on the other, cracked completely. Sitting in the dirt, her knees hugged tight to her chest, tears poured down her face while she stared into the distance.

Cole had gone to her side, rubbing her back in slow, comforting circles while, as gently as he could, reassuring her, "Don't worry, Toni, we'll take care of this. No one will ever know."

Brennon trembled beside me. "Maybe we should go get the Director..."

Only then did Toni make eye contact with Cole. "He'll call m-my father. And my father can never..." Her voice trailed off as fear and sobs took over once more.

Cole glared at Brennon and me, daring us to object as he said calmly, "We will make sure no one ever finds out." And that's the story of how three fifteen-year-old boys buried a staff member out in the woods one day. But that's not the version of the story on the recording.

No. On the recording, Toni recounts how Nick invited her out to the woods that day and skipped straight from kissing and flirting to pressuring her for sex. And when she didn't give in, he got angry, pushed her down, and tried to rape her. I sat and listened in horror as she described the assault. Her story matched with everything she'd told us that day, everything we'd seen, right up until she got to the end, and then she had looked out across the courtroom when the lawyer asked, "And what happened once he removed your pants, Antoinette?"

Her blue eyes sought me out, then Brennon, and finally Cole, seated in a line like her sad little soldiers waiting on orders that would never come. Her face was marked with tears but too far away to read much more than sadness in her expression. Then, with one slow blink, she looked away. And that was the moment I knew. Toni had lied.

She turned to her father's attorney, and with a harder voice than I would have thought she was capable of, she said, "I found a rock on the ground and I hit him with it. Over and over and over again, until he stopped."

She had known he was dead long before she came to find us. And then she'd made us unknowing accessories to a murder we didn't understand. Thinking about it now made me feel like a fucking moron. Only then did her father interject, telling the whole audience in the courtroom that his daughter was a troubled young lady, prone to making false claims, including ones about unwanted male attention and even abuse at his hands.

From there, it was easy enough for Franklin Barrett's lawyer to paint a convincing picture of a young woman whose mother had encouraged her to lie, all for the sake of covering up something as stupid as cheating. I didn't exactly believe that. Toni had always been too smart to fall for the regular lies and tricks adults use on children. But I didn't know what to believe, either. Not then, and not now, as the recording finally ended.

Somehow, in its aftermath, the staff team seemed unable to react. Cole made zero attempts to continue the pretence of the game, instead revelling in the awkward looks and whispers exchanged across the hall. Everyone's focus was elsewhere, so I didn't think anyone except me saw the way his smile curled into something smouldering, devious, and cruel as he stared down at a shell-shocked Toni.

Toni, age 15

5 years ago

Today was going to be the worst day of my life. As we got in the cab, Mum held my hand in solidarity, while Francis sat on her other side, letting rage radiate off him in waves. In the few weeks since we had left our home, he hadn't said much, and I still wasn't sure if he was angry at Father or me. When the car pulled up to the courthouse, Mum whispered, "Don't worry, honey. No matter what happens today, you did the right thing and I love you."

Her words bolstered me, right up until the car door closed and Mum went to speak to her lawyer. Unnoticed, Francis had stepped behind me, and when he gripped my shoulder uncomfortably, he hissed, "You've already ruined so much. Are you seriously going to make it worse?"

He didn't wait for an answer, instead following Mum and the lawyer up the concrete steps and into the building. I swallowed hard, wishing I had someone, or specifically three someones, with me to rally my strength, but I didn't, and all alone, I followed what was left of my family inside. I prayed for them.

Three months ago, I arrived home from camp. After the best summer of my life, going back to my family home in West Barrett Hills felt like a punishment I hadn't. deserved. Those summer months had felt like a dream. Every day I'd hung out with my three best friends, laughed, loved, and done the typical dumb shit that fifteen-year-olds do without the constant dread I lived with at home. But summers end. They always do. I had felt the weight of my father's presence the second I got off the long bus ride and was loaded into his personal towncar. Threatening me, forcing me to be 'his princess', the way I had been before. But now, I couldn't be. When I was younger, the summers away at camp had always been joyous, light-filled months, but chalk it up to the foolishness of youth. I had always been able to come home and slip right back into the carefully, if obscenely, constructed space my father had built for me. This time was different. Maybe because for the first time this summer, I had caught a glimpse of what love could look like, and it didn't, not even for a second, resemble the sick form of 'love' he swore to me was normal. And now, my brain and my body were rebelling.

So I did the only thing I could. I told my mum. The morning school started, I had stood in my room getting dressed, putting on my kilt and uniform. My hands trembled with each button. My father would be picking me up alone at the end of the day, and there would be no one but his driver Mikhael to stop him. Mikhael never stopped him. Then Mum came in to see if I was ready to go, and I broke down. I sobbed to my mother and ran through every interaction, every twisted moment my father had put me through, and to be honest, I think I almost killed her. Once the first words came out, she demanded the rest. At her request, I told story after story about touching him in ways that would make him happy, and make him feel good, and each one was like taking a battering ram to the naïve, country-club life my mother had established for herself. By the time I was done, I was out of tears, and she had vomited into my candy-pink rubbish bin at least three times. I half expected her to abandon me completely. Instead, my mum showed a strength I didn't know she possessed.

She let me stay home from school, and together, we curled up in bed while she held me securely as I slept and cried on a constant rotation. All the while whispering into my back how sorry she was, and how she would protect me from now on. When my father had gotten home in a rage, having gone to the academy to pick me up, only to be told I stayed home, I half expected my mother to cave, to back down in fear of him the way she had done in the past, but again, she surprised me.

He stood by the front door, yelling for me. "ANTOINETTE BARRETT! Where are you?!" I sat cradled against a wall at the top of our stairs, with tears streaking down my face. Guilt and terror at not answering mingled inside me, and I almost gave in.

But Mum was a superhero. She was so much more than I ever expected her to be. She stomped down the stairs step-by-step to where he stood in our foyer, and in a steely-edged voice, calm as anything, she said, "Franklin. My daughter will never be going near you again. I will never let you get near her, either. Not ever again."

He said nothing for a second, letting her words hang in the air. Then his face twisted into a horrific kind of smile for a second or two, before he picked up his briefcase and hurled it at Mum.

"You fucking cunt. How dare you? She's mine. MINE!" he shouted. "And I will get what I want from her. Always. There's nothing you or anyone else can do to stop me," he spewed, strings of spit flying from his open mouth as he yelled. Thankfully, Mum managed to dodge his briefcase as it landed, springing out, and paperwork spilt everywhere.

"I don't know how I missed it all this time. But now I see you, Franklin Barrett, and I promise, you will never, ever, hurt my daughter again."

Her calm response only heightened his vitriol, and he prowled closer to her. "If you dare to keep me from her, I will destroy you. I will ruin every scrap of your pathetic existence, and you will beg me for mercy. So, choose wisely, Diane." With those last words, he was finally close enough to reach her, and his hand snapped out faster than I'd ever seen him move and slapped Mum so hard her body ricocheted into the steps.

"I'm going to my office. You should send Antoinette to see me there." Somehow, almost like his outburst hadn't happened, he'd slipped back into his persona of a contained, well-mannered businessman. "However, Diane, if my princess isn't standing before me in the next fifteen minutes, then I recommend that neither of you remain in this house after that."

Fifteen minutes later, Mum was stuffing me and Francis into the back of her car with the small suitcases we had each managed to pack. It hadn't taken long for Father to capitalise on our leaving. Within a week, gossip had spread that Mum had an affair. Two weeks later, I was being bullied so mercilessly at school that Mum pulled me out. A month after that, newspapers were running with the story that my mum was a cheater, a liar, and some kind of sex maniac. Everywhere we went in town, together or alone, people were merciless and cruel. After all, my father was the town's namesake, a big employer, and a major benefactor of most of the charities around. He was a well-loved and well-respected, contributing member of society. Mum was just an ungrateful slut, at least according to them.

But she stood by me the whole time. Hugged me on the nights I cried, wailing that I had ruined our family and ruined her life. She swore every day, up and down, that that wasn't the case. Basically, she loved me through it, even though I wasn't sure I deserved it. Now, at the beginning of December, here we were on the first day of their divorce hearings. We had been living out of a hotel ever since we left our big house in West Barrett. Although, for how much longer, I wasn't sure. Mum had been paying the bills out of her small personal savings, and those accounts were drying up rapidly. She needed a cash settlement from Father to allow us to get back to some kind of life, and today was the first step to getting that for her. The lawyer had already warned me, given the accusations Mum and I had levelled against my father, I would likely have to take the stand. We had practised and practised and, as much as my heart ached and my stomach turned at the thought of admitting the truth to anyone else, I knew I needed to, for mother's sake more than my own.

Chapter Thirteen

Toni

If the trial were happening now, I was sure it would have gone differently. In the last five years, a lot has changed with how courts treat victims. Not enough, not nearly enough, but after a few high-profile cases in Hollywood and on Parliament Hill, there were more protections in place. Again, not enough; victims still lose nearly eighty percent of the time, but they don't have to suffer the indecencies of such public trials anymore. Names are protected. Identities hushed up, or at least for a little while. None of that was true five years ago.

Hearing that recording was a reopening of long-closed wounds. As my own words played out over the stereo, I shrunk, becoming smaller and smaller in the hopes that I could be nothing. Secure in the knowledge that I was nothing. Even though I hadn't said anything, somehow, the women around me had seen the recordings for what they were, an attack, and instead of abandoning me, Michele, Abbi, and Isabella surrounded me. Their voices were almost enough to block out the echoes of my memory—until they weren't. When the speakers popped and shut off, I swallowed and looked up at Cole. Surely, he wouldn't have done this. Surely, he knew me enough to know that was the worst day of my life, and though he might hate me now, he wouldn't taunt me with it. Boy, what a fucking idiot I was. His expression was one of pure delight. He was practically giddy at the reaction the recording had elicited, scanning the crowd with a smile I could only describe as proud.

It was that proud smile that got me out of my seat, that had me pushing my new friends off and running into the dark of the May night.

Although it wasn't that late, not even 10:30, night had come into its own outside the bright fluorescence of the dining hall, and spring stars covered the sky. Not that I noticed as I hurtled my way down to the Point until I stopped short at the water's edge. When I was a kid, there hadn't been a proper stage or even half the benches. Back then, Jack had just stood on the rocks under my feet and made daily announcements that way. At the campfires of my childhood, the flames had been visible everywhere across the point, orange and bright in the twilight. At our opening fire last night, I could barely see them over the platform and performers. There was more performance and less magic. But now, I was grateful that the stage hid me from sight, especially as I sat down on the cold grey stones and cradled my knees into my chest.

The rocks were damp, and I could feel the cold of it against my ass, even through my jeans. I let the feeling numb me, letting my mind drift away, out across the lake water to some place where my memories couldn't touch me. Usually, I was good at disassociating—at mum's apartment, in my sad little dorm room, fuck anywhere. It was my superpower—the ability to shove every emotion of my own into a box in my mind, one so small and so secret no one could get to it. But here, in this fucking place, that seemed impossible. There were just too many memories here battling for supremacy at the front of my mind. I tried my best to concentrate on the soft lapping of the water in front of me. Eventually, it worked, at least enough that I wasn't listening to the sound of footsteps behind me. Not until they were too close. God, their combined presence had a fucking gravitational pull. Even after tonight, I had to fight the urge to run to them, to race for a hug. Their arms were the only security blanket I'd ever known. Instead, I stayed sitting as they came closer until they penned me in. I let the weight of their eyes settle over my seated body.

Echoing his own words, it was Xavi who broke the silence. "I did promise you'd regret it. Time to crawl back into the hole you came out of, Nettie." My only reaction was a shiver, one I mentally blamed on the small gust of wind off the lake and not his deep voice.

That wasn't enough for Cole, who snapped, "Fuck this," and grabbed my arm, hauling me to my feet with one hand, like a paper doll. His other hand wrenched my head to face him, holding me by the neck and leaving me with no choice but to look directly at him. Hatred looked back at me. All the soft edges of boy-Cole's face were gone, replaced by the square jaw and the hard-set eyes of an angry man. "I swear to fucking Christ, Toni, if you stay, tonight will feel like a fucking dream compared to what I'll do. I'll ruin your fucking life."

Cole was certainly intimidating enough to send most people running at a threat like that. Maybe if I were a different person, with a different past, it would have. Instead, it was a dam breaking, and an ugly, jaded laugh bubbling from me. Confusion and momentary concern replaced the anger in Cole's dark eyes, and he dropped his hands from my body as I doubled over, letting the manic laughter ripple out of me again. I spun as I cackled, seeing similar looks of apprehension on both Xavi's and Brennon's faces. All pinched eyebrows and scrunched expressions.

When I finally ran out of air, I was looking at him again. I sucked in a breath. "Oh, Coley, there's nothing left to ruin."

"Fucking crazy bitch." He looked to the other two guys. "She's insane." I mean, he wasn't exactly wrong.

Despite the anxious way he chewed the silver ring on his lower lip, Brennon chimed in, "All the more reason to get her out of here."

"And how do you propose we do that, Brennon, because we tried my thing already?" Xavi asked.

I don't know why, but something about the way they were talking around me like I wasn't a part of their conversation, like I wasn't a factor, reminded me that I didn't have to be a bystander in this. I was a passenger in every other part of my life, but it didn't have to be that way here.

"Why do you all hate me so much? When did I become your enemy?" My voice sounded sadder than I had expected. "When did I stop being your friend?"

"Were we ever friends, Nettie, or were you the star, and we were just your collection of idiot fanboys?"

"Xav—" my voice broke. "How could you—"

As though the tears threatening at the edges of my eyes were offensive to him, Cole cut me off. "No, none of your bullshit tears, Toni."

Did they think I was lying? Holy shit. My eyes sprung wide at the realisation. Did they think I'd done all of this, spilled my guts in a public courtroom, for no good reason? No wonder they were pissed.

"They aren't bullshit, Coley."

Behind me, Xavier laughed harshly. "Of course they are. We were all there that day in the courtroom." And dropping his voice low so that his wrath wouldn't escape our little circle, "You played us, Toni. We helped you cover up a murder," he hissed.

My cheeks burned with a combination of anger and shame. "I lied for a reason. I had to. I did it to protect all of you," I pleaded, facing each of them in turn. My eyes silently asked them to understand. "I know you won't believe me, but you were everything. Everything."

I was fully begging now. "My father is a poison. I had to protect my mum. I had to!" I inched closer to Cole, willing him to see the truth. "We ran. After that day in court, Mum took Francis and me and ran. We sold my car, she trashed our phones and my laptop. Fuck, I don't even have a passport anymore! That's how I became Antoinette Hillis! My dad hunted us. He's still hunting us. That's why I had to disappear. But I tried to explain!"

Early in our friendship, we had been trying to figure out how far apart we all lived. Back then, I remember hoping that they lived far enough away that they wouldn't be able to visit. Remember knowing, even then, that my father wouldn't like it. The words came rushing out now, humiliating but honest. "I had the address here! So, I wrote to you! All of you! And then again that next summer, I wrote so many fucking letters. Sometimes I even wrote to you all together. I had this stupid picture in my head of the three of you sitting together, reading the letters and knowing I was missing you. Other times, I wrote to each of you individually. Over and over again I wrote, but not once did I get an answer." With that final admission, my tears overflowed.

Xavi's face was a question mark. "We never got a single letter, Toni. So, we don't know what the fuck you're talking about."

My mouth dropped open. How was that even possible? I swear, I'd written probably like fifty letters that summer. I had hoarded the money for stamps by doing odd babysitting jobs for the other renters in our crappy building. They didn't pay very well, because honestly, no one with the money to pay well lived in our building. It was nobody's first choice.

Snarling, Cole fired back, "Of course, we didn't get any letters, Xavier, because she's still fucking lying." His shoulders tensed and his fists balled at his sides, and suddenly, his hands were on me again. Only not my arms this time. Both his hands wrapped around my neck. "Always. Fucking. Lying."

Cole's anger was apocalyptic. Terrifying. And I could feel the pressure of his hands around me. It didn't hurt, not yet, but he was definitely strong enough to crush my windpipe if he decided to. A quick peek around was enough to tell me that the other two were as freaked out as I was by the rage burning off his athletic frame. For the first time in this whole fucked up fight, I genuinely thought Cole might hurt me, and I visibly flinched, the shock causing him to release me and sending my ass to the ground in the process. It was a hard landing. Guaranteed I would have a bruise on my left butt cheek tomorrow.

Brennon's hands went up in an attempt to calm Cole, the same way you would a wild animal. "Woah, woah, woah, Cole, man..."

"Coley—you need to calm down." Xavi used the nickname reserved for us alone. His voice was only slightly less edged than when he'd threatened me.

One slow step at a time, Brennon approached Cole, reaching out to lay a hand on his shoulder. "Seriously Puck Dropper—" that nickname, God, I hadn't heard that in so long, "Men who beat on women don't get to go pro, so maybe put the hands down, yeah?" The attempt at levity fell flat, more than flat. Cole moved with a speed I couldn't have anticipated, his fist cracking across Brennon's face and knocking him so hard Bren visibly recoiled.

"SHUT. THE. FUCK. UP." Cole's body heaved and sagged. "And don't ever use that shitty nickname again. Don't act like we're fucking friends." And on that note, he turned and stomped away without even a glance at the rest of us. When his back was swallowed by the shadows, a silent Xavi looked to each of us, pausing as he took in my wide eyes and Brennon's now bloodied eyebrow piercing, before wordlessly following after Cole. Together in the dark, Brennon and I stood staring after them.

"Not anymore, anyway..." he muttered, so quietly I barely heard it. I'm not sure he even meant to say it out loud. His long fingers came up, one running through his blue-grey hair, gripping the strands so his knuckles whitened. The other touched his brow softly, checking the silver ring was still there. Then his hands fell and our eyes connected. Matching sets of blue lost eyes. He sighed heavily, breaking the contact, and walked away, leaving me exactly where I was always destined to wind up, anyway—alone in the dark.

Chapter Fourteen

Toni

Two weeks had passed since I knelt in the dirt in front of the guys, willing, begging, hoping they would hear me out. Like every other fucking thing in my life, that turned to shit right quick. Since then, every day of staff training has been a mixed bag of torments. Jeers and taunts followed me everywhere. But none of it was as confrontational as that night, so mostly, I just kept my head down and focused on training. For the most part, it felt like the younger staff members were just doing their best to stay out of my way, maybe to avoid getting caught up in hailstorm Cole. Almost none of them spoke to me or would even make eye contact with me during sessions, which made things a bit tough, since I was pretty much the only senior staff who had to attend them. The others, like Abs and Michele, got to run them. The guys ran them, too, but thankfully, my newfound girlfriends knew who was leading which sessions and mostly kept me out of the line of fire.

Mealtimes and any of the staff gatherings were the hardest. Jack would usually be there to make announcements or welcome us to things, and then promptly fucked off, leaving the staff to police themselves. That didn't work. Like clockwork, the second he was out the door, there would be some sort of incident. Soup was dumped in my lap, and old newspaper clippings from the trial dropped like confetti from the lodge ceiling. And like I said, more trial recordings. Mostly, ones of my father talking about how fucked up I was. None of it was great, but all of it was survivable. The worst of it wasn't even the guys; it was Cole's posse of inane morons; shitheads like Greer, who seemed to get a thrill out of soliciting me and my mum for a creative host of sexual services or barely feigned coughs of "murderer" anytime I got within twenty feet of them. Again, not great, but compared to what I was used to, it was basically a cakewalk.

Now, on the last day of staff training, there wasn't much those assholes could do. As soon as campers started arriving tomorrow morning, there would be about 250 obstacles in the way of their torture at any given moment. Fuck whatever those guys said. There was a reason that Brennon, Cole, and Xav were all still working here. There were other jobs. They all had other options. But they chose this, and I felt secure in the knowledge they wouldn't do anything around campers that would fuck that up for them. That feeling was like fucking Teflon. I went to sessions and ate my meals for the first time without a constant fear that I'd be sent packing back to East Barrett, back to my mum, and our tomb of an apartment. The girls seemed relieved, too. After the last dinner, the four of us sat around on the dining hall deck together. We'd pulled four of the wooden deck chairs into a small circle in the corner and sat there talking shit and gossiping about what was to come over the next eight weeks. Michele, in particular, was reeling from Cole's actions over the last little while.

"I haven't really spoken to him since you got here. I don't even know if we're still..."

"Michy—" I had fully succumbed to calling her that because that girl was an angel. She's got girl code written in her fucking bones. "I'm sorry. I never meant for my being here to ruin your relationship."

"You didn't, Toni. Cole's doing a perfectly good job of that all on his own," she replied. "But forget him, let's talk about something more interesting than my pathetic relationship." Like she had flipped a switch, she was back to her peppy self. "Any prospects, Abs? Or Bella, what about you? Are any of those male cabin leaders worthy?" Isabella blushed furiously. Her already-tanned skin hid it better than my pale ass would have, but the spots of pink on her cheeks as she shook her head were easy to spot.

Abs, on the other hand, gave an uproarious laugh. "Oh, fuck yeah, I have."

We all laughed at her fox-like grin. I couldn't help but ask, "Well, now you have to spill, girl."

"Wellllllllll, you know that little protégé of Brennon's, Riley?" None of us said anything, all stunned. She laughed again. "What, he's cute, plus, he tries really hard." She lifted her eyebrows suggestively.

"Isn't he younger?" I asked.

"Yeah, and so what? I'm only two years older. If our genders were reversed, we all know he'd be getting a clap on the back for fucking an eighteen-year-old chick," she replied defensively.

None of us could say shit after that. It was true. Michele backed her up. "You know what, girl? You're right. Get some." And then they high-fived, which led to even more giggles.

Summer night descended around us as we stayed on that deck. It was such a joy to just be there. I couldn't have articulated it at the time, but being around those three women was like setting down a heavy weight I had been carrying for far too long. Everything felt lighter. My laughter felt more genuine in my ears than it ever had. But between the cold and my bladder, eventually, I excused myself, promising I'd be back.

Once I'd dropped off the deck steps, I pulled my phone out of my sweatshirt pocket. I had charged it earlier today, and ever since, it had been buzzing on and off at steady intervals, but I hadn't bothered to check because honestly, the signal out here wasn't great, so notifications came in, but every time I tried to open so much as a text message, the signal would drop out. The only spot in camp where the Wi-Fi functioned was, unsurprisingly, the office. I had to go past it on my way to the toilets, so I paused on the HQ steps to check back in with the real world. I figured at worst, Mum was trying to reach me to confirm when I'd get paid. Wrong in one, Toni. The first email in my inbox was labelled: "Urgent: Payment Due." from a Red Range University address.

Fuck. In the chaos of the last few weeks, my financial situation had completely slipped my mind. I opened the email and read through the notice. The gist: I was on the pre-payment plan, and when they'd gone to withdraw the first payment from my account for the fall semester, shocker, there hadn't been any money there to draw from. My legs sagged underneath me. I was sure most of the other staff here would just call their mums and dads and ask for help. Fuck, most of them wouldn't even need to because their parents were paying the bills, anyway. That wasn't an option for me. Not anymore.

There had been times in the last few years when I had wished so badly that I was still a Barrett. Not many, I grant, because remaining a Barrett would have meant remaining my father's princess. But still, there were moments. Don't listen to any fucker who glorifies being poor. If they did, they'd never experienced it. The endless grind, the worry, fear, and exhaustion are easy to celebrate when they aren't happening to you. My bootstraps are fucking tired. My self-pity didn't help or change things, so I gave my head a shake and instead re-read the email, paying more attention this time around to the alternative payment options the registration office has outlined. I was halfway through crafting a response when a man's voice called out of the dark, "Toni, Toni, Toni, sitting here all alone."

Fucking Mitchell Greer. He sauntered out the office door behind me, swinging his arm over my shoulder as he sat down. "What is a sweet girl like you doing out here all alone?" The question itself was harmless enough, but the lecherous look he shot me gave him away.

"Nothing, Greer, I was just reading an email." Thankfully, I had already locked my screen, so Mitchell didn't get a glance at the message I'd been drafting back to the school. I needed to finish it, but there was no way I was going to do that with this asshat looming over me, so I tucked my phone back into my sweatshirt and tried to stand. Predictably, he wouldn't let me, using his big arm to keep me on my ass. What was it with these hockey bros? Were they all juiced up or something?

"Running away so quickly, Antoinette?" He started to run his fingers softly up and down my shoulder. Because, at this point, it's basically a Pavlovian response; his touch made my stomach turn over. "I thought I could entice you to hang out with me for a bit. We could go to my cabin—no kids there yet." Ugh—I can't believe Jack thought this guy could be around children. His proposition was made even worse as his fingers drifted from my shoulder to my chest and then down to my right tit. "Or maybe you'd prefer to stay right here? Maybe a little slut like you would prefer to show off the goods in public, huh?" He squeezed my boob hard, and not in a pleasant way, either.

While the urge to vomit became stronger and stronger, I stayed silent, letting him grope and fuck with me. A lifetime's worth of lessons had taught me that the quickest road out of this was through. Greer was an absolute cretin, but I doubted he had the balls to take it too far, so if I just stayed quiet, he'd eventually get bored and leave so I could dive for the bushes and throw up in peace. I let my mind completely disassociate, retreating into my psyche while he continued to paw at me. It was the sound of another pair of footsteps that pulled me back to myself. I didn't need any more rumours flying around this place about me.

"Go fucking figure." I cursed internally at the deep voice as Cole came up the path. Of course, I wasn't going to escape this interaction unscathed. "Didn't even take you two weeks to start spreading those legs, huh, Toni?" As he got closer, the light casting out of the office showed his face enough that I could see his fury.

"Sorry, bro," Mitchell chuckled. "Didn't see you there. Not that this one seems to mind an audience. She didn't even fight back. Love that for me." Shame filled me. He was right. I didn't fight back, not at all. "Honestly, I bet she would let me fuck her right here on these steps. What do you think?" My cheeks burned, and it was taking every bit of willpower I had not to throw up right then and there. So I clamped my lips shut and stared at the ground. None of that stopped Greer, though. "What do you think, Michaels? Think she'd let me pound that pussy right here?"

"Honestly, a whore like her? Probably. But a word to the wise bud: make sure you wrap it up. Who knows where that shit's been?"

"WHAT THE FUCK DID YOU JUST SAY, MICHEALS?" Abbi. I made a mental note to tell her she was my hero as she stormed out of the darkness. "Did I honestly just hear what I think I just heard?!" She stomped right up to the steps, her face filled with righteous anger. "Didn't anyone ever teach you monsters about consent? Because that," she jabbed her index finger my way, "is not a girl who's consenting." Like the coward I knew he was, Greer immediately backed off as Abbi stepped closer to him. "Get the fuck off away from my friend. NOW." In seconds, he removed his arm and moved to stand. "Mitchell, I am going to report you to the Director." His eyes paled, but only for a second, before squinting back menacingly. Abbi didn't back down. She just smiled at his grimace, "Oh, and for future reference, Greer, if it's not a 'hell yes', then it's a 'hell no'." Her tone was a dismissal. She didn't even need to say so, and while he didn't like it, something about her protective stance in front of me sent him retreating into the night with a mumbled, "Fucking bitches," on his breath.

"And you!" Abbi turned her attention to Cole. "What the hell is wrong with you?" She really did jab Cole in the chest. I needed to take some lessons in badassery from this woman. "I can't believe I just sent your girlfriend to talk to you. After what I just heard, you absolutely do not deserve her. Apologise. Right now. And then get the fuck out of my sight."

Cole glared at me, but stayed silent. Instead, he spun on his heels and retreated the way he'd come.

"Right. Fine. You're as bad as Greer," she shouted at his back before helping me up.

"You okay, Toni?"

"Yep."

"Bullshit."

I couldn't contain it anymore, and so darted to the bushes that lined the building, and as subtly as I could, forced myself to be sick.

"Yeah, that seems about right. Feel better?"

I didn't answer her, but I did feel better. "Let's go back to the Village. I think we need to talk about all this." She pointed her index finger, circling it in my direction.

We were silent until we got through my cabin door, where I promptly plopped down on my bed, wishing I could just bury myself under the covers.

"Ready to talk now?" Abbi asked from where she sat on the floor across from my bunk. I nodded. "Good, because I think we've reached the point of no return."

"I get that they hate me. Fine." God, I sounded so fucking pathetic. "But the guys I knew never would have treated me, or anyone, this way. I don't know how much more of this I can take. But I don't even have a choice now." I squeezed my eyes, pushing back tears and wishing that somehow I would open them and things would be different.

"Alright, I think I'm gonna need you to explain." After the way she'd stood up for me, Abbi deserved an explanation. So I spilled. Not everything—I skimmed over my family's "particularities" and the full truth of what happened that day in the forest. The trial recordings had revealed enough about that day, as far as I was concerned. However, I did fill in enough of the story for her to understand how I ended up in a courtroom facing off against my father. I talked about the divorce, the disappearing act, and finally about school and my little money problem. By the time I had finished, I was exhausted, and Abbi looked haunted by the details I'd shared.

"Fuck girl. I figured you had some shit going on, but that's some heavy heavy." I nodded as I reached for the water bottle I'd left on the floor this morning. My throat was sore from my horrific story time. "So, clearly, you need this job, at least for now, but this shit with those guys can't continue."

I shook my head. "No, it can't."

"Short of teaching you to be some sort of badass revenge artist overnight, we need a plan." She ran her tongue across her teeth, clearly thinking. "So, we know why they hate you."

Shame curdled yet again in my still-fragile stomach. I couldn't exactly spill the beans completely, so I just confirmed what I was sure she was already thinking. "You mean because I killed somebody?"

"Sure—but, honestly, fuck that guy, Toni. How old was he, nineteen, twenty, and he thought a fifteen-year-old was fair game? You did the world a favour. Good riddance to bad trash." I looked up at her, aghast. She simply smiled back at me. "What we need to know is why they hate each other. If we crack that chestnut, maybe we can get them to turn on each other."

It wasn't a bad idea. And honestly, I was dying to know how those three boys had gone from best friends to barely speaking.

"You're saying we fight fire with fire?"

She just winked. But then got right down to planning, so it was well past midnight by the time we went to bed. It had taken us over an hour, but we had a plan. If my former friends were happy to use my past against me, then I could do the same to them.

Step one: find out what happened in the five years I'd been gone.

Chapter Fifteen

Cole

Fucking Abbi. What did she know? She barely knew Toni. She had no idea what that girl was really like. How dare she threaten me? As if she'd threatened to tattle on me to my fucking girlfriend. But thinking of Michele squashed those bitter thoughts. Abbi was right. Fuck. She was one-hundred percent right. If Michele had heard what I had said to Toni, she'd have broken up with me immediately.

The distance between Michele and me had started the day Toni showed up, and since then, her continued presence had made things worse and worse. Now, it had been days since we'd even spoken. Fucking Antoinette Barrett. Less than two weeks with her back in my life, and I was already a mess. Walking through the Centre Circle, then past The Point, I headed toward the boys' cabins. With campers finally arriving tomorrow, most of the leaders would be asleep in their cabins already, having spent today prepping and cleaning. Tomorrow would be long. The day would start with a 6:30 a.m. early breakfast and end with the opening campfire. And somewhere in between, this place would be flooded with families dropping off their kids for the next couple of months.

After thirteen years, tomorrow's schedule was a familiar one. One blink and there would be some middle-aged dad in my face, shaking my hand and congratulating me on my season at Michigan State or asking offside questions about college puck bunnies. The thought made me grimace. On the other hand, twelve years' experience meant I didn't have to think about where I was going right now. Even in the dark, these paths were as worn into me as the other way around. And because of it, I spent the rest of the walk to my little one-room cabin kicking rocks and practising the apology I knew I owed my girlfriend. As a Section Head, I had my own little space located near the section I would be overseeing all summer. The tiny unnamed cabin had belonged to the previous few Boys' Section Heads as well. I imagine because its proximity allowed them, and now me, to be nearby if anything significant happened in the night. Whatever the reason, I was grateful it wasn't in the Village, surrounded by all the other non-counselling staff. I appreciated the distance.

I could see the lights on inside through the small window and the door as I got close. A surefire sign Michele was still waiting for me, since I always check the lock when I leave, and she's the only one with a key. Locking doors—this one, my MSU dorm room, my childhood bedroom—it all started the year I met Toni, the year my mum left. And Michele was the only person in all that time I had ever trusted with any kind of key. Because she's great. Everybody always says it, and I know it's because I'm mostly a bit of a douche, so there's always a hint of surprise when they find out we've been together as long as we have. Over two years.

She's seated on my bed, legs crossed, right in the centre, so the Peterston Penguins', my favourite hockey team, logo was barely visible beneath her. When she looked up at me, her face was unreadable. I mean, not happy. I didn't expect happy, but it was hard to tell what else she was feeling.

"Cole. I think maybe we need to talk about the last few days."

"Uhhh..." I stuttered.

"And we especially need to talk about Toni." Five goddamned seconds. That's how long it took for Toni to come up.

And at the mention of her, every calm and reasonable thing I had rehearsed on my walk up here flew out of my head, so instead of an apology, I just grunted, "I don't want to talk about Toni."

Mich huffed, "Well, then, what do you want to talk about, Cole? Because lately, we don't talk about anything at all." She stared back at me, but where my eyes were angry, hers were nothing but sadness and questions. Her question had me stumped.

"Because I think this has everything to do with Toni and with your past. You won't tell me anything about it. About anything. Even after two years..."

"Like you tell me everything, Michele?" I demanded, my anger at Toni getting the better of me. And I instantly regretted it, as tears started to fill her blue eyes.

"Oh, fuck, Mich." I dropped to my knees in front of her and placed my hands on her thighs. "That was such a dickhead thing to say. Or way to say it, at least." We both sighed, and I lifted one hand so I could push my hair back. “I guess what I mean is that I’m sorry, first, and that second, we both have our shit, and sometimes, that’s going to come up. Right now is just one of those times.”

She nodded, accepting my explanation without making eye contact. Instead, she stared down at her lap, chewing on her thumbnail. I kept my hands on her, running them up and down her legs in a motion I hoped was comforting, putting to rest the distance between us all while watching her. When she finally did look up at me, her expression hardened. “That’s fine, Cole. You’re right. I’ve got my own shit, but Toni is my friend, and…”

“How do you know that? You barely know that girl!” I shouted, my anger back already. Fuck, I needed to get a hold of it. Otherwise, I would turn into my dad.

As if she was resigned to my anger, she exhaled. “Because, Cole, you might not see it, but I told you that first day, Toni is struggling. I’m not sure how or with what. I just know it.”

“So?”

“SO?!” She pushed me off of her. “So, Cole Michaels, I don’t know about you, but when I see someone struggling, I want to help.” She was off the bed by that point, storming her way to the door, but I grabbed her hand and pulled her back into me, unwilling to give up so easily. Toni might have her convinced for now, but that could and would change. In the meantime, I’d be patient. I would be a better boyfriend. I’d be the best boyfriend. Because being with her stopped me from giving in, from sinking into something that could never be.

"Okay, Michele, maybe you're right." I kept her close, brushing her blond hair behind her ear. "I'll try to see it your way."

She looked up at me, not letting me off the hook for a second. "You'll try to be nice to Toni?"

"Fuck." I wasn't sure if or how I could be, but there I was, agreeing to try, anyway. "Yeah, fucking fine. For you... I'll try."

She leaned in and kissed me on the lips. "Thank you, baby," she whispered against my mouth, and then she pushed off me and headed for the door.

"Wait, Mich—" I called after her. "You don't want to stay? Even for a bit?" We didn't have to have sex or anything, although, I hoped we would, and that it would go some way toward fixing our problem. I gave her my best attempt at the puppy dog eyes, but instead of falling for it as most girls did, she paled and gave her head the smallest, almost imperceptible, shake.

"Not tonight, Cole. I need to get some sleep before tomorrow." She looked back at me through the now open door. "Besides, you have some serious making-up to do before we have another sleepover."

Chapter Sixteen

Toni

All I wanted was to drag my ass to bed at the end of the day. I had known going in that the first day of camp would be a long one, but since this was my first time experiencing it from the staff perspective, I underestimated exactly how tiring it would be. My late night planning with Abbi, combined with the extra early morning, happy camper greetings, and putting more than 250 kids through their swim tests, meant the bags under my eyes had reached mid-exam student and full-time bartender levels. And now, instead of going to bed, I was back in front of the office again, connected to the Wi-Fi and reading the email I had received earlier today from one of the RRU registration officials.

When I had eventually finished the email I'd started last night at about the ass crack of dawn, or 6:00 a.m., I'd made every effort to be polite and professional, but the email I got back from my school this afternoon felt like a giant 'fuck you'. Like the two years I had spent there as a student hadn't earned me even a shred of decency from the finance office. I mean, I suppose I wasn't the first student to struggle financially, and I definitely wouldn't be the last, but you would think they could handle the situation with some compassion. Apparently not. Their response told me I had until the first of August to make payment, and after that, my registration would be delayed.

And I quote, 'Any payments made after August 1st will maintain your student status. However, you will not be able to register for classes until payment is received in full and class registration will be on a first come, first serve basis." Basically, the academic way of telling me that if I couldn't get my shit and my money together, they couldn't guarantee I would get into the classes I needed to graduate. I mean, it's not like I'm pre-med or any of that shit, so maybe I could figure it out, but I had a countdown on for my graduation because the sooner I finished, the sooner I could take Mum and run for real. I had plans. Instead of barely escaping to the other side of Barrett Hills, we'd go west. As far west as it was possible to go. My father might be powerful, but even his reach was limited at 3,000 miles away. But to make my plan work, I would need a good job, and to get that good job, I would need my degree, which I was two years away from collecting. In the meantime, I had just over thirty days to come up with over $5000.

That afternoon, I sat in a deck chair, wearing my shiny new whistle, a mesh vest with 'Lifeguard' scrawled across the back, and my least sexy one-piece, watching group after group of kids traipse their way onto the swim dock. Every single kid had to go through a supervised swim test. Cabin group by cabin group, I made them get in the water and swim the distance from buoy line to buoy line a solid ten times, and then immediately tread water for two minutes.

Kids who finished got a green string tied around their wrists, which meant they could go do any of the water sports or activities. The ones who didn't, or couldn't, finish got a red string instead and would have to wear a life jacket for any water activities at the dock until they could get re-tested at midsummer. Given that Agonde was bordered on all sides by water, the test just made sense and was something I took seriously. The thought of a kid drowning or even coming close made my blood chill.

I always loved the water as a kid, plus we'd had a pool at home that I could practise in, which meant that even at eight years old, I'd avoided the red string. Swimming was one of the few things I was good at. But that's not the case for everyone. Then and now, kids failed sometimes. And in the process, they were embarrassed in front of their peers. With every red string I tied today, I knew I was also making things harder for cabin leaders, too, who would have to work around the rules anytime they wanted to take their cabin groups swimming or out in the canoes.

More than once, I'd had to step in and pull a kid from the water before they put themselves at risk. One girl, I swear to god, almost sank, but she kept trying to finish the test. All the other girls in her cabin passed, and her desire to keep up was obvious every time her hands slapped against the water and she almost made it, until her head dropped under on lap eight. When she didn't resurface at a five count, in I went, pulling her to the dock-side and out of the water. The embarrassment you feel as a pre-teen girl is unlike any you'll ever feel again in your life. I remembered a thousand and one moments of my own, as her eyes and face flushed red. So, as I tied the same coloured string on her wrist, I whispered, "Go to the office and ask the boy there—his name is Brennon with the blue hair—to sign you up for swimming lessons."

"But... b-but...," she stuttered, "he'll call my parents." There was an anxiousness in her voice that I couldn't understand.

"Yes, but if they agree and you take lessons with me this month, I promise, by mid-summer, that'll be a green string on your wrist."

That thought seemed to steel her. She sniffed and nodded before joining the rest of her cabin group. Right now, I felt just like her, embarrassed and unsure, needing someone to reassure me that I could figure my shit out. I'm sure if I had hiked it to the Village and knocked on Abbi's door or found Cam or even Mich, any of them would have done that for me, but they'd already shouldered more of my shit than new friends should. I couldn't put even more on them, so that left me with my original cheerleader and the need to make a phone call.

Many hours later, after the opening campfire was doused and the kids were headed to bed, I made my way out to the parking lot. The staff payphone was tucked away in a little wooden box hidden in the trees in the far corner of the lot. It was the kind you used to see on street corners and in public buildings that had basically disappeared with the rise of the cell phone, but like I said, the reception out here amongst the trees was absolute garbage, so this was my best option if I wanted to have a real conversation with my mother away from the prying eyes of Brennon and the Director. Not like I regularly carried quarters or the change to make a call, but thankfully, we could get coins on credit from the office, and I'd gone with Abbi a few days ago to visit her little—uh—protégé as she'd called him, Riley, while Brennon had been elsewhere, and I'd gotten enough to make at least a few calls on this thing.

I dropped the coins into the slot and dialled my mum's number. She picked up on the fourth ring.

"Hi, Mum."

"Oh, sweetheart, hello! I didn't expect to hear from you. Wasn't today the first day for all the kids?" I'd sent her a couple of texts over the last few weeks, whenever I could get a signal. No details, just the headlines of what I was doing. "How did it go?"

"It was great, Mum. Tiring, but great."

"Oh, I'm so glad." But as if she sensed something, her response was followed by an awkward pause. And, to be fair, if everything was so damn great, why was I calling? Which, of course, was her very next question.

I winced as I explained about the email from the school, dreading the stress I was putting on her. "I'm just not sure what to do."

"Hmmmm..." I could practically see the thin angry line of her lips through the phone. "You could call your brother? He... he's back..."

"He's back with dad now, isn't he?"

"Yes," came her watery reply. "There was a picture of them in the gazette and everything. But now that he is, maybe he could help you?"

"No!" I blurted. That was just doubling down on the torture. "No, Mum," I continued more calmly. "I'll figure something else out. Something less risky. Anyway, I can probably save enough to hit that August deadline."

She drew in a big breath at that. "That sounds like a good plan, honey, and if you don't, well, you can always come home. There's a new place opening at East Barrett Plaza in a few weeks, a family place called The Clubhouse, and I've got an interview." Fuck me. She sounded way too hopeful about yet another shitty waitressing job. The Clubhouse was a chain that mostly catered to families and seniors because you could get the world's cheapest steak and feed a family of four for less than fifty bucks. But I wouldn't take her hope from her.

"That's so great, Mum. I'm sure you'll get it!"

Her voice was even brighter as she answered, "Yeah, and if I do get it, then maybe I can get you a job, and after you work for a few months, I'm sure you'd be able to afford to re-enrol at Red Range in January."

Now I heard what she was really saying. Don't go back to school, stay home with me and work. Help me pay the rent. Help me survive. It would make things so much easier. And it would, I would be there to help her financially and god-fucking-forbid, I'd be there to buffer Francis if he ever came back. I knew she didn't mean it, but sometimes, we all slip into selfishness. Holding the phone away from my face, so she wouldn't hear it, I sighed out equal parts frustration and exhaustion. "Okay, Mum, that'll be the backup plan. If I can't save enough money by August, then I'll defer until next winter." I scrubbed my hand down my face, and cursed the universe in my head as I said, "And if you get the Clubhouse job, can you put in a good word for me, just in case?"

"Of course, honey! I'm sure with your experience from Janie's, they'd hire you in a second."

"Okay, well, I've got to go, Mum. Need to get some sleep before another big day tomorrow. Keep me updated on the job, yeah?"

"Will do, sweetie."

After telling my mum I loved her, I waited, listening for the sound of her hanging up. When it came, so did my anger, and I slammed the handset back into its plastic hook. Once, twice, three times until the need started to dissipate. Breathing hard, I shut my eyes for a second, pushing the weight of my fear and worry away in the back of my mind. I would deal with them when I had to. But my moment was interrupted by rustling outside the phone booth. I hadn't heard any footsteps, but the last fucking thing I needed was for that conversation to have been overheard. Opening the door, I stepped out and searched the dark parking lot for signs of another person. There was no one there but Betty and the other cars. I had forgotten how noisy the woods could seem at night. It was probably just an animal. I shook it off. Clearly, I was overdue for some sleep, and with that thought, I could feel my cot calling my name.

Chapter Seventeen

Brennon

Overhearing Toni's call with her mum three days ago was the last kind of shit that I needed. Yet, it was all I'd been able to think about. The only reason I was out there was to speak to Este, my housekeeper. She was the only person who would give me an honest update on how Mom was doing. At the time, I had hoped my mother would be coherent enough for me to actually talk to her. Instead, I had to listen to Toni's voice—quiet, but forever recognizable. Burned on the inside of my brain, honestly. The desperate plea to her mom about working at that shitty chain place, God—there was one on the edge of West Barrett, near the public high school. I had never eaten there, because my private school cafeteria probably served better food than that, but I knew it was kind of a shithole. Add to that the pathetic sound of her voice as she said goodbye and the obvious fury as she hung up, and it painted a very different picture than the one me and the guys had put together of Birdie. When her head popped out of the phone booth, I was worried she'd seen me, but thankfully, I had tucked myself out of sight on the backside of it just in time. In the shadows, barely breathing, I watched her retreat into the village.

Staring at my computer screen every day since hadn't exactly kept me occupied enough to distract from the new knot living at the bottom of my stomach. A knot that screamed I had missed something in my assessment of Toni, of the threat she caused to me by being here. If I was honest, the first twinges of it came even before I caught the phone call. It had come knocking in the form of a sweet kid. When that girl, Holly, tapped her fist quietly on the door, I had barely heard it. But kudos to her, she hadn't given up. She just kept knocking until Riley heard it. My ears were shot from years standing side-stage with Blue, so it was no surprise I didn't hear shit. But when he had opened the door, and this tiny blonde imp of a thing had looked up at him, he'd simply turned to me, puzzled. I took one look at her big blue eyes, which honestly reminded me of another pair I'd looked into once upon a time, and I'd invited her over to my desk. Usually, kids just walked in, looking for pens or asking for the Director, but not this kid. She fucking knocked and waited outside until we answered the door. When she finally sat down beside me, she swallowed hard and asked, "Are you Brennon with the blue hair?"

"What do you think?" I asked, tugging at my spiked strands. She tucked her chin, maintaining a level of seriousness adults never expect from kids, like my display had helped her confirm something, and then she started talking. "The girl on the dock sent me to see you. She said you could sign me up for swim lessons." She shoved her wrist, with its little red string, out at me. There was so much hope in that little voice, but I had to check.

"The girl on the dock?" It had to have been Birdie. As Waterfront Director, she had to supervise every single swim test.

"The lifeguard. She said you would help." Toni told this kid I could help? After everything that happened during pre-camp, especially just a few nights ago, why would she believe I was capable of helping anyone? The kid looked downcast when I didn't answer right away. "Did I get it wrong?"

Fuck. Any thoughts of Toni's reasons were pushed aside. This wasn't about our shit. "No, no, no, kiddo. I just wanted to check. What's your name?"

"Holly. Holly MacPherson." I ushered for her to follow me inside, and once I sat behind my computer, it took less than a minute for me to find her camper profile. "Well, Holly MacPherson, it says here your parents have signed you up for Tennis, Music, and Sailing. We can switch you to swimming lessons, but we'll need to check with your parents."

At my mention of her folks, she brought her thumbnail to her lips and started to chew nervously, clearly anxious about that call. Fuck, I knew how that could be. Anytime camp or one of my teachers had called my house growing up, it had gone one of two ways. Either my mom picked up, but was so high she just listened without really taking anything in, or worse, my dad was home and answered.

"Hey, now, don't worry. What if I call and tell them sailing was full but our Waterfront Director..." at her puzzled face, I clarified, "the lifeguard girl. What if I said she invited you to swimming lessons and would they please let you join? Do you think that would work?" Her smile exploded onto her face. "Right, well, you sit tight, Holly, and I'll call." For this, I could turn on the charm. Ten minutes later, I sent Holly on her way, signed up for swimming lessons and happy as could be after I'd spoken to her father. One mention of my last name and an affirmative answer to the question, "Grace? As in Blue Grace?" and that asshole didn't even listen to my question before agreeing. That's how it always was. One mention of dear old Dad, and people just tuned me out. Sure, they almost always agreed to whatever I wanted, but it made most of my conversations feel like I was talking to a brick wall.

Maybe that's why, despite my love of music, I was currently studying for a degree in computer science. Instead of having to work with partners or talk to people, I did most of my talking with the zeros and ones of computer code. But being around the kids was refreshing. Nobody under the age of fifteen gave a single shit that my dad was some over-the-hill rockstar, so even though I worked in the office instead of out in the programmes, I did more talking to people, or at least talking to kids, in these two months than I would do for the rest of the year.

In the few days since I'd spoken to her father, Holly had come to see me every day, stopping by the office, popping her blond hair through the door and interrupting my work with a cheerful, "Hi, Brennon with the blue-hair," said quickly, like my blue hair had become part of my name somehow. The first time she did, just two days ago, I made the mistake of asking her about her swimming lessons. It became clear within ten seconds that this kid idolised Toni. It was all, "Toni's so funny. Toni's so pretty. Today, Toni taught me how to tread water, and I did it for a whole minute."

Not wanting to dim her enthusiasm, I think I gritted out a, "That's great, kid," before sending her packing. I hadn't asked again. Hearing someone, even just a little girl, sing Birdie's praises was doing my head in.

Meals were strange, too. How could they not be? Most of the non-counselling staff sat at the same table in the far corner of the dining hall. Meaning that for breakfast, lunch, and dinner, Birdie, Xav, and I have no choice but to eat together. Along with Mich and a few others. Birdie seemed to be handling it better than I was. She spent her meals speaking exclusively to Mich, or to the two older nurses who shared the table with us, and other than the odd dirty look, she was doing a bang-up job pretending I didn't exist. The way her eyes just passed me by, like I wasn't even there, made me want to grab her and force her to look at me and never ignore me again. Even with my forkful of salad, that thought sent heat licking up my spine. I wanted to bend her to my will. Hell, I wanted to bend her fucking body in half. I couldn't resist watching her profile—her brown hair, her too-slim cheeks that were only now just starting to fill in. Her whole body was trim and lean. Maybe a little bit too lean, but her eyes were something else. They spoke of hunger. One that made me hungry, too. Fuck. It made me horny. My dick was half-hard at the idea of forcing her to look at me.

Like a different kind of thunderbolt, though, I felt his eyes every single time. When I looked away from my wild girl and across the table, I already knew he was watching. There were Xav's hazel eyes, pinned on me through his curls. Swear to god, he let his hair fall on purpose so he could use it like a shield. And it always made me want to pull on it. There he was, staring, not at Toni, but at me. One corner of his smile tucked up and his eyes burned. Recognition flashed in them, like he'd read my wanting on my face, and mirroring me, he licked his lips and the rest of a sinister smile unfurled with it, making his dimples show.

Fuck these two. I needed a distraction. And of course, that's what I got. Courtesy of Cole fucking Michaels. Watching him stroll around the hall, pausing at the different tables and getting off on the attention. As Section Head, it wasn't an abnormal thing to do. He checked in with each of the boys' cabins from the youngest to oldest, saying hello and cracking jokes. What drove me nuts was the adoration, the way the youngest kids stared at him like the sun shone out of his asshole and the way the oldest boys, aged fifteen, and old enough to know better, saw nothing but the hockey star, the big man on campus, and not the needy little attention-whore underneath. And Cole took all of it. He ate it up, like his body was physically feeding off their affection. A new wave of desire hit me, the desire to slap him, to hurt him and make him see that regardless of his height and muscular frame, he wasn't Mr. Big Shot.

Goddammit. What I really needed was to get my fucking rocks off. That last thought about Cole was just tipping me over the edge. All this week, I'd barely made it through a meal without the internal clash of will versus want. I might not have Cole's showy personality, but when I wanted to, I could turn it on. Tonight during staff free time, I planned to find someone—guy or girl, I didn't much care—and give them the privilege of sucking my cock until I could finally breathe again, or at least eat a fucking meal in peace.

A flash of tanned olive skin caught my attention as Isabella approached the table and ducked down between Mich and Toni for a whispered conversation. She would do nicely. Petite, with a great rack, and full lips that would look perfect wrapped around my shaft. Add to that the double whammy of sending her back to her pal Toni with my cum on her lips as yet another punishment for Birdie. Too delicious.

When 10 p.m. rolled around, the cabin leaders trickled into the dining hall. Sometimes one-by-one, and other times in groups of two or three. Other than a few nights a month, there are two hours every evening where all staff get a bit of a break. Cabin leaders can leave their kids, as long as they've done the job of actually putting them to bed, while a team of four were assigned to the Night Watch, patrolling each of the cabin lines and listening for anyone and anything out of the ordinary. The rest of us, those without cabins, were usually here a little earlier. Normally, I might pop in just to grab a snack or stay and play cards for a bit, but it was rare that I stayed the whole time. Tonight, I made a point of being as early as possible, and I planned to stick it out for however long it took me to convince Bella out of the dining hall and into my cabin.

With no kids around, mealtime rules didn't apply, and there were staff scattered at tables and some outside playing ping-pong. My first stop was the walk-in fridge, where I grabbed leftover buns, some day-old bacon, and even some leftover brownies from tonight's dessert. Access to that fridge was in my top five favourite parts of this job. Now I was propped up on the laminate serving counter, my feet dangling and kicking into the wood base while devouring my beautiful bacon sandwich and watching the door each time it creaked open. It was almost 10:30 when my target finally showed up, sidled next to Michele, listening actively to her as she spoke. I couldn't quite hear their conversation, but judging by Michele's gestures and their shared giggles, it was an entertaining story. They finally broke apart, Isabella nudging her gently on the arm and pointing to the kettle and coffee machine in the corner. The two exchanged nods, and I tracked Bella, dropping to my feet so I could follow her. Sure, I'm normally a coffee guy, even when it's shitty camp coffee, and even late at night, since it's not like I sleep great, anyway, but just this once, I could have what she was having.

Coming up behind her, I started small by standing just a little bit closer than I normally would. I mean, I know I'm tall, but unlike Birdie, who was within a few inches of my height, Isabella seemed so tiny you would think she would have noticed my lanky-ass shadow coming up behind her. Apparently not, because when I open with, "Hey, Isabella, or do you prefer Is? Or Bella?" she practically jumped out of her skin.

In the process, she spilled the cup of tea she'd just finished making, sending boiling water across the table. "Oh, shit—sorry! I didn't mean to scare you."

"No, no, it's fine. I guess you just surprised me. I'm going to go get a cloth." She turned as if that were the end of our conversation.

"Here, let me help." I gestured her toward the kitchen. "It'll go faster with two of us." She eyed me warily but didn't find anything too suspicious in my gaze. And she followed me, each of us grabbing from the folded piles of extra cloths tucked into cubbies at the backside of the counter. We worked together quietly to soak up all the water, even where it ran under the coffee machines, and when we'd finished, I held my hand out to her, "Listen, I'll take the cloths and ring them out if you make me a cup of Chamomile," I said as my eyes slipped to the tea bag in her hand. "Y luego puedes responder mi pregunta, ¿Is o Isabella?" 'And then, you can answer my question, Is or Isabella?' I said to her in my accented Spanish.

Her eyes widened in shock, but she smiled, too. "Bien, chico blanco." We both laughed at her calling me 'white boy' before I headed back to the kitchen to ditch the rags in my hands. While I was back there, I watched through the serving window as she flicked the electric kettle on and made not one, not two, but three cups of tea. Instead of glancing my way, she was throwing quick looks over her shoulder to where Michele was sitting, chatting with Abbi. Hell, that's annoying. I could have just let her deal with her spill on her own.

Fuck, I was going to have to work a little harder. I should have brought my guitar. She passed me a mug. “Thanks for helping me clean up. And your Spanish is pretty good, you know, for a white boy.” She turned to leave, heading toward her friends. Not so fast, chica.

“Hey, you never answered the question. Is, Bella, or Isabella?”

She rolled her eyes. “I didn’t really answer because I don’t really care, actually. Either is fine.”

“Really? So, it’s cool if I call you Is?”

“Really. And sure.” She waved me off, again trying to break our conversation. Since she’d already heard me speak, I took another shot. “¿Hablarás español conmigo?” I ask if she’ll speak Spanish with me before switching back to English. “I practice with my housekeeper at home, but I don’t really get a chance to practice all summer, and then I’m rusty as fuck come September.”

She assessed me silently, her eyes narrowing slightly as she stared. “Por que yo?” ‘Why me?’ she asked, testing me.

“No creo que nadie aquí lo hable.” “I don’t think any other staff speak it,” I answered, hoping that scored me some points. “And,” well, here goes my shot, “I think you’re cute.” I gave her my shyest grin, chewing my lip ring as I did it. It was a look I knew worked. I’d managed to pick up one or two guys, a handful of women, and even one couple with that look alone.

Isabella just rolled her eyes. “Fucking hell. This is about Toni, isn’t it?”

I groaned and scraped my hands on my face, flipping back to English. “Look, you know better than anyone that we have a history with her." She folded her arms across her chest, silently saying, 'Not good enough.'

"So, yeah, maybe we've taken things a bit far."

She huffed, "Damn right," but that's not what caught me off guard. It was the ring of truth in my voice that I hadn't meant to be there. Did I mean it?

I shoved that thought aside. "But Toni did some things and told some lies back then that we can't let go. Maybe if we were better people we'd forgive and forget, but we're not. So, we haven't."

Her arms dropped, her eyes closed briefly, and she nodded. I'm not sure if it's my sincerity or something else, but when she looked up at me again, she'd dropped all of her previous annoyance.

"You're cute, too, Brennon." Success, I thought to myself, but it was short-lived because she sighed and a hint of struggle flashed on her face.

I took one more shot. "Look, what if we just went for a walk somewhere else? No pressure?"

Another flicker of something painful. And when she spoke again, she reverted to Spanish, "It's not that. It's more that you're, um... ah... not my type?" It's like she was asking herself a question. And before I could ask her what her type was, she grabbed the third mug and practically speed walked away from me. Leaving me standing in the corner with my metaphorical dick in my hand and a cup of tea that I had since realised smelled pretty disgusting. Watching her walk away from me, I wondered what the hell had just happened. I don't get shot down. Like ever. And this fucking girl just brushed me off like it was nothing.

Stalking her back, she set the first cup down and then the other when she got to the table, where Michele and Abbi had their heads bent together. Both girls looked up at her, and when Mich noticed the cup in front of her, she practically beamed with gratitude at her friend. And Isabella, well, she flushed at the appreciation, and try as she might to hide it by dropping her eyes to her own cup, I didn't miss the way they came back to Michele over and over again. Well, fuck me. I didn't owe Cole shit-all explanation, so I just snickered. And even though I was annoyed I wouldn't be getting any tonight, it cheered me up to think that fucker had some competition.

Chapter Eighteen

Brennon

Unsurprisingly, the next morning I woke up alone in my little one-man cabin. That didn't stop my morning wood, though. It wasn't like there was any access to porn out here, surrounded by nothing but pine trees, so it was just me, myself, and my imagination as I slid my right hand down into my boxers, closing my eyes when I finally grabbed hold of my cock. I gave a slight squeeze at the base and slowly dragged my hand up toward the tip, mentally picturing a pair of feminine lips taking me in instead of my own hand. I imagined the feeling of a mouth—warm, wet and welcoming—as it slid up and down, making me even harder. That mouth was joined by a set of hands, gently cupping and tugging on my balls, as pre-cum started to bead at the top of my slit. Then another set of lips, fuller and more masculine, entirely different to the first ones, kissed their way along my hip, moving ever downward. My hand moved faster, pushing me even closer toward my tipping point, and in my mind, I saw the moment when both sets of lips met around my shaft and worked in tandem to get me off.

Although it was a fantasy, it felt fucking heavenly, and all I could see in my mind's eye were two faceless sets of lips swirling together in the heat of the moment, followed by two tongues tracing the length of me. At that thought, I was so close my balls started to tighten. But unbidden, the lips became faces, one with blue eyes and honey-brown hair, the other with hazel eyes and even darker curls. Still, I pumped, my ending harder and harder to put off. It wasn't until my imagination conjured up their voices, both whispering my name, that I came completely undone. White cum spilt out and over my hand. I sat up and reached for the box of tissues on my small bedside table, tidying the mess I just made, but when I looked up, there was my mirror, and in that fucking post-nut clarity, I saw a guy whose eyebrow was still healing from Cole's punch, whose blue hair was growing out badly, and who might be totally screwed.

Most days followed a pretty prescribed schedule. Wake-up and breakfast at 7:30, followed by 3Ps, or 'three picked programs,' the ones kids, or more realistically, their parents, pre-selected when they registered. They were my domain. As admin manager, I oversaw the online registration process and did all the scheduling, so that to the best of my ability, every single kid ended up where their parents wanted them, be it sailing, swimming lessons, soccer, tennis, or whatever the fuck else. Each kid got three, and Monday to Friday, for four straight weeks, those three activities made up their mornings. Lunch was at 12:30, followed by an hour's rest, a free period, and cabin-based activities, all before dinner at 6:30 p.m.

Back when I was a cabin leader, I used to do all that shit. Since I had transitioned to this gig last summer, it had been a bit different. Generally, I didn't see much outside of the four office walls, since I was busy fielding parent phone calls, handling staff scheduling, and even managing the kids' medical records. Occasionally, or whenever I could really, I scheduled myself to help out with the free period activities in the afternoon. Every day, there was a whole list of different activities that the kids could pick from. Some are constants, like daily free swims at the beach, while others, like today's Rock Guitar in the Library with me or Beginner Climbing at the Adventure Park with Cole and Greer, appear at random on the schedule.

One of the perks of my job was scheduling however and whomever I wanted. Sure, Jack had final approval, but honestly, he barely glanced at every schedule I showed him. I hadn't expected it initially, but he was pretty hands-off on all the day-to-day shit. Sometimes I wondered what he did with his time. Not that I cared, because it meant the rest of the staff were basically at my whim. Which was how Cole ended up stuck with Greer today, his punishment for punching me in my fucking face. Thinking about it was enough to make me chuckle as I carted my guitar into the Library that afternoon. I had no desire to follow in my father's footsteps. Being a rockstar had never appealed to me. But watching a kid's face light up when they played their first chord—that was a joy I would happily experience every damn day. So, I spent the hour with a group of kids as we learned the first few chords for the Pistols' 'Running Backwards'. Sue me. It's a classic for a reason.

Some of them have their own guitars—nice ones, far nicer than they need, nicer than my own—but their parents had no issue buying them. Others used the camp's beat-up ones. Not that it mattered, since other than one or two who'd had lessons, they were pretty much all beginners. Not that it mattered to me, either. In a fit of rage, I'd smashed the expensive Fender guitar my father had gifted me for my eighteenth birthday, and the one I played on now was one I found at a thrift shop in West Barrett. Maybe the Fender would have played better, carried a note better, and tuned easier, but it would have always belonged to Blue. This one was mine.

At the end of the hour, I felt calmer than I had in days, and it was with a huge smile on my face that I sent the kids back to their cabins. Stood over the beat-up plaid couches in the Library, I had my case propped up on cushions and my guitar strapped to my chest. With the few free minutes I had before my daily check-in with Jack, I took the opportunity to tune the damn thing. Plucking away at string after string, letting my digital tuner do most of the work, I was nearly finished when the shrieks and happy screams of kids made it impossible to carry on. The sounds had me lifting my head, and I watched a crowd of campers rushed out of the forest, all headed for the main path leading back to the girls' cabins and the centre of camp.

The thing about the Library was that while it was solid enough, it was a summer building, so there weren't any proper windows, just mesh screens. That made it the perfect spot on a hot summer day, shaded and breezy. It also meant that the sounds from all around carried through it with alarming ease. And it was for that reason that I heard every syllable of Mitchell Greer's cocky voice.

"I'm telling you, Michaels. I overheard the whole thing."

Ugh, not only was Greer an asshole, he was also a gossip. It was well-documented from previous summers that he had no problem spreading every rumour and whisper of shit-talk he heard. "Not sure who she was talking to, but bitch is definitely hard-up."

I could see them now, carrying bags of climbing equipment and a tangle of clipped-together helmets. Hidden inside the Library it was easy enough to watch Cole make a puzzled face. "Not that I don't believe you, man, but like, that's just not possible. I know for a fact her dad is loaded as fuck. No way he's letting his little princess go without."

"Yeah, I mean, I thought it was weird. But the girl was practically in tears. Crying to someone about having to get a job."

There was no way he wasn't talking about Birdie. Obviously, I hadn't been the only one to overhear her phone call the other night. Then again, I hadn't noticed a single sign of another person out by the phone box. No breathing, no shadows, not a single clue, but how else would Greer know this shit? Whipping my guitar off, I dropped it into the case, snapping each clasp closed but leaving it behind. I'd come back for it later. Right now, I needed to follow Tweedle-Dee and Tweedle-asshole as they passed by. I slipped out the door and tracked behind them. The paths back here were mostly soft forest turf, and it went a long way to cushioning the sound of footsteps, and besides, those two were so bloody cocky they didn't even bother to look around for two seconds. If they had, they would have seen me following all of ten feet behind them. Instead, I eavesdropped without any bother.

"I'm sure you misinterpreted it. But then again, boo-fucking-hoo. If it is true, poor princess might have to learn how the rest of us have to fucking live."

"What are you talking about, man?" Greer says. Ah, so clearly, Cole wasn't telling his little band of cronies fuck-all about his real life. Too bad for him, some of us already knew.

"Forget it," he gritted out before changing tack with a question. "So, you're saying she's got until August to pay up or her school's going to drop her?" Cole looked thrilled but contemplative. He had slipped into full calculation mode, trying to assess how he could use this new information to get what he wanted: Toni gone.

Mitchell confirmed, and the two dropped into silence as they skimmed the edge of the Staff Village. Cole wasn't stupid enough to be overheard, and Mitchell was too dumb to carry the conversation on his own. That moron never had an independent thought in his whole life. I wasn't sure why I was still following, other than that I wanted to know what Cole was going to do with this information. We might have agreed to work together to get rid of Toni, but I didn't trust him to tell us anything. Then again, it wasn't like I was sending out a radio broadcast to my former friends about this same conversation, anyway. Still, I slunk along behind them, and it was worth it because once we were shot of all the staff cabins, Cole picked up again. Only his voice had a faraway sound, like he was thinking out loud instead of talking to anyone.

"If she's broke, then what the fuck is she doing here? There's about a million things she could be doing to make more money."

Because the concept of a rhetorical question is so far beyond Greer's mental bandwidth, he answered, "Yeah, I mean, hasn't she heard of OnlyFans?" Silently, I sneer at the contempt in his voice. As if this guy, who had probably had to pay for every pussy he'd ever seen courtesy of a monthly subscription, was about to put down sex workers. That alone made me want to throat punch him, then as we reached the edge of the Activities field, he kept going, "If it hadn't been for Abbi, I'm sure she would have let me plough her right there on those steps." He laughed, and the sound of it made my blood boil. Then I made the mistake of picturing it, seeing Birdie's lithe frame stuck underneath Greer's hockey-player body, letting him fuck her. Sure, he wasn't as big as Cole, but he also didn't have his finesse either on or off the ice. And it was that image—of her willingly subjecting herself to that colossal douchebag—that made me finally call out.

"As if, Greer. In your fucking dreams." And my voice had both of them turning. "Besides, you don't fucking know what you heard."

"Don't I?" He smiled, and there was so much unjustified confidence in it that I charged toward him. "She let me get to second base, no fucking problem. And let me tell you, Brennon, those tits felt amazing."

I'm not sure what came over me, but I saw red, sweeping my arm out and tackling him. I might not have anything on Greer's size, but that doesn't mean I can't throw a punch, and I managed to get in a good one. Specifically, the throat punch I had been dying to administer a minute ago. The force of the hit knocked us both to the ground. I straddled his body, letting my closed fists hammer into his face, and though I landed a couple of good hits, it didn't last long. A force from behind me whipped me off Mitchell, and even before I saw him, I knew it was Cole.

"He doesn't know what he heard? How do you know what he heard, huh?!" I stared into Cole's dead, emotionless eyes as he asked. The charming, personable version of him that coaches, the press, and kids see was nowhere to be found. My lips fixed together. There wasn't any answer I could give. In the absence of a response, his voice started quiet but picked up in volume as he asked, "Do you mean that you knew about this conversation? You're telling me you heard this same phone call?! And you didn't—?!" His voice might have cut off, but not before it had reached a full-on yell, and it wasn't exactly inconspicuous. The Activities field was full of kids and other staff, all making their way back from various programs, some in sports gear, some with tennis rackets, and others in bathing suits coming from the docks.

Fuck this guy. "I didn't what, Michaels?" I taunted. "You're not our fucking leader. I don't owe you shit." My verbal diarrhoea had always gotten me into trouble, and that moment was no exception. Maybe one day I'd learn how to shut my fucking mouth. But my comments had him gripping the collar on my faded Bent Knee t-shirt and using it as leverage to slam me back to the ground, making it my turn to be the punching bag. The difference was that Cole's fist connected. His knuckles slammed against my brow and cheekbones, against my ribs and collarbones, and I swear I could already feel the bruises. He was lost in anger when my nose started bleeding and my vision blurred. The only thing that kept me from passing out was a shout from the distance.

"COLE! STOP!"

And then Birdie was there, putting her hand on his shoulder like she could pull his monster back. He couldn't hear her, though. Cole wasn't there anymore. I doubted he even knew it was me he was hitting. "COLEY. STOP." Her voice cracked. She was sad for me. The thought was fleeting as the pain took over. Maybe it was the nickname, or more likely the crying and shouting from the mixed crowd around us, but I saw the moment Cole mentally snapped back into place. His pupils shrank to pinpoints and, although I couldn't see what I looked like, Cole's horrified face was a pretty big clue. The pause was enough to let Toni and a few others drag him off me. With his weight gone, I shifted slightly, assessing the damage and any potential broken bones. There was nothing beyond the dull aching of my left shoulder, although I was certain more pain would come later. Still, I didn't move.

The other staff, however, sprung into action. My wild girl sent some of the junior staff to deal with the kids hovering around. The quiet, withdrawn version of Toni she had been since she got here was nowhere to be seen. Right now, she was commanding, bossing people around. I always loved bossy Toni. She knelt near my head and her voice sounded muffled in my ears when she asked, "Brennon, can you hear me? I'm going to administer some quick first aid, and then we'll get you to the nurses."

Yet again, Cole fucking Michaels left me reeling in the dirt. One day soon, I was going to ruin that motherfucker's life. For now, I had to contend with the emotional minefield of Birdie leaning over me. Sure, she was doing a bang-up job of using those tiny steri-strip bandages to close the cut along my forehead and the ice pack she'd popped and placed on my shoulder felt fucking great, but it was the look of concern in those wide eyes of hers that was most distracting. So different from the heat and lust they had held in my imagination. Then I remembered how I got here, with the shit kicked out of me. She let that dickhead feel her up. She let him touch her. And that memory has me shoving backward out of her reach. I didn't need her help. Didn't need her here at all. Turned out, getting myself off this morning to an imaginary version of her was the fucking highlight of this goddamn day.

BRENNON, AGE 15

5 years ago

I climbed out of the cab alone and stared up at the modern monstrosity that was my house. It was all concrete and windows. It practically screamed Blue Grace, but to me, it felt more like a prison than anything else. Sure, a multi-million dollar prison, but even the nicest cage is still a cage. After paying the driver, I headed inside, knowing there wouldn't be anyone to greet me on the other side except Este. God bless that woman. My parents' decision to hire her five years ago, fresh off the plane from Argentina, easily ranked as one of their best decisions ever. It was higher up the list than their decision to get married, that's for sure. That woman's a fucking saint. And maybe if I was lucky, I thought as I pushed our black steel door open, she would have a plate of Alfajores waiting for me in the kitchen. I swear, I could live off those cookies alone. On Este's weekends off, I practically did.

Everything about this day had been so shitty. First, finding out Toni lied about Nick felt like a kick in the chest. All the while, she stared at me with blue eyes so empty I felt like she was gone forever. Then watching Cole and Xav bleed their hearts out for her after that.

It felt like the tethers that held our friendship together were being pulled taut, ready to snap at any second. I was pissed, heartbroken, and hurt, but nothing was worse than seeing Birdie climb into her mother's lap as the judge ruled in her father's favour, ensuring not only was their prenup being upheld, but that Franklin Barrett would have primary custody of Toni and her brother until they turned eighteen. Watching it all from the benches on the other side of the courtroom, not able to hug her or comfort her as she turned visibly green, had me all twisted up in knots. I wanted to scream at her and hold her all at once. And maybe if that had been it, I could have managed. But it was having to sit there by myself, sandwiched between Xavi and his parents and Cole with his dad. Xavi's family had flown all the from the west coast to be there with him today, whereas I actually lived in West Barrett, and anyone with a fucking Wi-Fi connection or the radio would know my dad was back on tour, so any outsider could rationalize that.

What they wouldn't know, what nobody knew, was that my mom wasn't on tour with him. She was at home, stoned out of her fucking face, or at least she was well on her way there when I left after breakfast. I watched her pop a pill bottle and swallow down three white pills with her coffee. I had tried reminding her about the trial. About the fact that I might have to take the stand to talk about Toni, and had practically begged, "Mum, please, not today. Please, just come with me. The other guys will all have their parents with them, so please?"

"Umm, not today, honey..." Her voice was already languid, probably from self-medicating the moment she got up. "I'm not feeling

very well today. Maybe tomorrow..." her voice trailing off as she set her coffee down. "Este, darling, I'd like to go back to bed, I think." And she gestured to where Este stood in the corner of our too-empty dining room. Cook, housekeeper, and full-time babysitter, Este rushed to my mother's side, taking time to give me a wince of concern and sadness, before helping my faded-out parent to her feet and escorting her from the room. Now, hours later, I expected my mother was still locked away in her room upstairs with the doors closed and the lights off either still flying high or crashing through a come-down. Neither was pretty, and I planned to avoid seeing that shit at all costs. At fifteen, I'd already had the joyous experience of holding my mother's hair back while she vomited more times than I cared to think about.

Heading down the main hall, I ignored the framed records and magazine covers with my father's smarmy face on them, pausing when I reached the kitchen door and heard Este's voice. It was less animated and more servile than normal.

"Yes, Mister Grace," the edges of her accent slightly turned up. Fuck. Shit. Fuck. I knew she only did it when she spoke to my father. He liked to be the big man in every fucking way, and making her feel small or implying that she should be grateful to work for him probably made his dick swell. All it made me feel was embarrassment. This woman had cared more for me than he ever had, and he always treated her like a fucking serf while he masqueraded in public as the good guy, the one who took a chance on her, blah, blah, blah. But Este knew as well as I did what kind of man my father was, so she did what she had to do. Don't we all? But I wanted to spare her, to give

her an out, and God knows I'm my father's favourite punching bag, so the second he saw me, he'd leave her alone.

With that thought, I swallowed deeply before shouting, "Hi, Este, I'm home!" and strolling into the kitchen like I didn't know shit but stopping just inside the doorway when I saw him just a little bit too close to her where she was washing dishes in the sink.

He stepped back to look at me, and it was just enough that Este could retreat. Placing the last dish in the rack, asked quietly, "Do you need anything else, Mister Grace?"

"No, Este, darling," he purred. "Thank you. I'd just like to say hello to my son." She nodded, never making eye contact with him, but she did with me. This woman knew me better than almost anyone, and with her stare, she was silently asking if I needed her to stay. I give a tiny, hopefully imperceptible head shake and let her run back to her rooms in the basement. I prayed she'd stay there no matter what she heard. If it wasn't too bad, I'd go find her later to say thank you. And, well, if it was, then I knew she'd come check on me later tonight.

My father didn't care about her exit as he turned his attention my way. "Well, boy, aren't you going to say hello to your old man?" He assessed me. The blue eyes that were identical to mine scanned my clothing, my black suit, white shirt, and skinny black tie, all the way up to my currently green hair and the new eyebrow piercing I got last month. Dad had been doing a week's worth of shows at some casino or something in the Middle East. And my then-bright pink hair had been enough of a distraction that Mum signed off on my piercing without even noticing what she'd signed. She was too high, and apparently, my hair looked like "tufts of cotton candy".

"Hi, Dad," I finally answered, trying to sound relatively cheerful.

"What, no hug? It's been months." He held out his arms like he really wanted to hug me, but his stare was all, "Hug me, or else."

"Welcome home, Dad. We weren't expecting you." Or at least I wasn't. I called his tour manager and left a message with him about the trial. It was stupid, but I thought maybe, given how high profile it was and how many paparazzi were swarming the courthouse, he might give a shit and show up. Wrong.

"What? I can't visit my own fucking house?" There was an edge to his voice that had me measuring my answer.

"Sorry, Dad, that's not what I meant." Time to change the subject. "Mom must have been so happy to see you."

"Hmmmm," he grumbled, but didn't elaborate.

Since he hadn't been outright hostile yet, I decided it was safe to walk deeper into the room. I was starving. I couldn't bring myself to eat this morning or during any of today's recesses. Plus, there was no sign of the cookies I'd been hoping for at the door. So, now my stomach was screaming at me to eat something. I peeled off my jacket and rested it on the back of one of the eight clear acrylic chairs that surrounded our rectangular glass and wrought iron kitchen table. My father watched me the whole time, as I headed to our stainless fridge and grabbed a bottle of sparkling water, the kind he demands we always have on hand, and a wrapped-up plate of last night's leftovers that Este set aside for me. Without saying anything more, I paused to grab cutlery and then sat down to eat. I would have warmed it up, but I honestly didn't have the stones to ask my father to move from where he was leaning in front of the microwave. I ate quickly as we held the same silence. The faster I finished, the faster I could get the hell out of here.

"How long do you think you'll be home for?" I finally broke down and asked, unable to stand the tense quiet any longer. Not because I wanted to, but because I needed to know exactly how long we were all going to have to live with his presence this time.

"Only a few days. We have an appearance at Tao in Vegas on Tuesday. But I had some business to take care of here." He didn't even bother to lie and pretend he came to see his wife and kid. I almost appreciated it.

"Speaking of which, you better have sold that girl up the river kid, otherwise..." The threat he was making was so obvious he didn't need to finish his sentence. He stalked closer to me, and it was clear in the way his whole body tensed, in the way he became taller so he could loom over me, and in the way his hands crushed into the marble of our kitchen counter. Because of his tour, I'd managed to go a whole semester without having to cover a single bruise, but if he was back now, it wouldn't be long before I was back digging through Mum's makeup trying to shade match.

"Don't worry, Dad, she did that all on her own. I didn't even have to take the stand, after all," I replied after swallowing my last bite of food. It was true, and I hoped it was enough to get him off my back.

"Good. Her father's an important man. His company sponsors a lot of your mother's charitable work." I fought back the urge to scoff. What charitable work? That charity was mostly his way of ensuring

he paid as little income tax as possible. Besides, Mom hadn't left this house in months. Honestly, the last time she did was probably for the Grammy's last year. Blue got her just cleaned up enough to make a public appearance and then promptly dropped her back into her doped-up depression as soon as he was done with her. "And we wouldn't want her to lose out on such an important partner just for some pathetic messed up girl, now would we?"

"No, we wouldn't," I replied, knowing it was what he wanted to hear from me.

"Excellent," he replied and his body relaxed, satisfied that he was getting his way. He turned and grabbed the refrigerator handle, pulling it open. "Oh, and Brennon, next time, pick a girl who's a little less crazy or one who's easier to control."

"What, like you did with Mom?" The answer flew off my tongue, dripping with sarcasm, and instantly, I knew it was a mistake. He slammed the fridge door, and I didn't even get a second to react before his palm flew at my face, cracking my jaw so hard I rocketed back into the sharp edge of our table before dropping to the floor. There was still a month before the Christmas holidays, so between my back and my face, there went my bruise-free semester. It was my last thought before I passed out.

Chapter Nineteen

Toni

"No."

Fucking boys. I rolled my eyes. "Fine, but you need the nurse, and it's not like anyone else is offering to help." My bossiness had taken over earlier, and in my rush to get the campers away from Brennon and Cole's macho throwdown, I had sent pretty much everyone else off to do damage control with the kids. This meant that now, it was just Brennon and me, alone in the expanse of the field. It might have taken him a second, but with a quick scan around, Bren caught on that he didn't have any other options.

"Fine. Help me up, and then I can make it there on my own."

Two could play his game. "No."

"What the fuck, Toni?"

Nothing tastes as good as petty feels. "I thought you didn't need my help? Big tough rocker boy can do it on his own?" I teased mercilessly.

"Fuck off. Fine. Toni, please help me." He dragged out the words like they were painful, but since he asked nicely, I grabbed his outstretched arm and leaned back on my heels to help him to his feet. Thank god Brennon wasn't quite as massive as Cole, otherwise, I probably would have dropped his ass right back in the dirt. He still looked a little unsteady on his feet, though, so I ignored the way he stormed away from me in the direction of the camp's heart and the Nurses House, and followed him. I didn't want to be there any more than he wanted me there, but the thought of leaving him bruised and alone made my stomach sink so I trailed about ten steps behind him as we lumbered along the beachfront and back up through camp letting him shout back at me and giving even snarkier responses.

"You don't need to follow me, Toni."

"What if you trip and fall and break off one of your pretty piercings?"

"Well, then the girls who usually fuck me because of all those pretty piercings will probably just ride my dick harder out of sympathy," he said it matter-of-factly, like girls actually did fuck him because of his piercings, or maybe because of his tattoos, or maybe because he looked far too tempting. He looked like a rebellious girl's fantasy come to life. Droolworthy and bad news, but oh-so-delicious. Yeah, even as I thought it, I realised that it was probably true. And that realisation made me blush first, and crack my knuckles second.

I bit my cheek and, annoyed at myself, I threw out, "Oh, I didn't think the hand-me-downs you got from Dad gave a shit about your piercings..." I let that cheap shot hang in the air, "or anything else about you except your last name."

We had been walking through the duration of our exchange, but that made him stop and face me. I sucked in a breath, waiting for a snarky response. Instead, his face was a stone wall. Kid-Brennon was all emotion; his face gave everything away. Every blush was a secret revealed. Every blink was a truth uncovered. The face looking back at me at that moment was empty of all feeling. He swallowed, blinked slowly, and without a word, turned back around and kept walking. I walked on, too, only now we walked in silence. No more trading jibes back and forth, and somehow that was worse. The silence gave me space to wonder and worry.

Brennon, still ahead of me, got to the door of Nurse House first. His long arm wrenched open the screen door, and I'm not sure what happened, but I squeaked out a concerned moan that prompted him to look back at me yet again. Brennon, Xav, and Cole might have cast the first stone, but throwing his dad's exploits in Brennon's face was equally inexcusable, so I gulped down my fear as we faced off. "I'm sorry, Brennon. What I said, what I just said. That was shitty, and I didn't mean it. I was... I am angry because I don't understand why you all hate me so much." Every piece of that sentence made my shoulders curve in on themselves, shame and embarrassment a lethal combination as I looked at him.

He still held tight to the screen door as he answered, "I don't hate you, Toni." A flood of warmth hit me, and I wanted to run a few steps toward him. Thank god I didn't. Brennon turned back to knock on the closed door, and without even bothering to look at me, he said coldly, "I pity you and I don't trust you. So, please, do us both a favour and don't mistake my lack of outright hostility for friendship." As far as dismissals go, it was like a punch to the chest, and I watched in an injured silence when the nurse answered, and with one quick look at his face, ushered him inside.

When I first made eye contact with Xavi those few weeks ago, his eyes had been full of regret and unsaid things. Every shared look with Cole was filled with anger and hate. Looking into Brennon's eyes in that doorway was the worst of the three. All he met me with was nothingness, no regret, no hurt, just a void. Somehow my musician, my artistic, soulful boy, had drained away the oceans of feeling that used to rage behind his stormy eyes. He meant it. I really was nothing. Not to him. Not now. Not anymore.

Embarrassed and frustrated, I held myself back from immediately running away. With all the gossip already swirling, courtesy of Greer's big mouth, the last I needed was for Cole or one of his posse to see me fleeing from Brennon. Bren and I had cut in from the side, but the main path to the Nurses House was a narrow dirt strip lined with small cedars that led you right back out to the main path. Brennon was a big boy who didn't need or even want me here. Pivoting to follow that path, I planned to head back to the Staff Village, grab a sweater, and maybe take a stop at the girls' toilets before turning right back around so I could stuff my face with tonight's dinner. No sooner did I turn away from the Nurses' building, as dirt slipped to gravel under my heel and sent me stumbling headfirst into a fucking freight train. Also known as Xavi running. Shirtless.

My only consolation, as my ass rebounded hard off the tiny sharp rocks, was the fact that I brought Xavi down with me.

"What the h—" he cursed, stopping himself just in time as a crowd of teenagers came up behind him.

The frontrunners, two girls in high school varsity shirts and running shorts, called out, "Xavi, are you okay?!" Their voices were high-pitched and worried enough to catch my attention, too. God, both of them were blonde, tanned, and California-beautiful, with long runner legs. Of course they were. One of them got even closer and extended her arm so she could help Xav to his feet. It took him a minute to accept her help. Initially, he was too busy staring daggers at me to notice, but eventually, he took her hand, jumping to his feet in one smooth motion.

"Thanks, Stephanie." He nodded, and she beamed, causing her friend to throw out a suggestive and knowing smile. Meanwhile, a boy from the middle of the pack now gathered around Xav, finally reached down to help me to my feet with a softly spoken, "Let me help you up, Toni."

"Thank you, uh—" I spoke loudly but paused, not knowing the kid's name.

"Callum. I'm one of the Land SEs. We all are." He gestured to the crowd.

Now the run made more sense. SEs were the "Sports Elite," the programme that was effectively half-leadership programme, half-athletic torture. Agonde celebrated what they called a 'culture of excellence', so once kids were old enough, they were expected to pick a lane, a sport or an art form and train like maniacs until they became experts. As Waterfront Director, I only ever saw the Water SEs, the swimmers, but there were lots of other types under the Lands or Paddles, and even more on the Arts Elite side, with music, visual arts, and drama. Most of these kids around me now would be high school athletes training for college scholarships, the Olympics, or hell, both.

"Well, thanks, Callum," I replied, dusting the last bit of gravel off my ass. A wide smile lit his face for a second until Xavi cut across. "Landies," he shouted, his voice lower than before, "Follow Heather, she'll lead the final half mile."

A girl I recognised, but didn't know, cut through the kids until she stood at the head of the group and called, "Everyone, follow me!" before she took off at a run.

Ugh. I mean I love to swim, but running seems like torture, I couldn't help but think as the kids followed her. Xavi stood beside me like a statue, saying nothing, but managing to glare at Callum when he eventually passed. Then he turned on me, sneering, "Toni, the boy is sixteen. Maybe take it down a notch."

"Take what down a notch?" I barked. "Common politeness? How 'bout you stop giving Stephanie your supermodel smile?"

"Oh, you think I have a supermodel smile?" He licked his full lips before biting the bottom one between his teeth. Something about the action forced my eyes to focus there, and then somehow they just kept drifting, down his tanned chest to the well-defined six-pack, and finally the angled v-lines and dark trail until they cut off at his shorts. When did Xavi get so cut? And why did it make heat bloom in my chest, or it did until he followed it up with, "Too bad I don't fuck sluts."

Seconds ago, my cheeks might have been red from a blush, but that turned to anger in an instant. "Fuck you, Xavi. I'm no slut."

"Could have fooled me. And everyone else. I heard you let Mitchell Greer feel you up right out in the open." He was still sweating from the run, beads of it running across his chest. And while he didn't wait for an answer, he grabbed the t-shirt he had tucked into his shorts at some point and dragged it across his body. He stepped closer, inches from my face. Close enough that I could smell him, and fuck, even with all the sweat, he smelled like vanilla and pepper. The scent was goddamn edible, even if his words turned sour. "He claims you gave him an all-access pass to those tits". He wiggled a finger at my chest. "That's pretty classic. Slut. Behaviour." In perfect time with the words, he flicked his fingers three times, hitting my right nipple hard each time. Hard enough that it tightened at the pain. He smirked, noticing my body's reaction. "See," he pointed at my now peaked bud, "I just call it like I see it." And before I could defend myself, he shot off, running to follow the tracks the SEs had left.

Fuck, he was fast. I watched him go for a minute, heated, annoyed with my own body and angry. Sue me—it took my brain a bit to catch up, but before he could round the tree line, I screamed after him, "You'd think you'd know better, Xavier Rothberg. Silence isn't consent!" My words must have reached him because he stopped dead. He'd heard me and that was enough. All these battles were exhausting. I was exhausted. Any response I got from him would just make me feel worse, so I dragged my bruised ass and hurt feelings away down a different path.

I skipped dinner, opting to lose myself in a book instead, but my little cabin felt stuffy and my book, dragons and all, failed to hold my attention. My cheap shot at Brennon and the coldness in his stare played on a loop in my head while regret and self-loathing danced in my belly. Add to that my confrontation with Xavi and yep, no dinner was the right call. That left me staring up at the ceiling planks, yet again wishing things were different. But the more I thought about it, the more the regret twisted and turned itself into anger and frustration. What I said to Brennon wasn't any worse than the things they had said or done to me in the last few weeks. So why was I sitting here feeling bad and punishing myself when they didn't have any remorse for being such dickheads?

Pushing off my bed, I dog-eared my page. Dragons would have to wait. I had a point to prove. They didn't get to just make me the bad guy. They weren't forcing me to run and hide. I did that all on my own. Maybe I was channelling Abbi, but I clung to my anger, stomping in the direction of the dining hall.

"Nice of you to join us, Toni." The Director deadpanned as I approached the crowd of staff gathered in a semi-circle around where he perched on the girls' steps. I ignored the comment and slipped quietly into the spot at the back of the group where Mich had shuffled sideways to make space for me. Jack's muddy eyes zeroed in on me, his lips creasing into a frown for a second, but then a gentle cough from someone in the crows had him remembering he was in the midst of a full staff meeting. He lifted his eyes and addressed the group loudly, "Now where were we?" Oh yeah - we were just going over the plans for tonight's evening!" The monthly schedule we were given during pre-camp had tonight labelled "cabin-based activities" which meant that hopefully those of us who weren't cabin leaders would be off the hook. It also meant I could tune out the Director and focus on Michele's whispered question, "Where were you?"

A quick check of the crowd confirmed everyone else was focused on the Director, as well as Cole and Abbi, who had joined Jack on the steps to explain the plans for each cabin tonight. Through tight lips, I said, "I had run-ins with both Xavi and Brennon today. Sharing a table with them didn't seem like the best idea after that."

Her eyes got wide. "Oh, no! What happened?"

As quickly and quietly as I could, I ran her through the speed version of my afternoon until she was shaking her head. "I don't know what's going on with Cole anymore, either." Her voice was barely more than a murmur. They say if you don't have anything nice to say, don't say anything at all. So I didn't, but I was desperate to comfort my friend. It wasn't like I could excuse Cole's behaviour, or even Brennon's or Xavi's. Hell, based on what I had said to Brennon today about his dad, I was pretty ashamed of myself, too. I reached for her hand and squeezed my support. We hadn't been friends long enough for me to do anymore, and having a taste of real female friendship for the first time in my adult life wasn't something I was willing to jeopardise by telling Mich her boyfriend was a world-class asshole. She offered me a small smile in return before we dropped our hands and lapsed into a comfortable silence, leaning into each other

Gradually, Jack's voice leaked through the bubble I was in with Michy. "So, cabin leaders and section staff, you're on your regular schedules tomorrow. Take off. Area heads, stick around." Huh. Clearly, I'd missed something. Beside me, Mich looked equally confused. Since cabin leaders and section staff make up a solid 70% of the team, our numbers shrank rapidly. Bella and Abbi were amongst the last to leave, waving joint goodbyes to Mich and me. Although I could have sworn her eyes caught briefly on where our shoulders touched.

There were only six programme Directors: creative and water, me and Mich, land and office, Xav and Bren, leaving just paddles and trips, manned by a guy and girl I knew were step-siblings, but whose names I could never remember. "So, as you all just heard from Cole, at least those of you who were listening," the Director explained with the quickest flash of angry eyes in my direction. "Our first camp-wide theme day is this Saturday." News to me. Serves me right for not listening, even though Cole didn't deserve my attention.

"The theme is 'Escape from the Zoo', and as our programme staff, you are responsible for planning the escape, and just in case it wasn't clear," his small smile widened into a sneer and his eyes found and held mine, “the kids are the hunters, you’re the prey. You have the rest of this week to plan, so plan well.” And with that sinister message and a wave of his hand, we were dismissed.

Xavi, age 15
5 years ago

My suit chafed. My skin itched. The lights in this godforsaken courtroom were too bright. The excess of stimuli around me was overwhelming, and I had to fight the compulsion to drag my hair over my eyes. If my father wasn't here, I almost certainly would have done it, but he hated the habit, and if he caught me doing it today, of all days, shit at home would go from bad to worse.

There was no escaping what I would have to do. What we would all have to do now that Toni had revealed the truth. The minutes we'd spent together, huddled like little kids in the toilets, felt like they were the memories of a different person. Now we were three people forced into a situation we wanted no part of. Brennon just had the shitty job of going first. He looked like a boy band gone punk rock when he climbed into the witness box with his pink hair, studded belt, and skinny tie. If it was any other day, I'd have probably laughed.

He explained the truth as we knew it. He detailed what she had told us, about how Nick was flirting with her and had invited her out to the woods, and how that was the last time we saw him. The rest of the truth wasn't worth telling. We had all agreed, especially since it was now clear we'd been unknowing accessories to a crime. So not one word about the three of us burying a man five years our senior in a shallow hole in the middle of a vast forest passed Brennon's lips. Cole went next, taking his seat without letting his eyes drift Toni's way even once. He stared right over her like she wasn't even in the room. Meanwhile, I could see the tears that streamed down her cheeks as she buried her face in her mom's shoulder. He repeated the same version of events Brennon had just spelt out.

When the judge finally called my name, it filled my veins with ice. I didn't move right away. It took my father squeezing my arm like a vice and hissing in my ear, "Xavier." The stern hazel eyes that I'd inherited bore into me. "You will move. Now." I couldn't ignore his command, so instead, I ignored the weight of dread I had been carrying since we got on the plane from Cali this morning. I staggered to my feet and slipped past my still-snarling father, defeated mother, and silent "cousins". Father had insisted that they come along, even though it would have been easier to leave them all at home. Surely they could have fended for themselves. Then again, that would have meant giving up control, even temporarily, and Daniel Rothberg could never.

My unsteady feet carried me up to the front of the courtroom. From there, Franklin's lawyer directed me into the small wooden box and closed the door behind me. I've never felt so caged in. But having seen my friends go through this, I had spent the last hour mentally preparing myself to be asked those same questions, about Nick, about Toni, and about that day that would probably haunt me right into the next life. Until today, I had never really thought about our friendship, about how or why a fifteen-year-old girl might only have three friends, and all of them guys. And I'd never really considered how that might be perceived. Until Franklin's lawyer grilled me about our friendship.

"Would you describe Antoinette Barrett as one of your 'best friends', Mr. Rothberg?"

"Yes."

"How many other female friends do you have, Mr. Rothberg?"

"None."

"To your knowledge, how many female friends do Mr. Grace or Mr. Michaels have?"

"To my knowledge, none."

"And, to your knowledge, did Ms Barrett have any other friends? Male, female, or other?"

"Again, to my knowledge, no."

"And none of you thought that it was strange that you were Ms Barrett's only friends?"

"No." I didn't know what this asshole was playing at. "We were best friends," I shouted. "Why would we need anyone else?" It was a genuine question, but one that made me sound like a naïve little boy.

"And that didn't strike any of you as odd?"

His derisive tone halted any answer I could offer. Looking out across the courtroom, the wincing faces of men and women forced me to see our friendship through a different lens. Forced me to ask questions I had never had reason to think about. I thought about my so-called cousins. After all, they were the only other girls I was exposed to regularly. They never really spoke to me. They seemed to rely wholly on each other, other than Rachel. Like Toni, Rachel never quite fit it, and well, when I had tried to be friendly, they'd seemed horrified. So, maybe there was something wrong with our friendship. Maybe it was weird that the three of us circled her like she was the sun in our sky. Quickly, I scanned the room for my friends. Cole sat red-faced and tight-lipped beside his dad, who seemed to be muttering at him nonstop. About what, I would never know. Cole probably wouldn't talk about it, even if I asked.

On his other side, Brennon was an empty mask. We, as in the three of us, all knew enough about his home life to know that he was an expert at putting on a show. He could be whoever someone else needed him to be. His dad showed up with the paparazzi and he yucked it up, charming everyone in sight. His mom needed him to speak for her children's charity, he'd slap on his most sombre face and speak to a crowd of hundreds about his privilege and his parents' hopes and wishes for every other child. Long story short, I had no idea how he felt right now, but no one else in this courtroom did, either. The only tiny sign he felt anything, and I'm not sure why I was able to pick it out amongst the thousand other things happening around me, was the way he's wrapped his pinky finger up with Cole's. The way their fingers squeezed together over the edge of the bench was strangely comforting.

It gave me the courage to look at Toni. She was still scrunched into her mother's side. Shrinking herself against the onslaught. But like she felt my eyes on her, she looked up, directly at me. She was stone-faced. Her tears had stopped running. She wasn't crying any-

more. And that made me angry. I wanted her to cry. I wanted her to cry for me and for us. For everything we'd all endured today, that she had put us through without ever having the courage to tell us the truth. If we were her everything, like she had always claimed, why didn't she just tell us the truth that day? I felt myself wanting to scream the question at her from the witness box. Sure, I was ashamed of us today, of me, of Cole, of Brennon. But I was furious with her. Yet there she was, holding on to all of her pride, while we sat up here and fell apart for her. How dare she? Here and now I couldn't punish her, but one day soon, I would.

The second the bailiff approached the box to free me, I bolted from the seat and the room. My breath was crushing in my tightening lungs, and I was desperate for air. The courtroom door slammed behind me as I sprinted through blurring hallways until I crashed through the grand entrance and out into the sun. Bent double at the edge of the sweeping staircase, I heaved against the sadness, rage and fear pushing me to the floor. After the way I tore out of there, my father would surely make me regret embarrassing him the second we weren't in public. But my fear of him is ever-present. I was used to it, so it wasn't what had me dropping to my ass and staring down the steps over the skyline of West Barrett Hills. I didn't know this town at all. This wasn't home to me. What little I did know about this expensive playground of Victorian mansions, private schools and old money came courtesy of Brennon and Toni. And just thinking about Toni was a final nail, hammering through the last wall of control I had. And like a fucking child, I sat there and cried.

Thank fuck, I was alone. And I stayed that way until an ominous voice beside me drew my attention. The voice was attached to recognizable dress pants and the well-contained rage I was oh-so-familiar with.

"Come, Xavier."

"What? But Father, it's—"

"It's done. And rightly done. Those women will think twice before they dare to step out of line again." He straightened his tie, even though it had never been ruffled in the first place. It was order first, always, with that man.

"Now get up. We are leaving," he said calmly.

The black limousine that had carried us here from the airport this morning was already waiting at the bottom of the staircase. The driver already stood, holding the door open for my father. He descended with his typical gravitas while my mother and the girls trailed after him, in a silent single-file line like naughty kindergarten kids behind a teacher. Not one of them, Mother included, spared me a glance as they trotted neatly behind him.

I scrubbed the last bit of emotion away with the heels of my hands and stood. I had to follow Father just the same as the girls or risk his wrath. It wasn't any kind of choice. That knowledge had me dusting my hands down my jacket and checking my shirt was still appropriately tucked in. It still itched, still chafed, but at least I once again looked the part of a Rothberg. Ready to join my family, I almost stepped down, but a firm pull on my arm launched me backward.

"Xav, wait!"

Brennon's voice was immediately recognizable, even as it cracked over the words.

"Wait for what, Brennon?"

"It doesn't have to end like this." I looked to where he gripped my elbow so tightly, and slowly roved up to his face, where his sadness and desperation were just as obvious as my own certainly was.

"Spit it out, Brennon," I snarled. "My family is waiting."

"Fuck your family, Xav. Something about this whole thing is wrong and you know it. Why would she lie to us?"

"Because she's a liar?" I questioned angrily, ripping my arm away from him.

His eyes were as damp as my own had been seconds ago as he reached for me again. "Please Xav, just listen," he begged.

"No!" I sliced my hands out. How could he be so stupid? Didn't he see her in there today? "Didn't you see the faces of everyone else in that courtroom, Bren? They all know we got conned. Scammed by a pretty face."

"That's not true," he flung back at me, just as angry. "They don't know anything about us or her, for that matter. Xav, I'm begging you, we need to find a way to get to her, to get the truth."

"No, Brennon. We heard the truth today," I sighed. "And the people in there, they're adults. Real-life adults. They know more about life than three naïve teenage boys."

"Says fucking who? Cole's already gone; his dad ripped him away so fast, but Birdie's still here. Stay, Xavier, stay and figure this out with me. Please," he pleaded, and though everything in me wanted to reach for him again, hug him again, just like we had done in the

bathroom hours ago, all I could see in my mind's eye was Toni's hard, unbothered face. So, all I did was shake my head and turn my back on one of my oldest friends, so I could follow after my family, who had left me sitting up here alone.

I got about halfway down the steps when his voice called out. "Is this what you would do if it was Cole up here asking?!" he screamed down at me, his deepening voice cracking a second time over Cole's name. Brennon was already so much taller than me, his teenage growth spurt coming early, but from where I stood now, he seemed smaller, more reminiscent of the eight-year-old I had first met. My mouth dried up, and no words came out of my swollen throat as I fixed on his tortured face in a silent showdown. "Of course not," he chided, as if my silence confirmed something for him.

There was nothing I could say to defend myself. Even to myself, I was struggling to deny that, right then, I was running away, and so I turned again and kept walking.

"You should know better than anyone, Xav, adults don't always get it right," he continued to shout at my back.

When I got close enough to the car, the driver, in his ridiculous guard-style uniform, reopened the door with a polite, "Sir." Any thank you I might have offered him was again cut off by Brennon shouts, "And they don't know fuck all about love."

"Yeah, well," I yelled back, even as I slid my ass into the town car, "after how we all behaved today, neither do we." And I slammed the door.

Chapter Twenty

Xavi

"Silence isn't consent." Fuck. She couldn't see my reaction, but those words Toni screamed at my retreating back had been playing on a loop for the past few days. Every meal, every staff huddle—fuck—every time she walked past smelling like sunscreen and starry nights, it was all I could think about. Those words and those letters. It didn't help that we were forced to spend the past few days practically huddled in the Creative Cluster's supply room. And here we were, yet again this morning, doing the last bits of prep for tomorrow's themed day.

The room was already claustrophobic as a result of the shelves stacked ceiling-high with art supplies, craft paper, and who the fuck knew what else Michele claimed was necessary for the various art programmes she had running out of here. On top of all that, there were six of us crammed in here like sardines and it was downright suffocating. This was why I stuck to Land Sports. No inventory other than footballs, volleyballs and tennis racquets. Lots of sunshine and no prep. Kids turned up, I handed them a ball to kick or throw or hit, and off they went. Easy. All this creative shit was not my wheelhouse and now, like I needed the additional layer of suffering, I had to sit in this glorified closet and watch as Toni laughed and made jokes with Michele. They had craft paper strung up along a whole wall, and paper cups in hand, they were traipsing back and forth across the room painting their versions of wild animals, jungle plants and who knew what else. Personally, I thought Michele's tiger looked more like a deformed house cat but that wasn't really what I was focused on.

She never was an artist, always too impatient to spend the time making things perfect, yet somehow now Toni was in her element. She followed behind Michele, painting grey bars over each animal and exclaiming, "Well, at least I can paint in a straight line. That's something!" Each time, the girls would collapse into laughter together. When we were kids, Cole, Bren and I would battle every day to try to make her laugh, mostly because if we could get her to laugh hard enough, she would snort and, I swear, it caught her by surprise every damn time. Watching her now was brewing a cocktail of jealousy, frustration and guilt churn in my stomach. I could have been the one making her laugh right now instead of trying to string ribbon, through the paper-plate masks we'd made yesterday. The holes Brennon had punched in them were too small, and my attempts at jamming the ribbons through them weren't working. Of the fifty we'd made so far, I had only managed to finish five of them. It was going to be a long day.

Toni's tiny jean shorts weren't exactly helping my concentration, either. In the four weeks since she'd arrived, her body had filled back out and now she looked more like the athletic version of her I remembered from five years ago and less like the emaciated girl who'd first shown up this summer. A little more oomph in those curves was a dangerous thing, though. With every brush stroke, she was either leaning up on her tiptoes making her perfect ass cheeks and toned legs flex, or worse, she'd bend over to reload the brush from the trays that littered the floor, and her baggy t-shirt would gape just enough for flashes of her tanned cleavage to tease me.

I was staring so intently that I didn't notice Brennon until it was too late. I had purposely snatched a stool so I could tuck myself into a corner. Naively, I had assumed that would guarantee no one would creep into my personal space. Fuck people. I needed my own space. Always, well mostly, always. There were a few exceptions. But nope, not today since Brennon somehow found his stool, and instead of picking a different corner, decided to slam his overgrown frame right into me. "Stop staring."

"I'm not staring." I retorted.

"Sure, of course, you're not." He rolled his blue eyes at me. "You're just sitting here doing fuck all."

In the four years since we'd stopped being friends, somehow, I had managed to forget how annoying Brennon could be. The last few days had been a stark reminder, and now I was about ready to clock him. "Fuck off." I picked up another one of his stupid arts and crafts projects. "I've been sitting here trying to put your shitty masks together." And, of course, in my annoyance, I pushed too hard, and the stupid overgrown paper plate ripped in half, leaving me holding a limp ribbon like a jackass. "Fuck this."

Of course, Brennon only laughed, his low chuckle making blood rush to my face, and he grabbed it from me. "I forgot how impatient you are. Here." He snapped his long arm to the shelf behind us, grabbing some tape as he set about fixing the mask I just ruined.

"Leave me alone, man. I'll fix it on my own." I tried to snatch the mask from his hands.

"No. You'll ruin all my work, dickhead." He held on tight, and laying the mask back in his lap, I watched as he picked up the ribbon I dropped, pinching one end and weaving it slowly through one hole and then the other. "Sit the fuck down, Xavier," he commanded.

Hell, he could be a real asshole when he wanted to be. Part of me wanted to give him the finger, but this shit needed to be done, so I fucking sat. I didn't miss the smug-as-shit look on his face when my ass hit my stool, either. Seated together like that, we were a magnet for Toni, her blue eyes flitting in our direction whenever she thought we weren't looking. They were filled with worry, like just the fact that Brennon and I were sitting together spelled out certain doom for her. It probably did, and she should have known better. I'm always looking and always plotting, except this time I wasn't the only one. Sequestered as we were in the corner of the room, no one else could hear when Brennon let out a low whistle, "Jesus, would you look at that ass."

"What ass?"

"As if your eyes haven't been glued to her this whole time," he answered. Might have caught me staring, but I wasn't about to admit it to him.

"I've been focused on other things."

"Sure you have," more sarcasm in his voice now. "Focused on the way those handfuls swing every time she dips down?"

God, he really never shut up. "You think you're so subtle, Xav, but I see the way you watch her. You did it then, and you do it now."

"What do you know?" My voice came out louder and more defensive than I meant it to. The whole room seized, and four sets of eyes bore down on us. It made the hair on my arms stand up and my neck itch.

"Everything okay over there?" Mich called out.

Brennon slapped on a fake smile and dialled the charm in his voice up to eleven. "Just fine, Mich." He thumbed at me. "Just trying to teach this grump how to string the masks." Then he waved his finished mask in the air.

I still hadn't managed to do another one. With that, the attention shifted off of us. All except Toni's. My wild girl continued to watch, her gaze appraising both of us, testing for the truth. Brennon licked his lips suggestively at her. "Keep watching us like that, Birdie, and I'll take a bite right out of you." And he snapped his jaws, like a goddamned animal. The jarring of his teeth clashing made her jump out of her skin and a blush rose on her cheeks as she turned away. I couldn't help my grin at the sight of it. Which faded pretty much instantly when Brennon leaned into my ear with a stupid smirk of his own. "I know, because you're not the only one watching." And again, he licked his lips, sucking his piercing into his mouth. His eyes narrowed in on mine, and it was my turn to flush, to turn away, to ignore him.

Camp is always a balancing act between chaos and organisation. Saturday morning's breakfast tipped those scales a little closer to the chaos. There was a kind of frantic energy in the dining hall thanks to the kids' excitement and nerves about the theme day. And the buzzing sensation of it continued to build throughout the meal, only cresting when Cole, Abbi and Jack took the stage to announce the plan for the day.

Thankfully, my morning would be my own. Days like today had cabin staff readying their kids, the costumes, the cheers, all that crap. That left the rest of us with setup time for the afternoon. Yesterday's disastrous mask-making and crafting had eventually given way to game and costume prep. Since all we were really planning was a glorified game of tag, it wasn't exactly a chess match to sort things out.

As Lands' Director, I had been allocated the job of sorting all the staff, excluding cabin leaders, into their "animal groups". Basically, I had to decide who could run fast, and who was lazy as hell, and then assign them an animal accordingly. So Brennon, with his stupid mop of hair and preference for lying on his ass, playing guitar or fucking with computers, well, he was a lion. Still a predator, but not one with any particular speed or stealth, whereas Nettie, who moved through the water with more grace than she ever moved with on land, would be one of our dolphins.

After lunch, the whole camp gathered at the dining hall steps where 'Head Zookeeper' Cole explained the game. At the sound of his horn, we, the animals, would escape. Then 300 kids would have to hunt us down, catch us, and drag us back to the Centre Circle. The faster the animal, the harder we'd be to catch, but the more points we were worth. Like any game ever, most points win. Dressed in my all-black jaguar costume, I was faster and deadlier than other animals, so I'd be the hardest to catch and worth the most points. Only Nettie was worth as many, mostly because kids would have to get in the water to catch her. When Cole finally finished showboating and blew the horn, we all took off.

Two hours later, the game was called with loud air horns sounding throughout the property. I was dripping in sweat and desperate to grab a shower as I dragged my ass back to the Centre Circle. This game had turned out to be the best workout I'd had in a while.

When I got there, all of camp, both staff and kids, were gathered again. The only difference was now we all looked exhausted. All except the Director, who had taken over Cole's announcement duties and looked freshly starched in khakis and a polo. Microphone in hand, he announced which cabin won the game. I wasn't surprised it was a group of senior girls, including Stephanie and Megan, who were part of the Land SEs and ran at pace with me regularly. They had also been the only ones who had managed to catch me. Others had given a good chase, but few could match my speed.

At the announcement, the girls cheered and whooped before Jack cleared his throat to interrupt. "Congratulations, ladies! As a prize, you get a special party in the Hive hosted by three of our escaped creatures." This news led to more teenage-girl cheering. "The staff—I mean, our escaped animals—of your choosing will serve snacks, provide entertainment, and play host for the evening. You have two minutes to choose!"

Barely twenty seconds went by, granted in a tense silence, as the whole camp waited for their decision. In that short window, the girls put their heads together, tittering and giggling at their choices, but it was Stephanie who stepped forward and shouted to the crowd, "We've picked!"

The Director beckoned her to the stage and with her head high and blonde braid swinging she pushed through the throngs of younger kids with the kind of smug smirk only teenage girls seem to master. She skipped up the wooden steps, extending her hand and snatching the microphone from Jack, swinging her body back to the crowd. "We would like Xavier to be our host." Not ideal, since it meant I'd be spending my night rebuffing poor attempts at flirting instead of cooped up in my cabin with a book, but at least I would be hosting and not entertaining. God help whoever had to do that shitty job. Or worse, serve these girls. Say what you want, nobody is more cutthroat than a teenage girl, and Stephanie proved it two seconds later. "For our entertainment, we'd like Brennon Grace to play for us." On cue, the crowd turned to the lake-side to where Bren stood, kicking rocks and ignoring the eyes on him. The only sign he heard her was a slow nod of his head. His muted reaction had everyone switching their attention back to Stephanie for her final name. Her eyes narrowed and her smirk went fox-like as she brought the mic right to her lips. "And we'd like Antoinette to serve us." And then she laughed. Nobody turned to look at Toni, well nobody except me and Stephanie, who scrunched her face in displeasure when Nettie's only reaction was a thumbs' up and a weak smile.

Nettie's absent reaction took the wind out of Stephanie's sails and from the deck, I could see the clenching of her fists in annoyance as the Director shouted out, "One more round of applause for our winners!" And a final chorus of cheers spread through the circle. When the applause trickled off, bit by bit, the crowd dispersed. Kids and cabin leaders heading off to clean up before dinner. When you live in the middle of the woods with limited services, showers aren't exactly an everyday occurrence and Saturdays were a prime shower day. I'd bet money that cabin leaders would be spending the next hour packaging up their kids and shoving them into showers. Easy enough with the girls, but a tough sell with the boys sometimes. Except me. Even at eight, I remember being grossed out by the boys in my cabin who refused to clean themselves. It was fucking disgusting.

I needed to beat them to the showers, if only so I could guarantee hot water, but kids are slow, so as long as I headed straight to my cabin, grabbed my shit and hustled there, I knew I would be fine. The fastest route back to the Staff Village took me along the path that ran just below the dining hall deck. It wasn't like I meant to eavesdrop, but Cole was so goddamn loud. And his baritone had me poking my head up at his back. With his back to the railing, he stood broad-shoulder to broad-shoulder with Mitchell. It meant he couldn't see me, and though I couldn't see more than his muscled back, either, I could hear his shit-eating grin that backed his words to Greer. "Serves the princess right. I hope those girls put her ass to work."

Between Brennon and Nettie, the last two days had already been a mind-fuck, and now we would be spending yet another night trapped in each other's company. I wasn't thrilled at the prospect, but when I hopped under the scalding water ten minutes later, I wasn't sure Toni deserved whatever shit those girls were going to throw her way, either.

Chapter Twenty-One

Brennon

I'm no athlete. Too much time spent on computers or with my guitar in my hands. The occasional blunt smoked during the school year didn't help my lung capacity much either. But if I needed to, I could be fierce, and I happened to have a spectacular head of hair, even if the blue dye job needed a top up on my next day off. That's why I just laughed when Xav stuck a big 'Hello, My Name Is' sticker on my chest with the word 'lion' scribbled across it in his neat handwriting.

Staying true to the role, when Cole blew the air horn to start the game, I did run, but not too far. There was the lovely spot out behind Valerium, one of the boys' cabins, where a bunch of trees had fallen during a storm a few summers' back, and now the clearing was one giant sun-trap that even included a perfect rock I could use as a lounger while I soaked up some heat, like any self-respecting lion would do.

That's where I spent most of the game, until two older girls stumbled on my hiding spot. They were both so fast they circled me easily. And as they escorted me back to the Centre Circle to claim their points, I realised that they were part of Xav's Land Elites group. If they could keep up with him, I'd never stood a chance. As we walked, the girls gossiped back and forth about how many points they'd accumulated so far and if it was enough for them to win. From the sounds of things, the only people they hadn't caught yet were Xav and Birdie. Not surprising. Knowing those two, I doubted anyone would manage to catch them.

Sure enough, when the game ended shortly after my capture, Xav was among the last people to return and join the throngs waiting for the winners' announcement outside the dining hall. He was sweating from the game. Knowing him, he'd probably used the whole thing as a workout, but I couldn't fault what it had done to his curls. Even as he tried to slick them back, they clung to the forehead, refusing to budge. I thought back to the way it felt to grab those curls not so long ago. Not that he noticed me watching him, anyway. Usually so observant, his entire focus was consumed by Birdie, whose wet skin seemed to be hogging all the sunlight from the rest of us. Sue me, I was jealous.

The last bruises from my face had faded, mostly, but not her words. Screw her for thinking I'd fuck Blue's hand-me-downs or ever cash in on that motherfucker's name to get laid. If that's the kind of thanks I get for defending her, she could go to hell. And with that thought, and another look at Xavi whose gaze was still honed in on Toni, I was reminded just how badly the three of us were failing. Other than some empty words, we'd done fuck all for weeks to try to get rid of her. Xavier might think he's the mastermind out of the three of us, and maybe he is, but so far his plan had failed, so maybe it was time I took a shot.

Cole and Abbi were slowly making their way through the crowd. Once they got to the top of the stairs, they'd announce the winning cabin. Part of all the prep work we'd done over the last few days had included brainstorming potential prizes for the winner, so I knew exactly what was coming. Searching the crowd, I spotted the blonde ponytail of the girl who'd done such a good job of catching me. She and her friends, likely cabin mates, were gathered together near the centre of the crowd, but her eyes were hard and hungry and entirely focused on Xavi. I obviously wasn't the only one annoyed by the attention he was lavishing on Birdie, meaning I'd just found a new ally. Silently, I wove through the crowd until I was close enough that I could tap her on the shoulder.

She turned to face me, confused, until I opened my mouth to ask, "Do you really think your cabin won?"

Either this girl was hella competitive or just a damn happy teenager, but I suspected it was the first when she smiled back at me. "I know we did. I was the only one to catch Xavier."

There was definite pride in her voice. Not that that was any guarantee, but I had nothing to lose if things didn't shake out in my favour. I was thankful for the roar of the crowd as, instead of Abbi or Cole, Jack's voice echoed out over the microphone, asking, "Ready to hear our winners?!"

Taking advantage of the extra seconds, I leaned in to the girl and quietly whispered the details of the prize.

"So, when it's announced, I don't care who you get to host, but pick me for your entertainment."

She rolled her eyes. "I would have done that, anyway."

"What about the rest of your friends?" She laughed quietly. "They'll go with whatever I decide. They always do." This girl might be helping with my plan, but she also seemed like a bit of a bitch.

"And pick Toni to be the one who serves you," I said, ignoring her comments. But her next one was hard to ignore, especially as her lips curled into a venomous grin. "With pleasure."

Seconds later, Jack called the winners and my quick work came together when the girl, whose name I discovered was Stephanie, as her friends shouted their approval, raced to the stage. I backed out of the crowd, lingering on the edge, and barely registered any notice as she shouted my name. The whole thing could have been an innocent coincidence.

Except, it was actually a sting operation. I was already making a playlist in my head of songs. Some were recent, but many were older, at least five years older. They were songs sung over campfires, side-by-side during sing-alongs, hummed under our breath during quiet moments at the Throw. Her continued presence here was nothing but a reminder of the past I'd rather not relive. But every summer has a soundtrack, and tonight I'd use music to make those memories hurt.

Chapter Twenty-Two

Xavi

The Hive, so-called because of its hexagon shape, was basically a giant tent with a raised floor and a fire pit in the centre. It was modelled on indigenous structures, the type of teepee that was probably here before some white guy like me turned up and stole the land. Tucked away behind the Creative Cluster, it was usually used for programmes and elite training during the day and junior staff hook-ups at night. During the in-between hours, it was typically dark and empty. The only exception was on nights like tonight, when it served as the venue for some sort of special occasion. Special occasions like my parents' wedding. Thinking about it made me scoff. They met here at camp when my father was a cabin leader and my mother was a fifteen-year-old camper in his tennis class. Barely six years later, they got married inside this stupid tent. And trust me, every part of it was, and still is, exactly as gross as it sounds. Not that I was alive when they got married, but I had seen enough photos and heard enough stories about the value of their courtship to try to avoid this place at all costs.

Last summer, I had managed to go a whole four months without stepping foot inside once. I guess I couldn't be that lucky twice. What I wasn't expecting was the fire already burning within the canvas walls. The only reason I came up here so early was to arrive first. Pulling back the curtain, I didn't expect to find Nettie, bare-legged but for shorts, and kneeling in the dirt in front of the fire pit. Her face glistened in the heat of the burgeoning flames and strands of her brown hair clung to her neck and shoulders. I watched her silently for a few seconds before my presence inside the tent registered with her. In the flickering shadows of the fire, she looked up as the tent flap closed behind me, fluttering in the faint evening breeze.

She looked beautiful. Worshipful. I wanted to keep her there.

"You're here early, Cinderella," I snarked down at her.

"Hello to you, too, Xavier," she said, but didn't bite back, instead re-focusing on the fire, adding another cluster of small logs around the edges. A classic technique that would keep the fire burning for a long time.

"What are you doing here?" I demanded.

She looked back up at me, her eyes shining, probably from the smoke. "I'm here *to serve,* or didn't you hear your little *friend*?"

"Oh, I heard. I just didn't expect you to get here early."

She placed a final log on either side of the fire, then stood, dusting her knees as she moved to press her back against the far wall of the tent, as far away from me as she could possibly get.

I asked again, "What are you doing here right now, Nettie?"

“I’m here,” she sassed, “because those girls and their cabin leader—”

“Alex?”

"Yeah, well, Alex is kind of a bitch. But, anyway, they told me they wanted the fire hot and their snacks ready when they arrived.”

“Alex is a bitch. So, why did you listen?”

This time she didn’t answer me, just shrugging off my question. Instead, she hugged the edges of the space as she inched toward the door where I still stood, blocking her exit. “They’ll be here soon. I have to go get their snacks.”

I let her sneak behind me and watched until she was out of sight behind the Creative Cluster. Probably headed for the kitchen to grab said snacks. Everything about it was so unlike my wild girl. No battle, no attitude, just downright submission. That wasn’t Toni. At least that wasn’t fifteen-year-old Toni, who threw a downright fit any time Cole tried to shove a sweatshirt over her bikini-clad body. Back then, she would accuse him of being a prude and shout that she could dress however she liked. Little did she know, he did it because seeing her in a bikini sent all three of us into a hormonal tailspin. Brennon and I didn’t exactly love seeing staff and campers alike ogle her, but we definitely handled it better than Cole.

Toni in a bikini at fifteen was one thing, but seeing her in the crowd at the end of the wide game today, wet-haired with beads of water catching the sun as they ran between her breasts and the black triangles of her swimsuit, well that was a new form of torture. So much so that the first five minutes of my shower this afternoon had consisted of me picturing my hands yanking those strips of fabric from her body before sliding my cock between the perfect breasts. I came so hard I almost lost my footing.

Lost as I was in that fantasy, even now, what drew me back to reality were the screeches and giggles that are the unique property of teenage girls. In Toni's absence, I had tucked myself just inside the tent's opening where I stood ready and waiting to play host. Not that that was all I planned to do. I fully intended to take advantage of Toni's circumstances tonight. The second these girls left this tent, I would pin her ass to the wall and demand to know why she had finally reappeared at Agonde. After all, it was the question that had been torturing me ever since she showed her face. And there was no way in hell Cole and Brennon weren't wondering the same thing. I put those plans on pause when Stephanie and Alex skipped inside arm-in-arm, giggling the way girls do. Behind them, a trail of other girls followed. All of them carried a mix of pillows and blankets and dressed in pyjamas like this was a regular old slumber party. Not that I would know. Teenage boys don't exactly do 'slumber parties', and even if they did, my father's rules meant no friends at the house. I watched them disperse around the tent, but Alex, Stephanie, and her friend, whose name I definitely should have known, but didn't, stuck together. Although Alex was the cabin leader and at least a couple of years older, the two girls honestly looked like sisters or twin dolls. And even though cabin leaders weren't supposed to, it was pretty clear that Alex had picked favourites.

It was Stephanie who spotted me first, her blue eyes catching mine across the shadows of Toni's fire. "Xavi!" she exclaimed, getting back up and leaving her cabin leader and friend on their asses as she stalked over to me. "Thank you for being our host, we're all so excited." Gesturing toward the other girls like a queen holding court. Stephanie was a talented sprinter, but because I generally led the SE runs in silence, I had never really noticed her condescension before.

One of the other girls actually raised her hands to ask, "Stephanie, what now?"

"Christ," I cursed, silently wondering why that question wasn't directed at Alex, since she was their leader, after all. But none of the other girls seemed surprised or affronted by the question, not even Alex. "Well, Miranda," she drawled, "Xavier here, and oh, Brennon!" Her mouth popped open in excitement as Bren's tall frame ducked through the open flap, carrying his guitar case. He surveyed the scene with all his usual unaffectedness. Until his eyes landed on where Stephanie stood beside me, her arm draped on my shoulder. Then his eyes narrowed. And it only got worse when Toni, because of course she managed to time her entrance perfectly, stumbled back into the tent. Forever graceful in the water, Toni was strangely like a baby deer on land sometimes. All limbs. It was worse now because she had a party-size bowl in each hand and was making every effort to salvage the popcorn they held. Toni's entrance only distracted the girls momentarily, as Stephanie sneered in her direction. "As I was saying, before I was so rudely interrupted," she swatted her hand dismissively at Toni, "these two gentlemen, Xavier and Brennon, are here to entertain us."

All the girls grinned, and a few even clapped. Meanwhile, I watched my wild girl as she just stood there, eyes downcast, looking unsure of how to move or what to do.

"Antoinette, here," Stephanie derided, her snarky voice breaking the spell Toni held over me, "is going to serve us. You know, like a maid." She laughed.

That wasn't exactly right. Sure, Toni hadn't been given a choice when Stephanie asked for her to be here. That's the thing about this job, we keep kids safe, we teach them shit, but at the end of the day, some of them know they hold the balance of power. We're basically all here to make sure they have a good time. So again, Toni didn't have a choice but to play serving girl tonight.

"Antoinette." Toni bristled at the use of her full name, but she looked up at Stephanie, anyway, as the girl continued, with a new level of cruel glee, "Make sure all the girls have popcorn. Brennon can't start playing until you're done stumbling around. Isn't that right, Brennon?" She turned to him now, moving away from me. Finally, I felt like I could breathe again with that girl out of my personal space, and I watched Toni weave her way around the room, passing out smaller bowls of popcorn to each group of girls. Eventually, she made it all the way around the room and had no choice but to skirt around Brennon, still standing near the entrance, and Stephanie, who'd moved on to cling to him instead of me. And while she might not notice, I was fully aware of the way Brennon's eyes followed Nettie in the darkness. Normally, our resident rockstar always acted like he didn't give a single fuck, but in that tent, his eyes glimmered darkly as he tilted his head down and whispered something to Stephanie. Her eyes shone just as much at whatever he said, and it meant nothing good. Sure enough, Nettie swallowed hard as she faced the fire and filled her last bowl with popcorn before turning to hand it to Stephanie. The girl gave her a far too saccharine smile as she reached out to grab it, only to swat it back in Nettie's face at the last second. Kernels sprayed everywhere, including on Toni's face.

"Oops." Stephanie shrugged, no trace of real remorse in her voice.

Nettie tucked down so she could brush the fallen snacks into a small pile on the Hive floor. And as if seeing her on her knees wasn't enough, just as she reached for the bowl to collect the now-ruined food, Stephanie's Nike-clad foot kicked out and launched the bowl out of her reach so that it skittered and landed in the ashes at the edges of the fire. "Sorry, Antoinette, could you go get us another bowl? I think that one is ruined. And besides, we'll need something bigger." She wasn't even making an attempt to hide her malice anymore, as she stared down at my wild girl. "Brennon and I are going to share."

"Oh, and Antoinette," Brennon finally chimed in. It was the first time in years I'd heard him use her full name and hearing it in his deep voice made both Toni and I stare at him. "Bring me a chair, too, so I can give these girls a proper show." Nobody but Brennon, Stephanie, and I could see it, but her cheeks blushed furiously, and she practically sprinted toward the exit. Not that I could see her face, but I swore I heard a sniffle as she passed me. The sound made my blood boil, although, whether I was angry for Nettie or at her, I wasn't sure anymore.

Eventually, she reappeared, dragging a bench along the dirt path with her. By then, Brennon and Stephanie had forgotten about tormenting her. Brennon, because he'd started playing, and Stephanie, because she was too busy staring at him while he did. All the girls were distracted as Bren played an annoyingly good cover of a current pop song, so I ducked out and strode toward Nettie's bent-over frame.

"Let me help you."

I swear, the girl practically jumped in fear. Something about that thrilled me and had me prowling even closer to her turned back. Regaining her composure a little, although not enough to brave looking at me, she grumbled back, "Are you really going to help me, Xav? Or just cause more problems?" The question was so soft, her voice so unsure, it halted me.

A strangled "Hmmmmm," was all I could reply, and to avoid answering for real, I stepped up behind the bench. She took a few steps back, not wanting to come too close, but my intentions weren't bad this time. I grabbed the small bench, one she'd clearly stolen from the dining hall, and lifted it easily. Without another word, but with one hell of a confused look, Nettie bent back down and grabbed yet another giant bowl of popcorn I hadn't noticed she'd left sitting in the dirt. Obviously, she'd been struggling to try to carry both on a single trip. Letting her go first, we walked back into the Hive in silence.

It was almost ten by the time Brennon finally seemed to be winding down the showman act. The firelight had dimmed, with only the last flames and embers still burning orange and the air inside the Hive had grown suffocating and tight from fifteen peoples' breathing. Some of the girls had fallen asleep, and even Stephanie seemed to have grown bored with staring at Brennon and torturing Toni. So far, she had "accidentally" kicked her twice, tripped her once, and thrown or dropped at least three bowls of popcorn. Toni looked increasingly weary each time, but for the last half hour, she'd finally been able to sit, crouched down against the canvas wall, and keep her distance from the girls. Every time the shadows of the fire moved, I watched her try to sink into the darkness more and more. I swear she would have melted into the corner if she could have.

Being tonight's host hadn't exactly been a demanding job. Most of my time was spent watching my former friends watch each other. When Bren finished the next song, one I hadn't recognized, he scanned the small space before announcing to the crowd, "Last song for tonight, girls. One you're all probably too young to remember, but it's an old favourite of mine." The words were nice enough, but there was a chill in his voice that wasn't there when he had started talking, and the way he looked at Toni was so vicious that she visibly shivered, which only made him smile.

Then he started playing, low melodic chords that matched his deep hum. At first, I didn't recognize the song, since he dragged out the intro, playing it softer and slower than the radio version. Only when he started tapping out the bass beat against his guitar did my gut churn in recognition. It was definitely an “old” song now, but back then, it had been newly released, and Cole had spent that entire summer singing it under his breath. He was obsessed with it. So much so that every time we hung out at the Throw, he would set up his stupid Bluetooth speaker on one of the rocks and play that song over and over again. The lyrics and melody eventually became the soundtrack to every conversation we had that summer. There was no way Brennon could know about my other memories associated with it, and as he sang out the stripped-back lyrics, “It was almost love. When the walls came down…” I half wondered if this was about me. But his eyes never left Toni, whose recognition of the song was written just as clearly on her face as it probably was on mine. Her mouth was hard and her blue eyes steeled, but there was an undeniable shine in them that spoke to painful memories called back to life. Ones she obviously couldn’t stand to relive. Showing her backbone for the first time tonight, she shoved herself past me and out the door into the night. Without missing a beat, Brennon watched her go right past me, and the asshole paused to look at me and wink. Like this was a fucking joke I was supposed to be in on.

I couldn’t stand it anymore. Not even halfway through the song, I cut him off. “Girls. Back to your cabin. NOW!” I couldn’t help but bark at them. They needed to be out of here. I needed them gone. The girls looked a mix of shock and worry at my sudden outburst. I ignored it, fixing my hardest stare at their cabin leader. “Alex, get your kids to bed. It’s already past curfew.”

She gulped and nodded before turning to the girls spread out everywhere. “Ladies, Xavier is right. Grab your stuff and let’s go. Time for bed.” There was a rush of activity as they gathered up all the supplies and blankets they had dragged in here earlier and started to make their way out of the tent. I pressed my back against the walls to avoid them as they passed me. Any touch right then would turn me violent. Only Stephanie even attempted it, reaching out like she was going to brush my arm, but I stepped back again. She eyed me suspiciously, but thank fuck, she kept walking. As soon as the last girl was out the door, so was I. I bolted like a skittish colt, until I rounded the back corner of the Creative Cluster, stopping to lean against one of the big trees back there so I could catch my breath and calm the panic inside me.

There was a trio of tall oak trees back there, with strings tied between them that were used as drying lines for kids’ artwork. And their trunks were big enough that I could hide out of sight while I regrouped. That stupid fucking song. I hadn’t heard it in years. Even now, though, it’s a reminder of that night, of skin on skin in the dark, of the shared whispers and of the empty feeling of being left alone afterward. Not content to leave me to panic in peace, Brennon stormed along the dark path I had just left behind, stopping a few feet away to stare at me.

“For fuck’s sake, Brennon, why that song?” I spat.

His face softened as he answered, “I don’t know, Xav, it wasn’t my plan, but there are just ghosts everywhere these days.” He shrugged. “Don’t you feel them? Because I’m fucking haunted by them.” I breathed, but the only sound came from the clatter of small stones rolling out of the way of his feet as Brennon took a few steps closer. "And I needed you both to know that I remember." I didn't move, but he took more steps. And more steps again, until we were only inches apart.

His voice dropped low and quiet. "I remember how it was and what I thought it could have been."

Somewhere in the last few years, I had lost my ability to read him, to know with perfect certainty what he meant and the why behind it. Now, I wasn't sure if he was being sincere or just playing the clown, fucking with Toni and with me because he could. Sincerity was dangerous. Something Brennon rarely exhibited these days. Him screwing with me, that made more sense. That I could handle. I knew how to respond to that.

"Cut this shit out, Brennon." I paused, a question hanging in the back of my throat. "Why are you fucking with me, man? Shouldn't you be directing this shit at Toni?"

He stepped even closer, pushing me so my back arched into the tree behind me. Downside was the curve in my spine shoved my chest forward toward his enough that our t-shirts skimmed against one another.

"Who says I'm fucking with you, Xavier?" His tone brooked no arguments as he took another step into me. Now we really were chest to chest, and I could feel the pressure of his muscles on mine. His long arms came around to rest against the tree bark behind my head, surrounding me on all sides as he leaned closer still. His face was so close to mine that I held my breath, and so slowly, so softly, his lips brushed the edge of my jaw. I said nothing, did nothing. I swear my body seized completely. And in the absence of any protest from me, Brennon's lips continued to climb, tenderly touching along my jaw up toward my ear. The warmth of his mouth clashed with the chilled metal of his lip piercing and sent shivers through my body.

Time was moving both agonisingly slowly and too fast as he finally brought the weight of his mouth to the sensitive spot behind my ear and his tongue laved my skin. With that, my confusion took a backseat as my brain and body reacted on impulse to the fire he was lighting. My eyes closed and my body tightened in anticipation. Of what? I wasn't sure. "Bren—" His name came out half question, half moan.

He stopped and instantly I missed the press of him, but he stayed close and his breath tickled my neck as he spoke. "I'm not fucking with you, Xavier. I'm not him."

I spluttered, "Wha— How—"

He rolled his eyes at me. "How about you spare us both the bullshit, huh?"

I let the rustling of the wind through the trees be my answer. "Look, Xav," he sighed impatiently, "I know who I am and what I want. And what if I'm just tired of being alone?" Again, his blue eyes fought to pin me.

Pressure, tension, conflict. All of it can make your brain do some weird shit. Even still, I wasn't prepared when I heard myself ask, "What about Toni?"

Was I surprised by my own question? Sure, but it made Brennon look sick to his stomach. Only for a second, though, then his eyes went from heated to twin icicles in no time at all.

"Fuck her. This isn't about her," he practically growled.

"Isn't it, though?" It sure sounded like it was at least a little about her. Maybe he had already forgotten his comments about her tits yesterday, but I hadn't.

"No." He kept his voice quiet, but too firm. "That bitch made her bed. Too bad for her, she has to share it with that shrimp-dick Greer." A dark chuckle made his opinion of both Nettie and Mitchell Greer crystal clear. Three days ago, I might have agreed. Thing was, now I wasn't so sure. Fuck, no. I was sure. I couldn't erase the past, but I could admit that maybe we got at least part of this situation wrong. That thought had me straightening.

"Thing is, Brennon. I don't think she did."

He faltered. "You know what she said to me?"

There was a pregnant pause that hung between us as he waited for me to fill him in. "Silence isn't consent."

He stepped back, disgust on his face. "Fuck off."

"I gave her shit about Greer, and her response was, 'Silence isn't consent.' And you know what? She's right." Usually, Brennon was pretty rational, or at least thoughtful enough to evaluate a situation fully. Not this time, though.

More disgust settled over his features. "Don't be such an idiot, Xavier. She's a liar and a whore. We know this."

"Do we?" I couldn't help it. Now that the questions were there on the tip of my tongue, I couldn't help but ask them. "I'm starting to wonder if we got it wrong. We were all just kids." He stared at me like I had grown a second head. "I'm not saying I trust her. But she is right, at least about Mitchell. The guy's a fucking creep and we both know it. So maybe Silence. Isn't. Consent." I punctuated every word, hoping he could hear the words, hoping his anger would clear. Shocker - it didn't. Instead, he recoiled from me as if I'd slapped him away. And in the newfound space between us, the motion-sensor light from the Creative Cluster kicked on, casting a golden halo around the only girl I knew brave enough to follow us out here. My wild girl. How long had she been watching us? In this dark, she looked like an avenging angel and I was in awe of her. Maybe that's what tipped Brennon off as his eyebrow quirked at me before turning to follow my stare.

With the shadows cast from behind her, it was hard to make out her expression, but not Brennon's. His ire burned ever brighter. He ignored Nettie, and turned back toward me, grabbing me by my t-shirt. Louder than before, because he was obviously trying to make a point, he lashed out, "Fuck this." And then he pushed me back against the tree, only this time he didn't follow. He simply stormed off into the dark. Without his tall frame blocking her, Nettie's body stood out even more against the black night. Now that my eyes had adjusted, I could see her mouth was open in uncertainty and her eyes blazing. But just like Brennon, she didn't stick around, darting deeper into the shadows of the surrounding forest.

There was still a fluttering of nerves in my stomach from when Brennon shoved me away, our moment totally broken. I wanted more than this. More than being shoved off into the darkness. Again. By yet another person.

Brennon had claimed he was watching us both yesterday, but not close enough. Anyone paying my level of attention wouldn't have run away from Nettie's stare. What I saw in those eyes was a fire I hadn't seen in years, maybe one that hadn't been alight since the trial. I smoothed out the wrinkles from Brennon's hands in my t-shirt and followed the path she darted down, knowing exactly where it led. Knowing I would find her seated on one of the rocks in Stones' Throw. Predictably, I was right. I approached the near-black clearing as quietly as I could, stepping lightly and using the thin moonlight as a guide. When I finally found her, I was frozen for a moment. Under the cool blue of a summer moon, seated as she was, knees pulled against her chest in the dark, I froze to take her in. I might not trust her, we might never be friends again, but it was impossible to deny that Toni was anything other than an angel.

Then she spotted me and immediately jumped to her feet like a spooked little bunny, ready to run. "Fuck, Xavi, you scared the shit out of me." Brennon had left me turned on, on edge and angry, and something about seeing that tiny bit of fright in Toni fed the beast inside. After being chased around all day by hordes of shouting kids, it was my turn to do the chasing.

"You should be scared, Nettie." I purred back.

Always so responsive, she sucked in an audible breath, but she was still my wild girl, after all, so it didn't take her long to recover, to slam her brave, I-don't-give-a-shit armour back on as she drawled, "Why? Do you want to hunt me, Xavi?" She would regret that sarcasm soon.

"Oh, Nettie," I said low and heated, as I prowled toward her silently, thanking the moon and stars for shining bright enough to let me see her properly even in this dark of the trees. "I'm going to do so much more than hunt you." My threat made the blue of her irises recede as her pupils dilated. It seemed my wicked little angel liked the threat.

"You're going to run as fast as you can, little Red Riding Hood," I teased and smiled. Nettie swallowed nervously. "I'm the big bad wolf in these woods, so when I catch you, I'm going to press you into the dirt and devour you until you cry for me to stop."

Her fingers curled tight around the hem of those tempting jean shorts of hers. She might not understand why yet, but if I had to bet, she was already wet and wanting just from words. On cue, she shifted her hips so her thighs clenched together, unconsciously seeking to alleviate the feeling. I sympathised. The need to push her further, the urge to make her give in had me nearly in a frenzy myself. Watching her try to tamp down her arousal had me half-hard against my sweatpants, so I pushed some more. "And only once you're begging me for release will I give in. Do you know what that means, Nettie?" Her eyes were so wide, so uncertain, and even before she gave the tiniest head shake, I knew I would need to explain. Saying the words out loud made my heart pound even more. "Hmmm, well it means that you're going to beg me to fuck you, right there in the dirt," I point to the centre of our stone circle, "and only once you beg, will I fill you with my cock the way you so obviously need." I bit my lower lip, craving her reaction.

She stared at me in stunned silence. I watched the rise and fall of her chest. She wanted to speak, to say something, but clearly didn't trust herself. I'd fix that. Closing the space between us slowly, just like Brennon had done with me, just like you did with a wild animal, I pushed a loose strand of that honeyed hair behind her ear. We both noticed her shiver at my touch. Still, she said nothing. "Don't worry, Nettie, I know my wild little thing is in there somewhere. I'm going to bring her out again. Just not tonight." And I quickly stepped back from her thin frame and walked away, back up the hill toward the lights of the lodge in the distance. I battled my need to touch her the entire way.

Chapter Twenty-Three

Toni

A week later my skin still burned anytime I thought about Xavi's words or the predatory look in his eyes. Every night, despite how exhausted I was from the day, I couldn't stop myself from thinking about the two of them, either. The way their chests seemed glued together against that tree. God, I wanted to be in the middle of that sandwich. And every time the image crossed my mind, it brought a newfound heat to my core. One I had never experienced before and didn't completely understand. Working at the campus bar, my manager Amanda would regale us with tales of her conquests and orgasms. Honestly, I thought she was full of it. But I swear, just watching Brennon's lips press on Xavi's skin like that had caused my belly to fill with heat and a slickness between my legs that was totally new. The feeling was worse every single night when Abbi or Mich inevitably dragged me to the dining hall, and I was forced to watch them both. Sure, they avoided each other the same way they had been avoiding me, so it wasn't exactly the same but seeing them move in the same physical space, circling each other with a new kind of cautiousness made me want to pick them up like dolls and force them together. Not that I could have, because they would both overpower me easily.

One good thing did come out of that night. Xavier was at least willing to look at me again. It was clear as crystal he didn't trust me and wasn't willing to let go of whatever it was that made him so angry at me in the first place, but three cheers for small victories, right? Now, I could feel his eyes on me every time we were in the same space. Always the watcher, that wasn't new, although there was a heat to his stares now that I hadn't noticed there before. Also new were the growing number of appearances he seemed to be making in my everyday. In the last seven days, I had caught him lingering outside my cabin door more mornings than not. Greeting me each time with his dimpled smirk and a, "Good morning, wild girl."

The first time it happened, he caught me completely off guard in a ratty old tank top and sleep shorts. I had been heading to the toilets to brush my teeth but one look at him, in low-slung grey sweatpants, the universal female kryptonite, and my breath caught. There was also no hiding the way my nipples hardened instantly. Something Xav obviously noticed, given the slow scan of his eyes up and down my body, followed by a low, pleased laugh. "For me, Nettie?" he joked, and I'm sure I turned tomato-red.

I managed to squeak out, "No, I'm just cold." Right, great defence, Toni, I cursed myself.

"Mhmmmm." He bit his lower lip, and as if it was even possible, my traitorous body reacted even more, my chest flushing a blush pink under his gaze.

He followed me almost to the bathroom door. We walked in silence the whole way, and only when I climbed the steps into the girl's bathroom did he finally say something else. “Great chatting with you, wild girl. See you tomorrow morning.” I looked up in surprise, about to ask what the hell he meant, but the instant I did, he just winked and sprinted away.

Just in case, that night, I recruited Abb's help and the next morning she knocked on my door. “Toni, I'm here.” Relieved, I finished tying my shoes. “But so is your new stalker.” At least I had been prepared for that possibility and had on a bra, a sweatshirt, and full pyjama pants. No more free shows. Except, when I stepped outside, it was somehow worse than the day before. Xavi had obviously just finished his run and was leaning shirtless and sweaty against the outside wall of my cabin. His tanned skin and lean muscles shone, and very unfairly, he didn't even seem to stink. Instead, he smelled like sugar and spice. I felt the temptation to lean in and sniff him. That thought had me questioning my own sanity and turning to Abbi for help. She simply lifted her brows and shrugged, equally unsure what to make of the whole situation. Then we both watched him pull an apple from his pocket and take a bite, really driving home the temptation metaphor, which had me rolling my eyes while also trying not to drool or be jealous of an innocent apple.

“Morning, ladies,” he said simply, before inviting us to go ahead of him. Abbi and I walked together to breakfast, with Xavier following silently behind us the whole way. He disappeared without any goodbye when we got there, and I was grateful for the everyday busyness of programming to keep me distracted the rest of the day.

Sure enough, every morning since, he had been right back outside my door first thing. I didn't know how he was managing it. I even tried getting up an extra hour early one morning, confident he wouldn't be there and I could take advantage of the extra time to squeeze in a proper swim. No such luck. There he was, seated on the small platform steps with his back to me. Nor could I ignore the way my body hummed with pleasure when his eyes blazed at the sight of me in my very unsexy training bikini. The whole situation was getting more confusing and overwhelming by the day.

However, if the situation with Xavi had question marks flying in both my body and mind, at least we seemed to have achieved a kind of truce. We definitely weren't in friendship territory, but there weren't any more barbs or insults being shoved at me. Things with Brennon, on the other hand, seemed to have gone from bad to worse. He no longer sat at the staff table during meals. Every meal that week, he just grabbed a plate of food and carted it outside. Then proceeded to eat it, alone on the deck, like he couldn't stand to be in the same building as me. There were no more biting or sarcastic comments from him, either. The only acknowledgement I got from him after that night out at the Creative Cluster was after one staff meeting when I had been distracted talking to Michele and slipped on the deck steps, knocking into his back. He lurched around, and seeing me, his face contorted into an ugly smile. Before I could stutter out an apology, he spit on me. Not at me.

On me. A thick glob of saliva landed squarely on my cheek. What do you say when something like that happens? I was speechless. Michele's shouts on my behalf sounded hollow and distant as I focused on the feeling of his spit dripping down my face and then on his disappearing frame, walking away from me yet again.

In his own words, Brennon had said he felt nothing for me, though that had obviously changed. Somehow, in catching him and Xav together like that, I'd committed some sort of transgression, and his indifference had shifted to Cole-level hatred.

Between the two of them, I was ready for a change of scenery and so fucking grateful that my days off for the month were coming up. Forty-eight undisturbed hours off camp property away from the two, or really three, of them and I didn't even have to go too far. Abbi had invited me to her parent's summer house. And not just me, but she had somehow wrangled it so that the two of us, Bella, and Michele, all had the same time off. When I asked her about it, she simply smiled and wiggled her eyebrows at me. I let her maintain her air of mystery, but I suspected she had pulled some strings with her little office boy-toy, Riley, likely while Brennon wasn't looking. If it was up to him, I probably wouldn't get a day off at all. Screw him. There was fuck all he could about when the schedule was posted five days ago and even less he could do now that I was safely tucked into the back of Mich's Volvo SUV. We opted to take one car since Abbi said the house was nearby and Michele's car was big enough that all four of us and our mountains of laundry could fit in easily. It also saved me the embarrassment of trying to squeeze anyone else into my clunker.

Abbi wasn't lying when she said the house was close by. We stopped about half an hour into the journey to pop into one of the little cottage shops that peppered the country roads out here. It was a combination post office, grocery, liquor and hardware store. Abbi waved off mine and Bell's attempts to buy food, claiming her parents always kept the house stocked, but she did let us spring for some booze and junk food. I was not a big drinker, so I let Bella pick out a bunch of different things from the small selection in the store. A mix of wine, fruity coolers, and a small bottle of vodka. Meanwhile, I grabbed several bags of popcorn and the greatest chips of all time- Ruffles All-Dressed. I might also have let Michele persuade me to pick up a king-size bag of Sour Patch Kids. Despite our pit stop, it was less than an hour later and Michele was turning down a dirt driveway, pulling up alongside a pale blue house that looked like something out of an old movie. Half-lap covered the exterior walls and as we pulled around the last corner, a large white deck spanned the entire width of the house, facing out over a lake that I immediately recognized. Jesus, Abbi hadn't been kidding about being close. We were only on the other side of Lake Ganawen. You could practically see Agonde from here, and when I opened the car door, I could practically hear the noise from the dining hall echoing across the water. Each scooping up armfuls of stuff, we headed up the steps onto the deck and into the house.

After showing us around and letting us pick our bedrooms, Abbi and I headed down to the basement so we could get started on our laundry. There were two large front-loading washing machines and two huge clothes dryers. I wasn't sure how two scientists and their only child produced enough laundry to necessitate such a setup, but given how many clothes we all packed into the car earlier, I was also pretty grateful. As we stuffed our clothes into the machines, I asked Abbi about the proximity between Agonde and this place. Normally such an open book, she just shrugged, "How do you think I ended up at camp in the first place?" She said it casually, but the way her face scrunched as she said it also said there was more to the story. It was at least a half-lie, and it took one to know one. A liar, that is. But one lie didn't take away from the fact that Abbi had been nothing short of a rockstar friend since we met and add to that this invite and the fact that I didn't have to haul my shit-kicker car back home. She definitely deserved to keep her secrets. We all do.

That night ended up being one of the most wholesome nights I have ever had. Abbi wasn't kidding about her family's fridge being full. The house had a chef's kitchen and there was fresh summer corn, thick steaks, and pre-prepared salads all waiting for us. At my wide-eyed stare, again Abbs just shrugged and explained that her parents hired a housekeeper to make sure the place was ready for us or for anyone visiting. On the deck, there was a giant barbecue and big, cosy loungers, large enough that all four of us could fit on one together. The perfect spot to eat and watch the summer sunset. As a team, we carried the food and a bunch of the booze we bought outside, and while Abbi cooked, Bells made us all laugh with stories about her Mexican mum trying to convince her white-as-anything Oklahoma dad that real tacos did not come out of a box.

The thing about a job where you're moving all the time and where you have to be the happiest, most positive version of yourself is that it is tiring as hell. Which is why all four of us didn't last long after eating. The need for sleep pulled us all under much earlier than any self-respecting twenty-year-old would like to admit. The next day, however, was a totally different story. We all slept late, and one-by-one crept into the kitchen for coffees and leisurely breakfasts, before embracing the heat of the July afternoon. That meant hours on Abbi's dock with our smallest bikinis so we could actually tan properly before we finally wandered inside. Then, after a meal of burgers, the real debauchery reared its head. I absolutely blamed Abbi, who disappeared inside to put her dinner plate in the dishwasher only to return with a platter of lemons, a bottle of vodka and four shot glasses.

Slamming her offering down on the deck table, she proclaimed, "Never have I ever!"

"Never have I ever what, Abbs?" I asked, naively. The three girls looked back at me like I had just spoken in tongues.

"Are you serious, Toni?" Mich asked.

"How have you made it to twenty without ever playing Never Have I Ever? Not even at school?" Isabella laughed like she didn't believe me.

Embarrassed, I tried to justify my ignorance. "Ummmm, I don't really go out a lot." I couldn't stop my eyes from drifting floor-ward in an attempt to hide my frustration with myself. But the feeling doesn't last long. The girls don't linger on my lack of typical college-girl knowledge and instead, make quick work of explaining the game. "One by one, we'll call out a scenario to the group starting with 'Never have I ever...' and finish the sentence with something we've never done. And anyone who has done it has to take a shot," Abbi explained.

Good thing I haven't really done anything exciting in the last five years unless you count holding down two jobs. That's probably why an hour later, I had only had one and a half shots. The half shot was choked down to Bella's, "Never have I ever had a man's dick in my mouth." Abbi and Mich swallowed theirs without missing a beat, but I guessed they didn't have the same baggage around the act that I did. When I didn't swallow the whole shot, I answered their questioning looks with a shrug and a simple, "A boy's dick, sure. A man's? Not yet." And it set off a chain of cackles from the girls that instantly relaxed me.

But it's like my answer cracked open a door and round by round, the statements just got filthier until we abandoned the 'Never have I evers' altogether and just started throwing out questions. Predictably, Abbi's been the most adventurous of all of us and had the most shots. She's also showing it the least. So it wasn't surprising, at least not to me, when she was the first to answer my next question. Wanting to play along with my friends, who so far hadn't shown any signs of the kind of hang ups or shame I had around sex, I trickled false confidence into my voice and asked, "Best lay ever?"

Abbi just giggled and answered first, clear as day. "Riley. I'm not sure where he got the skills, but that boy lays some good pipe." The rest of us shook our heads and laughed at her confidence. Then I turned my attention to the other two.

"Ladies?" I zeroed in on Bella while she tried to avoid my attention by looking anywhere but at me, the table now laden with lemon rinds and small clear spills of liquor and the very full shot class sitting in front of her. "Bells?" I probed.

"Uhhh, my ex, Samantha." The name slips out like a whisper from her lips, but still manages to make our previously light-hearted conversation seem about ten times heavier.

It only lasts a second before Abbi bursts out, "Holy shit! Bells, are you gay?!" And before she can even answer, she smiles and looks around at Mich and me. "Cool! Obviously! But like, how did we not know that?!" Abbi looked from me to Michele, confirming that we were just as in the dark about this as she was.

She must have seen our mutual surprise because she dropped her voice back to normal levels, "Sorry." She winced. "Are you okay with us knowing? Are you out?"

"I'm not out-out, so keep it to yourselves, please, but I'm out enough to have dated a few people."

"Like, this Sam?" I ask gently, reaching to squeeze her hand at the same time.

"Yeah, Sam, she was my assigned lab partner in first-year chemistry and also my first real girlfriend. But we broke up when she found out I'd be gone all summer. Turns out she had some trust issues." She squeezed back before releasing my fingers. Retreat and annoyance were lacing her voice as she finished explaining, but she threw back her shot and dropped the empty glass with a smile and a shrug. "Life's too short, ya know?" Abbi and I both nodded our understanding. "But for a minute there, the sex was something else."

"Sounds like it." Abbs giggled. Laugher aside, there was still a cloud of tension that hung around Isabella after her admission. Seeking to alleviate it, I flipped my eyes to Michele, who hadn't uttered a sound since Bella's confession.

"Alright, that's one answer out of the way. Got one of your own for us, Mich?"

She blanched, her normally bright smile fully absent. Instantly, I wished I could retract my question, but Abbs pushed, "Don't be a prude, Mich, come on."

"And don't say Cole," I groaned before I could stop myself.

She bristled and dragged her blonde locks out of her face. "Well, I don't know what you all want me to say, then." Her voice, an octave higher than normal already, continued to pitch higher and higher even as she snapped back at us, "I've only ever been with Cole. I don't have anyone else to compare it to."

It was my turn to blanch. Cole was her first. Was she his? I couldn't ask that. And thinking about the potential answer made something ache in the back of my heart. After all the shit he had put me through in the last month, I shouldn't have felt any type of way about Cole, nor give a single shit about his sex life. But judging by the way it continued to thump painfully in my chest, my heart knew my mind was a liar. And I couldn't think about what that meant or the way bile was already creeping up my throat, promising that control could be found through a quick trip to the bathroom for one good purge. It had been weeks since I felt that impulse, but now it was almost unbearable.

Michele shivered on the couch, and beside her, Bells was chewing her fingernails distractedly. Somehow we had stumbled into something even heavier than Bella's revelation and none of us were quite comfortable with it. Except Abbi, who for all her wonderful qualities, didn't seem to pick up on the temperature shift the rest of us experienced. "So, is it good, then?" she rambled. "Because I'm so curious. Like you're such an angel and he's such a dickhole, but I feel like it's gotta be good. I mean, the guy is built like a brick wall, and that's gotta—"

"Abbi. Stop," Isabella cut in abruptly.

Without saying anything, Michele ripped herself out of her seat, and ignoring our calls and apologies, stormed down the deck's stairs and out into the darkness.

Abbi looked frantically between Bella and me, "I didn't—"

"I know you didn't, Abbs, but not everybody has your confidence about this stuff." The other girl sighed, lifting out of the sofa cushions. "I'll go talk to her." And she followed Michele's path.

Thank god she did. Much as I felt bad, I couldn't talk to Michele about Cole. Not properly and definitely not right now. I would end up asking too many questions and getting answers that she didn't want to give, and I didn't want to hear. Was she Cole's first? What was it like? When did it happen? Did she love him? Were they happy? There was something dark and sick inside me that longed for the answers, that wanted those details, even if only to torture myself with them. Thankfully, I stayed glued to my seat as my more rational side, the side that cried I was tortured enough already, won out.

"I really didn't mean to upset her."

"Me neither, Abbs. I never should have asked the stupid question." We both shook our heads regretfully. "Let's take this shit inside, and we can wait for them in there." And together, we gathered up the mess we had made and headed back into the well-lit kitchen.

We waited for over an hour for the girls to come back, but by two in the morning, Abbi was yawning loudly and I was losing a battle against both a headache and a whole-body tiredness that had crept in as the vodka slowly left my system. The two of us, resigned that they weren't coming back anytime soon, promised each other we'd apologise to Michele properly in the morning and dragged our now hungover asses to bed.

Our chance for apologies never came. The next morning, over coffee, I repeatedly tried to broach the previous night's escapades with her, and Michele shut me down every single time. It was as if, for her, none of it ever happened. She was right back to her bubbly smiling self, humming peacefully as she poured coffee into one of the many oversized mugs housed in this cottage. She did the same when Abbi came down the stairs and pulled her aside for an attempted whisper of, "I'm sorry." Only when Bella joined us did I finally catch my bubbly friend's mask slip. Isabella sidled up beside her at the breakfast bar, a plate of coffee in one hand and cereal in the other and softly whispered, "Morning." Without looking up at her, Michele's phoney grin flattened, and she answered with a clipped, "Morning," before promptly dumping the rest of her coffee down the drain and pasting that smile back in place.

"Who's up for another beach day?" She clapped like we had already said 'yes' and ran back upstairs, presumably to change into a swimsuit. Abbi simply shrugged like she wasn't sure what to make of it before doing the same.

I was happy enough to go with the flow. I had already rocked the boat of my still-new friendships enough last night, so I headed back toward my temporary bedroom to grab my suit, too, shouting a quick, "You coming, Bells?"

Back to me, where she still stood, she called, "In a minute," and if I hadn't looked back, I would have missed the way she sank her face into her hands and sighed.

The rest of the day passed much like the previous one, all of us revelling in the sunshine and taking it easy. But unlike the day before, all the easy camaraderie was gone and in its place was this air of pretend. All of us stuck to surface-level chatter until 5 p.m. rolled around. We loaded up the car in near-silence. As quick as the drive here had felt, the drive back to camp felt much longer. Two days ago, I had been desperate to get away from Agonde, but there was so much anxiety colouring the air in the car on the way back, that I found myself thankful to be stepping out of it and back into the routine that came with day-to-day camp life.

Chapter Twenty-Four

Cole

Michele was acting weird. She had been acting weird for the last few days, too. Ever since she had gotten back from her big girly day off. I hadn't mentioned it to her because thinking about her and Toni cooped up in some cottage together made me want to grill her with questions. It also gave me an uncomfortable, guilty feeling in the pit of my stomach. Which seemed pretty fucking unreasonable, considering I hadn't done anything to feel guilty about.

My bad mood infested the Section Office. This tiny sweatbox mostly went unnoticed by the kids, sheltered as it was by trees. Only Abbi and I really used it, and thank fuck for that because technically any Section head could too, from Lands to Sports Elite to Waterfront. This hobbit hole was already too small for my six-foot-three frame. Add in the attitude from Barrett Hill's number-one princess, and it would probably burst. And there was that bad mood again. Actually, now that I was thinking about it, my pissy attitude seemed to have spread through the entire boys' section and was now contributing to my day from hell. The whole reason I was in here, sitting in front of my laptop and the old landline phone, was because I had to make several unpleasant parent phone calls. One to the parents of a kid who was being bullied so cruelly he had started to fake stomach aches at night just so he could sleep in the nurse's office. The cabin leader and I had been trying for the last two weeks to deal with it, and it only seemed to be getting worse. Hence why I would also be making another two calls to two separate families. All because a bunch of twelve-year-old boys couldn't sort their shit out.

Normally, I thrived on responsibility. It's why I wanted to be a Section Head after spending the last two years as a cabin leader. It's why I was captain of the Michigan State Bears. I was always happy to plan rookie recruitment days, make plays, lead team huddles, all that stuff. It was the touchy-feely stuff that I hated. Some captains I knew did the whole rousing inspirational speech thing, but I was never very good at consoling my teammates after a difficult loss. I was too busy critiquing my own performance for that. Calls like the ones I was making now were a million times worse. The first call sucked. So did the second. But the third was the worst. It rang and rang, and when the call finally connected, a hard masculine voice answered, "Hello."

"Hello Sir, my name is Cole Michaels, and I..."

"Cole Michaels, the Bears' player?"

"Yes, sir. That's me, but I'm also calling about your son."

Even over the phone, the man's attitude shift rippled down the line. Defensively, he asked, "What about my son?"

The next ten minutes were painful, as I tried to explain to this man that his son was a bully and he alternated between cursing his kid and cussing at me. Either way, it was a whole lot of denial.

At some point during the call, Abbi must have skipped in behind me, and when I slammed the phone down with a frustrated groan, she spun her old grey office chair to face me, the old metal frame and bearings clanking together at the move. "I was just wondering, big guy, what does hypocrisy taste like?"

"What the hell are you talking about now?" I sighed. This right here was why I avoided this office whenever Abbi was in it. Because the girl never shut up.

"Oh, just the irony of you giving those parents shit about their kid's dick-ish behaviour when you're the biggest dickhole of them all." She chortled, amused by her own shitty joke.

"Fuck off, Abigail." I shot back. She just laughed more, grabbing something off the desk in front of her before sauntering back toward the door.

"On that charming note, toodles, asshole." And she swung the door open and slammed it shut behind her. The silence resumed, and with no more calls to make, the voice in my head filled it instead. Yeah, okay, I might be a meathead some of the time, but I have enough self-awareness to know that Abbi had a point. I was being a bully. The difference between me and those kids was that I knew my target deserved it. Not only was Antoinette Barrett a liar, *Hillis* my ass, but she was also a master manipulator and a murderer to boot. Back then, Dad had been one of Franklin Barrett's most respected foremen, working on his most high-profile projects. New bank buildings, tech company HQs, and large estate-style developments for the nouveau-riche flooding into West Barrett back then. Dad oversaw them all. Until he didn't.

Less than a week after the trial, Franklin Barrett summoned Dad to his office downtown and then had his VP of Operations explain that his expertise was needed elsewhere. And by elsewhere, they meant strip malls and low-grade gas stations in East Barrett, where getting good labour was nearly impossible and where jobs got delayed and shut down almost constantly because of violent crime and vandalism. He had always been tough on me, demanding to the point of extreme. When I was young, more than one hockey coach had to have him removed from the arena for shouting either at me or at kids on the other team. But ever since his job shifted, he had been taking the blame for cancelled and stalled jobs, ignored at work, and never promoted. Mum leaving turned him angry, but that had turned him goddamned spiteful. Not at Franklin Barrett–fuck knows why, but Dad still thinks the sun shines out of that guy's ass–but at me.

The few times a year when I came home, he never missed an opportunity to remind me that his shitty luck was all my fault. In his twisted mind, Franklin Barrett was punishing us both for my friendship with his daughter. Every time something went wrong on a job, he would scream, curse and throw empty bottles my way. Although never at me. He couldn't or wouldn't risk any physical damage that might affect my game. As if his fat ass was still strong enough to do any real damage. Reining in my wandering mind, my thoughts returned to the girl who was really at fault. Toni had always managed to wind the three of us around her pinky finger, and I was certain she pulled the same shit with her father, begging his forgiveness despite the horrific thing she had done. She probably batted those big blue eyes at him until he did whatever she asked, which was how she basically got away with murder. Getting my dad demoted was just a way of making sure I didn't say anything about it.

It all circled back to her, the fact that my father had turned into such a bastard, the things I had done to fuck up my friendships with Brennon and Xav, and now she was wreaking havoc on my relationship without even lifting a finger. That shit needed to stop. All the weak shit the three of us had been doing to get Toni out of here wasn't working. In fact, she just turned up her nose at all of us and now she had a new little cult of hangers-on surrounding her all the fucking time. That couldn't stand. Maybe it was time for more drastic action. Something to bring that bitch to her knees before me. I grabbed my notebook, usually reserved for notes about campers and cabin leaders, and began to jot down ideas to ruin her life. As the ideas started to flow, I smiled for the first time that day.

Turns out plotting revenge is good for the soul. Once I'd gotten a few delicious ideas out on paper, I left the section office feeling like a new man. To celebrate, I spent the rest of the day hanging out with a bunch of the different boys' cabins. I checked in with Mitch and his campers playing flag football on the activities field, then went to the paddling docks where two younger cabins were squaring off in a vicious game of canoe pirates, where three boats of kids against three battled to sink the old metal hulkers the camp kept down here just for games like this. It was a mix of screaming and laughter and watching ten-year-olds scramble around the things like monkeys, and honestly, it was downright fun to watch.

By the time I was climbing the small hill back to my little hut that night, after saying goodnight to each boys' cabin in turn, the sour feelings from this morning were all but gone. Later tonight, I was going to pull Xavier and Brennon aside to discuss my ideas, and together the three of us could finally purge her poison from our lives. Permanently, this time. It was nearing the end of July and the nights were coming in faster, but I could always find my way in the dark, feeling for the familiar roots and rocks that marked this path from the wider gravel ones that flowed through the main parts of the property. But I didn't have to rely completely on feeling my way since the single light in my cabin was on, and through the few windows I had, it illuminated enough of the forest and path to keep me from stumbling. Certain I had turned that light off this morning, its flickering now hopefully meant Michele was inside waiting for me. Maybe this day had worked its magic on her too and we could be done with her giving me the brush off. Hell, maybe if I wished extra hard, she would be down to have sex. That thought had me running the last few metres to my door, and bursting through it, with maybe just a touch too much excitement.

There she was, though. She had obviously been lying down on my bed, blond hair spilling over my navy sheets, but my entrance had surprised her and she bolted upright. The hand she brought to her chest relaxed and finally fell as she registered it was me.

"Sorry, babe, did I scare you?" I asked with a smirk.

She yanked one of her flip-flops from my floor and launched it at my chest. Her poor little toss had no power behind it, and I just let the shoe hit me and fall away as she gave me grief. "Yes, you did, Cole!"

Shrugging, I kicked my own running shoes off and sat down beside her, reaching for her as I did. "I didn't mean to. I just pictured you all tucked up in my covers and I guess I got excited." I gave her my best puppy-dog pout, and she rolled her eyes but leaned into me just the same. We sat snuggled into each other against my pillows, neither of us saying anything for a few moments. Bit by bit, I felt some of the tension in her shoulders ease, and once it was mostly gone, I brushed my fingers against her chin, tilting her head in my direction and placing my lips on hers for our first kiss in days. It took a second, but slowly her lips unlocked against mine, giving me silent permission to deepen our exchange. I turned her in my arms, so I was positioned above her, holding my own weight while we made out in earnest. Or, I guess I was attempting to make-out. Michele kissed me back, but there was no heat behind it. Our kisses had never been exactly porn-worthy, but these were lacklustre, even by our standards. Still, it had been too long since I had rubbed one out, so now even this small physical connection meant my cock was getting hard against the fleece of my sweats and

I was sure she could feel it too, so when I skimmed my hand to the bottom of her t-shirt, she didn't resist. But wherever my fingers touched bare skin, her body flinched away, running from the feel of me. As my hands traced up toward her chest, she pushed me back, taking her own bra off without a word rather than letting me do it. When she was finally bare, she lay back down and our kisses restarted.

Despite the weeks without sex, I tried to take it slow, not wanting to spook my girlfriend even more. After a few more minutes at second base, I reached down to skim my hands into Michele's shorts; any hope I had for getting laid died a quick death as my girlfriend shuddered beneath me. Michele is such a great girl. I really did love her in a way, but there were times I knew things weren't quite right. Looking down at her, beautiful as she was, she looked faded out. Like a teenage movie star I was looking at through a screen. She was there, present, but she was playing the part just a little too perfectly. It just didn't read right. Like the colours were off or something.

"Christ," I muttered, pulling back from our kiss. She deserved better than this watered-down version of love we were giving each other right now.

"What's wrong?" she asked, pulling back herself, concern for me etched on her features. She was always more aware of my emotions than I was of hers. Sometimes, I was a shitty boyfriend. I promised myself I'd pay more attention in the future. Right now, however, we clearly needed to talk about this. I scrubbed my hand through my hair before reaching for the sweatpants I had discarded during our make-out. I could not have this conversation with my dick out. Standing, I yanked them back on, not even watching for my erection, which had faded to nothing faster than I liked to admit. Feelings were a fucking mood killer.

"I don't know, Michele," I snapped. "You tell me."

She shrank a little at my obvious anger. And internally, I cursed myself again. Fuck, I'm not the guy who snaps at his girl all the damn time. I'm not my dad. More softly, I continued, "It's just that lately, you're either a million miles away or you're giving me shit about your new little gal pal." I didn't even say her name because I knew it would just make me angrier. Opting instead to sit back down, I focused on Michele's semi-naked frame, still curled up under my covers. She'd wrapped them around herself like a security blanket. I reached for her to explain further. "And lately, every time I so much as touch you, you shut me down." As if on cue, her body shivered and retreated away from the smallest brush of my fingers on her bare shoulder. It's undeniable. I saw it. She saw it, too. Her eyes widened at the realisation.

Wordlessly, she reached for her own t-shirt and the bra she'd removed, giving me her back as she slid both back on. "Cole I—" she said, her voice barely audible but cracking just the same. She was on the verge of tears, and I fucking hated it when she cried. She hadn't done it in so long, not since her family dog died last year. And the time before that, well, that was my fault and a long time ago. I'd worked hard to make her forget about that. I'd worked hard to forget that night myself.

Doing my best to speak gently, I reached out again to soothe her. "Did I do something wrong, Michele?" My mind scrambled for things I might have done to upset her, and I stammered and stuttered uncertainly, "I-I know I've been an asshole, and I haven't really explained, b-but I promise you, Toni's not who you think—"

This time she cut me off, her voice still shaking from the effort of holding back tears, although she finally turned to look at me as she said, "This isn't about Toni." There was a finality to her tone that said she truly believed that, but I could practically taste the flavour of Antoinette Barrett all over this. I snarled. Shit, I might have even growled. Toni always had the power to turn me feral. Michele reached for my hand, succeeded in dragging my thoughts from Toni, and her watery eyes peered up to mine.

"It really isn't. I promise, Cole. This—" She paused, chewing her lip as she searched for words. "What's been eating at me, well," she stopped again, swallowing hard, "it's about me."

"What about you, Michele?'

More silence. Christ. It was taking everything I had not to lose my shit.

"I'm just..." she stuttered. "I'm... there is... I think I..."

"Just spit it out."

"I think there's something I've been burying for a long time, and last week, I, well, I realised I can't really bury it anymore."

She went quiet again, and I stayed that way, waiting her out. It wasn't like there was any good way to respond. I barely understood what she was trying to tell me anyway, so shutting up seemed like my best choice. We stared at each other and I swear, I saw the flash of determination in her eyes when she rolled her shoulders back and said, "Cole, I'm so sorry, but..."

"No," I grunted. "Just no. Whatever it is you're about to say, don't."

"I have to."

"Says fucking who?"

She never answered who. She didn't need to. What she did go on to explain was that she needed 'space'. The words 'break' and 'time' were also mentioned. I didn't really listen much after that, too busy trying to keep the volcano of my own anger in check. Michele wouldn't do this. This wasn't her. She was being manipulated into whatever the fuck this was, and so she didn't deserve to be the target of my ire. I let her finish her little speech, delivering the message she thought she needed to, and when she finished, I waved her off with little more than another grunt.

From the window in my cabin door, I watched Michele walk away in the dim shadows cast by my outside light. Her shoulders sagged and her pace slow. I knew she felt horrible. She's far too nice of a person not to. Meanwhile, my rage was a barely contained thing. The second she was far enough away, it exploded. My hands shot out uncontrollably, battering the walls and the door. Each punch carried five years' worth of anger, and fuck, maybe even a little self-loathing. I tried to keep this part of myself locked down. The red cloud of rage all too reminiscent of my father. Still, every once, and a while, I couldn't stop it, and once the rush started it became unstoppable. I was lost to it. So lost, I didn't even pause as my right fist connected with the window. Granted, the doors on these cabins were old reclaimed things salvaged because it was the cheapest option, but it wasn't until sharp edges of glass were spilling out over my bare toes that I even registered I'd smashed through it.

And when it finally sank in, the last flames of my anger burned down, and the last of my restraint shattered right along with the glass. In the absence of heated fury, there was just cold, calculating awareness. I was going to destroy her. The torments I had brainstormed earlier that day were a shopping list of cruelties, but there was one worse than all the others. An idea so bad my hand shook while I wrote it down. It wasn't the one I had planned on executing, and lord knows, I was probably going to hate myself afterward. Then again, I hadn't anticipated that Antoinette Barrett would rip my whole life to shreds not once, but twice. So here we were.

The thing about knowing someone as long as I've known Barrett-Hills' resident princess, even if she is a lying little whore, is that you *know* them. What makes them happy, what makes them tick, and what will make them lose their goddamn mind. And for all her many faults, Toni always had a soft spot for the lonely, the damaged, fragile, and broken creatures. Lord knows, that was why she collected the three of us. Break one of her toys completely and she would crumble. And if it was her fault, well, she'd be fucking destroyed.

I snatched one of my ratty old team shirts from the floor and used it to shove the broken window shards into the corner by the door. I would deal with them tomorrow. Then I grabbed a hoodie from my laundry pile and shoved my feet back into the shoes I had been so excited to shed when I stormed in here. With black shoes and a black hoodie, nobody would see me pull together the things I needed to make my plans work. It was going to be a long night, but dawn would come. And with it, Toni's complete and utter humiliation. And the second she was gone, I could set about rebuilding my life. I'm Cole-fucking-Michaels and I'd already done it once. You better fucking believe I could do it again.

By breakfast time the next day, my plans were firmly in place. Although it left me running on only one hour's sleep, I was downright giddy knowing what the day would bring. Or at least I was until I caught Michele's eyes across the dining hall only for her to frown and scurry away in the direction of the staff table in the corner, where I watched her slide herself in beside Toni like that was where she belonged all along. Bullshit, she wasn't involved in this. Pivoting, I watched her instead. Her cherry red swimsuit, while obviously meant for real actual swimming rather than tanning like your average bikini, still showed off all the curves she'd filled in. Frankly, I hated to admit it, but even from where I stood by the stage, her tits looked delicious. I wanted to rip the straps from her shoulders and pinch her rosy little nipples until she screamed from the pain. Fuck. No. That wasn't what I wanted. I wanted to hurt her, to grip that honey-brown hair in my fist and force her to do what I wanted. I needed Antoinette Barrett to break for me.

Before any of that could happen, I had work to do. Sure enough, there was no sign of the Director, so only Abbi and I stood by the sound system, meaning one of us would be making this morning's announcements. Thinking about Toni's inevitable submission had my cock fighting to stiffen in my shorts, so it wouldn't be me. I jutted my chin out at Abbi, who took the cue and stepped up to the platform.

The Director was becoming increasingly erratic. He was supposed to meet with senior staff every other day, but it'd been at least five days since I had seen the whites of his eyes. Not that I could complain. His absence only made it that much easier for me to manipulate today's plans. But, it was becoming downright negligent, so I made a point to question Brennon later today. I mean, the two of them practically share an office, so I'm sure our resident rockstar slash computer nerd has seen him.

Abbi tapped the mic as she flicked it on, and the static echoed across the open wood beams of the building. After almost four weeks, the kids knew the meal routine and at the sound of the mic, all the nearly four hundred people in the room turned to face her way. My eyes flicked back to Toni, where they would stay fixed. She was smiling, fucking really smiling, at Michele. It was the exact same smile she'd had at fifteen, the one I always thought was reserved just for us. The lips around it had become fuller, lush, and useful for a few other things I could think of, all of which would replace that grin. So much about her had changed, but that smile was still the same. That smile was mine, and it had no place on her face anymore.

I tuned Abbi out for the most part, letting her get into a rhythm before she shouted, "And one last thing, Agonde... How do you think we should celebrate the start of our Mid-Summer Weekend?!" She cupped one hand around her ear in an exaggerated movement that demanded answers. And a whole chorus of voices replied, chanting, "All-Along-Mara-Thon! All-Along-Mara-Thon!" The shouts, hoots, and hollers of it got louder and louder until applause and cheering drowned out any words. Minutes later, when the commotion finally died down enough, Abbi continued, "So, remember, dinner starts early tonight, right after afternoon programmes, to make way for the big race. We will see you there!" One final cheer soared from the crowd while cabin leaders started the difficult job of wrangling their excited kids back to their cabins.

The All-Along Marathon was a longstanding camp tradition. Every year at mid-summer, the regular schedule was tossed out the window and there was a series of events where kids and staff all competed for bragging rights and domination. And that all started with the giant race, where everyone, including staff, had the opportunity to take part. It was an opt-in thing, but I couldn't help it if there was also a fuck load of pressure to take part and a hell of a lot of competition too. Those things just worked in my favour.

The marathon took all day to set up since it spread across every program area. This meant any staff not assigned to programmes or responsible for cabins were put to work getting the different obstacles ready. There was everything from speed climbing through the treetop ropes course and hitting an archery target at a specific spot to retrieving a mystery item from the depths of the swim area or winning a paddle via canoe sword fight. Mostly, the different tasks were designed to test the different skills kids should have picked up over the last month. It wasn't just physical tasks either, since that would be unfair considering kids as young as eight could be competing too. So there were also creative challenges like a three-chord songwriting race or others where small limbs or short stature were a huge advantage, like the Low Limbo contest or Body-Shelter-Build. That one in particular was so much easier when I was a scrawny nine-year-old. All in all, it was a pretty even split, so that just about anyone had a shot at victory. When the race was done, the winners in each bracket would see their names make it onto the "Winner's Circle", a giant crown-shaped plaque mounted in prime position over the dining hall stage that listed all the previous winners. Including my win from two years ago, and Xavi's from last year.

There was also the secret staff betting pool that usually came with a pretty hefty cash prize. After all, summer camp pays like shit, so most of the staff working here weren't in it for the cash. They usually had the kind of bank accounts that let them piss money away on stupid crap like betting on a silly ass race. Not me. Firstly, because I was usually too busy planning to win and secondly because I wasn't in the business of throwing the little bit of money I did have into the wind. This time, though, I wasn't competing, and in my absence, I knew who the winner would be, or at least, I was ninety-nine percent sure. So, if everything went to plan, I would be winning double today, watching Toni fail miserably and padding my wallet at once.

By dinner time, early as promised, an anxious excitement pervaded the entire camp. You could tell the kids planning to compete. They were either amped to the point of shaking or they were stiff as statues in their seats out of fear or determination, or both. The staff competing weren't any different. At his cabin table, Mitchell was bragging to his kids and anyone else who would listen about his training regime and how he would be 'crushing it' tonight. We might be friends, but it was that bravado that had me betting against him. On the other side of the equation was Xavier, who sat nearly stock still in his usual corner spot, as far from any boisterous kids as he could be at mealtimes. Especially since Chef always kicked him out of his kitchen hiding spot once food service started. He had foregone a shirt and already had his running shoes and racing shorts on. His trim frame, sculpted courtesy of varsity soccer and golden skin from a month of daily runs along the camp road, were all on display. Once the race started, I knew exactly how those muscles would move. I could already picture the sweat that would soak his curls and the way lake water would bead and trail between his shoulder blades. I was only thinking about it because he had always been my biggest competitor. Both of us had started participating in the marathon together when we were twelve. Each of us tried to one-up the other and impress Toni in the process, even though she was racing too and never seemed to care.

After she was gone, we kept on racing. Together at first, and then against each other. We traded off wins year after year. For the first time though, I wasn't playing our usual game, meaning Xav's win was all but locked in. He didn't know it yet, which was probably why his hazel eyes were so far away right now, focused entirely on what was to come. People have a bad habit of underestimating Xav, even now after so many victories. But never me, which was why, when the pool was called, I'd be betting on him.

COLE, AGE 15
5 years ago

Everything about today was a test of my patience. From the moment I had put on my suit this morning and the shoulders of my jacket squeezed just a little too much, I had felt like screaming. It was partially due to a summer growth spurt that had me cracking six feet. The other problem was hockey training, which had started the second I got back from camp, with my dad forcing me into our garage weight room nearly every day. "Can't let yourself go in the off-season, boy." Or, "Slackers don't make Captain." And maybe he was right, but it wasn't like he could afford to buy me a new suit every time I outgrew one, and with the training he had me under, today was inevitable. Being a foreman at Barrett-Hill Construction wasn't exactly raking in the big bucks for dear old Dad. Just keeping our place in West Barrett was stretching him to the limit, but he would do anything to keep me at West Barrett Collegiate, the "good" high school, and playing for the Badgers. So, I'd put on my too-small suit and let Dad load me into his company car, the one Franklin Barrett gifted all his foremen, and drive us down to that hellhole building.

Once we got there, things only got worse. There had been a huge lineup of photographers and reporters outside the building. Their flashes popped off every five seconds and made my eyes sting. Then, when we finally got inside the actual courthouse, we still had to wait in the stupid hallway with crowds of people, and even more photographers and reporters. All of these strangers were just waiting to hear what Toni, or I guess really her mom, had to say. The whispers and rumours traded back and forth over and over again. All the same things I'd been hearing every day at school ever since news of the Barrett divorce hit the front page of the local paper. Since then, Toni's whole family had been a regular feature on primetime news, too. The only relief came when Brennon broke through the crowds to come and stand with me and Dad. Until I noticed his suit. Neat, black, fitted, and complete with a skinny tie and belt, it had probably been custom-cut just for him. He looked like the male lead in a teen movie. Next to him, my own suit looked like someone's bad hand-me-downs. But at least Brennon broke the silence between me and Dad as he clapped me on the back. "Hey, man, I'm glad you're here. I was worried I'd be sitting alone."

"You're here alone? Where's your mom?" He grimaced and I knew what that meant. His mom's always in rough shape. He doesn't talk about his family much, but he's said enough for me to guess she's got some kind of substance abuse stuff going on, and it's not like his dad's ever home. When we were younger, Brennon would always defend Blue, but in the last few years, he'd just stopped mentioning him at all. Sometimes I think one of the reasons he and I have stayed friends–the jock and the artist–was because we're both latchkey kids.

One parent is gone, the other too fucked, or in my case, too busy with work and planning my NHL career to give a shit. True to form, Bren grumbled something about his mum not feeling well, and I let it slide.

We waited for my dad, sweating in his suit, to leave us alone as he headed in search of a vending machine, and as soon as he was out of earshot, he asked, "Have you seen Xav? Is he here?"

I had seen him alright, and we turned together as I pointed. At the end of the long tiled hallway, near the doors of the closed courtroom, was Xav. He looked just like he had six weeks ago when we'd left camp, his skin still tanned, curls still loose around his face. And as if he could sense it, he turned to look our way. "Let's go, dude." Brennon stepped out in his direction, until I grabbed his jacketed arm.

"We can't." His blond eyebrows knit together in confusion mixed with annoyance. I sighed. "We can't. Look." This time I didn't need to point, as a dark-haired couple, both dressed fully in black, came to stand beside Xavi. They weren't alone either. Dragging behind them was a line of girls of varying ages, also decked out in black. His cousins, he called them. Apparently, his family had some pretty weird, but hella strict, religious traditions that meant he always had about a million cousins living at his house. They weren't allowed to come to camp, not since his sister Rachel had disappeared, so it wasn't like we'd ever met any of them before. Now, seeing them standing together, they looked like some little goth troupe. I couldn't hear it over the roar of the crowds, but as Xavi continued to lock eyes with us, his father was obviously yelling at him, his wife, and all the cousins.

The girls all dropped their chins to stare at the floor. Fuck, even his mum did, too.

Xav's cheeks reddened, but he didn't look away. All he could do was give the smallest shake of his head. A silent gesture of "no, you can't come over here, and I'm sorry." Brennon and I looked at each other for a second before both nodding back.

Before we could say much more to one another, two things happened that stopped any further discussion. First, my dad came back, and then the courtroom doors were thrown open and we were ushered inside along with the other fuck ton of people. It felt like being a sardine as strangers' shoulders and bodies jostled against me and pushed me forward, until we were able to sneak into one of the hard wooden benches in the fourth row, right behind Xavi and his family. I wouldn't be able to speak to him, but at least he'd know Brennon and I were close by.

What followed were the worst hours of my life so far. Worse than the day my mum "went out for coffee" and fucked off forever instead. Watching Toni be subjected to question after question, then learning that we'd been sold one horrible lie after another from someone I loved more than I could explain made me want to tear the tie from around my neck. I wanted to shout across the room at her and hug her all at once. Dad didn't help, whispering under his breath the whole time, "Little lying slut," "Takes after her whore mother that one.." And even, "These women. They're all the same. Don't ever let that little twat trick you, Cole."

I couldn't even say anything back. Toni and I had been friends for so long that my brain was doing somersaults over her lies. All I could do was grip the edge of the bench so hard my knuckles were white and my fingers ached. The only thing that held my anger in check was the press of Brennon's pinky finger against my own. When the judge declared a recess, I booked it out the doors, not even waiting for him to follow, and practically ran to the washroom. Thankfully, it was still empty, so I could duck into a stall and throw up the peanut butter toast I had for breakfast. Using toilet paper, I wiped the corner of my mouth and flushed it before turning to check my face in the mirror. To my left, the heavy bathroom door creaked open. "Cole?" Xavi asked. "Is that you?"

"Yeah, Xav, it's me." At my answer, he stepped inside, letting the door swing closed behind him. He didn't come closer, just leaned back against the door and stared at me, those hazel eyes probing my own for a second. "Are you okay?"

"I'm fine, bro." I have a lot of experience faking confidence. Locker rooms are basically full of it, but spewing that crap to Xav sounded phoney as hell. Even to me.

"Oh, right." He paused. "Just wanted to check." He turned, like he was going to walk right back out there, and something about that made my stomach drop.

"Xavi." I reached out toward him.

"Yes?" Hazel eyes found mine a second time in as many minutes.

"Fine. I'm not okay." Caught in a moment of honesty, my voice became more accusatory than I'd meant it to be. "Are you?"

"No. Obviously not. Nothing about today is okay." Finally, he stepped away from the door and closed the distance between us until we were side by side, looking at ourselves and each other in the mirror.

"I'm here with my fucking parents, and because they're crazy, I can't even talk to you guys."

"It's fine, dude. We get it."

"Do you? Because I don't." His body turned my way, but his eyes stared into the marble toilet floors and he sounded almost as sad as I'd ever heard him. "My father hates me."

A voice from behind us made us both jump for a second, until recognition kicked in. "That's cool man, my father hates me, too." Brennon looked completely chilled out. Like today was just a normal day as he leaned back against the bathroom door, simultaneously sealing us in and keeping anyone else out. People were going to worry about what we were doing in here if we didn't cut this shit out. One look at Xavi booted that thought away. There was a small glimmer of something that wasn't sadness on his face as he looked at Brennon.

Wanting to bolster him even more, I added, "Pretty sure my dad doesn't think I'm any great shakes, either."

Somehow, our moment of honesty embarrassed us all. Maybe if Toni was here, we would have blamed her for making us all girly and emotional. But thinking about Toni just brought my anger rushing back and saw me slamming my fist against the ceramic sinks.

"Fuck."

"Toni?" asked Brennon, and all I could do was nod.

"I know. Me too." Brennon wasn't normally one for anger, but one look at him in that bathroom, and I could see a new kind of coldness sweeping over his face and into his shoulders.

Xavi broke our rage. "What if she didn't have a choice? What if she had to lie to us? What if she had to? Or what if..." His voice was so desperate, I hated to drag him back to this hell, or at least reality.

"Either she lied just now, or she's been lying to us the whole time."

"Cole's right, Xav. She could have told us the truth right from the hop. Instead, she made us criminals." Brennon's words hung like radio static between the three of us. It practically echoed off the walls. And maybe that's what brought us all together, three fifteen-year-old kids way out of our depth, huddled together in a courtroom toilet. Only it was less of a huddle, and more of a hug. Each of us holding on to the other two, our foreheads pressed together. I'm not sure how long we stood together like that. I only noticed how close we were when Brennon, that lanky fucker already taller than both Xav and I, squeezed his arms just a little bit more and kissed the top of Xav's forehead, and then my own. "See you both back in there. Cole, I'll stick with your dad." And he turned and left the two of us still holding each other.

I'm not sure why, but I had to close the gap Brennon left behind. Our noses just an inch apart, he whispered, "What's going to happen, Cole?"

I whispered back, my breath so close it made his curls dance, "I don't know, Xav. But I do know that now we have to protect each other."

A second before, I had no clue his hand had slid down my back, but when he dropped it and lifted his face away from mine, well, that I noticed. "What's going to happen to us, Cole?" His eyes were back on mine, so unsure, so many questions hiding in them. My brain screamed at me to answer him. To give him hope. To promise him everything could still be the same as it has always been. For me. For him. For the three of us.

"Cole Michaels!—" My dad's shout from outside had me jumping away from Xav. "Finish your shit and get back out here! You're due on the stand." His words were one thing, but the hurt that flashed in Xavi's face was worse. It made me flinch.

"Coming, Dad!" I shouted at the still-closed door. Turning back to Xav, I tried to scrub the gruffness from my voice as I croaked, "See you later, dude." And I turned my back on my friend.

"Sure, dude. See you later." His words were spoken only to my back.

Hours later, with my testimony sitting in my stomach like a rock, Dad dragged me from the courtroom the second the judge released us, leaving Brennon and Xavi behind. I didn't even get a chance to say goodbye.

Chapter Twenty-Five

Cole

The last dinner dishes were being dumped into the plastic basins the kitchen team would later shove through the industrial dishwasher. And that signalled the end of the meal and the start of a hurricane. Surprisingly, Jack actually showed up this time around, to announce registration and revel in the glory of the race, even if it was from the sidelines since he had never taken part. Not in the more than ten years I'd known the guy. At his declaration, a hoard of bodies clattered out to the deck, where several long tables were arranged with sign-up sheets for each age group and the staff category. Sure, the winner was the overall star, but since that was usually a staff member, there was also a tradition of acknowledging the best finishing kid in each age bracket. Brennon, along with his office monkey, Riley, and a few of the other support staff supervised the flurry of signatures.

I watched the last kid, some girl whose name I didn't know, as she finished adding her name to the seniors' list before strutting past Xavier only so she could drag her ratty little fingers along his bicep and lean toward him, saying something to him that I couldn't catch before shimmying her ass away. What she missed was the way Xavi shook her touch off. With her gone, only staff remained on the deck and now the real chaos of betting could begin. The crowd of us drew a collective breath, but it took Bren a second to catch on. He stood stock still, his expression was intense but unrecognisable with his mouth a thin grim line and eyes fixed on her for far too long as she walked away. Maybe our pervy little rockstar had developed an inappropriate crush, but I wished he would get the fuck over it and focus.

When he did finally snap out of it, I waited near the wall, leaning against the timber frame as other chumps placed their bets. I already knew the odds on Xavi's win wouldn't lead to big money, which was confirmed when Riley jumped his ass onto one of the tables to announce the odds. Xavier was last year's winner, after all, and this wasn't exactly Brennon's first book. He started running bets on the race and the other camp-wide competitions the same summer the rest of us started racing. It was my secret side bet that would make me the real money. No one else would ever think to make it. That would leave Brennon with no choice but to offer me good odds. The crowd finally wound down as staff headed out to either prep for the race or take up a spot manning a particular obstacle. Any staff member not racing would be assigned an official position courtesy of Abbi and the Director. There were only a few minutes before the marathon started with an air horn blast from the start line across the Centre Circle.

It was time to place my wagers. Ignoring the few stragglers, I sauntered up to Brennon, who was too busy jotting something in his notebook to notice. "Ahem," I coughed lightly, "I'd like to place a couple of bets." At the sound of my voice, he looked up and immediately his expression morphed into something wicked. His icy eyes gleamed and a sinful smile cast along his lips as he drawled, "Not man enough for the race this year, Michaels?"

"Get fucked, Grace."

He leaned into the insult. "Maybe I'll see if Michele's up for it since she's single now."

Ready to tear that stupid ring right out of his face, I reached for him, but he had anticipated the move and had already jumped backward, just out of my reach. Full of mirth, he tsked three times. "I don't think so, *pal*, not if you want me to take your bets."

My desire to rip his head off didn't disappear, but I did back down. I needed the cash this bet would bring. It would give me some leverage to push back on Dad when Carl Michaels inevitably came bearing down on me with his shit, so through gritted teeth, I seethed, "Fine, whatever. Just take my bet already. I'm sick of your shit."

Apparently, that fucker needed to have the last word, though. As always. He grabbed his pen, but before I could spell out my bets, he looked me dead on, and still with that stupid smirk, said, "One day, Michaels, someone's going to teach you a lesson in humility. I just hope I'm there when it happens."

I rolled my eyes, and without waiting for him any longer, gave him my bets. Let that fucker grin and wax sarcastic. We'd see who was grinning in the end.

It didn't take long for swarms of kids and cabin leaders to gather again, walking in clusters along the main road. Every snippet of chatter I overheard was just gossip about who was racing and who wasn't. My own name was whispered more than once, in shocked undertones, as news spread that I wasn't participating. I did my best to ignore it as I jogged past them. After giving my bets to Brennon and seeing his eyebrows lift in surprise at my little side bet, there was just enough time to check on my hard work from last night before things kicked off. Anyone not racing was already lined up along the edges of the main road out past the staff lot, right up to the wrought iron main gates. Some of the staff helping with the race were already in position, including Riley and Colin, another junior staff. Stood on either side of the gates, they each held a large wooden branch, more akin to torches really, with Camp Agonde flags hung on them. These flags, and the gates, marked the starting line and part of their job would be to wave the flags the second Jack blew the horn.

Slowly, racers joined the throngs. The youngest kids approached the front, where the flag-bearers helped arrange them by age. Each age group got a few minutes' head-start before the one above it, which of course meant staff would be the last to start. That's why, as more and more runners got into position, I scanned the stragglers for two particular faces. I didn't see them at first. Instead,

I caught the faded blue tips of Brennon's hair as he ducked near the front line to have a whispered conversation with a little blonde slip of a thing. The girl couldn't be more than seven or eight, so I had to admire her gumption for even trying to compete. Brennon placed his oversized palms on her shoulders and gave them a squeeze before ruffling her hair. Then he let her ruffle his strands right back. He's always been particular about his hair. Even when we were kids he didn't like us touching it, quickly swatting Toni's hand away any time she tried. So, even though he was an office monkey and didn't spend a ton of time with campers, this little girl had obviously wormed her way past his defences. Good to know.

Moving on, I resumed my search and was quickly rewarded when I spotted Xavier. He was already in position and bobbing up and down on his toes, readying himself for what was ahead. But it was the sight of a high brown ponytail and defiant blue eyes striding up beside him that had me huffing out in relief. Toni was going to race. I needed her, too, but any encouragement from me would have only raised concerns, and after all these years, I wasn't even convinced there was anything left of the competitive little brat she'd been before.

Xavi's eyes practically bugged out when he finally noticed her. Toni had bent forward at the waist to stretch, and as a result, her tiny running shorts had stretched to capacity over her round ass. Honestly, it was distracting as hell, but I ignored her and watched his reaction instead. He clearly wasn't immune to her, either. His gaze followed the long lines of her legs all the way up, and as he finally looked away, his eyes were hungry from the look of her.

I snorted. Xavi was probably cursing his oh-so-human reaction. Then again, in those shorts and her red racing bikini, she really was something to look at. Even though he couldn't have heard my laughter from back by the tree line, as if on cue, his stare locked on mine over the crowd. It was only for a second, but his jaw ticked before his focus shot forward away from me, and from Toni, too.

At the front of the crowd, Jack was waiting, air horn in one hand and a wireless mic in the other.

"All runners to positions!" he called down the microphone. As the last runners moved, he watched the crowd, lips curling in displeasure when he spotted Toni. It was his fault she was even here. If he didn't want her to race, didn't want her here, he should never have brought her back in the first place. He didn't linger, though, casting instead back to the larger crowd. "Alright, Agonde, are youuuuuu ready?!" A shout of approval answered back. "In that case, and now that our runners are in position, let's count this thing down!" He paused, taking a deep breath. The kids and staff competitors lowered as one, readying themselves to move. "On the horn, the first wave goes. Three!... Two!... One!" The crowd had joined in the count and cheered as the horn's shrill sound blasted through the otherwise quiet evening air. With it, a small group of maybe fifteen kids, all under the age of ten, sprinted off the line as fast as their little legs could go. I noticed Brennon's little favourite amongst them.

The race would take them about a kilometre up the gravel road away from the main property and out to a road marker where one of Xavi's land sports leaders would issue them their first challenge.

They would be tasked with finding the old logging railway tracks that, if followed correctly, would lead them right to the ropes course and back onto camp land. But theirs wasn't the race I was here to watch, so while some of the younger cabin groups moved off to wait out the race, I hung back with most of the crowd. Next went the under-fifteens, then the Elites, and finally, the last horn sounded the start of the staff race.

Both Xav and Toni were ferocious, launching themselves forward like there was no one else in the race. And for them, there probably wasn't. Toni was fast, but she had never been an endurance runner like Xavi, making her ability to keep pace all the more impressive. She was probably running on stubbornness alone. It wasn't until they started to round the first bend in the road that he began to pull ahead of her and the rest of the pack. That was my cue to leave. I had somewhere to be, vengeance to strike, and bets to win. All that good shit. Hopefully, Toni would still be near the front of the race by the time they reached me. Ripping the lead away from her would be the chocolate sauce on my revenge sundae.

Just like the other spectators, I ditched the starting line once the last racers were out of sight. Most cabin leaders were already cajoling their kids back to their cabins to wait out the hour when the race would be close to done. Many simply scattered. Small pockets of friends sought out different spots all over the property from which they could watch the different parts of the race. The beach, the Point and all along the shoreline were always popular spots because you could catch some of the challenges on land and the ones that happened out on the open water, too.

Sure enough, when I ran through the activities field and past the swim docks, every gap in the trees was lined with people watching eagerly for any sign of the competitors. In the distance, I could hear cheers of encouragement, and not knowing where they were coming from, I put on an extra burst of speed. There was no way of knowing how much time I had before someone got to the boat dock, where I would be overseeing the final challenge and making sure no one fucked up my plan in the process.

The dock pieces bobbed under my heavy footsteps as I hopped between the kayaks lined up along each long edge of the nearly thirty-foot forked dock. Normally, each piece was lined with canoes. They were cleared away earlier to make space for the race. There were twenty of them prepped and ready to go with paddles and life jackets tucked into each cockpit. There were also the same number of extras lined up along the shore and in the tall metal racks set back from the dock. I would pull those out as and when I needed them, except for one very special boat that I was going to make damn sure got used. Knowing I had time to spare, I turned back to shore and checked that specific boat. My work last night was nearly perfect, and even up close, it was hard to identify the hole I had shorn in the boat's hull. In the heat of the race, no one would notice the faulty patch I had done or the weighted rudder that would make it nearly impossible to push the thing forward.

Sighing with satisfaction, I retraced my steps so I could watch for the first signs of racers. I didn't have to wait long before two boys, twins I recognized from the Ironweed cabin, darted out onto the dock. Both looked smug as hell when they realised they were in the lead. I clapped my hands for their attention. “Right, boys, you know the drill.” They were almost fourteen and had competed for at least the last three years, as far as I could remember. The final stretch of the marathon was always the same, so instead of waiting on my explanation, they each raced for boats and began strapping life jackets into place. Moving quickly, they shoved their respective boats over the timber edge and into the water, picking up their pace as they went. Maybe because they already knew this last challenge was a rough one. It was a full-out paddle to the island in the middle of the lake where a treasure box waited on its rocky beach. They would need to grab a token from the box, carry it back with them and keep hold of it until they crossed the finish line up at the Centre Circle. The real reason for their hustle became obvious a minute later when the unmistakable sounds of shouting and sneakers slapping against the earth reached my ears. The other racers were coming up quick.

My eyebrows shot up when the next face to sprint onto the dock was the little girl I had seen with Brennon. Hell, she was a determined little thing to have held on to an overall third at this stage. Though, I could see that wouldn’t last much longer as more and more faces peeked out at me over her head. At least twenty of them. Fuck. I had counted on things having spread out a bit more than this. Normally, by the time folks reached this last obstacle, they had faced enough bumps, stops, starts, and hurdles to create distance between the athletes. Now, I was definitely going to need those extra kayaks. And some help, too. I cursed internally again as my eyes fought to find Toni in the crowd. She had to be here. No way she had fallen behind this many others. But as people flooded onto the dock, I was forced to focus on helping as many as I could. In my periphery, I spotted other staff, including Brennon and Riley, pulling more boats off the racks and starting to load some of the older kids into them. My pulse skyrocketed at each boat they reached for. As long as they didn't touch the last blue boat on the rack, my plan could probably still work.

There was a rushing sound as the first kayakers pushed off, but more and more racers kept pouring onto the dock in their place. There was no time to think or to plot. I just loaded one after the other into boat after boat. It wasn't until I heard the high-pitched yell, "Hey!" From the other end of the lineup I even paused long enough to register my surroundings. It was that same little girl again, her small face irate as a male camper dropped into the water in front of her. "That was my kayak!" she shouted down at the boy. I knew his face but couldn't name him. It was hard to remember the names of nearly eighty-five kids. Whatever his name, he just looked back at her, stuck out his tongue, and started to paddle away. I gave a shove to the Elite I was helping and stood. I would grab her another boat before the waterworks started, but in lifting to my full height, I finally spotted Toni across the crowded dock. That was my sign. I needed to move now or all my efforts would turn to shit. Running down the docks, I passed Xavi as he dove for one of the last ready boats. I would worry about how he got caught up in this mess later. Right now, I needed that blue boat.

The last of the day's raging sun stung my eyes and kept me from making out much until I ducked past the last competitors and into the shade. As soon as I was under the tree canopy, though, I could see it. Empty. The boat racks were empty. My blue boat, gone.

Frantic, I spun in place, my eyes blinking as I searched for any sign of the boat I spent all of last night sabotaging.

The previous night, I had sat down here in the dark, with nothing but a flashlight, using an old hand drill borrowed from the camp's maintenance shed to drill holes into its hull and then filled them in with newspaper, flour and water, laughing to myself about revenge a-la-papier mache. Then, I waited hours for it to dry before painting it the perfect, matching shade of blue. It had taken multiple trips to the Creative Cluster supply closet to make it happen. One of the benefits of dating the Creative Director, I knew where the hell to find all the shit I needed. All of it, all that work, so the boat would float for a while before starting to sink mid-race. I had pictured the flour mixture slipping away as Toni struggled and fought to keep herself afloat. But if Toni's ass never made it to that boat, then it would all be for nothing. Not to mention, I was going to lose my fucking shirt to Brennon when my little side bet didn't pay off.

So, where the fuck was that boat?

The dock was starting to clear, and finally, my eyes latched on to a swath of bright blue. It was the last boat of that colour, and that had to be my boat. Only, I was too fucking late. I sprinted, choking on a yell as I ran, "Nooo—" My stuttered voice went unheard over the lingering spectators, and none of the staff members on the dock even looked my way. Instead, I watched in horror as Brennon pushed that sweet little pal of his out in a blue boat I knew was destined to capsize. My stomach lurched. A potent cocktail of regret and wrath. Normally, my anger spews out, violent, on the ice and off. Now, for the first time ever, I was frozen with it. I watched, helpless, as she paddled away from Brennon and the docks with all the strength in her small arms out to where a watchful Toni's boat floated metres away.

My palms were slick and clammy even as they clenched, containing the roar I felt clawing at the inside of my throat. I had just sabotaged a child. A child. One who definitely didn't deserve it, and the fear of what would happen to her had my whole body shaking where I stood. I didn't want this. I never wanted this. As the girl caught up to Toni and the two of them began to paddle out to Bakwe Island together, I couldn't do anything to stop it. I prayed the girl would be okay. I would never forgive myself if she wasn't. And when that boat eventually gave out, my only hope was that the girl I planned to punish would still be with her to save the day.

Chapter Twenty-Six

Xavi

She was such a fucking distraction. The second she strolled up to the starting line, my victory became a slippery, distant thing. And once the race started, I had to battle my way through every obstacle to get here. Last year, they had all been a breeze. Now I couldn't focus or stop my eyes from drifting her way. I beat her by one arm's length on the climbing wall. Predictably, she destroyed me on the swim from the docks to the beach. We couldn't seem to escape each other. But when I slipped into my kayak, I knew I finally had her and had the race too. This was where I had won last year's race, too. Cole was the only one who had even come close to matching my speed and only because his arms, like the rest of him, were so damn big.

Without the weight of her so close, my muscles seemed to move properly for the first time since Jack blew the starting horn. I was going to get this race back on track. My arms started to pivot around the paddle's axis, pushing against the blue-grey water. The effort of it catapulted my narrow fibreglass boat forward and away from the chaos still criss-crossing the dock. In the distance ahead,

I could just make out the edges of the comically large treasure box stationed on the rocky shoreline of Bakwe Island. It had been the same stupid box since we were kids. Around the time we turned twelve, they had stopped bothering to remove it and instead bolted it directly to the rock. I let everything else fall away as I zeroed in on that box, pushing my muscles harder until my shoulders started to burn with the effort. Now that I had broken whatever curse had kept me tied to Toni, it was nothing to push past boat after boat, until only a few remained in front of me. They would likely beat me to the island, but I could overtake them on the turn. And once we were docked again, no one could beat me in the final sprint.

That knowledge made me smile, even as I dug deeper, using my whole body in the movement. My core braced so it could share the effort with my arms. The distance ahead of me shrunk rapidly, and I was only metres away from the island when from behind me a piercing scream broke my concentration. "Xavier!" I ignored it. It came again, tighter and filled with fear and desperation. "Xavi! Help!" I would know that voice anywhere, normally filled with sass and bravado, or more recently, a steely determination. But the terror in her scream now stretched across the water and all the boats between us to tear my heart right out of my chest. Something about her cries reached across time, and suddenly, it wasn't twenty-year-old Toni calling out for me but my ten-year-old best friend, my twelve-year-old first crush, and my fifteen-year-old first love. It was every version of her I'd known and loved, and for that girl, I turned my boat around.

Pressing one blade of my paddle into the water, I shoved against the resistance and spun my kayak in place. The sun setting over the forest and horizon, coupled with the flurry of other racers, none of whom seemed to care about the screams behind them, made it hard to make out Toni's position. My hand shielded my face, allowing me to see, search and find her just in time to watch, horrified and confused, as she stood up in her boat. Kayaks aren't known for their steadiness, and it wobbled and rocked uncertainly under her as she ripped her life jacket off her body. She looked up for a second, right at me, and cried out again. Frantic and near tears, she called for me, "Xavi—" her voice breaking over my name. "Please!" She begged and then dove into the lake. I watched her slip under the dark surface, leaving her life jacket floating and empty. Only then did I spot a second, child-size life preserver floating beside the one my girl had just discarded. Fuck. A kid. There was a kid in the water somewhere. Of course, Toni was going to go after them.

With that, there was no stopping me. Arching my back, I used every ounce of effort I had just used to put distance between us and hauled ass back toward Toni's empty kayak. I cruised past the last few racers, all staring at me like I had lost my damn mind but not giving enough of a shit about me, Toni, or anyone other than themselves to stop. Clear of them, I could finally see exactly why Toni was so terrified, as her head broke the surface and she screamed again. Not my name this time, but, "Holly!!" and dove under again.

My heart raced as I waited what felt like a thousand too many minutes while I sat there, useless, on the water, waiting. The small force of Toni's jump had sent her own boat drifting. She would need my help to get it back, to get back to camp. Even she wouldn't have the endurance to swim the distance, not while carrying a child in her arms. Assuming she managed to save the kid in the first place. I gulped at that thought. Each of my breaths felt too shallow, none fully reaching my lungs, and right then I understood how tragedies could snowball because that wild girl had five seconds to get her ass back to me before I went into that water after her.

My silent prayer was granted when, with an echoing splash, Toni's head and shoulders burst from the depths. She leaned back in the water and clutched to her chest was the tiny form of a girl. The child's body rested against Toni. She might have been sleeping, but for her unnatural stillness, the absence of even the smallest of movements. I positioned my boat close beside the two and urgently reached out my arms. "T, give me the girl."

"She's not breathing. She needs CPR," she panted.

Still, she let me grab the girl–Holly, I gathered–and lift her out of the water and into my arms instead. Then I reached back for Toni, too, assuring her, "On it," as I used my other hand, the one now holding the girl, to guide and force her hands to grip the frame of my boat. Speed was key now. I didn't need anyone to tell me that as I moved us toward Toni's boat as fast as I could, then held it steady as she lifted herself back in.

Working in tandem, we used the twin bows as a makeshift table, laying the girl out flat across them. Soaked and pale, the kid looked so frail laid out in front of us. It was like seeing a ghost, and that wasn't a thought I wanted to dwell on, so I shifted my attention to Toni. Balanced on her knees in the hollow of the boat, she could just about reach across the girl's rib cage. My only job was to follow her directive, to keep us as steady as possible while Toni, that wild, strong, fierce woman, used her own breath and her whole body to press down on the girl's rib cage. Toni became the girl's heartbeat. She took over the girl's breath. I held us firm, but it was agony to watch. Toni never stopped. She never rested to catch her own breath.

Another round of breath. Another round of chest compressions.

And another.

And another.

Those were among the longest minutes of my life, and I was little more than a bystander.

Still, the girl didn't move. I saw the moment Toni's last bit of hope slipped away. Her shoulders slumped, her head sank, and the burning urgency in her eyes, fuelled by adrenaline and fear, waned into an empty exhaustion. Even hopeless, she moved, unthinking, hammering out a rhythm on the girl's unresponsive body.

Suddenly, she stopped. Her arms dropped and slow streams of lake water and tears ran down her face. Then, just as suddenly, she tilted her head skyward and roared. A hoarse, angry, incoherent scream was the only sound rippling over the otherwise still lake.

And a cough. A small, quiet, beautiful cough. So tiny, it almost didn't register, coming from a body that still hung limply over our boats. But it was enough. The soft sound hurtled Toni back into action. She rolled the girl onto her side. It didn't look comfortable. The angles of the boat hulls forced the girl's body to arc strangely. And I was sure it didn't get any better as Holly vomited. Bile and water crept from her lungs and trailed down the fibreglass back to the lake from which it had come in the first place.

Unsure of what to do, I looked from Holly to Toni. My wild girl was crying even harder now, all while smiling with relief. She waited, the same patience she had alway, and only, displayed in the face of pain and hurt well intact. When the last spits and coughs ceased, she dragged the girl back against her own body. Toni herself was shivering and shaking, but she cuddled the girl tightly, keeping two fingers on Holly's throat so she could feel the beating of the kid's pulse. She nodded to herself a minute later, obviously satisfied with whatever she felt there. Then she looked up at me. Her blue eyes still shone with worry but also the tiniest sliver of hope as she so gently said, "Xavi, please take us home."

She could have asked me for anything in that moment. I would have fished stars from the sky or bowed at her feet. So, of course, I would get us home if that was what she wanted. Directing her to hold on, I pulled the strap from my own life jacket, handing it to her with a command to hold on while I tied the other end to one of my boat's anchor points. Once I was sure the knot would stay, I retrieved my paddle, which through some miracle had floated so neatly beside me throughout this whole shitshow, and with it back in my hands, I began the work of getting us safely to shore.

The docks were nearly empty as we finally scraped against them. No cheering crowds waited for us. The race was long over, and I couldn't even find it in myself to care. Only a handful of lone figures waited. Cole, Brennon, Abbi, and the Director, all towering over us. But I didn't care about any of them, either. I pulled on the tie holding Toni to me, and drawing her and Holly into the dock, as well, my eyes stayed glued to the girls. Toni still held the child like precious cargo, and the girl, still barely moving beyond the small rise and fall of her chest, slept against her. Both bore the signs of what they had just endured. There were deep lines under Toni's eyes and her shivering had gotten worse. Yet it was with nothing but softness that she looked up at Abbi and whispered at our watchers' evident distress, "She's breathing. But she should still go to the hospital right away." There was a small cottage hospital in town that every summer dealt with a series of stitches, broken wrists, and concussions that are a somewhat regular occurrence at an athletics and competition-driven summer camp.

Abbi nodded, ducking down to lift the girl away from Toni and into her own arms.

"I'll take her right now," she answered solemnly, making to turn.

Her path was immediately blocked by the director. His doughy face and soft flat features often tricked people into assuming he was a nice guy. But all of us who'd been around a while knew that it was just an act he puts on for parents and occasionally, kids. Really, he doesn't do fuck all unless there's something in it for him. Usually, it's about glory, attention, or adoration, so I guess Holly's situation must have tugged on whatever few heartstrings the guy still had because he stuck his arms out too and demanded, "No, Abigail. Give me the girl."

She visibly bristled at the use of her full name, but the guy was still her boss, and ours, after all. Jack took the girl from Abbi, awkwardly shifting as he lifted her. The guy could obviously handle it. He'd played college hockey for Michigan State long before Cole ever tried on a pair of skates, but he bore the soft middle of someone who hadn't bothered to keep up with his training. It was common knowledge that a full MCL tear had ended his game before it ever got off the ground. Carrying the kid was probably the closest he had gotten to a workout in years.

The dock stayed silent as we collectively watched him leave with the girl. The sun was setting quickly now. Only the last hints of the day remained and it wouldn't be long before the five of us were in total darkness. And neither mine nor Toni's stress-wracked bodies would be able to handle that. My shoulders screamed as I lifted myself out of the kayak. After the efforts of the race and getting us back here, the muscles down my arms and back were also cramped and stiff. Toni had to be feeling it, too. Or even worse. I would help her out of her boat and back to her cabin, and that was all. I was done playing her hero after that. Then I was going to take a well-deserved shower.

Before I could step toward her, Abbi beat me to the punch. She eyed me wearily while she once again stooped. This time, helping Toni step from the boat to the dock. Any help I could or would have offered was rendered pointless. Abbi continued to stare us all down, seeing us for the threat we were. Or had been. She wrapped my wild girl up in a towel, Toni's teeth chattering audibly, and tucked her under one shoulder protectively. And with muffled whispers of comfort, Abbi led her off the dock and away from me.

For the last hour or so, it had been me and Toni against the world, or the water in this case, but under the weight of stares from Cole and Bren, and shit, Abbi, too, the reality that we weren't a team at all bled back in, and it felt colder and lonelier than before.

The tension across the dock didn't lessen with their departure, either. If anything, it seemed to amplify. The seconds lingered like they do between a crash of thunder and an inevitable lightning strike, or maybe that was just Cole's wrath I was sensing. It was hard to miss, honestly, his square jaw, even more angular as he clenched, and his whole body shook and flexed unconsciously. A surefire sign that he was about to spout some angry bullshit in my direction. Mere moments later, he snarled, "What the *fuck,* Xav?"

I didn't need his shit. I was emotionally strung out so all I did was shrug and huff back at him, "I don't know, Cole," wanting nothing more than to be done with this day. But stepping away from Cole sent me colliding straight into the silent wall that was Brennon at my back. I spun to get away and instead, I was confronted by yet another set of eyes that I could read far too easily and unfortunately, could read me back just as well. There was another question in his eyes. He just let Cole ask it for him though as the meathead yanked me back toward him.

"Don't give me that shit, Xavier." His free hand already lifting, preparing to choke answers from me like he'd done to Toni all those weeks ago.

"What happened out there?!" he shouted. With none of the noise pollution of a city night, his voice exploded across the top of the water.

Much more calmly, Brennon asked, "What he really means is how did you lose so badly? Isn't that right, big guy?" It was a taunt. One I didn't quite get, and Bren must have read my confusion as he smirked and filled in the gap, "You see, Xav, our boy here bet on you to win, so now, he owes me all his pocket money." It was another taunt. Actually, more of a potshot. A reminder to Cole that the two of us knew he needed every dime he made. He played at fitting in with his wealthy hockey cronies, the Mitchell Greers of this world, but in fact, he hoarded his dollars out of necessity, saving himself from begging for help from his dickhead dad. He never bet on the marathon before, not even on himself. And right now, I was too tired to grapple with the knowledge that he had bet on me. Worse was the warmth in my chest, the flush of pride I shouldn't have felt and the disappointment and guilt at having let him down. All of it was fucking unwelcome.

I tried to fight it, force myself to focus on anywhere or anything else, but still, I looked to Cole even as the night descended around the three of us. The burning anger I saw reflected at me was so predictable I couldn't even return it with anger of my own. It did have me internally berating myself for being dumb enough to think I might find anything else. I sighed and the last of my fight left me as I explained, "Fine, Cole, you want to know what happened so damn badly—" and I started to recount the events of the afternoon. Most of it secondhand, told to me by Toni during our long journey back to shore in response to my own demand for answers.

She had broken free of the mayhem on the docks, only to hear shouting from a voice she recognized. Holly's. From out on the lake, she watched the girl she had spent the last month coaching find a boat and begin her own paddle.

"I was scared for her, Xavi," she admitted to me. "We've been working on her endurance, but still, I knew..." Her voice trailed off as she cast her eyes down to the unmoving girl in her arms. It was that worry that had caused Toni to abandon the race. Her caring trumped her competitive nature. She let Holly catch up, or at least get close enough that she could keep an eye on her. And good thing, too, because somewhere out there, halfway between the dock and the island, Holly screamed her name. The girl's boat filled with water, sinking fast. And, of course, the kid panicked, screaming and crying and moving too fast. All of it only sinking her boat more rapidly. Toni tried to get to her through the crowd of other boats, just like I had fought to get to T. She succeeded, but not before she had had to watch in horror as the tiny slip of a girl slid out of her too-big life jacket and under the water. Never coming back up.

Brennon flinched as I wound down my story. When I looked at him, I saw his eyes flash for a second before he let whatever feeling that was fall into the void inside him. Cole's anger was an inferno. Bren's was cold and empty as he cut me off, "And Toni saved her."

It wasn't a question. He knew. Still, I nodded for confirmation. When he spoke again, his voice was icier than I had ever heard it. And his glare didn't leave Cole the whole time.

"Well, now we know what happened. But what I'd like to know, Michaels, is how you knew a boat would sink?"

Cole's spine went ramrod straight. He was pinned in place under Brennon's stare. His jaw was still grinding, but now there was guilt threaded in there, too. His brown eyes jumped around, looking anywhere but at either of us.

"But you bet on the wrong racer there, too, didn't you?"

The implications of Brennon's question became clearer as he accused, "Why would you place *such* a specific bet? A bet that Toni would lose? That her boat would sink?"

I couldn't help the sharp inhale.

"You knew it would happen," I gasped. It was Brennon's turn to nod. And both of us turned on Cole. I screamed, "That girl nearly drowned, Cole!"

I wanted to smash his jaw in. I plummeted toward him to deliver the punch he fucking deserved so damn badly. All he did was shove me back.

"It was an accident!"

I shook off his pathetic defence. He repeated, bleating, "It was supposed to be Toni in that boat."

Brennon's face morphed into a picture of disgust.

"You're a bigger idiot than I gave you credit for." Rarely one to use his fists, the fight from weeks ago aside, Brennon used his words to tear Cole's plan to shreds.

"What did you think would happen, you fucking moron?" he ploughed on. "You thought you'd just ignore the fifty other racers and hand Toni into your perfectly sabotaged boat like, 'Hey, I know I've spent the last two months torturing you, but here, let me help you'?"

Cole's anger surfaced again. Confronted with the stupidity of the whole thing, it was like that was the only way his body knew how to respond. But Bren wasn't done lambasting him. He was determined to break him as he drilled, "And then, rather than admit what you'd done, you coward, you let that sweet little girl risk her fucking life!" And then he said the words. The ones perfectly designed to worm their way into Cole's psyche.

"Your daddy's right, Michaels. You're nothing but a little bitch."

Cole exploded. He shoved past me, the force sending me stumbling and crashing into the water. When I surfaced, Cole had both hands wrapped around Brennon's neck.

Red-faced with spit flying, he screamed, "Shut the fuck up! I'll fucking kill you!" And just because he's either a total shithead or just completely devoid of any instincts toward self-preservation, Brennon just offered up a twisted smile, "Do it, then."

I was officially the only non-moron on this dock tonight. Quickly, I scrambled back onto the dock, rushing to tug on Cole's shoulder. To stop him the only way I knew how.

"Do it, and you won't just be the loser your dad claims you are. You'll be worse." My words must have broken through the fury. Not enough for him to drop his hands, but I saw the pressure ease off Brennon's throat.

"Keep going like this, Cole, and you'll become exactly like him." I kept my hand pressed on his shoulder, watching as he chewed the inside of his cheek, eating up my advice and swallowing it whole. His hands flexed once more, an itch to continue, but they dropped just as fast. Unprepared for Cole's mercy, Brennon's legs didn't hold him. His ass hit the wood planks with a thud and there he stayed while, for the third time, we watched Cole Michaels leave us both behind.

Chapter Twenty-Seven

Toni

After steering me away from the boys and their shouting, Abbi guided me toward the bathroom. We both knew I needed to get warm and quick. It might still be summer, but as August got closer, so did cool nights, and as the adrenaline fled my body, I was left with shivers and a palpable unnatural heat blazing under my skin. Both symptoms that hypothermia could set in any minute. With chattering teeth, it was a real challenge to get Abbs to let me shower by myself. The girl was determined to help me, and most of the time, I appreciated it, although I wasn't really sure why she went to all the effort, but I needed to be alone. I needed to fall apart with no one there to witness it. My stomach was heaving and there was an itch in my mind that I didn't want to scratch at. One that wouldn't stop clawing at me to find the nearest toilet and let the burn of bile in my throat push away the horrors of this afternoon.

It took a repeated promise that I would go directly from a hot shower to my cabin and to bed to finally convince my stubborn friend I would survive on my own. And then it took a scalding shower, so hot that my skin flushed red under the cascading water, to get the shivers to subside. No one would ever know that in addition to warming up my frozen body, I spent the entire time sobbing over the events of today, and I definitely wouldn't be telling anyone how those tears eventually stopped being about the girl I had rescued and became tears of longing. Having Xavi play hero with me today was nothing but a cruel reminder of what I used to have. I didn't need them the way I used to. The girls were proof positive that I could make other friends. But none of that stopped me from missing them.

"So. Fucking. Unfair!" I screamed against the white shower stall, smashing my fists against the fibreglass walls until they shook back at me. And then I found myself sinking until my bare ass hit the floor and my knees folded in on me. And there I stayed, curled up, like a beaten puppy, until the water ran cold. Which was when I finally regained enough sense to reach for the dial and turn the water off. Then I crawled my dumb, and once again, frozen butt to the towel Abbi had thrust at me before she left. Curled up against the soft cotton, I thought about Holly and how thankful I was that she had survived. I also couldn't help but feel like Xav and I had turned a corner. Only time would tell, but no matter what happened from here on out, I would always be grateful to him because he saved us both today.

The walk between the bathroom and my little cabin took way too long. My aching limbs were slow to move and the night wrapping around me under the clouds and canopy felt close and tight, forcing me to take even more time. The last thing I wanted was a bruised ass from tripping over an unexpected tree root. Eventually, though, I made it to my safe haven. The second the door closed behind me, I tossed the towel away and stuffed myself into my warmest clothes. Sweatpants, my old RRU sweatshirt and the thickest pair of socks I owned. They were ratty and had holes in the toes, so I grabbed a second pair and put them on top. By the time I was clothed, I resembled an overstuffed doughnut, but I was finally warm. And besides, late as it was, I wasn't going anywhere except under my blankets.

Despite the bone-deep weariness I felt climbing into bed, I knew I needed a distraction. Without one, my brain was going to replay the events of today over and over again, even in my dreams, and whatever sleep I managed to get was going to end up being useless. Normally, I would have reached for my book, but tonight, I wanted mindless fun, and the only place to go for that was the internet. I slapped my hand down on my phone. It was basically useless to me around camp, so it stayed plugged into the single socket in the cabin most days. With the way the signal was out here, it was unlikely I would be able to load more than a video or two, but hopefully that would be enough. My thumb unlocked the screen, and instead of the distraction I craved, I was confronted with email notifications. Marked 'URGENT' and 'FINAL NOTICE', all from the university's finance office. Except for one from Mum. I skimmed the contents, my brain struggling to take in the words. The only bit that did register was a date. I had three weeks to make a payment or I would be unenrolled. Meaning, even if I did eventually scrape the money together, I was going to have to re-apply and hope RRU would admit me a second time. I scanned the email again and noticed a minimum payment amount. Five hundred dollars. Paycheques for July were due in a day or two. I set a reminder to make the payment as soon as the money hit my account.

Once that was set, I opened Mum's email. It had been weeks since we had spoken, but based on our last conversation, I was certain it was an email to fill me in on all her news, the new job, and gossip from the waitressing staff. I smiled at her greeting.

"Hi, Sweetie - I miss you!"

The grin faded quickly as I kept reading. Mum's tone was light, but there was no mention of the new job, except one line to say that she was still looking and hopefully something would turn up soon. She repeated that refrain over and over, telling me not to worry. How could I not, though? I was already doing the math in my head, calculating how much money she was going to need for rent on the first of the month and a little extra for other bills. I needed to know. It was going to come down to a choice: helping her or helping myself. But maybe, just maybe, if I got lucky, I would be able to do both. Skipping from the email app over to the keypad, I dialled her number multiple times. I hit call over and over and over again, and each time it disconnected before even a single ring drummed in my ear. Either it was the signal, or the bill had gone unpaid. My money, what little I had left of it, was on the latter.

Just when I managed to scrape myself out of hell, there was always something that dragged me back in. Back to him. Tomorrow, I was going to stop by the office and use the computer there to transfer the money to Mum, but that wouldn't solve my school problem. It only made it worse, leaving me with the one option I really and truly dreaded. There was no chance I was sleeping tonight. I'd rather just get this over with as fast as humanly possible.

Several futile attempts to call my brother later, I gave up fighting against the shitty reception. There were two options: the staff pay phone or the phone in the Director's office. The thought of being overheard or having anyone witness the emotional wreckage that was sure to follow my call narrowed my options to one. Office, it is. I hadn't seen the director since he left the docks with Holly. And knowing how slow that cottage hospital can be, I doubted they were even back yet, so the office should be deserted. I swapped my school shirt for my ratty old Agonde sweater and slid my feet into my ratty sneakers before sliding out into the dark. Most of the time, the door to my cabin creaked, but I used only the gentlest of pressure to close it, and thankfully, it shut with only the barest click from the latch. It was already late, after eleven, which meant most staff would be in the dining hall or in cabins of their own. Either way, I was not exactly keen to make small talk with anyone right now. I drew the hood up over my hair, moving as fast as I could down the path. At the split, I contemplated taking the direct route to the office. It would be faster, but it was also more likely to be used by any staff who were still up or were heading to their accommodations for late-night hookups. My other choice was to go the long way around, via the activities field.

It took me a good ten minutes longer to get to the office. Partially because I stuck to the edges of trees that separated the Staff Village from the field. The stars were bright over the wide open grass and there was almost nowhere to hide, but the starlight overhead also meant that the trees cast shadows and I hugged tight to them. It was a challenge, but the lack of sheltered spots in this part of camp also meant it was usually deserted at night, and tonight was no exception. Once I was across the field, it wasn't far to the office and the only other tricky bit was the small path that ran right beside the section office. The two offices sit side by side and are backed by thorny bushes. I crouched in the brambles, and from that hiding spot, I saw the lit windows in the section office and I heard multiple male voices. The glass wasn't exactly double-paned, so it was easy to make out Cole's deep baritone amongst the others. He was cursing loudly. His temper was just as riled as it was a few hours ago, and he was clearly bitching to his friends about me. I couldn't tell who was in there with him, but a guy's voice said, "Too bad it wasn't her in that boat. Dumb bitch would have done me a favour if she drowned instead." It wasn't Cole, but he spoke up next.

"What a fucking shitshow. She fucked me over. I wish someone would do the same to her." It might have been easier to hear him call me a 'dumb bitch' like his friends had. Hearing him make the terrible events of today about himself got me to my feet. I didn't want to hear another word, so I used the laughter of his idiotic friends as cover to make the last dash to the main office.

The lights were off, and when I got inside, I was plunged into near-pitch black. Only flickers from the small porch light outside penetrated the cheap vertical blinds. My body pressed back against the closed door behind me. I sucked in a few deep breaths and let myself give in to the shaking. Again. Fucking great. I knew it was down to the combined adrenaline and dread. My last hurdle was the door between the staff office and the Director's private one. He always kept it locked. When I was younger, I would often run through this space and rap on the door over and over again until he let me in. And then, I would talk his ear off about me and the boys and all our adventures. If it was locked now, I was screwed. Real talk, I was pretty much fucked either way, but at least if I could get my brother to pony up some of the cash our father was almost certainly giving him, then I could buy myself time to breathe and figure out another solution long-term.

I sent a silent prayer up to a god I didn't believe existed, then marched across the space, staying as far from the windows as possible until I could reach the knob. When it twisted against my clammy palm, I wanted to lean in and kiss it. Instead, I dove inside the dark room, and the second my body was all the way through, I closed and locked it behind me. Because I'm a paranoid bitch, I gave the dark room a once over, even though it was too small of a space for someone to have been hiding. Besides, who hides in a dark, empty office? Except for desperate idiots like me, I guess. Now that I was here, with the desk and the phone on top of it right in front of me, I needed to prepare myself.

Over and over again, I whispered to myself, "You can do this. He's not here. He can't hurt you." And each step I took toward the desk felt robotic, clunky, like my knees were refusing to work.

Eventually, I dropped my ass in the old office chair, just like I'd seen Jack do a thousand times in my memory. My emotions had been yoyo-ing back and forth since I opened Mum's email, but with the phone so close, the hurried need to get it over with returned. Pulling my cell out of the front pocket where I had stashed it, I frantically scrolled through my contacts list for my brother's number. Once I landed on it, my other hand proceeded to hammer the digits into the old office phone and the pressure in my chest built and built with every unanswered ring until, finally, the call connected.

"Hello." My hearing tunnelled and my heart stuttered. The stony voice on the other end of the phone didn't belong to Francis, which would have been scary enough. It was all business, as always, but chilling to hear after so long. It had been nearly five years since I'd last heard my father's voice live. There had been the odd voicemail when he tracked down a number, never, not once since that day in the courtroom had we had a conversation. I forgot how to breathe. Forgot the reason I was making this call. Even when I was a child, conversations with my father were a rarity and they were never easy. He used words like minefields of manipulation where one wrong word or misstep would send me running in exactly the direction he wanted me to. I finally exhaled, "Hello, Father."

"Antoinette?!" His voice was filled with a false excitement, a clue he wasn't alone.

"My darling daughter!" he continued. "It's been so long!" I could hear movement in the background, ending with the click of a door closing. He had moved somewhere private. Now the monster could come out to play.

"My beautiful princess," he hissed, and my skin crawled. "I knew you would call your darling brother, eventually." Darling brother my ass, but it figured. Since Francis had my number, my father had probably taken over monitoring his phone from the second they were reunited. Earlier, I had been annoyed by Agonde's terrible cell reception. Now, I was grateful. It was probably the only thing that had kept my father from finding me. He continued, "It's coming up as an unknown number, my darling. Where are you?"

"Does it fucking matter?"

"YES, IT FUCKING MATTERS!" he cannoned down the line. Then, much quieter, like he remembered whoever was listening in the other room, he snarled, "Where are you, Antoinette? Your brother and I have been searching for you..."

Fuck. Shit. Of course, they were looking for me. I had gotten too comfortable. Father was always tracking me. I had just deluded myself into thinking he wouldn't care now that he had Francis back, but then again, for Franklin Barrett, my twin and I had always been a matching set. One of us would never be enough. In his sick head, he needed us both to secure his empire. That sickening thought had me shunting around the dark office, checking the locked door and the downed blinds. Hiding from him, even all the way out here.

Once I confirmed I was really and truly alone in here, my tight lungs were able to expand properly. Less than five minutes on the phone and already he had managed to twist both me and our conversation in knots.

"Focus, Toni," I whispered to myself, before hardening my voice to speak to him again.

"Cut the bullshit, Franklin. You don't give a fuck where I am."

Ten thousand miles away, I could feel his fingers clench around the edges of the phone, squeezing it to near-cracking. Tension fused my spine in place as his ironclad voice gripped me.

"That is *not* how you speak to me."

My eyes closed as if that could battle my thundering heart.

"Good little princesses respect and love their fathers." His tone was both sarcastic and chilling at once. My throat was so clogged up with fear, I couldn't speak. "If you can't show me proper respect, then perhaps I really do need to track you down. Returning to my home would do wonders for your attitude."

To anyone else, those words would sound innocent enough, but for me, they recalled the nightmares of my childhood, the ones I kept forever locked behind my own mental gates. Now they rattled for freedom. My voice shook as I replied, all my previous bravado gone. "That's not necessary, Father. I wouldn't want to trouble you."

"Better."

"I apologise for my rudeness." There was nothing his ego loved better than hearing someone humble themselves before him.

"Hmmmm," he hummed as if considering. "Better. Insincere, but better."

I fought the urge to hang up and run even further away than I already was. Desperation makes hypocrites of us all, though, so instead I boxed up all my pride and hatred for him and put it somewhere far away in the back of my mind. The sweet voice that spoke next wasn't one I would ever associate with myself. Unfortunately, that didn't stop it from belonging to me.

"I was hoping to speak to Francis, sir." Calling him that left a sour taste in my mouth.

"Your brother is not available at the moment. What did you wish to speak with him about?"

"I was just calling to ask him for a favour."

Silence hung between us on the line, but when my father finally spoke again, his pleasure was obvious.

"I see. And what is the favour, princess?"

More of that curdled taste filled my mouth. There was every chance of me vomiting right then and there, but I swallowed it back. I needed money. Badly.

"Well, sir, I was hoping Francis could help me with school..."

He laughed. Or I guess cackled, would be more accurate. It was such a cold sound.

"Yes, I'm sure you were calling your brother, who has yet to get his GED, for help with school." Dread made my stomach plummet to the floor. "My guess is that you were hoping your brother, who loves his sister *so very much,* would come to your rescue?"

I blanched.

"It turns out, I was able to track down one Antoinette Hillis at Red Range University, who failed to pay her tuition on time. It's amazing what information becomes available when donations are on offer."

I could practically feel the noose tightening even before he said, "Unfortunately, Francis *Barrett,*" he stressed the name like he wanted to imprint it on my skin, "well, he won't be able to assist such an ungrateful little cunt until she tells us where she is."

With that declaration, the prison walls of my world, that I had pushed to their very limit over the last eight weeks, pressed back in on me. Heavier and taller than ever, suffocating the little bit of hope I had carved out by being here again.

"Nothing to say, princess?" he asked, so nonchalantly, his voice regaining its business-like composure. My father was eternally confident he would get what he wanted. He always did, eventually.

There was nothing I could say. Revealing I was at Camp Agonde would only end badly. For me. For my newfound friends and especially for three boys who hated me. Even though I had made a promise to myself so long ago that I would do anything to protect them. So, silence was all I could offer my father.

Frustrated by my reticence, he snapped, "Fine. Then I suppose we both know what happens now." And with a click, rather than the slam I expected, the line disconnected. I dropped the handset, and it clattered onto the desk. The rattling noise made me jump, and my deep breath afterward was accompanied by the tears I had held back for the duration of the call. I was going to need to drink about eight litres of water tomorrow after all the crying I had done today. Using the sleeves of my hoodie, I wiped my face and stood on unsteady knees. Tomorrow, I would wake up, eat breakfast and come up with a plan to save my ass, but for now, I was so over it.

I left the director's office, making sure to close the door behind me. It was open when I got here, and it's not like I have the key to lock it, so closing it was all I could do. Cautious of being caught again, I ducked beside Brennon's desk so I could scan the office deck before popping out the front door. The desk itself was littered with loose papers. From the little bit of light coming in, I saw a mix of printed guitar tabs for punk bands like Modern Anarchy and The Preaching Pistols and his own scribbled notes, likely the actual administrative jobs he needed to do. Brennon was organised chaos and his desk was no different. But I wasn't here to rediscover his musical tastes. Poking my face inches from the glass, I stared outside, looking from the paths to the road and back again. I did a few scans of the area and reassured myself that the coast was clear. Another run-in with Cole was the last thing I needed.

When a minute or two passed and no signs of life appeared, I deemed it safe to leave, and moving just as quickly as I did getting to the office I slunk out the door and halfway down the steps when a solid black mass swung around the lower railing and collided with my frame. It felt like I ran into a brick wall, and I skidded backward, landing on my ass, winded from the hit.

"Whoa, whoa, whoa. What have we here?"

Talk about fucking déjà vu. I was starting to wonder if Mitchell spent all his free time loitering around this damn building, waiting for unsuspecting women or something. That giant oaf leered down at me and shoved his hood back to expose his face. The overhead light cast a shadow across his forehead, and I had the chilling feeling I was looking at Francis' kindred spirit.

He didn't bother to help me up. He just kept talking as I stood up and dusted myself off. "You know, you cost me a lot of money today."

I was vaguely aware that some of the other staff, even Abbi, placed bets on tonight's race, so I could only guess that's what he was talking about, but he basically confirmed it in his next breath. "Rothberg would have won if he wasn't so busy saving your ass."

What a cretin. "Um, you mean saving a kid. That girl nearly drowned out there."

He rolled his eyes. And unprompted, my lip curled in disgust. Like saving a kid wasn't a justifiable enough reason for him. "As if you couldn't have done that alone. Some shitty Waterfront Director you are."

"First off, I did save her. But I never would have made it back to shore without Xavi. And second —"

"Bullshit," he scoffs. "You just like having those boys at your beck and call again. You always did. You probably don't remember, but I was there all those years ago. I know exactly who you are, Antoinette *Barrett*, and I know you played those boys like a slutty little fiddle."

Snapshots of the past flashed through my mind, like I was flipping through an old photo album, trying to catch a glimpse of a young Mitchell. But nothing registered. He must have seen it on my face, because his eyes pinched tight as he explained, "Of course you don't remember. I was small back then. Too insignificant to register on your little group's radar, but I watched you. I used to hide up in the bushes and spy on your little gathering spot in the woods you all loved so damn much. I used to dream that one day you would see me and invite me to join you."

And now I remembered. Mitchell. Cole told me his name only once, one day when he had caught the boy spying on us at the Throw. He was in their cabin that summer and the guys used to complain that he was kind of a creep, always watching them or trying to intrude when they were having private conversations. Now, as an adult, I understand how hard loneliness can be, but back then, all that sneaking around had given us all the fucking creeps. So, when Cole caught him, both he and Bren, who had already had their teenage growth spurts, threatened to kick the crap out of him if he ever did it again.

Jolted back to reality with a shake, it dawned on me that I'd missed a whole monologue from Greer, but I did manage to catch the end of it as he said, "Now I'm glad I'm not one of your pussy-whipped little bitches." Before stepping uncomfortably close. On instinct, I backed up a step or two.

"Then again, I would be a whole lot happier right now if I had my thousand bucks back. Care to help me with that?" He stepped toward me again.

I stammered, "I... uh, look, Mitchell, I'm sorry. About back then, and about the money, too."

"Oh, so you do remember."

"Now, I do. And I'm sorry. We were pretty cliquey back then and should have been nicer." His eyes blazed at the apology, but he didn't back off.

"Thank you for the apology, Toni." The words were nice, but belied by a contemptuous smile. "Now, what are we going to do about my money?"

The answer he had in mind became increasingly obvious as he continued to press closer. We were only a few inches apart when he reached up to paw at my chest. I slammed my eyes closed and jumped backward like a frightened animal desperate to get away from a predator. Stupid Toni. When had that ever stopped any of the other predators in my life?

"You play like you're some innocent victim," Mitchell growled out, stalking toward me again. He was already a big guy, not as tall as Cole but nearly as broad, so maybe it was a trick of the paling office lights behind me or the oversized sweatshirt he was wearing, but he looked even more domineering than normal.

His chest hit my own, and he pressed me backward with force until my back smacked against the cedar shingles of the building's exterior. It hurt. The corners dug into my shoulder blades. Still, he kept pushing. My back was going to be bruised tomorrow, and it would be just another thing to add to the catalogue of hurt I was already dealing with. When his hands found my hip bones and his nails pinned me, I cursed myself for letting worry about something as stupid as a school, a hundred miles away, for sending me scurrying from my bed in the middle of the night. Even worse, I'd let fear of my father drive me from the office. A few more minutes at Brennon's desk would have avoided this whole thing. At least in the director's office, I was contained. There was a locked door. Out here, with the door at my back and nowhere to run but deeper into the black-shrouded corners of the office deck, I was starting to feel like a rabid creature caged. Even the one sad light above me wouldn't reach me if I moved.

I was trapped in the same nightmare I'd lived a thousand and one times before when his clammy, oversized hand began to tear its way under the waistband of my sweatpants. I squirmed and tried to kick my feet out at his shins, praying that I could manage one good hit, one hard enough that he let go and I could run. It didn't happen. Instead, his hand continued to wind its way into my pants. Pushing and forceful, he finally crammed his fingers into my underwear, and the feeling of his fingertips on that sensitive skin had me spitting, screaming, and snarling in his face.

"Get the fuck off me!" I shrieked, attempting to shove him away.

He just laughed. "Nah, I don't think so. I think you owe me, and I intend to collect, princess." And then, with one last painful slam, he shoved his fingers inside me. He pumped in and out of me roughly. It burned and hurt, and I couldn't be sure, but I thought I heard a cry.

From there, I had no control over what happened. Maybe it was the use of my father's preferred nickname. Or maybe it was PTSD. Actually, not a maybe. It was definitely trauma-induced, and that nickname coming from his mouth snapped something deep within my psyche. Suddenly, I was twelve again, hiding in my bedroom closet, and it was not Mitchell bearing down on me.

It was my father. And my mind did what it had always done to protect me. It retreated.

Chapter Twenty-Eight

Brennon

"Throw. Tonight at eleven. We need to talk." Xavi's last words to me as he dragged his soaking wet frame off the dock a couple of hours ago. It's like we couldn't stop reliving the past. Somehow I was always the last fucker standing, whether it was on courthouse steps or a goddamn dock. Maybe that made me some sort of chump.

At least I was a much richer chump than I was a couple of hours ago. After the marathon is over, every year, I always made a point of heading straight to the dining hall. Since I didn't have to put any kids to bed, I could grab a cup of coffee and wait for all my punters to turn up and either collect their winnings or settle their debts. And tonight, it was definitely debts. The wad of cash in my hands should have felt glorious. I leant back, letting the edge of the Formica countertop cut into my spine while I counted out the bills I had collected tonight. Normally, I would have revelled in all that sweet, sweet money. As staff turned up in the dining hall, in groups or one-by-one, most of them made a pit stop to pay me. Tonight had been my most successful take ever since neither Xav nor Toni had won, or even finished, the race. Both were popular contenders, so the staff that had bet on them found themselves shit out of luck, and despite my, shall we say, contemplative mood, it was hard not to enjoy watching them approach me one by one to fork over their money. Most, like Isabella, or even my boy, Riley, had been good-natured about it. Both had bet on my wild girl and were paying for it. Others not so much. That fuckface Mitchell had been particularly churlish about handing over his cash. As if his banker daddy wouldn't just serve him another helping via his silver spoon the second he asked. What a prick.

Maybe as the only child of a rockstar, I was being a hypocrite. I hadn't exactly grown up wanting in any material way. Then again, I hadn't taken a dime from Blue since I had turned eighteen. Between small hacking jobs during the school year, the kind where you forge a doctor's note here or change a Psych 101 grade there, and running books all summer, I managed to pay for school and a pretty decent apartment without having to ask for a handout from Daddy Dearest. I also didn't make bets. My money was exactly that. Mine. So I had no pity for Mitchell or those other jock-bros. Once they all paid me, they had gathered in a huddle in the far corner. Except for Cole, who hadn't shown his face yet, and in his absence, it was like they didn't know what to do with themselves. None of them looked happy, staring me down, and I could see their lips moving fast, probably bitching about me or the race, but at least they were far enough away that I didn't have to listen to whatever shit they were spouting.

I glanced over my shoulder at the large clock in the kitchen. It was almost time for me to meet Xav. I would already be out at the Throw if I wasn't still waiting on Cole. No way was I letting him off the hook for the cash he owed me. Not after the shit he pulled today. Every time I thought about it, about what could have happened to Holly because of him, my fists clenched and I had to fight the urge to wring my former best friend's neck.

It was less than five minutes to eleven when he finally showed his face. He at least had the decency to look like shit. His shoulders were hunched as he shuffled over to me. He couldn't seem to look me in the eye, either. It made me want to chuckle. So much for all that bravado. I snapped my hand out and tapped his cheek twice. "Where's my money, Michaels?" He jerked his chin away and frowned. He finally looked at me, and his eyes were ringed red. Good. I kept my hand extended toward him, my palm open expectantly. "Still waiting, Cole."

"Fuck off, Brennon," he grumbled, but he dug his hand out of his left pocket and it came out full of loose bills, which he slammed down on the counter beside me, ignoring my hand. I turned and grabbed it, counting out each bill in my head. Once I was confident he had given me the full amount, nothing was stopping me from letting some of my rage vent his way.

"Good to know where you draw the line, Michaels. Drowning people is fine, as long as you pay your debts?"

He reacted like an angry bear, launching at me before remembering we were not alone. The gasps from other staff stopped him before he ever laid a hand on me. Cole had worked hard to craft this jovial nice guy personality that he shows the world. Most of the people here had never seen him lose his cool, which was hilarious to me because Cole Michaels was one of the angriest fuckers I've ever known. He jumped back from me, shaking his head. Whether to clear his rage or to dismiss my comments, I wasn't sure, and I couldn't resist another jab. "You should really do something about that temper!"

He was already walking away, though, to join his little posse, all of whom crowded around him. They looked like they were waiting for his instructions, which he clearly gave because the next second they filed outside and away into the dark. When the doors closed behind them, it was time for me to jet, too. Rather than follow them, I slipped into the dark kitchen and out the back door. Thankfully, it was a short journey through the woods to the Throw from here. Once I was outside, the silence of the night overwhelmed me. It was such a sharp contrast to the background music of laughter and gossip inside the hall. It was too quiet and in the silence, there was too much space for my own thoughts to dominate. The last thing I wanted tonight was to be left alone with my own mind. To fill the silence, I started to hum. I wasn't even sure what song I was mumbling, maybe the Dread-Nots, but who knows? My fellow computer science major turned petty criminal pal, Gibbs, calls it one of my tics. We've run a few bigger hacks together, and he's had to give me shit about it every time. Apparently, it was distracting. I reminded him that was kinda the point. As the notes skated across my lips, I retrieved my phone from my pocket and turned on the flashlight function. Unlike Xav, who probably made his way out there in total darkness, I would rather have a little bit of light.

He was leaning against the tallest stone when I got close, his arms and legs crossed and staring into the forest. When my light caught up to his face, his lips thinned with displeasure.

"Turn it off, Brennon."

"But then I won't be able to see your pretty face, Xavi."

I couldn't help my grin as he clicked his tongue, dismissing my perceived joke. Thing was, even in the blue cast of my flashlight, Xavi's sharp jaw and soft curls really were pretty. Downright touchable. But that didn't mean he was in charge. I flashed the light over him. "Ask me again. Say, 'Please, sir,' and maybe I'll listen." He rolled his dark eyes at me and didn't answer for a beat. Then he cleared his throat like he couldn't help but answer me.

"Please turn the light off, Brennon." My pulse stuttered a beat. I would have preferred 'sir,' but I listened immediately. My finger was already extended, hovering over the button. I was always going to turn it off. I wasn't a complete asshole. I didn't want us to get spotted, either, so I was more than happy to have this little chat in complete darkness.

"Thank you," he replied. "And thank you for coming."

My eyes started adjusting to the blackness enough that I joined him in the stone circle. We were no more than three feet apart. And in the dark, the space between us felt smaller, more intimate than it did during the day. I leaned against another one of the rocks opposite him. The heel of my right foot started kicking against the rock over and over again impatiently. "Why did you want to meet?"

"I think we need to talk about what Cole did to Toni tonight."

"Cole Michaels can go fuck himself for what he did tonight."

Across from me, he took a deep breath. "I don't disagree, but, Brennon..." he paused. "It's more than that. It's more than Cole."

My brows drew together. What more could there be? He sighed into the silence. "It's all of us."

"All of us?" I questioned.

"Think about it. About us. How we've all been acting since she showed up here again!"

I tried not to. That's the truth. I'd spent every day since she showed up trying to erase our history. But my memories of her, of us, were a blessing and a curse and every cruel word I said, every nasty thing we'd done to Toni since the start of staff training was like taking a seam ripper to the only happy patches of my past. I didn't say that, though. I didn't tell Xavi any of that.

Instead, I just asked, "So, what, Xav? You want to just forgive and forget?" Wishing it was that simple.

He hesitated. "No, I..."

Except he did want that. It was written all over his sad face and in his puppy dog eyes. Truthfully, I did, too. But it wasn't that easy, and he knew it. That was there in his features, too. It was in the grimace and the way his face crumbled when I reminded him exactly what went down.

"She swore! Swore it was an accident! And then there we all were, burying a body for a girl who didn't give a fuck about us. We were nothing but useful pawns in some chess game between her and her parents!"

He winced like I had hit him.

"I know, Brennon. I know." He sounded so tired. I was, too.

I pushed off the rock with the heel of my Vans, and now that I wasn't leaning back, I was close enough to Xav that I could smell his cinnamon scent. It was almost certain proof that he had showered after Cole shoved him in the lake. Of course, he did, because Xavier hates messes of all kinds. That's why this situation with Toni was driving him so crazy. With so little distance between us, it would have been so easy to pull him into a hug. To breathe him in. I wanted to. It's all I wanted. I fought the temptation but couldn't resist dropping a hand onto his shoulder and giving what I hoped was a reassuring squeeze.

He looked up at me and before I had time to think about the concern I read in his brown eyes, I heard a man's voice in the distance. "Bitch!"

It came from back toward the dining hall. I lit up my phone screen to check the time. 11:43 p.m. Less than twenty minutes until staff curfew. By now, most people had probably left the dining hall to head to bed or brush their teeth or get dicked down. So a shout like that was definitely strange. One look at Xav and I saw his wide-eyed alarm. I turned my flashlight back on and the two of us walked back toward the dining hall.

The lights were off inside the lodge when we came alongside it. Yet, we stopped to listen, waiting for any other indications of a problem. For a second, nothing came, and then there was another muffled shout. Or a scream. And my stomach lurched in recognition. That scream belonged to my Birdie. With the quickest shared look, both Xav and I took off running. We skirted the edge of the dining hall and once we hit the road, there was enough light from the office and so little distance that I could see my little bird. And I could see the man standing over her, crushing her against the building. I turned to my side, but Xavi was already ahead, runners' legs outstripping mine as he sprinted toward the office and shouted, "Hey!"

I stopped. I froze, completely unable to bear the idea of seeing my little bird with someone else. That was right up until the moment when Toni's legs gave out, and then I followed Xav. The distance across the gravel road from the dining hall to the office steps was probably the furthest I had run in years because, well, fuck running. Ahead of me, Xavi jumped the guy from behind and ripped him off Toni's collapsed body. They both fell backward, and in the fall, his face was exposed. Fucking Mitchell Greer. Xavi was on him, straddling his prone frame and hammering hit after hit into Greer's skull. Once I closed the distance, I could see the blood on Xav's fists. I ignored it and headed straight for Birdie. She hadn't moved or said a word. I knelt beside her, and it was like kneeling beside a corpse. She wasn't there. Her eyes were open but unfocused. I called her name. Over and over. "Ton? Birdie? Little Bird?" I begged her to answer me, but she just stared into the night. My hands shook even as I reached in to hug her to my chest, sheltering her from the sights and sounds behind us. I had no idea what to do or how to help her. All I could think to do was beg for help.

"Xavi," I called quietly. "We need you." I heard one more thud of a fist connecting with bone and tissue from behind me and then Xavi's voice, more bitter than he had ever sounded before.

"Get the fuck out of here, Greer." His voice dropped even lower, quieter and even more threatening, so I couldn't be sure, but I thought the next words out of his mouth were, "If I hear one word about this tomorrow, I'll fucking kill you."

Out of the corner of my eye, I could see Xavier standing over Mitchell, where the fucker still lay bleeding in the dirt. Xavier's arms crossed his chest as he stared down at him as if waiting for Greer to put up a fight. He didn't. Whatever he saw on Xavier's face made his eyes go wide for a second before he spat a hunk of blood at Xav's feet and muttered a garbled, "Fuck you." Then he scrambled to his feet and ran off.

Turning back to Toni, I gave her shoulders a gentle shake, willing her eyes to focus on me or on anything. When the weight of a hand pressed against my back, I shifted just enough that Xavi and I were shoulder to shoulder as we huddled around her. He forced some of the heaviness from his voice as he pleaded with her, "Please, Toni? Wild girl? Tell us what happened?" No response. Panic was starting to set in for both of us. She was practically catatonic, and when Xavier looked at me, his brown eyes begging me to do something, I did the only thing I could think of.

"Stay with her."

"What?!" he replied with quiet shock. "Where are you going?"

"I'm going to find out what happened here." His brows furrowed with confusion and he watched me, puzzled, as I walked into the office. The door was unlocked. Either I forgot to lock up or Riley did. Not normally a big deal, although the director was a real dick about it and would definitely give us grief if he knew we'd left it open. All the lights were off inside, and I left them that way. I spend enough time in this building to know exactly where shit was. Rounding the corner of my own desk, I dropped my ass in my chair and clicked my mouse over and over again until my sleeping desktop lit up and I logged in. Once I did, it didn't take me more than a minute to find what I was looking for.

I wasn't sure what prompted me to do it. Fuck that, yeah, I do. Even the small hacks that I did were enough to teach me how easy it is to access information online. That's why it always rubbed me so wrong that I couldn't find anything about Toni online after the trial. Not a Facebook page or email or anything. So, when I took over from the previous administrator, whose recordkeeping was frankly shocking, I let my own paranoia be my guide. Especially after I realised just how flaky Jack Walker was. During my first week as admin manager, I set about installing motion-activated cameras over my desk, around the office, and even outside. I never told anyone they were there. To date, I'd never had a reason to. But now, I watched in grainy black and white as Toni snuck through the front door. It took her longer than I expected to go from there to the director's office. On the cameras, I could see her whole body practically vibrating until she disappeared behind Jack's door. I sped through the footage, only slowing it again when I saw her re-emerge fifteen minutes later. Like I said, in the dark, the quality is shit, but her distress was obvious, and when I zoomed in on her face, there were visible tear tracks down her cheeks.

There was no audio and no cameras in the boss' office, so I had no way of knowing what went down, but I kept watching for clues. She once again snuck around, this time up to my desk, past the chair I was sitting in, only to duck and stare out the window. Eventually, she nodded to herself and stood, making a break for the door. I flipped to the other camera view. I only had one set up outside, and I prayed it had captured enough to tell me what the fuck went on. It did. I watched Greer encroach on Toni, my stomach turning over as he did, and when he shoved his disgusting hand inside her pants, I reached for the small waste bin under my desk and retched for real. The vomit burned nearly as bad as my own disgust. Toni's resistance was obvious. She fought him at every turn, kicking and thrashing against his hold until he leaned over her. I could just make out his lips moving against her ear, though I had no idea what he said, but whatever it was made her legs give out. My little bird just crumbled underneath his gargantuan frame.

I only watched a little more. Just enough to see Xav and I show up on camera. I watched Xavier beat the ever-living-shit out of Greer, mostly for my own personal satisfaction. Then I erased it permanently, saving only the video of Toni's assault. I vowed to myself that I would never show it to another soul unless I had to, but at least it was there as insurance. I clipped the video file and saved it to my secure folder before shutting the computer down and heading back outside. On the deck, Toni was still out of it, but

Xav had lifted her so she was cradled in his lap. He held her with one arm, and his other hand was smoothing along her long hair. I looked down at them together, and despite the circumstances, they looked so beautiful. While I watched them, I noticed the small signs of life in our girl that weren't there when I went inside. Her fingers had locked onto his sweater. The tension had eased from her neck and shoulders, leaning on him for support instead. She was still in there. She was just buried and maybe she needed our help to dig herself out again.

I wasn't sure if Xav noticed me right away. It was possible he didn't because he never stopped his soft whispers into her hair. I closed my eyes and took a deep breath, knowing we couldn't stay there any longer. Toni couldn't stay there.

When my eyes reopened, I gave a small cough, and in the gentlest tone I could find, I repeated the thought out loud. "We can't stay here."

He pulled her even closer and looked up at me helplessly. "I won't leave her, Brennon."

"I'm not suggesting we do. Let's go." I gestured for him to stand. "You got her?"

He didn't even acknowledge the question. He simply stood up with Toni in his arms as if she were weightless. "Okay," he nodded.

We stuck together, and it took us a bit longer than normal, but with no one around, our walk from the office to Toni's cabin was uninterrupted. It was a blessing and saved us from any awkward questions. I went inside first and flicked on the single light. Her cot in the corner was made up with cheap sheets and a scratchy-looking duvet. Clothes and shoes were scattered across the space. Toni and I always had that in common. We thrived in our own personal chaos. I also wasn't surprised by the stack of books littered on the floor near the top of the bed. Once a bookworm, always a bookworm. Even when we were ten, Toni would usually have some sort of paperback in her pocket. 'Just in case,' she'd always say.

Xavi slipped past me toward the bed, lowering her softly until her head rested against her single pillow. Stepping back, he kicked off his shoes and stripped down to his boxers. They were tight around his soccer player thighs, and everywhere else, too. My lips parted before I even noticed, until I realised what he was doing. He climbed in behind Toni, tucking himself between her body and the cabin wall. I stared at him and he just shrugged and said matter-of-factly, "I'm not leaving her," before pulling her back into his chest and drawing the covers over them both.

"I know, Xav. Me either." He nodded at me and nestled into her again.

"We'll figure it all out tomorrow," I muttered as I turned off the light and sunk down against the opposite wall. I was going to watch over them both tonight, and tomorrow, well, tomorrow I would figure out what was going on with my little bird.

I'm not sure when I fell asleep, but I woke with a start. It was still mostly dark outside, but the first shimmers of dawn were peeking in through the single cabin window. And when I looked over to the bed, Toni's ocean eyes were open and boring into me. "Brennon," she mouthed, barely loud enough to register, and I crawled over to the edge of the bed. Our faces were so close I could make out every freckle on her nose. "Brennon," she said again, her voice cracking over my name. A single tear ran from her eyes.

"What can I do, Birdie?" I asked in a hush.

She drew the duvet back just enough; her invitation clear. It wasn't exactly a queen-size, but she and Xav were pushed so close together that there was just enough space for me to crawl in beside her. With a soft push, I turned her so she was facing Xavi. I wasn't sure why, but I didn't want to fight the impulse to hold her close. To hold them both close. My top arm draped all the way over her and landed on his side. He didn't budge, obviously deeply asleep.

With my face pressed into the back of her head, I mumbled my question over again, "What can I do, Birdie?"

"I don't know, Bren. I don't feel..." her faint voice lingered on the words before pausing on her inhale. On an impulse, I kissed the nest of her hair.

"Rest again, sweetheart." She exhaled and softened against me. And deep inside my chest, something unspoken and unsettled decided to rest, too.

It didn't take long before I was drifting back to sleep, but just before my eyes closed, I heard her whisper hopelessly, "I just want to feel something good. For once."

"Shhh, little bird, tomorrow, I'll make sure you feel something good."

Chapter Twenty-Nine

Xavi

Waking up in the same bed as Toni Barrett was everything my fifteen-year-old self could have dreamed of. The morning light shone through the single window in her cabin, just enough that she glowed beside me. She didn't move at all, but on the other side of her, I heard Brennon stirring. Three of us in a bed this small was a tight squeeze, and I almost felt it when he fit his body around Toni's. I didn't care. It was enough to watch her.

There was a small rustling sound that obviously came from Brennon. I couldn't see what he was doing, but I noticed when Toni's perfect pale lips parted, even as she remained asleep. Her long brown hair draped over her shoulder. It was shinier than it was when she got here, and longer, too. The ends of it long enough that they traced across the top of her perfect tits, skimming the edge of the tank top she had kept hidden under that frumpy sweatshirt. At some point during the night, she'd stripped it off. Probably because the body heat from the three of us meant it was sweltering in here. The warmth didn't stop her nipples from peeking out at me through the thin fabric. I was fighting the urge to reach out and pinch them between my fingertips, if only to watch her skin blush from the slight pain.

Apparently, Brennon wasn't hampered by the same restraint. He whispered against her skin, "You want that good feeling I promised you, Birdie?" Her eyes didn't open, but her head nodded gently. Seconds later, his smirking face appeared over her shoulder, and when he noticed my eyes open, he mouthed, "She's soaked." I raised my eyebrows in a silent question, which was answered by him dragging his right hand from under our shared covers and showing me the slickness glistening on his index and middle finger. He dipped them into his mouth, clearly savouring Toni's taste, before letting them drift back down. All while I watched in fascination.

I could tell the moment he pushed them inside her because her lips parted, a pleasured "oh" crossing her lips, even in sleep. The sound crumbled the last of my resistance, and I reached for her. My voice was still rough with sleep or maybe lust.

Caressing her soft skin, I whispered loud enough for Brennon to hear as I reached out to pinch one of those hard buds between my fingers. "So beautiful. You're such a perfect little whore for us even when you sleep, huh, baby?"

She didn't really respond, other than a faint moan. I didn't expect her to. But her body was moving between us now, writhing from our combined efforts.

From her other side, Bren purred appreciatively, "She liked that Xav. A lot. She's gripping my fingers so tight," he groaned. "Keep talking."

Those were directions I would happily take.

"So perfect, Nettie. I bet you'd let us have you just like this. Would you let Brennon slide his cock all the way into that tight little pussy? Want to wake up cumming? I bet you'd like that, pretty girl." She stirred slightly at my compliment, giving us a little pant that made my dick impossibly harder than it already was.

"Keep moaning like that, little bird, and Xavi's going to have to fill your mouth."

I smiled at Brennon's dirty thoughts, so close to my own. Not right now, but soon, I was going to do exactly that. For now, for this morning, this was about bringing our wild girl back to life. To that end, I dragged my left hand down her soft body, keeping my touch feather-light, almost a tickle, until I reached her core.

"You going to help me get our girl there, Xav?" Brennon teased, and I smiled in response.

"Well, then," he nodded, "I think her clit could use some attention." With pleasure, I gently pressed my fingers between her legs. Brennon hadn't lied. She was dripping, and part of me wanted to drop even further down the bed and eat her instead, but again, this moment called for patience. So I sought out her small bead, rubbing gentle circles over it, gathering her wetness as I went.

Brennon groaned. "She's getting tighter. She's squeezing my fingers so hard, man."

I leaned even closer. My bare chest pressed against hers, and it was all I could do to get the words out. I fought my own desire, but I managed to whisper my plea against her ear. "Come for us, wild girl." Her legs tensing and flexing made it clear how close she was, as I kept up my circling, moving just a little faster until she was right on the edge, and then I pulled my hand back. It was only for a second. Then I brought my palm down in a light slap against her swollen clit.

Her eyes popped open at the contact, and I got to watch her come completely undone. Her pupils blew wide as she shouted out her orgasm.

"Good morning, Nettie," I said innocently.

Picking up my tone, Brennon chimed in, keeping it light. "Hello, little bird. Did you sleep well?"

She didn't say anything at first, merely darted confused looks between Brennon's face and my own. I could see the moment it dawned on her exactly how caught she was between the two of us. Her cheeks reddened and twitches of last night's panic reappeared in her doe-wide eyes. She gripped her comforter and yanked it tightly to her chest. The wariness that had replaced her ecstasy so quickly pissed me off, but when she started to falter and trip over her words asking, "What?... How?... Did we—" I remembered exactly what state she was in when we had found her last night.

Fuck. What a couple of pricks we were. Judging by her questions, she had no idea how we got here or how we got here with her.

"Shhhh, wild girl," I soothed. "Other than what you just experienced, we just slept." Her blue eyes found my own for confirmation.

Brennon, asshat that he is sometimes, rolled himself from the bed and snatched his jeans from the floor, slipping them on casually.

"You asked me to make you feel something good. This was the easiest way I could think of." He shrugged and grinned at her surprised gasp and my own snort. "The most fun, too."

Toni blushed even more. The colour gave away her innocence. It also made me want to run my tongue along every inch of her lit-up skin. Brennon must have had a similar idea because his smile turned slyer. Lust dripped from his voice as he rumbled, "I would be happy to repeat the experience, sweetheart."

She blanched. And as much as my dick was on Brennon's side about a second round, I didn't want to overwhelm Toni right now. I never wanted to see her fade away like she did last night ever again. I shuddered just recalling her vacant expression as I carried her here. It felt like I was carrying her corpse. I coughed softly, breaking their rapt stare, and pulled their attention back to me. I was still in the bed beside Toni, although I shifted to give her some space even though my back and shoulders were now pressed against the cold wooden corner.

"I think we should talk about last night," I said to the room, and pointed to her sweatshirt in its heap on the floor. "And, Bren, if you can pass that to Toni, I think she'd prefer to be at least mostly dressed for this." It was a guess, based purely on her continuous efforts to cover herself, even though she wasn't really naked.

Brennon nodded and tossed it to her. She visibly relaxed as the ratty old thing slipped over her head. Once she had it on, I pet her shoulder gently and prayed it comforted her. She didn't flinch or push me away, so I kept at it as I asked, "How much of last night do you remember?"

Her shoulders stiffened against my palm. Brennon didn't say anything, obviously content to let me lead this little chat, but he never took his icy eyes off Toni. I asked another question. "Do you remember what happened with Mitchell?"

"Mitchell." She breathed his name, but it was full of terror. And she shivered. Leaning against the opposite wall, a still shirtless Brennon cracked his knuckles. My own tingled, too, bruised from last night, and I could feel it every time I stroked across my girl's back. That didn't stop me, though.

"Yes, Mitchell," I replied.

"I remember... I remember he—" she paused. "But I don't remember you guys there." It was a guarded answer, and again, her eyes shifted questioningly from me to Bren and back again.

This time it was Brennon who answered her. "We were at the Throw and we heard you scream." His voice was hollow and his inflexion didn't change as he then described the scene we stumbled onto. He skirted over the damage I did to Greer's face and his own pit stop inside the office. Since we didn't exactly talk on our way here last night, I was also in the dark about whatever it was he went in there for. Now wasn't the moment to ask, either.

When he finished the story, repeating Toni's pleas for something good, his eyes and tone finally softened. I sat up to check on our girl and the panic was gone from her eyes, replaced with the glassiness of unspilled tears. Bren's voice broke a little as he pleaded to her, "I just wanted you to have something good, Birdie."

It was a justification, if not an apology, for the events of this morning. Toni nodded and, thankfully, gave us the smallest of smiles.

"Thank you," she mumbled, "for last night."

"You're welcome," we both murmured back solemnly. I couldn't speak for Brennon, but I would repeat the actions of last night and this morning a thousand times over.

She didn't look up at either of us, and I worried we might have fucked this up again until she softly blurted out, "And for this morning, too. Thank you. I mean." In another fit of embarrassment, she dove under the covers to hide her face.

Neither Brennon nor I fought our smiles. I tugged the blankets gently until she released them with a huff. Then I tipped her chin to look at me. "Anytime you want a repeat performance, beautiful, we're here."

She blushed again, and on her tanned skin, it was absolute perfection.

"What he said, Birdie," Brennon grinned. "But right now, I think it's time Xav and I got out of your hair."

He nudged his chin to the door, and I nodded, squeezing myself past Toni with only the softest brush of my skin against her now-covered body. It was an immediate tease, but I resisted.

Brennon and I each scooped yesterday's clothes from the floor, dressing quickly. I felt Toni's eyes on us the whole time. None of us spoke a word, but when Brennon and I waved goodbye from the door, she squeaked and hid her face again. Our girl was embarrassed we had caught her ogling us. We both chuckled as we headed outside, Brennon first and me right behind him. I caught the door so it closed with only the quietest click instead of slamming. There were no other sounds around the village, so it was obviously still early.

Brennon and I drifted silent and aimless away from her cabin door. It was so early the cooks likely hadn't unlocked the dining hall yet, but going back to my own lonely cabin at the other end of the village didn't feel right. So, I just walked, and Brennon followed. Uncertain of what to say to him about last night, or anything else, I latched my mouth shut. Hell, I practically held my breath. And instead of looking at him, I focused on counting every pebble and root in the dirt under my feet.

When I had my wild girl to focus on, it was easy to ignore everything else, but now I was shaken and unsure. And I fucking hated it. Watching Toni climax like that was the hottest thing I had ever seen, but the further we walked away from her, the more the reality of what the three of us had just done was crashing down around me. It had me more twisted up than usual. Brennon was never someone I thought about that way, but ever since he had pushed against me that night weeks ago, I've had questions. And now, they wouldn't stop swirling in my head. Was I jealous? And who of? Him? Her? Both of them? I didn't have any answers, and that was the worst part.

"Xav?" I heard him call for me. But I couldn't bear to hear what he was going to say. He wanted her, of course. We had all always wanted her. Even before we knew what that meant. But seeing them together sent my imagination lurching forward in time. Their tall, lithe frames, wrapped around one another, matching blue eyes so focused on each other there would be no space left for anyone else. They looked beautiful. They were perfect together. A work of art. And just picturing it left me empty.

"XAV!" he called again, shouting this time, and his long arm yanked on my shoulder, pulling me back.

"Where the fuck are you, man? I've been trying to talk to you!"

My mouth gaped when I looked at him, like an idiotic fish. But I couldn't help it. His fading blue hair was completely and perfectly dishevelled. Combined with the tattoos and piercings, his inner rockstar was on full display. I'd never doubted that if Brennon wanted to, he could eclipse his father's fame in every single way.

Finally, I managed to untangle my tongue. He was half smiling, watching me while I struggled to get words out.

"Bren, I..." My voice barely trickled before trailing off and still, he wouldn't stop watching me. If he would have just looked anywhere else, maybe I could have fucking said something. Or if he wasn't stood so close, maybe I could have focused on the present instead of picturing him holding me against that tree and the feeling of his stubbled jaw edging against my neck. Suddenly, my confusion made sense. And with that realisation, came anger.

"What the fuck are you doing, Brennon?"

His eyebrow, the pierced one, peaked in curiosity. And still, he smiled. If anything, it morphed from a half smile to a true one. And it annoyed me even more.

"You want me? You want her? What?!" My volume rose as I went on, and for a second, I became anxious someone was going to come bursting out of one of the other cabins and see us, so I dropped my voice to a frustrated hush. "Or is it just another way of fucking with her? Or are you screwing with both of us now?"

His smile twisted and his fingers twitched at his sides. It was the first reaction that didn't irritate the fuck out of me.

"Is that what you think I'm doing?" he replied sternly. I didn't answer, and he didn't speak, either. He did push, though. With one hand, he shoved me back, making me stumble a little. He didn't stop, pushing us off the path. He kept at it, ignoring my curses and half-questions, until we were deep enough in the woods that the back of Toni's cabin was just barely visible through the brush.

I'm strong and athletic, sure, but Brennon's height sometimes gives him an advantage. When we finally stopped, he used that leverage to shove me to my knees. I fought to get up, but with both hands on my shoulders now, he easily held me down. The forest floor was damp and started to soak through my sweats as he kept me there with one hand, circling me, while his other hand ran along my neck and jaw until he was right in front of me. Then, he tilted my head, so I was forced to look up at him.

"You think this is about torturing you, Xav? Or my little bird?"

Harsh and clipped, he spoke, "Maybe I do want to torture you both. But not in the way you think."

Before I could respond, he stepped closer. His hands slid into my curls and using an almost painful grip, he forced me to look forward, directly at his hip level, where his low-slung jeans showed the top inch of his boxers and the rock-hard outline of his dick. The tip of it was visible, nudging out of his boxers. It was swollen and leaking pre-cum. Holding me there, he started to pump his hips so his cock rubbed against my face through the rough denim and through his thrusts he gritted, “This is how I want to torture you.”

I fought to move. Or maybe to listen. But it was hard to concentrate on anything but what was in front of me.

“I told you weeks ago that I knew what I wanted.” There was a sinister laugh as he continued, “I was wrong. I want her. And you. I want you both.” He picked up the pace, his hips rocking into me faster.

“And I will have you.” He grunted before retracting just as fast and easing his hold on my hair. I missed the force, and I couldn’t stop my eyes from following his movements. Quickly, he unzipped, and in one motion, dropped his pants and boxers so his dick hung free in front of me. It was long, longer than my own, and thick, but that was all I had time to notice before he pulled me back toward him. The tip of him played at the edges of my lips. My mouth watered, but I couldn’t stop a shiver of worry. My cheeks felt hot when I looked up at him.

“Bren, I haven’t... I... not since...” His heated eyes softened and so did his hold. And for some reason, I hated it. I snapped, “Don’t. Don’t look at me like that, Grace.”

He licked his lips and smiled with satisfaction. It was like he was just waiting for my attitude.

"Oh, Xavi," he said, his thumb dropping to my face. His calloused digit ran along my cheek and over my mouth. "You don't give the orders around here. Now open," he commanded and pressed my lips apart. For some reason, I let him, and when he shoved his cock roughly onto my tongue, all I felt was relief. He was hard enough that he filled my mouth completely. His tip notched at the back of my tongue and I resisted the temptation to hollow my cheeks and take him even deeper. But the need to tease him was there, too. I wanted to drag this out and make him beg me for it, so instead of any quick movements, my tongue moved languidly around his head first, then traced a slow path along the vein at the back of his shaft. When I got close to his base, he groaned and thrust deeper.

He growled, "Xavier."

I popped my mouth off him, half-smiling at his torment. When I looked up at him, his eyes were burning down into mine.

"Xavier. I am not in the mood to be teased."

"Oh, really?" I taunted. My blood rushed, and my own cock was painfully hard, waiting for his response. He dug his hands into my hair again.

"No," he replied, slamming back into my waiting mouth. I relished his grunts as my mouth pumped up and down properly. I swallowed his length down as far as I could. Each groan of pleasure from him egged me on. He tasted and smelled smokey and warm, like wood and good whiskey. It was intoxicating and comforting. Breathing him in, all of my worries from minutes ago slipped away as I concentrated on him, on making him give in to me, the only way I knew how to.

It wasn't long before his thighs went rigid against my hands and he grunted, "I'm going to cum. And you are going to swallow it. Every damn drop." He punctuated each word with a hard thrust, and on the last one, I tasted spurts of warm, salty liquid even as it hit the back of my throat. It felt like a victory. When he sagged slightly, it felt like I had somehow conquered that ever-present wall made of sarcasm and indifference that Brennon kept around himself these days, even if I had to do it from beneath him. When he finished a series of softer thrusts, I gave his shaft one last lick before he slipped from my mouth and tucked himself away.

He reached down and softly stroked my jaw. With an awed whisper, he praised, "Amazing!" I couldn't handle the way his eyes focused on me, so I looked down instead, readying myself to stand. I was so hard that even the soft fabric of my sweatpants brushing against me felt agonising. Brennon helped me up, and I needed his steadying hand because my own erection was all I could concentrate on.

Once I was standing, though, he spun me to face the path we had left behind. And it wasn't empty. Toni was frozen fifteen feet in front of us. She was staring at us with parted lips like she was going to say something. Instead, she bit her lower lip for a second before sprinting away.

Flustered, I looked at Bren.

"She saw us?" My voice quaked and my worry was obvious.

He was so fucking casual in his response. "She did."

"Fuck!" I cursed, preparing to chase her down and explain.

Brennon stopped me. "Relax, Xav. She watched the whole thing, or most of it, anyway."

He smiled. "And I swear, I could smell how wet she was from here. Our girl likes to watch."

"How the hell can you know that, Brennon?" I croaked. "What if we scared her away? What if I...?" I asked miserably.

"We didn't. You didn't." He turned me to face him again, caressing my cheek softly.

"I'll talk to her. But right now, we should definitely talk about last night."

Quickly, he rushed through an explanation about his cameras, Toni's dip into the boss' office, and everything that led up to our arrival on the scene we witnessed. And while it definitely raised questions about what Toni was doing, I was done doubting my wild girl. I might not know everything, but then again, I hadn't done anything to earn her confidence yet. I would, though.

Chapter Thirty

Toni

It had been two days. Two days since Holly nearly drowned, since Mitchell tried to force himself on me, and since Brennon and Xavier woke me up with the most intense experience of my life. Maybe if I were a different, more normal, person, those first two things would have been my focus, but I've been so fucked up over those boys for so long that they were all I had thought about since.

Anytime I had thought about it, of them hovering over me or of the two of them together, mouths on skin, that same warmth I felt pulse between my legs seemed to roar back to life. More than once in the last forty-eight hours, in my moments alone in my cabin, I had dreamt about what it would be like to do it again. To be awake for all of it, while they traced their hands up and down my body. To be right there, by Brennon's side, as he kissed Xavi's jaw or while their lips battled for dominance. And every time, I had ended up bringing my own hand to my core, running my own fingers along my slit and wishing they belonged to Bren, or Xav, or both. I had brought myself to the edge and fucked my hand over and over, thinking about all of us together, in all sorts of combinations.

The only problem was afterward, when I had to leave the safety of my cabin and confront the reality of what it might mean. I was too chickenshit to deal with it, to deal with them, so I had been keeping my distance. I avoided the dining hall during meals, opting to eat leftovers in the kitchen long after mealtimes had come and gone. I ducked out of staff meetings and huddles early, running away or feigning the need to be somewhere. And when those weren't an option, like all-camp gatherings, I hid myself between Abbi and Michele.

That was exactly where I found myself this morning during announcements. I had purposely dragged the girls to the bench at the very front of the Point Campfire, knowing that Xavi would never willingly put himself in front of everyone, exposed for all the kids and staff to see the way we were here. Brennon might consider it, but I just hoped that the presence of my friends was enough to stop him from getting close. When the director got up on the small stage, I breathed a momentary sigh of relief and focused on listening to what he had to say. Every time I had caught sight of him since the accident, which truthfully hadn't been often, I had to basically chase him down for an update on Holly. The two whole times I had seen him since he got back from the hospital, he pawned me off. He offered up trite explanations that she was fine, "She's recovering," before slipping away with some excuse. Now, it had been a few days, and I was desperate for an update on the poor girl. Hopefully, this morning's updates would include some information. I knew her cabin mates and even her cabin leader had been pestering Abbs for information. She didn't have any. I had asked, too, and the director had told her the same thing he'd told me.

The director launched into his usual updates, listing the optional games and activities that would run this afternoon. I would be overseeing a free swim at the beach. That was followed by the same flag-raising that happened every morning, and I gave up hope of hearing anything until Jack coughed and shifted on his feet. Normally, the flag went up and that was that, but he cleared his throat again, eventually regaining everyone's attention.

"I know many of you have been worried about our fellow Agonde family member, Holly."

The still nattering crowd hushed and listened in near silence as he explained, "I've spoken at length with Holly's family. She is doing well and has left the hospital, but her family have decided it's best she finish out her recovery at home."

An audible mix of gasps and other surprised, if whispered, exclamations at this news forced Jack to stop talking for a minute. When the initial shock tempered, he continued on as if nothing had happened. There was no further information, just a thank you before sending us along to breakfast. The tenor of his voice never changed, but he dropped the small step from the stage as quick as he could like he was fleeing his own shadow, and though I stared after him, he never met my eyes.

A hand grabbed my shoulder, making me jump in my seat on the hard bench, my ass crashing back down with a thump. It was only Mich, asking, "Coming, T?"

I looked back for the director, wanting to race after him for more details, but he had vanished just like every other fucking time. When had he become so erratic? These days, the man was the master of the disappearing act, rarely around, and even when he was, he barely seemed to care about what was going on around camp day to day. He never used to be like that. When we were younger, he was always around. The guys and I would pop into his office between programmes or he would come and sit with us at campfires or show up in our guitar class with tabs he had printed just for Brennon. Now, he never seemed to spend time with the kids. Lately, I could swear he wasn't even on the property half of the time.

"Toni." Michele tugged again. I stood up, ready to follow her and grab some breakfast, but we didn't get two steps before Brennon stopped right in front of us. His arms were stretched out so he could fully block our path. So fucking tall that it worked.

I panicked as he said my name. "Birdie? Can we—". I didn't even hear the rest. I just bolted sideways. I think I might have managed to mumble an excuse as I ran away from both my friends and Brennon. Maybe something about needing to pee, because I was just classy like that. I didn't have any planned destination in mind. I just followed the shore around its curve, past the beach and the field, and all the way to the swim docks. My home away from home, really. Most of my past three months were spent down here.

When programmes weren't running, there was a safety gate across the first boards to stop any of the campers from wandering out onto the water unattended. Part of my gig as Waterfront Director was to manage access, so I carried the key with me most of the time. I slipped it out of my pocket now and unlatched the gate, tucking myself through before locking it behind me.

Everyone else was at breakfast, and until it was finished, I had this space to myself. I intended to use the time to sort my shit out. Enjoying the gentle rocking of the timber frames as I stepped, I strode a few metres out and sat facing the boating dock. I slipped my sandals off and dropped them at my side before letting my toes, feet, and ankles dangle into the water. It wasn't exactly deep here, like it was further out at the end of the dock, but it was deep enough that I would have to get all the way in to touch the bottom. The crispness of the August morning made the water feel deceptively warm on my skin and for a second I was tempted to slide beneath the current. Under the water there would be nothing to run from, no Brennon, no Xavier, no Cole, no school emails or calls from Mum, and definitely no Francis or Franklin Barrett. Just the muffled sound of water moving exactly the way it wanted to.

As quick as that thought came, it was replaced by another, much more pathetic one. We didn't kiss. I mean, they had kissed me, or parts of my body, at least. But I hadn't kissed them back. I had dreamt of kissing those boys since I first saw Devon Sawa kiss Christina Ricci at the end of Casper, since I learned what kissing was, only to chicken out at my first, and probably only, chance. What a fucking coward I was. I cursed myself over and over as

I watched the distant tree line sway in the morning breeze, and promised myself that even if it fucking backfired like everything else in my life so far, I still deserved a kiss. One perfect kiss, on the mouth, from someone I actually gave a shit about. Nick had tried to kiss me, sure, and if you had asked me back then, I would have sworn up, down, and all around that I wanted him, too. But in that moment, I realised that his kisses weren't the ones I had wanted at all.

Later that afternoon, under the hot sun, I watched nearly a hundred kids of varying ages traipse, jump, scream, and laugh their way through the free swim. The greyed-out wood of the guard chair, dulled from years of sun and summer storms, made my thighs itch. I tried to ignore the feeling and concentrated instead on watching the kids. There were five of us staff spread out across the beach area, all doing the same thing. Two in the water, one, a junior staff named Peter, stood out on a floating dock while Bella strolled along the water's edge not ten feet from me. As the head guard, I was in the chair, but only because I would be the one in charge if anyone got hurt today.

Anytime I was lifeguarding, whether from this chair or at the university pool, I did this thing where I counted the people. I would pick a random section of water and count the people swimming in it over and over and over again before I moved on to another section and did the same thing. Like if I just kept counting them, there was no way I would miss if, or when, something bad happened. That's what I was doing, counting the players in a water wrestling match. Two boys, scrawny pre-teens, had girls hoisted on their shoulders and they scraped and scrambled at one another until they all collapsed into the shallow water before repeating the whole thing over again. There was a mix of laughter and bravado that was so uniquely teenage that I found myself caught up in daydreams of doing something very similar with Cole. Me on his shoulders, parading across this very same swim area, challenging any takers to a game of chicken. It's why Abbi's curls popping up at the bottom of the stairs caught me off guard before she swung herself up to sit beside me in the chair.

Her dark skin glistened compared to mine, even though I was much more tanned after weeks spent under the summer's hot sun. And she had somehow managed to wrangle one of the red tank tops labelled 'Guard' that only the real lifeguards were supposed to wear. She grinned widely at me as I rolled my eyes at her, even though I moved over and made space so she could sit beside me comfortably. I had a suspicion of where she got the shirt, and when I looked down at Bells, she was staring back at me and laughing.

"We needed to pin you down somehow," Abbi said into my ear.

"Huh?"

"You've been all over the place the last couple of days. Like a wild animal that's been spooked."

From the bottom of the guard chair's stepladder, I heard Bella confirm, "*Está como una cabra,* T. You seem a bit crazy, honey."

"What's going on?" Abbi gestured from Bells to herself. "We're just a bit worried. You've skipped, like, the last four meals?"

"Ummm..." was all I managed to reply at first, but it was not long before the whole story came flooding out. Or most of it, anyway. Bella moved to stand closer to the guard chair, leaning against it so she could hear everything without me shouting it out in front of everyone. I left out the phone call to my father, but otherwise gave them a pretty complete picture of what had happened with Mitchell, my freak out, and waking up in a three-way cuddle. Again, there, I kept some of the details to myself, particularly about catching the boys together, but shared enough that they were both staring at me in shock when I finished.

"Mierda!' Bells cursed. "I wondered what the hell had happened to Mitchell's face. Boy looked properly fucked up the next day. Still does."

"I'm glad." Abbi nodded, agreeing. "Now that I know what happened, that scumbag deserved it. Did you tell Jack?"

"No." I averted my eyes, ashamed that I hadn't even thought to report Mitchell for what he tried to do to me.

Abbi shook her head softly. "You should, you know. The guy is a creep. He shouldn't be allowed around children."

"I'll think about it," I shrugged.

"I'm sure Brennon and Xavier would back you up! Think about it!"

"I don't know," I answered, my voice shrinking under layers of embarrassment. "I haven't really spoken to them."

"You what!?" Abbi exclaimed. Loud enough that several kids lying in the sand looked up at us, before she whispered, "You haven't talked to them? Like at all? About any of it?"

"Noooo..." I whispered, sounding exactly as cowardly as I felt.

"Jesus Christ, girl—"

"But I'm going to!" I proclaimed. "Tonight! I swear!"

"You'll get your chance. The director's called a staff meeting for tonight, so everyone will be in the dining hall for that, even the shy one." I knew Abbi was referring to Xav, since he rarely appeared during staff free time, and when he did, he didn't exactly engage with anyone, mostly hiding out in the dark kitchen alone. I chewed my lip, but nodded to confirm I'd heard them. Both of my friends watched me for a second before looking at one another in disbelief, like neither of them really believed me. I couldn't even be upset, because I didn't really believe me either. I may have promised to be brave to myself this morning, but making that promise and actually fulfilling it were two different things.

Just as my friends predicted, I completely chickened out. I took a page out of Xav's playbook and was now hiding alone in the darkened kitchen. There wasn't a single light on back here, and it was only thanks to the bright fluorescents in the dining hall shining through the serving windows that I could see enough to avoid running into the industrial appliances that were spread across the kitchen.

There were still another ten minutes before the meeting was due to start, but most of the staff had arrived. The benches from various tables were pulled down and arranged to face the stage.

Most were full now. From my hiding spot, I watched people fill them over the last half hour. I got my first glance at Greer since that night. The girls were right; he looked awful. He had two black eyes in a mottled shade of purple and there was an obvious cut still healing across his swollen lower lip. Add to that the miserable face the fucker was making, and I couldn't help but smile. Abbi and Bella came in together and sat down facing the stage. A few minutes later, Mich joined them, waving quickly at Bells before sitting down on Abbi's other side.

The director arrived late, nearly five minutes after the meeting was supposed to have started. He scanned the room like he was taking some kind of silent headcount. He must have realised there were still a few of us missing because he grimaced and sucked his teeth before opening his mouth to speak. I still had not seen Xav, Brennon, or Cole, for that matter, but whatever Jack wanted to say must have been important, because he didn't wait any longer.

It was a talk about camper safety. About our responsibility to protect the children in our care. I didn't need to hear it. Not from him. I had done everything I could to protect Holly, and he had belittled my concern for the girl ever since. So I tuned him out, opting instead to watch the other staff and the doors for any signs of Brennon. I always thought I was a good listener, but apparently not because I didn't catch a single hint that someone was behind me until a palm clapped down over my mouth, stopping my surprised shout before it could come out. You would think I'd have been more scared given my history, but when I looked down at the hands holding me, the finger tattoos gave him away. Even if they hadn't, barely five seconds went by before Brennon's raspy voice put me at ease, whispering into my hair, "Shhhhhh, Birdie. It's just me."

Brennon's no athlete. He's much leaner than Xav, and definitely Cole. But he makes up for it with height. He's so tall that he dwarves even my lanky frame, and so standing there together, in the unlit kitchen, I felt completely wrapped up by him.

"Can you be a good girl for me and stay quiet?" he whispered again.

I looked out at the crowd of staff, all listening attentively to Jack's updates, and nodded. Immediately, his hand slid down until his fingers caressed the column of my throat. His other hand snaked further, wrapping around my exposed hipbone, where his thumb began to trace slow circles on my skin. Everything about his touch was soft enough to feel kind, but firm enough to keep my hips pushed against the counter's edge. Everywhere his fingers moved felt on fire, and just like the other morning, there was a new kind of heat unspooling in my lower belly. He kept talking through his caresses. "You have been avoiding me since the other day."

"B—"

"No talking," he cut my protest off before it could even start. Although, what could I say? The confusion, the joy, the passion of being between them like that had made my brain short circuit. And now I didn't know what to do or say. "Don't deny it, Birdie. You've been avoiding me. And Xavi. And after we showed you how much fun you could have with us." His hand slid from my hip toward the centre of my belly and over the button of my shorts.

With that one hand, he managed to pop it open, and again, I had to fight the urge to pull away, to run, even as my body craved his hands lower still.

"No, no, you aren't going to run away from me again." He slid my zipper down. And I looked back between him and the crowd gathered under the lights in the heart of the dining hall, slightly frantic we would be seen. Brennon must have picked up on my fear and soothed me yet again. "Don't worry, sweetheart, no one can see us back here. I know because this is Xavi's favourite hiding spot. And you know our boy likes to watch." My body relaxed. He was right, Xavi would only hang out where he could do the watching, not the other way around. At the easing of tension, his fingers teased at the edges of my panties. "Now, Birdie, remember to be a good girl and stay quiet for me," but as he said it, his fingers dipped inside my underwear and easily found my centre. He groaned against me, and I felt even more wetness between my legs at the sound. "Sweetheart, your pussy is so wet. Is that all for me?" I nodded, and he rumbled his pleasure and rocked his hips against the back of my ass so I could feel his body's response to me, too. And ever so slowly, he started to swirl his middle finger, spreading me just the tiniest bit so he could move my wetness where he wanted it. I was so unused to feeling, the sensations his hands were able to build in my body, that I moaned. But then he stopped. "Birdie," he chastised, "if you can't be quiet, I'll have to stop. Do you want that?" He couldn't stop. I would go crazy. I shook my head violently, internally promising to stay quiet as long as it meant more touches.

He got the message and again began to tease. If anything, I was wetter than before, and when he pushed one finger inside of me, I bit my lips together to avoid yet another moan. Soon he added another and my hips began to rock against his hand, seeking more of him, more of this. “Mmmmm, look at you fucking yourself on my fingers. You look so beautiful.” His praise made me move even faster. “Do you need more, baby?” Again, another nod. “Okay, here you go.” And his thumb found my clit and made more slow circles. I couldn’t stop my body from moving now. I was chasing a high that felt so close, and my teeth were digging into my lips so hard I could taste the metallic tang of blood. “One day soon, my little bird, it will be my cock inside you instead of these fingers. And when you come apart for me, I am going to fill that beautiful pussy until my cum drips down your thighs.” And that was it. His dirty words and the image of Brennon with me like that tipped my body over the edge. My legs gave way as my orgasm rocked my body. And Brennon held me through it, only withdrawing his fingers when the last tremors of pleasure left me.

Spinning in place, his blue eyes burned into me even in the darkness. I watched, equally shocked and fascinated as he brought his fingers, so recently inside me, to his lips and licked the taste of me from them. “Oh, Birdie, you taste so perfect. Like strawberries and honey.” That couldn’t be true, and yet I felt my chest flush with pride at the thought that he might actually mean it. And maybe it was his eagerness or his sincerity that had me dropping to my knees in front of him. I wanted to taste him, too. He had lit me up from the inside out, and I was desperate to do the same for him. He clearly didn't realise what I was doing until I took my turn to work his zipper down.

"Birdie, no, you don't—" I stopped and looked up at his face, riddled with concern. Did he not want me to do this? Was this all some kind of game? The hurt of it punched me in the gut. I was so stupid to think they might believe me now. That I finally got back to two of the only people that ever mattered to me.

Stuck between his legs and the countertop, I couldn't even run away before the tears started to come. Choking on them, I mumbled, "I'm, uh, sorry. I'll just go. I thought—"

"Sweetheart, that is not what I meant." I hesitated. "Toni, look at me." From the spot on the floor, which might as well have been the bottom of a pit for how I felt, I swallowed my tears and did as requested. His eyes were softer, less worried, and he used his thumb to rub the tear from my cheek. "I was going to say, if you would let me finish, you impatient girl, that you don't have to. This wasn't about some kind of quid pro quo. I just wanted to make you feel good. Please don't run from me, Toni, I just—" and his voice cracked and fear replaced the worry on his features.

Twelve years later, I was still the girl slapping on a brave face, and he was once again the boy who didn't want to be left alone. Maybe neither of us had to be those things anymore. We could be something new, together. "You made me feel good, Bren, so good." Keeping my voice low, I let warmth and my own desperation flood into it. "And I just wanted to make you feel the same." The tiniest bit of my confidence returned, and I placed my hands back on his denim-clad thighs. He groaned as I knelt closer to his hardness.

"Birdie... Toni." his voice deepened again, egging me on. He let me shimmy his boxers down and his cock sprung free. A moment of hesitation at how big he was had me hauling in a deep breath, but still, I wanted this. Wanted him. Wanted to touch him and unlike the dread I was so used to at the thought of this act, now I felt only desire, so I decided to be brave. I wrapped my hand around his smooth shaft and brought the tip closer to my lips. Brennon's hands stopped me again, and yet again rejection burned, but only for a second as he forced my face up to his.

"I want to see my cock pass those sweet lips more than anything, little bird, but just know, if you do this, I will never be able to let you go again."

"Maybe I don't want you to," I whispered against his hot skin and slid his tip into my mouth, causing him to groan yet again. The sound only urged me on, taking another inch or so deeper into my mouth. He was so big, bigger than I'd ever seen. I cut that thought off before it could take me somewhere dangerous, and instead, refocused on the man in front of me. Brennon was all I wanted to think about in that moment. I let my tongue swirl and roll around him, tasting every bit of him and relishing the way his hands sought my hair, gripping me in place. Still, I felt him holding back, and I wanted to break him open. Just for me. With that thought, I plunged my mouth deeper until his cock was so far down my throat I couldn't breathe around him, and then painfully slowly, I pulled back.

My retreat prompted him to whisper, "Don't you dare stop, little bird. I need that pretty little mouth. Now." The last word was a command that told me he was close, close to where I wanted him. I wanted him wild for me, and so again, my mouth descended on him. This time I moved faster, took him deeper, and pressed my tongue firmly against the vein in his shaft. When his hips started to rock into me, and his hands pulled harder at my hair, almost to the point of pain, I relished his desire for me. Despite having just come on his hands, something about taking him like this–here–was making me wet all over again. My panties were practically soaked through because of it. Since it was his filthy words that had undone me, a filthy idea of my own filled my head and had me pulling back one last time to look up into his eyes. He growled, his voice low and rasping. "Birdie..." he scolded down at me.

"Bren," I paused to lick the pre-cum from his head. "I want to taste you." Another lick, and another moan. "I want you to fuck my face." No more licks, I dove back into sucking him off. Only this time, there were no casual hip thrusts. Once I had him in my mouth, he set a punishing pace, holding me in place by my hair as he slammed into my mouth over and over again.

"You want me to fuck your face, sweetheart? I can do that. You want me to slam my cock down your throat? My pleasure." My eyes were watering from his efforts, and I probably looked like hell, but Brennon still looked at me with nothing but lust, as he whispered, "You look so beautiful with my cock in your mouth like this." I hummed under his praise, which only made him pump harder. "I'm going to cum down your throat if you keep doing that, Birdie." I nodded and hummed around him again. "You want that, pretty girl? You want me to fill that hot little mouth of yours?" That was exactly what I wanted. What I needed. I swallowed around him and the dam broke. "Toni, fuckkkk." Warm liquid spurted across my tongue, filling my mouth, as Brennon kept thrusting. "Such a hot mouth. So perfect." His words dragged until they were just a mix of sounds. I swallowed the last drops of him and popped him free. Quickly, he tucked his dick away and did up his jeans before dropping to his knees so we were face to face.

"Birdie, that was..."

"Oh, it was something alright," a cruel voice cut across whatever Brennon was about to say. And shocking us both, one lonely light flicked on at the back of the kitchen, revealing Cole. His face was hard and arms crossed, as if unimpressed to find us here.

Without another word, Cole paraded down the narrow lane between the prep counters and the industrial stove, passing right by us. And only when he was within inches of where we sat cradled together on the floor did I hear it. He never even looked our way, but he did spare a second to feign a cough of "Slut" before he pushed on the door, letting it swing on loose hinges as he headed out to join the meeting. The label stung, and my shoulders shrank in on me as I sagged back from Brennon to lean against the open cubbies beneath the countertop.

"Don't listen to him, Toni."

I didn't answer. Instead, my shoulders clinked against the restaurant-style napkin dispensers and I twisted my body around, slapping my hands on each one to muffle the sounds. I didn't look back at Brennon, but I did listen.

"You are not a slut, Toni, and don't let Michaels make you feel like one. That's his jealousy and his dad talking."

I hummed noncommittally.

"No, I'm serious Birdie." He turned me to face him again. "You and me. And me and Xav, and all of us, it's something—"

"It's what, Bren? Because I saw you the other morning."

He chuckled lightly. "Oh, I know you did, sweetheart. Did you like it?"

Warmth flushed across my face.

"I'll take that as a yes." He laughed again before rubbing my cheek gently. Then he cursed and scrubbed his hand through his mop of shaggy hair. "God, I wish Xav was here. Stupid patrol duty." He cursed. "But I guess I'll have to do my best to explain alone."

I looked at him, slightly shocked by his offer of any kind of explanation.

"I wanted you both." He paused. "Want you both. Have done for a while now. Probably much longer than I wanted to admit."

I was stunned at the admission and struggled to do more than just blink to acknowledge I'd heard him.

"Truth is, you're not the first girl and Xav's not the first guy, but I think maybe you were always supposed to be." His voice dipped uncertainly. "I think maybe it was always supposed to be all of us?" There was fear behind the question, and without thinking, I reached for his hands, squeezing them between my own.

"We fly together?" I asked nervously. It was a new spin on words we had said to each other so many times before.

"Or not at all," he confirmed and leaned toward me, pulling my face to his and pressing our mouths together in a firm, sure kiss. His lips moulded to my own, and before I knew it, I yanked on his flannel shirt, pulling him in tighter and he deepened it. His tongue slipped into my open mouth, and the taste of Brennon overwhelmed my senses. He was warm, and I was home, and together with Xav, maybe we could regain some of what we'd lost.

Chapter Thirty-One

Cole

She was on her knees for him. My heart beat pounded against my rib cage. Fury at Brennon for giving in, fury at her for forgiving him. She shouldn't be on her knees for anyone but me. On her knees while I make her pay for all the ways she's ruined my life. Maybe then she'd run. Maybe then I'd never have to see her look at someone the way she looked at Brennon tonight. Like that metal-faced asshole was some kind of king. It made my stomach churn.

I don't think I listened to a word of Jack's dumb lecture. Forget that I was late because I was too busy dealing with a couple of homesick seven-year-olds, but my mind couldn't focus on anything other than the image of Toni with Brennon's dick in her mouth. Even my harsh words didn't seem to shatter the warmth that surrounded them and, though it didn't look like they'd fucked, I couldn't help my jealousy. Not of them. Never. Because I would never fuck that lying bitch. My stomach did yet another weird flip-flop at that thought. But witnessing it was a slap in the face. In the two years we had been together, all the times we'd had sex, Michele and I had never managed to generate anything close to that level of heat. We'd gotten to lukewarm at best.

I was going to fix that, though. Across the huddled crowd of staff, Michele laughed quietly at something Abbi whispered to her, and I swore I was going to get her back and show Toni what love really looked like. She said she needed time to figure things out, but in the weeks we had been apart, I still had no idea what she meant. It was all wrapped up in Toni. Somehow, she had conned my girlfriend into believing her shit, and I had let it all happen without so much as a fight. What I saw tonight just confirmed exactly what kind of girl Antoinette Barrett was. Brennon could have her. I was going to concentrate on getting my girlfriend back.

After far too long, Jack finally shut up and sent us off to bed. Fuck sleep. I launched from my seat at the back of the crowd, intent on catching up with Michele. Since she hit the pause button on our relationship, we hadn't spoken at all, and at this rate, we would never get back together if I couldn't convince her to talk to me. Halfway through the crowd and across the lodge, I jostled yet another cabin leader out of my way just in time to watch Michele's back disappear out the door and into the dark. My eyes charted a path between her and the remaining staff. If I could get out of here, I could definitely catch up to her before she got too far. I kicked off my back foot, ready to give chase. But barely one step into my sprint, I was forced to stop abruptly when Mitch slid between me and my goal.

Under my breath, I muttered a quick curse at yet another cock block. Then I looked at Mitchell's face and any further complaints were stopped short. I hadn't seen him in a few days. He had swapped days off with one of the other junior staff and vanished like a ghost. Despite the time off, he looked like shit. He was sporting a fading black eye and a patched-up, but still obviously split lip.

"Fuck, what happened to you? You look like hell," I sneered.

His lips curled back in some distorted snarl. "As if you don't know." He rolled his shoulders back, hardening his posture. "I'm sure those good little soldiers of yours couldn't wait to report back."

We might be something like friends. That didn't mean I was going to let Mitchell give me any kind of shit in front of all the junior staff still surrounding us. I grabbed hold of his sweatshirt and hauled him out onto the deck, away from any prying, or worse, gossiping, junior staff. The doors shuttered closed behind us, cutting off the lingering chatter from inside. Roughly, I shoved him against the railing.

"What are you talking about, Greer?"

He brushed his shoulders off, straightening out his sleeves. He didn't look at me either, at least not right away. It took a minute or two of him posturing before he was willing to face me. Even then, his eyes snaked side to side. My thin patience gave out.

"Get on with it," I grumbled.

His tongue dragged over his teeth, and then he finally opened his mouth. "Look, bro, I know you and those two dickweeds have some sort of history with the Barrett girl, and we're friends." We're not. We never have been. The only thing we have in common is hockey. I gave up on friendship entirely five years ago. Best decision I ever made. Not that it mattered since it was clear he had some whole sad story to tell me. "But that girl's hot as hell, so when I bumped into her outside the office real late at night, I figured I'd shoot my shot, ya know?"

I gritted my teeth and swallowed the rising need to choke him. He must have seen something in my expression that spooked him because his story began to spill out of him much quicker.

"Well," he gulped uncertainly. "She let me. Fuck man, she probably would have let me fuck her right there against the wall." As he kept talking, his voice became wistful, like the asshole was reminiscing. "I had just got my fingers right where she needed them..." The audible crack of my knuckles cut him off. I never wanted to know the end of that sentence, and the only reason I didn't crush Greer's windpipe right then and there was what he said next. "It never went any further though because Brennon and that weirdo Rothberg appeared out of nowhere and jumped me from behind. Before I knew it, they were kicking my ass and..."

"And what?" I snarled.

"Look, it's embarrassing, okay?"

Like I gave a shit about his embarrassment.

"It was all I could take to get away before those two beat me up even worse."

I barked a laugh. "Xavier and Brennon did this to you?" But then the images of Toni sucking Brennon's cock resurfaced in the back of my mind. Snapshots of the way he had towered over her, proprietary, owning her while I stood on the outside watching and any humour I might have found at Mitchell's pathetic story soured. It was probably a good thing because he looked seconds away from trying to kick my ass. Not that he could, but that was the last thing I needed right now. I adopted a reconciliatory tone. "Sorry, man, I didn't mean it like that. I really didn't know."

He let his own anger slide away. "Yeah, well..."

"Seriously, bro, I didn't. And honestly, that pussy is not worth the hassle. Trust me."

He quirked an eyebrow.

"She's been slutting it up all over the place. You're not the only one who's gone there, if you know what I mean." I raised my eyebrows at him suggestively.

"Seriously?" he asked with wide eyes.

"Seriously," I confirmed. "And sticking your dick in crazy is never the move. Believe me, that girl is a one-way ticket to an STI." I slapped my hand against his shoulder and turned us both to look out over the Centre Circle. The sole sources of light around us were the large exterior lights that hung from the dining hall roof. We stood together in silence. Tonight had been full of unexpected feelings and new information. It didn't start out that way, but with a little reflection, I couldn't say I was angry about what I learned. I was also feeling more charitable toward the asshole beside me so yet again, I patted his back.

"I'm sorry you got your ass kicked." I wasn't, because the thought of him finger-fucking Toni made my jaw tighten. "But I want you to know this won't go unpunished."

He smiled cruelly. “Hell yeah, bro,” before giving me a slap on the arm in thanks and leaving me to my own plotting. The idiot never stopped to question who I planned to punish. Not Xavier or Brennon, because honestly, I was impressed. I didn’t think either of them had the stones for that kind of fight. The only person I would be punishing was Toni. She flaunted around this place like she was untouchable, surrounded by her little pack of friends. Let’s see how invincible she feels when I tore them away from her.

The thrill of victory thrummed in my veins as I jogged along the path toward my cabin. My plan was to grab the MSU rugby shirt Michele had bought me for my birthday back in April from my cabin floor before dashing back to the girls' section. She would almost certainly be in Foxglove, so tracking her down wouldn’t be too hard. Except, when I rounded the corner from the dining hall, an unexpected light from the Creative Cluster caught me off guard. It was nearly midnight, well after even senior staff were supposed to be in bed, so there could only be one reason those lights were still on. Michele was nothing if not committed to her job.

Three skipped steps were all it took to carry me from the main path to the edge of the big square windows that lined all four sides of Agonde’s creative headquarters. The interior of the building was fully illuminated. All the overhead lights were on and from the shadows, it was enough that I could watch Mich move gracefully through the space. Her hands were full. The left held paper plates she was dropping one by one like she was setting the table for a meal, while the right was full of stacks upon stacks of folded tissue paper. Every few steps, she paused and dropped the lot, but just long enough that she could arrange the various colours of the delicate paper in neat stacks along the table. I watched her for a few minutes. When she finished setting up the last of the tables, only then did I stomp inside.

She jumped a whole foot in the air. “Holy crap! Cole!” She rubbed her chest. “You scared me!”

I apologised, stepping further into the well-lit room. I had spent many an afternoon in this pine box as a kid, mostly with Toni, but it was never my domain. Brennon’s maybe, considering the screened-in deck that lined the back half of the building was home to most of the camp’s guitar collection. But never mine. Xav and I only ever stepped foot in here because of them. Now I was here for something and someone entirely different.

“Sorry again, Mich.” I softened my expression as much as I could. “I just wanted... no, needed to talk to you.”

She froze in the centre of the room and sucked in a deep breath before replying. “Okay, Cole.”

“You can keep setting up.” I jutted my chin toward the supply closet. “I don’t want to slow you down. I just...”

My nerves got the better of me, and I had to swallow thickly around the words before spitting them out, gruffer than I’d initially intended. “I wanted to talk about us. About getting back together.”

With every syllable out of my mouth, her posture drooped and her whole body seemed to retreat further away from me, one step at a time.

"Cole..."

"No." I cut her off. "Just listen, Michele. I know you said you needed time, but we're right together. I know it." I stomped my foot. The floor shook beneath my sneakers. "I know it! You just let your friends convince you that wasn't true." I had planned to keep my cool, but now that the words were out there, I couldn't seem to keep the frustration from my voice.,

"But you should never have let them brainwash you. Especially not Toni..." and the story Mitchell had told me tumbled out faster than I could help myself, "...and then after leading him on, tonight I caught her with Grace's dick in her mouth! Like one guy wasn't enough for her! Mitchell had no idea! I bet Bren doesn't either! She's a..."

I paused, only because Michele's normally open expression pinched tightly. Her blue eyes shrunk to pinpoints, and she pulled taut before popping open in a shocked 'O'.

"Did you come here tonight because you thought slut-shaming Toni would make me want you back?" she shouted, incensed.

"No! Mich, I..."

"Because you can fuck right off with that attitude, Cole Michaels." I knew she was serious because I might swear like a sailor, but I've only ever heard her do it a handful of times. In our entire relationship.

"Michele—" I tried again, pleading her name, but she wouldn't let me explain.

"No, Cole. I told you Toni had nothing to do with this. I told you I needed time."

"I know. I know," I begged. "I swear, Mich, but I love you, and I can't stand to see her poison that. She's tearing us apart." My voice was cloying and desperate by the time I stopped talking. Not that it did any good. With every word, Michele backed away from me until she was practically pressed against the closet door.

"No, Cole, she isn't," she said, starkly calm. "All these months, Toni's never said a single negative thing about you. Not one. At least not in front of me."

I tried once again, advancing on her, "But she—"

"Cole! Stop!" she yelled, a thin needle of fear piercing her voice and stopping me, too. There was a note of hysteria there, and her arms banded across her body protectively, "This isn't you! This is your father talking!" Her mention of him sent blood rushing to my neck, and I wanted to shake any thoughts of Carl Michaels right out of her. Without noticing, I took even more steps in her direction, but she finally cried my name a second time. "Cole! You're... you're... scaring me," she stuttered, and it paralyzed me. She was afraid. Michele. My girlfriend of more than two years was scared. Of me.

The adrenaline rush that came with the anger drained, like flames that had been doused, and I immediately backed away. My arms dropped. I didn't even realise I had raised them. No wonder she was scared of me. My posture was a mirror image of one I had been on the receiving end of way too many times.

"Mich... I—"

"I think you should go." She flicked her eyes between me and the door. "And I think you should ask yourself who you're really mad at, Cole."

Horrified at her reaction, at the terror I had caused someone I cared about, I listened and backed up toward the door. "I'm so sorry, Mich. I'll go," I promised.

She breathed a sigh of relief.

Before I turned to grab the doorknob, I croaked one more, "I'm sorry, Mich," and then let the flimsy hollow thing close behind me. The lights from inside threw my shadow out in front of me, a hulking, ugly thing stretching to join the dark. I should have headed east toward my cabin rather than retracing my steps back toward the Centre Circle. It was a slow trudge, more than a walk, each step filled with remorse and a desire to kick my own ass. The last of the lights in the dining hall were off once I got there, and I moved along the path purely by memory. The dark hides the buildings and the small pockets of trees that surround them, but that didn't stop me from picturing the look on Toni's face that first day back in May when she stood in front of the office with Jack or from imagining the sounds she made when she let Mitchell press her against the wall of that same building. My ire pistoned back through me at every step.

I tried to protect us all from falling back under her spell, to stop this from happening, but I could admit now, I had failed at every turn because I was too soft. Too weak to do what I now knew needed to happen.

There was a reason Toni stopped using the Barrett surname. Deep down, I had known it all along. Too well did I remember the newspaper and TV interviews that followed the trial. The ones where a desperate-sounding Frank Barrett pleaded for the return of his children. Eventually, the news reports faded, but Toni never reappeared. She'd been too busy hiding in plain sight ever since, as Antoinette Hillis. And with that knowledge, I was confident I could finally fulfil the promise I'd made back in May; the promise to ruin her life.

Despite the clouds obscuring any starlight overhead, it was a short and easy walk to the staff parking lot. I scrounged a few measly coins from my pocket and ducked inside the small wooden box that framed the staff payphone, dialling a number I hated to know by heart. The line connected after five rings, and without waiting for a greeting, I spat a greeting of my own.

"Old man."

True to form, my father's slurred voice groaned down the line. "Well, if it isn't my ungrateful son." I didn't even say a word before he yawned, "Does this call have a purpose, Cole? Your old man is busy."

"Busy getting wasted?" I retorted, unable to help myself.

"Listen here, you little cunt, I work fucking hard to make sure you have a shot at something, so you don't turn out as useless as your whore mother." His mention of her threw my heart into a vice. I almost hung up, just to spite him, but his payback would come later. For now, this was about a different vendetta.

I barked, "Shut up, old man. I have something important to tell you."

And he panted like he just pissed himself. "Finally. Who called? A scout? An agent?"

"No, nothing like that." I could practically feel his drunk, overweight frame sag against the fridge in disappointment and it made me smile. And though I'd felt so sure of myself as the phone rang and rang, now that I had to say the words, it felt like I was trying to swallow around a golf ball. I cleared my throat, willing away a newfound chill that crept across my shoulders, and finally managed to say,"I found Antoinette Barrett."

Chapter Thirty-Two

Francis

I found her. My sister. She ran from me. And sure, it was exhilarating trying to chase her down, but after months of trying to find her, I was nearing my breaking point. Then our father got a call. Thanks to one of his idiotic staff, we finally knew where she was. And now she won't escape me, not ever again. And if she tries, well then, she'll live to regret it.

In the back of the plush town car, I reached down and patted my gun, a Combat 9mm, affectionately. Dad gave it to me when I went back to him, as a welcome home gift. Picking up that phone call was the best thing I ever did. When he finally found me back in April, he made me an offer to rule at his side. He reminded me that my mother was selfish, a whore. She didn't deserve us and had never taken care of us properly. If we had stayed with him, I'd be a prince of Barrett Hills by now and no one would have dared take my sister from me. He swore that if I joined him now, Antoinette and I would never have to be apart again. The months when she went off to that school were the worst. I hated them. Hated the people she met and talked to and worked with.

With Dad's help, she'd be entirely mine. And his. My father would use her to secure the future of our empire. His other interests lay elsewhere, while there would be nothing to stop me from chaining Antoinette where only I could hear her scream beneath me. And when she cried, I'd use every tear. It would be perfect. Father had even gifted me a special room in the penthouse. "Soundproofed," he'd said. "I know you'll put it to good use, son."

He was also teaching me the ins and outs of the company so that I could join him in ruling our empire. The lessons he'd started with me so long ago were finally being given space to flourish. And soon, we would take Barrett Holdings to the next level and do it with Antoinette at our sides. My beautiful, angelic sister. Eventually, she would realise the only place she was meant to be was beside me. Until then, though, I would do what I had to do to make her see. If it meant killing those idiotic boys who had tried to weasel their way into her heart all that time ago, so much the better. Really, I would kill anybody who got in my way today. Mikhael had shouted a while ago that we were less than an hour from Camp Agonde and with every mile we got closer, the thrill of seeing Antoinette, of having her all to myself for our long drive home, crawled up my spine. I was having trouble controlling myself, picturing her brown hair wrapped around my fist, her cherry pink lips and soft skin. I almost–no–I would wait. Show her that I'd waited for her. I'd make her see how much I needed her.

She was going to come home. Dad had a plan. For both of us.

Chapter Thirty-Three

Toni

The next two weeks with Xavi and Brennon were like something out of a dream, or my childhood memories, if I had ever dared to dream of my future. Every second we were alone, they were tasting me, or I was tasting them until we were all left sweaty and panting, exhausted and sated. But that didn't even come close to the best part–it was the smiles, laughter, and joy. It was a homecoming after a journey that was never supposed to last as long as it did. And sure, maybe in the darkest parts of the night, when I lay beside Brennon or curled into Xav, I could feel our hearts thumping out a collective longing for a boy-turned-man with chocolate brown eyes. We never talked about it, though. We didn't even say his name. It was just one on a list of many things that went unspoken between us, including the torture they'd put me through, the trial, and all the years between then and now.

Still, we dove into each other and time passed like it was nothing, except for the nights that got colder, even as the August days stayed warm. In the far north, the leaves start to change earlier, and all over camp, green became yellow became gold. Every day on the dock, the kids complained about the shifting temperature of the water, but still, we all remained swept away in the magic of summer. That uniquely distilled feeling that this is time set apart from our real lives and real worlds. And I revelled in it, right up until it came crashing down around me.

One morning, just a week before the summer was due to end, after yet another night falling asleep between Brennon and Xav, I woke up with a start at the sound of my phone buzzing against the hard cabin floor.

"Ignore it," grumbled a sleepy Brennon before kissing me on the shoulder and pressing me back down into the mattress. I hadn't told them about my little money problem or the fact that I had likely already been kicked out of school for not paying my tuition, so they couldn't understand the anxiety each vibration was pigging through me. "Can't," I mutter, "Might be my mum."

Neither of them had ever been early-risers. Even when we were kids, I remember them both complaining about having to get up for breakfast. And camp breakfasts are like a kid's dream–pancakes, bacon, sugary cereals, and everything you could ever want. Still, these two complained. And not much seemed to have changed. So, when I untangled myself from between them, they shifted a little, but once I was free, I turned to see their bodies drift together in my absence. Xavi pressed his bare chest to Brennon's, and Bren's long arm draped around Xav's waist, pulling their bodies tight together.

Meanwhile, my pyjamas, normally so comfy, felt like a poor substitute for being in the middle of that man-sandwich. I reached for my phone without looking at it. The second I was done listening to the stupid voicemail, probably letting me know that I was officially booted from RRU, I was going to crawl back into that bed and console myself by kissing their perfect pecs and maybe the rest of their bodies, too. But when I lifted the phone from the floor and the screen lit up with his familiar number, a feeling of wrongness, of dread, crashed down over me. I darted for the door and snuck outside. Pressing my back into the wood, I sunk to the ground and curled my knees to my chest before pressing the phone to my ear.

I cued up the message and hit play.

"Antoinette," his voice took me to task. "I've been looking for you. *We've* been looking for you. I love you, sister. More than Father. More than you deserve. And still, you hide from me?"

His voice got icier and crueller as the message went on. "But we finally found you. And now I'm going to come get you. 9 a.m. tomorrow, I'll be at those camp gates. Be there. Because if you're not, I won't be happy."

My blood froze in my veins. I had just over twenty-four hours before Francis showed up. My mind flashed to images of Xavi and Brennon. I considered explaining, telling them the whole truth. Maybe there was some hope that what we had found over the last few weeks was enough to keep them from hating me again. But Fran's message wasn't over.

"Oh, and sister, come alone. I know those bastards who tried to take you from me back then are still there, and if they try to stop me, this time Dad says I can kill them. And it would be my pleasure." It's said almost jokingly.

I could practically hear his sinister smile over the call.

"You are mine."

In what was becoming a recurring theme in my life, another man who tortured me hung up on me and, just like with my father, left me reeling. My lungs constricted and even though I was already seated in a small ball, I hugged my knees even tighter. I cast a useless prayer that I was still asleep and the call had just been part of a nightmare I was about to wake up from. But I knew already the nightmare was real, and as I sat there expecting to break, no tears came. Just shivers, and a telltale flip-flopping in my belly that would probably be with me for the rest of my life. I was cold, and now I needed to be empty. I needed to purge the terror of my brother so I could get the hell on with today. Shoving off the wall, I tip-toed around the side of the small wooden building and leaned my hand against the wall. I bent at the waist and drove the fingers of my other hand into my mouth. It took less than five seconds for bile to rise and vomit to follow. I threw up over and over. Until there was nothing left and my ribs ached from exertion. I wiped my mouth against the bottom hem of my tank top. I had no idea what I was going to do or what the hell I was going to say to the two men in my life, but I had twenty-four hours to figure it out.

When I went back inside the cabin, I squeezed some toothpaste on the tip of my finger, hastily brushing away the taste of sick. After a quick pop outside to spit, I stripped off my sick-covered tank and snuggled back between the two men still asleep in my bed. Not long after, Xavi showed signs of waking. It was almost breakfast time, and Brennon still snored beside us. The second Xav realised my breasts were exposed, he turned me and brought one nipple and then the other into his mouth, kissing, sucking, and eventually nipping each between his teeth. The sharp bites made me chew my lower lip to restrain mewls of delight, as his teasing caused heat to spread between my legs and a low pressure to build in my abdomen. It didn't take long before I couldn't fight back the sounds, and when I broke down and begged, "Xavier, please, I need—" My voice woke our sleeping bedmate.

"What is it that you need, Birdie?" growled Brennon in his sleep-soaked voice.

"She wants to cum, Bren," replied Xav, briefly lifting his lips from against my left tit. "But I'm not sure she's earned it yet."

"Please!" I begged again.

Brennon blinked a few times before sitting up to survey the scene. I was sure I looked like a desperate slut splayed out for Xavi the way I was. But under Brennon's heated stare, I was more turned on than ever. After a few seconds of misery, he shook his head and said, "Uh-uh. I can't help you." And then he launched me over him and replaced me in the centre of the bed.

"You're both bad, getting started without me, and now you both need to make up for it."

I knew there was something between them. I mean, I had seen it with my own two eyes, and then Bren and I had even talked about it, but I hadn't really experienced it up close and personal yet. So far, the nights we had spent together, they had been focused on me. I guess I had gotten a bit spoiled. Not that I was complaining about the idea of them being together like that because watching Xavi and Brennon in the woods had been one of the hottest things I had ever seen. I was absolutely up for whatever Brennon was about to suggest.

He pulled my duvet down to reveal his cut lines and the top of his boxers. The head of his hard dick was already poking out the top. I looked across him to Xav, who looked back at me, uncertainty and worry written all over his face.

I wanted to put him at ease, to show him I wanted to see this, so I brought my hand to rest along Brennon's length and asked, "How?"

"I want you both. Both your mouths. Together."

I gulped, and my pussy gushed at the idea and the order. I pushed down his shorts so his hardness was fully exposed before gripping it in one hand. Then I leaned over him.

"Xavi?" I asked tentatively.

"You sure, T?" His voice riddled with nerves.

"So sure." I nodded back and smiled up at him as excitement at what we were all about to share took over. Then I leaned down and kissed the head of Brennon's cock. I lifted up, reaching over Brennon, and kissed Xavi's mouth. I hoped my kiss was enough to show him how much I wanted this. When I pulled away, he blushed, gave me a shy smile, before sliding his body down so he could lick along Bren's expose hip bones.

Slowly, one tentative kiss, and then one lick at a time, we tasted our rockstar until neither of us could resist and both of our mouths found his shaft at the same time. Moving in sync, we kissed and sucked, sometimes letting our tongues find each other around him. When that happened, Brennon, who watched us both rapt, groaned with pleasure. He let us take our time until we found our rhythm, and then he took over, holding the back of our heads and ordering, "Mouths open. Tongues out." And then he started to buck his hips, faster and faster until his movements grew jerky and with a final thrust he came against my tongue and Xavi's.

"Clean me," he ordered again. And I couldn't help it. Neither could Xav it seemed, as we each licked the mess from his lower stomach. While we did, he petted our hair and hummed his satisfaction. "Such perfect toys. You both do that so well." I looked at Xavi, whose cheeks were flushed pink again thanks to the praise, and smiled. He gave me a shy smile back, and I leaned across to him again, this time kissing his soft lips. He tasted like Brennon.

When the guys left thirty minutes later, after they took turns using their fingers and tongues to make me cum, I got dressed for what would be my last day at Agonde unless I could figure something else out. If I couldn't, then I would leave with Francis, because I could never, would never, let him hurt them. Not even Cole. And besides, there were too many other people here, kids and other staff, who might end up as collateral damage if he decided it didn't matter. My brother was a loose cannon at his best. After months in our father's company, what little impulse control he had was probably long gone.

After breakfast and our usual staff huddle, I zoned in on one person–the Director. I needed answers about what happened to Holly. His response from two weeks ago still didn't sit right. The last time I had asked, he had practically barked, "She's fine. Gone, Toni. Focus on doing your job with the kids who are still here!"

Now, heading into, potentially, my last morning here, I couldn't shake my need for answers. The second the director dismissed us, I ducked and headed after him. He moved fast, and even though I was faster, I got caught up in the crowd as the other staff mingled together in pockets. Before I could get to him, someone grabbed me and tugged my arm until I spun in place. When I stopped, I stood in a circle with Abbi and Michele, both of whom eyed me with concern.

With a nervous giggle, Mich asked, "Did those two boys of yours keep you too late, Toni?"

"What she means is that you look like crap, girl," Abbi cut in matter-of-factly.

"Thanks, Abbs."

"Sorry, girl, but it's the truth."

"I know. It was a late night."

"Details?" She grinned and lifted her eyebrows suggestively.

I shook my head. It wasn't the boys who had worn me out. It was fear. Thankfully, she let the subject drop, maybe because of my response or because Bella came bounding up to join us. In her softly accented voice, she inquired where we were all headed. "I have a free programme period this morning, wanna hang?"

With a cough, Michele was first to answer. "Can't. I actually, uh, have to dash now. I have a lot of prep to do before kids show up." And before any of us could say anything, she jogged away in the direction of the Creative Cluster.

"Sorry, girl, I can't either. I've got my level three kids' class first period. Speaking of which," I turned to Abbi, because if anyone other than the director would know about Holly, it would be her. "Have you heard any updates about how Holly is doing?"

Abbi frowned. "Not much. After you asked, I spoke to Jack. He suggested I call her house and even gave me the number. I spoke to her sister."

"Sister?" In the month I had taught the girl, she never once mentioned a sister. Mum, Dad, sure, but never a sibling.

"Yeah, her older sister, Elizabeth. She was kind of a bitch. Refused to let me speak to her, but promised she was doing well." She shrugged. "Sorry, girl, wish I could tell you more."

I shook my head again. Something wasn't right, and now I might never get a chance to figure it out.

"If you get a chance, call again for me, would ya? I just want to make sure she's okay."

Abbi and Bella both looked back at me with touches of pity on their faces. I could live with that if it meant Abbi followed through. "Promise, Abbs?"

"I promise," she sighed, before turning to Bells. "I've got some planning to do for the final section campfire next week, but you can come help if you want?"

"Sounds good," she answered. "Between you and me, we'll make sure it's not just sad white people music."

We all laughed, even though we all knew sad folk music was my sweet spot. As my chuckles faded, I looked around the Centre Circle. The groups of kids and staff that usually hung around after meals were breaking apart and heading off in various directions. It was a sign that there wasn't much time before I had to be at the dock, but I lingered, anyway. There was a weight in my gut that reminded me over and over I might not get another chance to thank these girls for the way they'd embraced me.

I cleared my throat. "Listen, I gotta go, but, um, I love you both, okay?"

"Toni, are you okay?" Bella asked me again.

I nodded around the lump rising in my throat. If I thought too hard about saying goodbye to them or about what my brother would do to them if he knew how much they mattered to me, well, my last shreds of control would come apart completely.

As if she sensed my uncertainty, Abbi reached for me and pulled me into a hug. Her newly conditioned hair smelled like coconut and she whispered to me, "I know we don't know what's up, but something is and you can talk to me. Talk to us."

I froze against her and mumbled, "It's nothing."

She let me go and when I stepped back, her face was worried but resigned. "We love you too, girl. But I guess you better get going."

Equally worried, Bella reached for my arm and whispered, "Find us later if you need to talk, okay?"

"Okay," I replied and then waved them off as I headed for the trailhead that would take me toward the Activities Field and the docks.

The rest of my day passed by in a blur. I tried to take moments where I could, to appreciate the gifts the universe had given me this summer. The kids I helped, the friends I made, all of it. But mostly, I kept to myself. Too much time with the girls or with Xav or Bren, and one of them was bound to realise something was up and I was one question away from spilling, of putting someone I cared about at risk, and I had made a promise to myself that after mum, I would never do that again.

It wasn't until later that night that Xavier finally caught up with me. I skipped socialising, complaining to the girls of a migraine and the need for some extra sleep. I made a brief appearance at tonight's senior social, a game of co-ed Pictionary, before heading back to my cabin to pack. I wasn't about to leave all my shit behind, so I had started with my bedding and toiletries, carrying them out to where Betty still sat so comfortably in the parking lot. Surely Francis would at least let me drive her back tomorrow. I couldn't just abandon her here, after all. That would be a bit suspicious. As I shuffled along the dirt path, I collided with something solid, and before I knew it, my bedsheets were being scooped out of my arms, leaving me staring at Xavier's smiling face.

"Wild girl, you're not leaving me, are you?" he joked.

"No," I lied. "Just starting to pack. I've got my spare sheets on the bed."

"Let me help you! Brennon's got late-night patrol duty tonight, so somebody's got to keep you company."

"I get you all to myself?" I smiled and a child-like grin spread across his face, and he nodded. He let me lead as I continued toward the parking lot. After all, I needed to check that the old girl would start if I needed to drive her off tomorrow. When I dropped my toiletries bag on the closed trunk and whipped out the keys to unlock it, Xavier blurted, "That's your car?"

"Uh, yeah, Xav, meet Betty."

"Betty?"

I tapped the lid of the trunk gently as I opened it. "Yep," I popped. "This is Betty. She's not much to look at, but she's been my ride or die for a while now."

"This is the car you drive?" he asked again with shock in his voice.

"Yes? Why are you so surprised?"

He stared at me, and then at my crappy car, and back again. His smile faded bit by bit before it disappeared entirely and stone-faced, he asked just one of the questions we had been avoiding for so long.

"Didn't your dad buy you an X5?"

I didn't answer.

"Toni," he lashed out. "Where have you been for the last five years? Why did you disappear after the trial?"

I couldn't answer. I had waited five years for a chance to get the boys I loved to listen to me and now, here one of them was, asking the question I always wanted them to ask, and all I needed to do was meet him halfway. A short explanation would do the trick. But getting my mouth to open, getting any sound to leave my lips, was fighting a lifetime's psychological battle.

He dropped my bedding in the dirt and neither of us reached for it. Instead, he snatched my arms and hauled me until my back pressed against Betty's doors.

"Tell me, T."

"My father is a monster," I croaked. He stared at me, brows knit as I looked away from him while I explained. I couldn't stand to watch the love leave his eyes when he found out how damaged I actually was. "The first time my father came into my bedroom unannounced, I was five years old. The memories are fuzzy, but back then, he just wanted me to... to... touch him. But eventually, that wasn't enough." Those horrific images didn't need to haunt anyone else, so I didn't go into too much detail. Just enough for Xavier to understand.

"But when I turned fourteen, I started to age out of his *preferences."* I gagged over the word. "But that didn't mean he was done with me. Turns out, he'd been grooming his replacement for years, and just before I left for camp that last summer, my brother took over where my father had left off. When I got home, I finally broke down and told my mum. That's what kicked off the whole divorce, not any affair."

I watched my normally stoic man break. His knees buckled even as he used my crappy car to hold himself up. "Oh my god," he cried, reaching for me. I stepped away. Now that I had started, I needed to tell him everything.

"I did kill Nick, Xav, you should know that. But only because he tried to..." I couldn't say it, so I skipped ahead hoping he would get it. "It triggered me. I blacked out. The last thing I remember even now is reaching for a rock on the ground. I couldn't tell you. I loved you all so much, and I was so scared."

I finally looked at him again, and he seemed to be struggling to hold himself up. He tried to speak, and his voice broke over the words. "Toni, I-I... Oh my god, we..."

"It's okay, Xav."

"No. No, it's not." He seemed to stagger in place. "How can you look at me? At us?" He was spiralling into the past, and I needed to put a stop to it.

"Back then, I couldn't." I squeezed my eyes shut for a second as memories of the days and weeks after the trial threatened to drag me back.

"But that's why I tried to write it down. I poured so much truth into those letters. About what happened to me, what happened with Nick, all my regrets about that day in the forest. I wrote to tell you all I loved you. That I couldn't face kissing Nick, not really, because your faces wouldn't stop flashing through my mind. And when he touched me, I just wanted it to be you."

I paused to catch my breath. "But Xav," I grasped his solid forearm and pulled him until his arms surrounded me, barricading me against my car, "none of that was your fault. We were all just kids. There was nothing you could have done," I pleaded.

"Toni. I—" his voice broke as he pushed out the words. "I'm sorry."

Tears were welling in the corners of his eyes. I hated his sadness. I knew tomorrow would likely bring more. I still hadn't come up with any solutions for my Francis problem, but I didn't want to feel any more sadness tonight, so I implored, "There is nothing to apologise for. I'm not sad, Xav. I'm grateful.

He looked at me like I had lost my mind, but I continued, "I'm grateful we found each other again. Look at where we are. For the last five years, I didn't even dare to dream that this was a possibility!" He tried to pull away from me but I tore him back. "No! Look." I gestured between us, and the way my chest was pressed against his hard body. He didn't say a word, and I knew it was a lot to digest, so I turned my back to him briefly so I could unlock the car doors.

"Come sit with me." I opened the door and directed him into my backseat. He squeezed his body into the car and sat with his head in his hands. I got in behind him and neither of us spoke for a while. Eventually, I tucked my knee into the seat and faced him. "Xav—"

"You don't seem to get it, Toni." He sighed, dipping his forehead to mine. "You were our sun. We orbited around you. God, it was like I needed you to breathe back then. When you left us, our whole universe fell apart." He paused and swallowed. "And now that I know what you went through. That everything you did back then was because you didn't have a choice, and worse, that we didn't see it or do a fucking thing to stop it. How can I ever forgive myself?"

I didn't have any answers for him. The heaviness of his emotions smothered me and sadness for the boys I loved so much filled my eyes with tears. I just held him and put every bit of love I had ever had for him into our touches. When his body softened into my touch, I knew it was time to ask a question I had wanted the answer to for a long time. I wasn't sure either of us could handle talking about it, but tonight was a night for truths, so I worked up my courage and asked anyway, "What happened with the three of you?"

"Nothing. And too many things, really."He sighed. "It happened really slowly at first, but the empty space where you used to be just kept getting wider and wider until none of us could reach across it."

"If that's true, then why do you still work here, Xav?" I whispered. "I see you, you know? You're almost always alone. You don't join in. You haven't made other friends. So, why?"

"Same reason as always, Nettie."

"Rachel? Still?" I ask. "After all this time? You haven't got another option?"

"Did you, when you came back here?" he replied, and it shut me right up, because no, I didn't. And the knowledge that we were both in the same boat hit me like a gut punch. We were still just carrying the weight of the fucked up nonsense our families put us through. Wanting to bridge the gap I had made between us with my questions, I extended my open hand toward him, hoping he would understand.

When he slipped his fingers between mine, in the back of my junker car, I smiled my first truly weightless smile in five years. Holding Xavi's hand had the lonely fifteen-year-old inside me cheering. God, how I had missed him. Missed them. Since that night in my cabin, it felt like he and Brennon had coloured in the empty lines of my life. Hell, it wasn't just them, either. Abbi, Bells, Mich–each of them had painted unique colours back into the black-and-white world I'd been living in. And now, I just wanted more, a full kaleidoscope of colours. I wanted everything. Including sex.

Sex had always been a powerful weapon in my life, just never mine to wield. It was always something used against me, foisted upon me unwanted and never, not ever, chosen by me. Just once, I wanted to be the one to choose. And as I looked at Xavi, I knew my choice was already made. To get what I wanted, I manoeuvred my body over his, so that I was straddling his lap with our hands still clasped. His free hand slipped beneath the mane of my hair to cradle the back of my neck. His touch felt like an invitation. Granted my car was pretty tiny, so he was probably also keeping me from knocking my head against the roof.

I leaned toward him. "Xav," I prayed his name, "I might have been your sun, but you three were my Junes, Julys, and Augusts. My stars, my moon, and my whole damn universe. I loved you. I still love you."

His brown eyes shone in the pale, yellowed car light as he whispered my name. "Nettie—"

"No. Let me finish." I pressed my hand to his chest. "None of us can go back and change all the moments we missed."

He let out a sad laugh. "If I could, trust me, wild girl, I would." His smile and words were tinged with regret, then he smirked and said, "I could have had years worth of Toni-related material in my spank bank." We both laughed softly. Then he moved our joined hands down my body with the lightest of touches. It was teasing and comforting all at once, and I couldn't help but smile. I swatted him softly. "Jerk-off material aside, Xav, I don't want you to say something you don't mean just because, but I need you to know, I really mean it. I love you."

He looked down at me with those shining dark eyes. "Look at me Toni," he urged. I did, and with a certainty I couldn't deny he stared back and said, "I love you, too. Always have."

His words were like a match, burning hot and wild inside me, giving me the courage to ask for what I wanted.

"Xavier," I stuttered. "I want everything we've missed." I pushed forward, putting all my determination into a kiss as our lips connected. Hopefully, he tasted my meaning as my mouth opened for him. When my lips parted, he sat up higher against the seat, kissing me back even harder for a moment before breaking away.

"Nettie," he said, so earnestly, his eyes grilling mine. "Everything?" I could see the doubt and concern. Just a little while ago, that question would have sent me spiralling with fear and rejection. But I was learning a different way of being with them. And it helped that I could feel how much Xavi wanted me, his cock hard beneath my heated core. Talk about a confidence boost. So, I weighed his question and nodded. "Yes, Xav, everything."

Confirmation from me had him diving into action, pulling me back into our kiss while his hands roved over my body and down to my hips, where they gripped tight and started to roll me along his hardness. Every part of it sent sparks through me. He kept up the movement for a while, each arc fuelling more and more desire inside me. Once he was confident my hips could follow the rhythm he'd set, his hands roamed back up my body, shifting under my tank top so he could peel the cups of my bra away. Finding my nipples already hardening, he rolled, pinched, and squeezed to a point of exquisite pain. Every movement had me moaning into his mouth.

When he finally pulled his lips back again, he zeroed in on my movements, and with so much reverence in his voice he muttered against my skin, "My perfect little whore." He then reached for the zipper of my jeans and I lifted my hips trying to create enough space for him to remove my pants, but my car wasn't exactly made for this kind of backseat action, so even once my zipper was undone, we both fumbled for an angle.

"Enough!" Xavi ordered after two minutes of struggle. "If we're going to do this, it's sure as shit not going to be like this."

I wasn't exactly full of solutions. Between my need for him and my own inexperience, I didn't exactly have any practical suggestions to offer. Apparently, I didn't need them either, as Xav took complete control.

"Fuck it," he said, lifting me off his lap and reaching into his pocket. A quick beep sounded nearby before he explained, "Get that sweet ass over to my car." He gestured toward the over-the-top matte black Range Rover I'd been wondering about all summer long. There were other extravagant cars in the parking lot, but none more so than that one. I shouldn't have been surprised it was Xavi's.

"Anddddd?" I dragged out the question, biting my lip in anticipation, remembering his promise to hunt me from so long ago.

"And, my perfect little whore," I still wasn't sure why I liked it when he called me that, but this wasn't exactly the moment to question it, "you're going to drop those jeans so I can taste you properly. You have ten seconds. Now run," he commanded.

Don't ask me why, maybe because there is something wrong with me, but every time Xavi threatened to hunt me down, my pussy throbbed with need, and I couldn't help but obey. So I ran. I practically bolted toward his SUV. I ripped open the door and did my best to tear the pants from my body as quickly as I could.

Slapping my bare ass to his backseat, I couldn't help but notice how buttery soft the leather was against my skin. What a contrast to Betty's. My momentary distraction ended as Xavi stalked toward me, like a moving shadow across the dark. Still, a few feet away, I couldn't see his eyes, but from the angle of his chin, his focus was entirely given over to the apex of my thighs, still clad in my plain cotton thong. What could I say? Fancy underwear was for fancy people, and I hadn't been one of them in a long time. His eyes burned as he got closer.

"Lie back. Panties off." It was another order and one I was happy to obey, although, without the thin layer of fabric, I felt more vulnerable and exposed. It was a reflex to squeeze my thighs together in an attempt to shield myself from view.

Xavi tutted at the action, close enough that he reached out and pushed my thighs apart. "You will not hide from me, beautiful."

"But, Xav—"

"No," he fought back.

"You are mine. This pussy is mine, and you will not keep it from me." His tone was both worshipful and bossy. He continued to spread my legs wider with the demanding press of his hands, and I couldn't help but open for him.

"Perfect," he sighed with devotion against my most sensitive skin before kissing his way up my inner thigh. Each soft press of his lips made me squirm. There was so much wetness between my legs that I was leaving a puddle on the expensive material of his seat. Turned on as I was, I was definitely not prepared for the feeling of his mouth covering my pussy. His tongue slid between my folds, lapping at my taste, and I couldn't stop as I got wetter and wetter with need. When his lips circled over my clit and he started to suck, gentle as he was, there was no stopping the pornographic moan of pleasure that climbed out of my mouth.

He lifted his face and smiled. "That's it, baby. Give me all your moans." Then he dove back in. The feeling became so overwhelming that within seconds, I was bucking and writhing against his face, chasing my release. And he let me. Right up until he didn't.

He pulled back from my body with a mischievous smirk and I panted at his absence.

"Still want me, baby?"

"Xavierrrrr," I practically snarled at him, desperate to regain the high I was chasing.

"Okay, then." He chuckled, before commanding, "Watch."

I looked down my body to where his face was just seconds ago, but now his hard cock was there instead, lined up perfectly against my entrance, and with one hard, fast motion, he thrusted inside.

It hurt. It had been so long. But this was so different from the twisted experiences in my past. Less confusing, less painful, less ruining. It was also so much more. More caring, more heated, and more of everything I could have ever wanted. As he seated himself fully inside me, Xav leaned down over my body and kissed each bit of skin he could reach as softly as possible. He murmured against me, "Fuck, baby, I'm sorry for the pain." And then he pulled back, and looked down with frightened eyes to ask, "Are you okay?"

I focused on him, wanting to put his fears and my own to rest. "Xavier, please!" I begged.

"Please, what, baby?" he answered, concerned.

"Please move!" I cried out, desperate after all the teasing.

He laughed and relaxed against my hips. "Okay, wild girl. With pleasure," before slamming his dick back into me. I felt every inch of him, and with each movement, I craved more and more. Eventually, my hips chased his as our movements synchronised and our touches and kisses got wilder and wilder. I swear at one point I bit him as he shoved back into me, until finally, he pressed his thumb down on my clit and I lost all control, flooding around him before collapsing completely. He continued to thrust into me, praising me the whole time.

"Beautiful girl."

"Your pussy is squeezing me so tight."

"Your body was made to take me."

Each sentence was groaned out until his own release finally caught up with him and he filled me in a way that felt so satisfying another orgasm snuck up on me hard and fast. When it too subsided, all I could do was lie against the car seats and kiss his arms and shoulders as his body rested against mine and his heart pounded into my own. Minutes passed as we stayed like that, until, eventually, he pulled out of me, eliciting one final shiver of pleasure.

"Stay right there, wild girl," he ordered when I attempted to sit up. I did as I was told and laid back, watching as he pulled up his jeans and circled to his trunk. I couldn't see what he was doing, but when the back seat retracted underneath me, I found myself fully laid out. It was like he turned the back of his car into a bed. He then came back around, and using the softest towel and his own soft lips, he gently cleaned up my body and the seat. All the time he murmured about how beautiful I was, and there was no stopping my furious blushes even in the dark. It wasn't long before he was finished. He handed me back my own clothes before returning to grab something else from the trunk. Sitting up, I got dressed and prepared to leave. I didn't want to leave Xav. Not ever again. I wanted to stay here, at Agonde, with him and with Brennon. But it was easier to leave now, to spend tonight apart. Or so I thought.

When he returned, carrying my pile of blankets toward me, I meant to say my goodbyes, but he dropped them around me and ordered, "Lie down, Toni." As he climbed in behind me, I didn't say a word. I shifted deeper into the seat to make space, and because this car was so absurdly large, of course, there was space for him to slip in behind me. He pulled my body against his own until my hips were against his lap, and then he drew several blankets over us. Sleeping beside these boys was like taking a sleeping pill. And before I knew it, I drifted off completely.

When the first rays of sun broke through Xavier's tinted windows, I woke to find his toned arms still wrapped all the way around my stomach. If the sun was up, it meant there wasn't much time before Francis got here and the last thing I wanted was for him to see me with Xav. Knowing Fran, he would kill him and I would do anything to prevent that from happening. Even if it meant lying. Again. With slow pushes and pulls, I shifted out of Xav's hold until I lay beside him. I extended my face to his and kissed him. He woke a little at the sensation because he slowly kissed me back with a satisfied, "Mmmmm."

"It's morning, Xav. I have to go."

"No," he grumbled, like a little kid. And I couldn't help but laugh softly.

"Yes," I said, kissing him again, before I steeled myself and lied, "But I'll see you later today." He smiled before relaxing back to the car bed and back to sleep. It took a few tries, but I finally hauled my body up and over his so I could get to one of the doors. I pushed it open and stepped out into the crisp morning air. I was rapidly running out of time, but I couldn't stop myself from taking one look back at the sleeping man I had no choice but to leave behind.

"I love you, Xav," I said out loud to no one since he was already fully back to sleep, but I prayed somehow he would hear the words or remember them either way. I pushed the car door closed, as softly as I could, and walked away. After the guys left yesterday, I spent most of my free time packing. I was not stupid enough to keep Francis waiting or let him loose on camp property, so I had to be ready to go. I was headed toward the Village when the bleating of a car horn cut me off just as I passed the pay phone where I called Mum all those weeks ago.

I turned to see a familiar black town car, tinted windows and all, lining the camp road. It parked and my brother exited. He was dressed like our father. All in black and formal. Like he was going to a business meeting for demons. His sharp eyes pinned me across the parking lot and he shouted, "Time to go!"

My whole body resisted what was obviously a summons, and my heels dug into the loose gravel of the lot. "I have to get my things!" I shouted back at him.

His brows narrowed, and he unbuttoned his jacket, reaching into the waist of his pants only to grasp the handle of a pistol. "Now, Antoinette," he ordered, pointing the barrel of the gun directly at Xavi's SUV. "It's time to come home, sister. Father has big plans for both of us."

Every cell in my body revolted. My chest seized at thoughts of Brennon and Xavier standing down the end of a gun's barrel. Momentarily, I considered defying him, considered running. And then other faces, Bells and Abbi and Michele and all the innocent kids I worked with all summer, stopped those thoughts. And so my feet started to move, step by step, toward the car until I stood at the door beside my sick excuse for a sibling. He drew his fingertips down my spine and purred, "We're going to have *such* a good catchup on the drive home." I felt the urge to vomit. I didn't. I swallowed the bile and got into the car.

Brennon would hate me for this. Xavi, too, most likely, and Cole, well it would likely just be another reason to despise me. But I would make the same choice a thousand times over. If it was a choice between me and them, I was going to pick them every time. Every. Damn. Time.

When I arrived back here all those weeks ago, I had been so sure that I knew the bitter taste of hopelessness. Things really could always get worse. As I stepped past my brother, who reached for me and stroked my side, unwanted and uninvited, I knew that the past version of me was an idiot. The car ride ahead was going to serve as a final, devastating eulogy for the education and morsels of independence I had fought so hard for, the friendships I had tried to make and remake, and the freed woman I had eventually hoped to become. I was burying her today. That was real hopelessness, and only now had it truly found a home in me.

Chapter Thirty-Four

Brennon

Last night was a late one. Emotions always run high at the end of the summer. Especially amongst the SEs, who've been training hard and playing hard all summer together, and were now just a week from being split up, and heading back to their regular lives. The ones where their parents and trainers controlled every damn aspect, from when they took a shit to what they put in their mouths. That's why I wasn't surprised when Natalia, my co-patroller, and I stumbled across a giant make-out session in the woods behind the Hive at nearly midnight last night. We broke it up, and she dragged the girls back to their side of camp while I dealt with the boys. I couldn't exactly blame them for wanting to get their dicks wet, my dick got hard anytime anyone even looked at me too long when I was their age. Fuck that still happened every time Toni or Xav looked at me now, so I was definitely sympathetic.

None of that showed on my face, though. I slapped on an angry expression and proceeded to spend the next fifteen minutes laying into them about safety and irresponsibility, as I escorted them back to their cabin. And once I slammed the door on their asses, I spent another half hour sitting outside in case they decided to sneak back out. They didn't, and I was eternally grateful when I crawled into my own bed around 1:30 a.m. We'd been mostly staying in Toni's cabin, so it had been a while since I slept in my own bed, and as much as I was craving the feeling of her tight body against me, I needed to sleep. When I woke up the next morning feeling properly rested, I knew I made the right choice.

I guess that the three of us trying to squeeze into one single bed hadn't exactly made for the best sleeps. As I got dressed, throwing on a faded Preaching Pistols t-shirt and black Dickies, I considered dragging another mattress into Toni's cabin this afternoon so we could all get some proper sleep for the next week. As a side benefit, the extra space would give us more room for the very best kinds of activities. Thinking about that kept me smiling all the way to breakfast. The meal was already underway when I arrived.

The staff table, for those of us who weren't assigned to cabins, was on the far side of the room, and I could already see the brown curls I seemed to search for all the time lately. When I wasn't searching for long honeyed hair instead, that was. I strolled up to the table and flicked my eyes sharply at the nurse sitting beside Xav. She squeaked before shifting over to make space for me beside him. Once I dropped down onto the bench, I used my left hand to load my bowl with rice cereal, milk, and several swirls of sugar. Sue me, I've got a sweet tooth. Plus, I was starving after last night. My other hand, meanwhile, snaked its way under the table and onto Xavi's thigh. He had his usual running shorts on, which I appreciated since their loose material made it too fucking easy to glide my hands under their hem and onto his warm skin. I flexed my fingers and squeezed his leg possessively.

He didn't look at me. He just pushed another mouthful of scrambled eggs into his mouth. The only hint of recognition was a slight lift at the corner of his lips. I took that as permission to leave my hand where it was, and while I recounted last night's adventures, my hand continued to exercise my ownership over him, squeezing on and off. Only when I got to the end and found myself chuckling alone at the horn-dog behaviour of teenage boys, did I look at him more directly. He was scanning the room, clearly looking for Toni, since she normally sat at this table, too, and there had been no sign of her so far. I was late. This was something else. She's normally an early bird, and if she didn't show up soon, she would miss the whole meal.

I broke down and asked him directly, "Where's Toni?"

"I don't know," he replied too forcefully, his frustration with her absence showing, before blowing out a breath. "Then again, we had a late night, too, so maybe she's just sneaking in some extra sleep." But the way he started to chew on the inside of his cheek, all while letting his eyes wander back to the main doors, said he didn't believe that at all.

"She'll turn up," I promised, pulling my hand from his thigh to squeeze his shoulder instead, then dropping my voice to little more than a whisper, I teased, "Especially if it was the kind of night I think it was..."

That made him smile for a second.

"It was, Brennon... or at least I thought it was..."

The way his smile dropped again, as quickly as it had come in the first place, had me asking, "What happened?"

"Not here," he bit out. It was a harsh reminder we weren't alone. There was always at least a handful of other staff and nurses who shared this table with us, and this morning was no different. I flashed my eyes around the table, and even though no one was obviously staring at us, the lack of other conversations made it pretty damn clear we were capturing everyone's attention.

"When?"

"Tonight. At the Throw. We need to talk for real."

"For real?" The seriousness of his statement caught me off guard. A low ripple of nerves crawled up my spine. And there it stayed, right through the rest of my morning, making it hard to focus. Which was a real bitch, since I was supposed to be processing final payment invoices for parents, and after making multiple mistakes, I finally broke down and got Riley to take over while I stared out the office windows wondering what the hell went down between Xavi and our girl last night.

When lunch came and went and Toni still hadn't appeared, things only got worse. Xavi's anxiety ramped up to new heights. He squeezed the cutlery so hard that his fork bent in his fists. His whole body vibrated, and his eyes never moved off the dining hall doors. I tried to distract him, unsuccessfully, and when the meal ended, he darted after Abbi and Michele as they headed outside, and I followed suit. We caught up with the girls on the dining hall deck, where the post-meal mob of kids and staff were still circulating. Using the noise and chaos of the crowd to cover the details of our conversation, the two of us whispered our frantic and worried questions. After quizzing them and listening as they swore up and down that neither of them had seen her today, we let them go, both of them now sporting concerned looks that nearly matched our own.

Their lack of information only fuelled more worry, and as they walked away from us, Xavi turned to me with full-blown panic written all over his face. “Where is she, Brennon?”

“I don’t know, Xav.” But questioning Toni’s friends hadn’t been totally worthless. “We should do what they said. Go check her cabin.”

“Nurses first,” he countered. “What if she ran into Greer or something after she left me this morning?”

I blanched for a second before growling, “Xav, I think I really need to know what happened last night.”

“And you will. Later,” he huffed, already a few steps ahead of me and picking up speed as he jogged in the direction of the Nurses' House. I’d never catch up to runner-boy, but I didn’t want to be too far behind either in case she was there.

But no dice. The nurses were nice enough to let us poke our heads into every room, including the treatment rooms. Well, that was after Xavi gave them his most ominous death stare, and maybe I cracked a knuckle or two.

From there, we booked it across camp to the Village, and practically launched ourselves through Toni’s door. There was no sign of her there either, but the fact that her bed was a mess, and her stupid fairy books were still scattered across the floor soothed something in my chest. The one she had been reading for the last two weeks lay in the centre of her bed, bookmark visible between the pages. She hadn't disappeared. She wasn't gone. The Toni I know would never leave her books behind.

Xavier clearly thought the same, and some of the tension dropped from his shoulders beside me. I yanked him into a hug, roughly breathing against him, "She's here somewhere. We'll find her."

He drew back to reply, "We have to, Brennon." His voice shook momentarily before he carried on, "We need to talk to her."

"About what?"

"The past, man, the past."

"No."

"Yes. She and I talked last night. And you–Fuck!--You need to... Have you seen her fucking car?" It was hard to follow his frantic words and that question stumped me.

"What about her fucking car?" He didn't answer. His mouth was downturned and his eyes laced with regret.

"It's...It was... she didn't have a choice, Brennon. Nick. Us. She didn't have a fucking choice." It was my turn to reel backward. I felt as if he'd slapped me.

"And we abandoned her for it!" His volume rose fast and hard.

The obvious rage there pulled me back. Anger like that was much more Cole's speed than Xav's. "Bullshit, Xavi. The trial. We were there!"

"I know," he insisted. "After last night, I just know..."

"You just know? How?" Now I was going to demand an answer. "What the fuck happened last night?"

The answer I got was not the one I ever expected.

"I love her."

"You..."

Before I could choke out any more words or think about what Xav's feelings might mean, the door behind us bolted open, and we turned both expecting Birdie and found Michele instead. Her breathing was ragged, like she had run here, and the same worry we'd left her with was still visible on her features.

"Guys... The director called a senior staff meeting. In his office. Right now."

"What?"

"Why?" Xavi and I both shot back in near unison.

She just shook her head and signalled for us to follow. The three of us jogged to the office in silence. Senior staff meetings were scheduled things, once a week, and always at the same time. In the last three years, we had never had a single one called at random like this. It made my skin itch.

We were the last ones to arrive. Except for Toni and Jack. All the other senior staff were spread out around the director's office, either sitting in the few available chairs or leaning against the walls, bookshelves, and filing cabinets that lined the space.

"Where's our Waterfront Director? Too high and mighty to come when she's called?" Cole grumbled in my direction. He was so full of bullshit. He was just as aware of her as Xavi and I were. Had been this whole time, and ever since he caught us together,

I had noticed him watching her more and more. Now, his brows were creased, and he was just as confused as the rest of us by this meeting. And her absence.

Xavi pulled no punches. “Shut the fuck up, Cole!” And it caught everyone in the room by surprise. All around us, eyebrows shot upward and eyes widened with surprise. Xavi normally sat through these meetings in abject silence, only speaking to answer questions immediately directed his way.

“Well, where the fuck is she then, Rothberg?”

“She’s gone.” It was Jack who answered as the door to his office slammed closed behind him. The whole room stilled. I swear no one even breathed. Except our boss, who strolled behind his desk and sat down, as if he didn’t just drop some bombshell on the rest of us. Fucker.

“Her father called me shortly after breakfast,” he explained. At the mention of her father, a low snarl tumbled from Xavi’s throat beside me.

“It seems Antoinette *Barrett*,” He stressed, like we didn’t all already know Birdie’s true identity, “has been missing for some time and her Father has been desperately trying to find her. He heard a rumour she was back here, and called. She needed to return to West Barrett urgently, and he sent her brother to collect her this morning.”

“Why?!” Xavi barked.

“That’s private, Mr. Rothberg. Her father wishes it to remain so.”

I slammed my arm out, across Xavi's chest, before he could leap at our boss. Jack might be a grade-A asshole, but he's still our boss, and Xavi punching him in the face wouldn't help this situation.

I continued to hold him back while everyone else in the room watched in silence. Only Cole stared directly at us like he was trying to solve some sort of puzzle.

It was Abbi who was finally brave enough to break the silence. "When will she be back?"

"She won't," he replied, making Abbi stiffen and the rest of us flinch. "That's why we need to meet. Although there are only a few days of programmes left, we need to discuss a plan to cover Antoinette's role. Any suggestions?"

Slowly, the other staff begin to speak up, offering ideas and putting forward names of other people with the necessary training to take over for T. But neither Cole nor Xavi nor I say a word. The room might as well have been fucking empty, but for the three of us. And even though it had been a long time since I'd called Cole a friend, our past was enough of a bond that the three of us exchanged looks and a silent message passed between us. There was a conversation to be had between the three of us the second this meeting was through.

It took the better part of an hour for us to parse through Toni's responsibilities and reassign them to other staff members. I didn't utter more than a handful of words. And Xavi didn't speak at all. The longer the meeting went on, the darker his gaze seemed to get, and I couldn't help but be grateful when the whole shitshow finally wrapped up. The only piss-off was that it was now just before afternoon programmes were due to start, and Xavier spent every afternoon with the SEs doing track and field shit. Today was no exception, and it meant that any discussion about what the actual fuck had gone down between Toni and Xavi would have to wait.

And wait, it did. The busy schedule and structure of camp days were usually something I appreciated. Structure was something I craved, whether it was in the patterns of music and the way my hands were forced to move just so to hit the needed notes or sitting in a class where there was an exact order to the zeros and ones to give life to a particular program. It wasn't that I had any issue with mess. One look at my cabin floor, smothered in laundry, or my desk littered with scraps of paper, would tell you I didn't. But I did take issue with having a disordered mind. That afternoon, mine was a mess. I couldn't concentrate on anything or focus beyond the energy it took to pick at the calluses on my fingertips. It was a relief when dinner finally ended.

Xavier left the dining hall first, and I practically threw myself out the doors after him. I was only a couple of steps behind him when we got to Stones' Throw. He was heading toward the rocks, but I grabbed him and pulled him back toward me, slamming my lips into his.

He shoved back at me like he didn't fucking want this. I didn't care. I needed this. If she had fucking disappeared again, I needed to know he wasn't going anywhere. I doubled down, drawing his bottom lip between my teeth to hold him near me. He bit me right back. We were both animals, after all. I pulled back for a second, only to lick the small trail of blood from my lower lip with a satisfied smile.

He frowned and ground out, "I don't know how this happened!"

"I do," I replied beneath my breath, but I could tell right away he either didn't hear me or didn't give a fuck, because words continued to pour out of him.

"We have to fix this."

"This is seriously fucked up."

"He can't do this."

"I'll stop him. I'll get her back."

That's when I finally cut him off., "Xav, there is no fixing this." I reached for him again. "It's just you and me now!" I promised before forcing another kiss onto his mouth, even more passionate than our last. My tongue pressed against the seam of his lips, demanding that he open for me and let me deepen our kiss yet again. I could feel the frown on his face even in our kiss, but I ignored it and grinned back at the feeling of his cock hardening against my thigh. He could moan about Toni all he wanted, as long as he was still here. Still with me. Keeping one hand on his neck to hold him still, the other traced along the edge of his shorts, teasing the lowest parts of his abdomen, but before it could sink any lower, crashing footsteps and a violent roar stopped me in my tracks. My own erection practically fucking wilted as Cole shouted, "What the fuck?!" from behind me.

I tried to hold on to Xav, to ignore Cole and cling to him instead, but he jumped away just the same. His skin was flushed, whether from the heat of our kiss or shame, I couldn't tell, but even thinking it might be the latter made my shoulders tense. Xavi continued to back away from me until his ass was resting on one of the stones, but he didn't look up. Not at Cole and not at me.

"What the fuck did I just see?" Cole asked again, his voice carrying around the Throw like the breeze rattling the trees that surrounded us. One more quick glance at Xav told me he wouldn't be saying shit, so it was on me to say something.

"If you don't know, then it's no wonder Michele broke up with you." I laughed darkly. There was also a smug satisfaction at seeing his fists clench.

"Shut the fuck up, freak."

"Jealous, Michaels?" I taunted. Colour drained from his face, and I took even more joy from watching him panic and choke on any kind of response. Talk about 'protesting too much'. Cole was the definition of it. I wasn't even sure if he was aware since we were still tossing insults back and forth, but I saw it. His whole body angled in Xav's direction and his hazel eyes were full of questions.

When Xavi didn't look up, opting instead to grind his palms into his eyes in frustration, Cole finally tried to steady himself. He rolled his overgrown shoulders back and snapped back at me, "Does your little whore know about—" He couldn't seem to get the rest of the sentence out, though, just jabbing his finger wildly from me to Xav and back.

"Oh, she knew," I answered. A confident smile unfurled on my face while his jaw hung slack for a second at my answer. Credit to Cole, he caught himself quickly, schooling his features into his normally callous mask.

"That's... that is..."

"Not fucking important!" Xavier kicked angrily. Seemed he finally regained his voice.

"We need to talk about what she told me last night!" He leapt to his feet and stomped toward us, stopping in the middle of the ten feet that separated us. I waited for him to turn my way. He didn't. He turned to Cole instead, and I couldn't see the look that passed between them, but I could see Cole's expression. And whatever look Xav shot his way, for the first time in five years, I swear I saw real pain on Michaels' face. That didn't purge or even soften his anger, though. He just cursed us both.

"I don't really want to hear about what you sick fucks get up to..."

"Pffffft... as if you don't," I snorted back, causing the Neanderthal to stalk several steps toward me. My reflex was to brace for the tackle I knew was forthcoming, neglecting that Xavier still stood like a wall blocking us from one another.

"Enough!"

His harsh snap shut the both of us right up. We froze, still feet apart, and like good little soldiers, shifted our focus from each other to him.

"You don't understand!" Xavi screamed at us both. "I was with her last night!"

Cole scrunched his face, but played it off as confusion, shrugging. "And so what? How's that any different from what you freaks have been doing the last few weeks?" Cue my extreme eye roll.

"That's not what he meant you prude! He was *with* her last night." He stared at me.

I explained, "They were *together* together. Neither of us has done that with her yet."

It took a minute, but I could tell the second my words sunk into Cole's hockey-addled brain. His expression blanched, and he tried to launch himself at Xav, but I stepped into the space between him.

"Cole." I commanded. "Before you fly off the handle, fucking listen to what he is saying!"

That shut him up, and together we listened as Xavi talked us through what they shared. Some of it is stuff I had heard this morning, how he woke up alone after the two of them spent the night asleep in the back of his Range. He's a gentleman, so he glossed over their actual fucking, not that it stopped his pupils from dilating nor did it keep the obvious heat from his voice. What he concentrated on was everything that led up to it. He told us about her car, and about what she told him, about the supposed truths she had confessed to him.

The whole thing didn't take long. Maybe five minutes from start to finish, but when Xav finally stopped talking, his eyes shot between my face and Cole's. It was obvious he was anxious for Toni, and for what our response would be.

Cole's reaction spoke for itself. He paled, but he didn't say a word. All he did was turn his back to us both and strode out of the stone circle and off into the forest. His steps were heavy and slow, but not once did he turn around to look at either of us, and soon enough, he was gone, lost behind the thick tangle of trees and underbrush that kept this place hidden for us.

The two of us didn't say a word to each other until the last muffled sounds of his footsteps faded. That didn't mean I didn't feel Xavi's eyes on me the entire time, waiting, expectant. I had no idea how to explain. I didn't know how to do this to him. The truth of our situation wasn't fair, and I was furious that I was left to be the one to break it to him. He was still living the lie. It was etched in his worried features. I, on the other hand, knew that we had been conned. Twice. By the same fucking girl.

"Bren," he begged. "We have to help her! I know something bad has happened, and I know it was her father's doing." He stepped toward me, and I let my arms drop open. What I had to say was going to make him hate me, at least temporarily, and I couldn't resist one last opportunity to have him close. My arms wrapped around him. Xavi's no shrimp, but I'm still a good few inches taller than him, so as I leaned down, my face pressed into his curls, and I inhaled the warm cinnamon smell of him.

"Something bad did happen, Xav," I finally said, squeezing him just once more while I could. "She happened. To us. Again." My words were croaked and my voice hoarse, but he reeled back violently all the same.

"What are you talking about?" he demanded.

"I don't know why she came back here, but it wasn't for us. She was probably here because Daddy Dearest wanted to check on his investment. Or because she missed playing with her three favourite puppets." I kept talking and watching him. His jaw was tightening and expression hardening with every word I said, but that didn't stop me. "She's probably been laughing at us from the start."

He went feral for a second. "You don't fucking get it, Brennon. You didn't see how she was with me!" he insisted.

I had no desire to break his heart any further, but I couldn't seem to stop myself as I let out a pitiful laugh. "Oh, but I do get it. I'm sure it was something. She always was an incredible actress. She fooled me, too. Again."

"You are wrong!" he shouted. "This was him! I know it! He's done something to her."

"She probably just got bored and had his driver come and pick her up."

"What the fuck is wrong with you?" he asked. "Where's the guy who stood on those steps and begged me to give her a chance to explain? To listen? Don't you remember?" he screamed, his voice growing hoarse. "You always fought for her, Brennon!"

"Right until I stopped," I answered, weary with the guilt and self-hatred that had sat so heavily inside me for so long. "But Xav, when I stopped fighting for her, I realised it wasn't worth fighting at all, and I stopped. It didn't seem worth it anymore. I guess it still doesn't."

His face turned bleak. He didn't even try to hide it when his eyes turned glassy and he retreated with hurt.

"So, our friendship wasn't worth it? Isn't worth it? This isn't worth fighting for at all?" The questions were heartbreaking, and

I waited for the tears to finally spill as he was met with my silence, but Xav had always been stronger than people, mostly his father, gave him credit for and the tears never came. At least not his.

When he realised he wouldn't be getting any answers from me, his shoulders slumped with a resigned sigh. "Somehow, I never am worth it. Not to Cole. Not to you. But maybe I can be for her." Without meaning to, I scoffed. Close as we were, I heard his teeth grind. "Silence isn't consent. If it's not an enthusiastic yes, then it's a hell no. She reminded me of that." He barrelled on over any of my half-worded objections. "No. I've lived so long without her voice of hope in my ears that I'd forgotten. Never again."

"Then you're an idiot," I snarled. "She's been playing us this whole time." And then I shoved, pushing him away from me. Steeling his body, he stepped back into the space I had just created between us and fisted the shoulders of my tank top. Xavi, normally so calm, so patient, always content to wait and watch, now showed me a rage I didn't know he was capable of. The corded muscles of his arms shook with it.

"Five years ago, you begged me to listen, to hear her out," he screamed, his disgust with me evident in every word. "And now you can't be fucked?!"

I heard his words, saw his pain, and all I wanted to do was reach for him, to soften and soothe the anger eating him up. Even now, when he couldn't hear the truth, couldn't face the reality that Toni was a deceitful bitch, he was beautiful. Like a fairytale prince, and right now, I was the villain in his story, but soon he'd see it wasn't me. Or at least I hoped so.

For now, he needed someone to vent his anger at because the girl who needed to hear it wasn't around to listen. Classic Antoinette Barrett. Plant dangerous seeds and don't stick around long enough to watch them poison everything.

"I should have listened to you back then, Brennon. Fuck!" he yelled sharply. "I should have been paying more attention. I didn't see it. I didn't want to see it!" He wrestled his hands away again, gripping his curls instead of my shirt. His next words were wistful and desperate. "We could have had all this fucking time. Just think about it." His sad hazel eyes clung to my own and, God help me, I did see it. Instead of five lonely years, the three of us–fuck, maybe even Cole, too–would have laughed and loved and been everything to each other in the same way we always were. Together, we were so much more than the sum of our individual parts. A thousand perfect, imaginary moments flashed through my mind. But that's what they were–imaginary, pretend, not real.

"Or would it all have been a lie?" I asked, knowing it was never meant to be.

He spit at my feet like I was worthless.

"Believe what you want, Brennon. I abandoned her once, and I was wrong. I won't do it again." He blinked slowly, and when his eyes reopened, any warmth–hell, any feeling at all–he'd shown me was gone. With a flick of his hand, he brushed everything between us away. He didn't have any words left for me. I wasn't worth them.

Chapter Thirty-Five

Cole

The flames from tonight's fire should have felt warm. It was certainly fucking big enough. Dave and the crew of site staff piled and stacked wood so high that the thing looked more like some kind of Viking pyre than a folksy campfire. This time last year, I was seated beside Michele right at the front. The two of us held hands while the Director waxed poetic about the summer. Back then, and every summer before, the girls and boys, the juniors and seniors, and even the fucking Elites had found a way to squeeze and mix together across the rows that lined the natural amphitheatre at the Point. Friends sat with friends. Siblings found one another in the dark. This was our night to be one camp. Now, five days since Toni disappeared, not so much. We were a camp divided.

Tonight started with separate section fires, as it always had. I hosted the boys in our small area at the far east end of camp property. The girls and the Elites had done the same, until each group wrapped with a torch-lit ceremony. When the oldest boys' cabin finished their song, part of my job as Section Director was to carry a birch torch, wrapped in gas-soaked towels, to the fire pit and set it alight. Once those flames had flickered to life, I guided most of the camp's male population down the main path, past their cabins, the Hive, the Creative Cluster, and right to the Point. Then I directed them down toward the bonfire already burning away. In the far-cast orange of the firelight, I could see that most of the camp was already there.

When I carried my torch down the slanted hill, I was met by Abbi and SE's director, Natalie. Together, the three of us had added our flames to the one already raging behind the stage. From there, we each navigated to find seats. This time around, Michele ignored me and sandwiched herself between Abbi and Bella. I couldn't be sure, but it seemed like the female staff were doing their damnedest to send a very clear message. Like word of my actions, my role in Holly's accident had got around. Not that I had anyone to blame for that. For the last three weeks I've been plagued by nightmares of that day, waking to the screams of a little girl who isn't there, only to be sick outside my cabin door. I was reaping what I'd sewn tonight. On the left side of the Point, all the girls lined the benches, the youngest at the front and the Elites and Seniors in the final three rows. Except for the very front bench, where all the female staff were seated together, like a line-up of Generals leading an army into battle. They even left an empty space in the middle. In it was a lifeguard's vest and a single whistle, screaming to me and the rest of us on the other side of the campfire exactly how they felt about Toni's absence. Meanwhile, the boys' section's front bench was sparse. Two figures noticeably absent.

Tucked into the shadows at the far side, I expected to find Xavier. Instead, Brennon's spiked hair just barely caught the light. If it hadn't been for Riley seated beside him, I doubt I would have even registered his presence. There were a few other guys sprinkled across the benches, seated alone or in pairs. None of us really sat together, and the spaces between us felt like failures on my part. Looking over my shoulder, my dark eyes roved over the crowd, looking for Xavier, now that I knew he wasn't hiding in his usual shadows.

Songs played, poems were read, and speeches were made before I finally caught sight of his curls. At some point, he had snuck in amongst the girls. He had even placed himself front and centre. A place he always hated to be. He was so close to the fire that the flickers caught every edge of his jawline and the crux of his fingers where they were wrapped supportively with Abbi's. I stared, but he never, not once, turned to look my way. When the director drew the night to a close, thanking us all for another magical summer, I watched my ex and my... I watched her thread her arms through Xavi's and they melted together into the darkness as a singular unit. It was only then that I flipped my attention back to Brennon, only to find that he was gone, too.

For the first time in a long time, I was completely alone when I made my way back to my small cabin. Last year, Mich and I had attempted to have sex, and before that, well, before that, I had made some mistakes. But at least I hadn't been alone. The last day of camp was always a long one. Besides the bonfires, there were programme awards during the day and closing ceremonies at dinner. Kids and cabin leaders alike ended up in tears. The whole thing was an emotional marathon, so it wasn't like my body wasn't tired when I finally leaned back against my pillow. My mind, on the other hand, felt fractured. My own feelings, Michele's words, and the faint sounds of an argument between Brennon and Xavier played on a loop in my head. But the soundtrack that overrode them all was the conversation I had with my father a few weeks back.

It was to those memories of hollow thrills, shouted drunkenly in my father's voice, that I eventually drifted into a shallow sleep.

The next morning came far too fast. August mornings were darker, and even when they arrived with the sun, it was a faded cool thing. Sleeping on top of my comforter meant that even my small cabin, normally warmed so easily by my body heat, was freezing. I swapped my jeans, which stunk of last night's bonfire, for a pair of tan Dickies that would make me seem pulled together when the parents started to roll in a few hours from now.

Breakfast was earlier than normal. It always was on this last morning, so kids had time to track down their lost and found, collect their medication from the nurses, and do any last-minute packing. It was a busy morning, but one wracked with a kind of heaviness. Sadness. That's how it used to feel, anyway. Throughout the dining hall, friends were hugging and so many tears were being shed. That used to be me. Five years ago, it had taken every bit of restraint I had to keep from sobbing my way through breakfast. Today, I just wanted a cup of coffee.

Three cups later, the meal was over. Without a cabin of my own or any programmes to prep, I had nowhere I needed to be. I thought about packing my own crap, but that could happen later today. Instead, I sat on the boys' steps outside the dining hall, throwing stones toward the oak trees lining the Centre Circle. Soon enough, I would have to stop because the coach buses would pull around the path, parking and opening their storage compartments for the duffel bags and suitcases belonging to the campers who lived too far away for their parents to come and pick them up. One bus would take kids to the airport and the other to downtown West Barrett. From there, they would stop being Agonde's problem and become their parents' responsibility once again. For now, though, they were still our–my–responsibility.

I left the steps twenty minutes later, eventually weary of being alone, and wound my way through the Boys' section. Cabin by cabin, I checked in on the campers and staff as they packed up and began to move their bags from their spots under bunk beds to the lawns and loading spots spread out across the property. Each bag left a ring of dust, the shadows of a summer spent outside, in their place. My progress was slow as I said a thousand goodbyes and gave hugs, back slaps, and handshakes to these boys I had seen every day for the last two and a half months. By the time I finally reached the last cabin, it was nearly eleven, and when I looked back down the pathways, there were handfuls of parents knocking on doors and calling their children's names.

The older boys played it cool. I still caught a couple of tears and hugs out of the corner of my eye, but I was out of there in less than ten minutes. I retraced my steps back down the cabin line, and though I threw a few waves and friendly smiles at parents and kids, no one stopped me. I was thankful, too, because all these sad partings and joyous greetings were grating on me. I managed to make it all the way to the nurses' station before running into a dad who finally stopped me for a chat. He had his arm thrown over his son's shoulder affectionately, and the kid, whose name I couldn't fully remember, but I think might be Ben, looked up at his dad like he was a hero. I was jealous of the way they stood beside each other. The father held his hand out toward me.

"Mr. Michaels, great season last year."

"Thank you, sir."

He slushed off my response. "And thanks for taking care of this one." He ran a palm through the kids' hair. "He had an amazing time this summer."

"I'm so glad, sir. It's been a great summer," I replied before turning to the kid and asking, "What was your favourite part?"

I instantly regretted it when he answered, "Swimming lessons! Toni taught me how to dive." I sucked in a breath at the sound of her name. Since she vanished, it had become practically taboo. Not that the kid noticed. He kept right on bragging. "She said I had the best dive she'd ever seen!"

His face fell a second later, though, and I caught him fiddling with the thin red string on his wrist. “Then she left. She promised to teach me how to dive without my lifejacket, but she never got the chance.” There’s nothing like a kid’s sad voice to kick you right in the heart. I didn’t want to, but my stomach churned with how upset the poor kid sounded, so I explained, more to the father than the kid, "Our Waterfront Director, Toni, had to leave unexpectedly. She had a family emergency.”

The father nodded with understanding and squeezed his son a bit tighter.

“Not to worry, kiddo, sounds like you’re almost there. How about we practise in the pool at home?”

The boy’s eyes lit up again, his disappointment from seconds ago completely forgotten as he nodded. I said goodbye and wished them a safe drive home, not that I was the one who moved. They turned away from me first and walked off together, chatting quietly. The dad, whose name I never caught, just listened as the kid proceeded to talk his ear off. I couldn’t hear a word with the jealousy ringing in my ears.

In all my years as a camper, no one ever came to pick me up. I was always a bus kid, riding the nearly ten hours back to West Barrett before Dad would begrudgingly collect me from the Barrett Fields Community Centre. But I was never alone. Toni was a bus kid, too, and every year, we had sat huddled together in the big coach seats, alternating between games and laughter. Around hour four, she would fall asleep. Her honey-brown hair and small head tipped against my shoulder. I would sit completely still, even against the rocks of the bus, so I wouldn't wake her up. That last summer, that last bus ride, I'd even wrapped my arm around her while she slept and thought about asking her to be my girlfriend when she woke up. But I chickened out, and then, well...

Thinking about that version of her clawed pits into my stomach and filled them in with memories from months ago, of her too-thin frame, of the names I called her, the things I did, and worst of all, the sound of my own angry voice, calling her names down the phone line to my overjoyed father who was all too happy to hear them. Names that my fifteen-year-old self, that bus kid with a crush on his best friend, would have fought me over.

CARL MICHAELS

2 weeks ago

When I first picked up the phone, my son's gruff voice caught me by surprise. That little shit never called me, not willingly, even though his old man had given everything and done everything to get him where he was. I shook my head to clear it of the five–no, seven–beers I'd enjoyed since strolling through my door tonight. No doubt I'd be having a few more after listening to whatever my pussy-ass son had to say.

"Old man."

"Well, if it isn't my ungrateful son."

He swore back at me, and I ignored it in favour of grabbing another can from the fridge, kicking the door shut behind me. My son had a history of temper tantrums. He definitely got that from his mother. God, that woman could bitch. Cutting him off before he really had a chance to get going, I groaned, "Does this call have a purpose, Cole? Your old man is busy."

"Busy getting wasted?"

"Listen here, you little cunt, I work fucking hard to make sure you have a shot at something, so you don't turn out as useless as your whore

mother." My mention of her shuts him right up. No backbone, that boy. So fucking soft it's a miracle I've managed to make him into the hockey player he is. He should be getting on his knees and thanking me for it. Instead, all I get is this bullshit.

"Shut up, Carl. I have something important to tell you," he snarled, the seriousness sobering me a bit, and I couldn't keep the relief in from my voice. "Finally. Who called? A scout? An agent?"

Either would have been great, and both would have been better, but what my son told me on that short phone call was beyond what I'd dared anticipate. He'd just gifted me my ticket out of the penalty box I'd been thrown in the second Frank Barrett realised my son had been pussy-whipped by his precious princess all those years ago. After the trial, rumours had flown about the Barrett girl. The Barrett children had disappeared from the public eye overnight, and it became a scandal. Rumours swirled that Frank had done something with them or that their mother had vanished. No official statement was ever made, and eventually, the media lost interest, but still, the gossip flew around all Frank Barrett's sites and offices. The children were ghosts, and Franklin would do anything, give anything, to get them back. That was until a few months ago, when the boy, Francis, suddenly reappeared at his father's side. Now, he was everywhere Frank went. He appeared in every photo, was at every building opening. The kid was front and centre in the news, but still, there was no sign of the girl. And behind the sealed doors of Barrett Holdings, everyone, from the front desk girls to the senior managers on the sixteenth floor, knew that Frank was still searching for his daughter.

Before I knew it, my freshly opened beer was forgotten on the table and my hand was dialling a number I had been too chickenshit to call for five years. It was nearly midnight, and I wasn't even sure he'd still be at the office, let alone pick up, but when the call connected, my pulse jumped as Franklin Barrett's voice rippled down the line.

"Carl Michaels. It's late. What the fuck is this about?"

I liked that about Frank. He might be a billionaire, and he might put on an act in public, but in business or behind closed doors, the man didn't fuck around.

"I know, sir, and I'm sorry to bother you, but I just got a very interesting call from my son..."

DANIEL ROTHBERG

2 weeks and 2 days ago

The doorbell buzzed. Then again, and again. I grit my teeth at the sound. I was trying to concentrate, penning this week's transactions into my ledger, and at yet another buzz, my fountain pen smudged. Fuck. This house was going to shit. I shoved back from my desk and ripped open my office door.

"Marissa!" I shouted down the long central hallway. No response except for the echo of my own voice off the white walls. Where the fuck was my useless wife?

"Girls!" I barked again, as I started to make my way toward the main entrance at the front of the house. While I walked, I grumbled. What the fuck was the point of all the women in this house or all the work I'd put into those girls if they couldn't show up when I called them? The ludicrous floral display Marissa had arranged in the foyer irritated me. It was ostentatious and absurd, so as I stomped past it to the front door, I swiped my arm across it, sending it clattering from the table to the marble floor. A satisfied grin spread across my face at the sound of shattering ceramic and pooling water. I supposed I should be grateful that pointless activities like decorating

our house kept my idiotic wife out of my hair, but that should never come at the expense of my own needs.

Then again, she did serve a purpose. Sometimes. Although, obviously, she was failing at her basic responsibility right now. I made another mental note to remind her of her duties later as I yanked on the wrought-iron doorknob, pasting on my customary smile. It dropped the second I recognized the pasty-faced moron waiting on my doorstep.

"Jack Walker."

"Daniel," he replied with a cursory nod. His face was tight, and it's only when the muscles in his right shoulder flex that I realise why. Standing elbow-high beside him is a perfect little blonde. Her large blue eyes are focused on Jack. She's watching him like he's trustworthy. If that were the case, he never would have brought her here. It had been five years since Jack last appeared at my door, and while I wasn't about to complain about the little prize he'd brought me, particularly in light of the failings of my current crop, I certainly had questions.

"Hello, sweetheart, who are you?" I asked.

Her eyes narrowed, uncertainty written on her young face. "I'm Holly. Who are you?" The question came out like a demand. Spoiled little thing. I'd soon fix that.

I ignored her question and asked, "How old are you, Holly?"

She curled her lips inward tightly, chewing on them before looking to Jack for confirmation.

He answered forcefully, "Tell the man, Holly."

"I'm nine."

Behind me, I finally heard the telltale shuffling of one of the girls. Glancing over my shoulder, I could immediately tell it was Elizabeth. Of course, it was Elizabeth. She was not quite Rachel. No one could be. Even at age eight, Rachel had been perfect. My magnum opus would never have disappointed me by being so late to my summons. But she's long gone, I think with a sigh.

Her replacement comes to stand perfectly behind me. Her head bowed to mine wordlessly, and my discontent dimmed. Quickly refocusing on my new arrivals, I flicked my eyes to the girl before staring back at Jack's nervous face. He was sweating in the West Coast sun, or maybe it was fear of my personal cameras, the ones he knew had been watching his every movement since his car pulled onto the property. My own form of insurance. He inclined his chin toward the girl just an inch.

I nodded back with a hum of approval before ordering, "Elizabeth, escort Holly upstairs."

On the quietest feet, she stepped forward and reached for the girl before asking softly, "To our room, sir?"

"No," I paused, considering both the girl and Jack again. "Not just yet. Please put her in bedroom three."

I didn't bother to mask my anger when Elizabeth let out the smallest frightened gasp in my direction. "Now," I commanded, and at the snap in my voice, she grabbed the girl, Holly, by the arm and dragged her inside.

Credit to the girl, she screamed, smart enough to recognize she was being separated from the only person here she knew. Or thought she knew. As Elizabeth hauled her away, both Jack and I listened silently as she shrieked his name over and over until they turned from yells to confused tears, and finally back to quiet once the two girls had retreated into the bowels of my house.

I turned on my heels and motioned for the other man to follow me. We headed to my office at the very rear of the house. Marissa greeted us at the door with a brittle smile.

"I'm so sorry, Daniel. I did not hear the doorbell," she bullshits, watching my reaction closely.

"It's fine, Marissa. We will discuss it after my associate leaves." I gestured to our guest and she practically jumped as she too recognised him. "Please wait for me downstairs." As she passed me, I whispered closely, "Bring the new girl in bedroom three. Your punishment will make for an excellent introduction," which sent her tiptoe-ing away from us as fast as she could.

We entered my office, and I directed Jack to sit while I returned to my recently vacated chair. Once seated, I planted my elbows on the desk and tipped my chin against my pointed fingers, staring back at this man I hadn't seen in so long.

"Why now? It's been five years."

"He said to call. The old number. He'll explain everything."

"Hmmm." I tap my fingers against my upper lip, considering this explanation. "Say I agree," I licked my lips. I had already decided, but he didn't need to know that yet. There was something satisfying about watching this little minion stew in his fear. "Can you confirm that the girl's untraceable?"

"Yes," he answered in a panic. "Moved from the camp to a hospital. I called her parents from the Emergency Room. Even took a picture and emailed it to them."

"A start. Not enough," I growled.

"There's more," he panted, desperate for my approval. It was very gratifying to watch him twist and squirm for me. "I registered her under a fake name, waited until the parents confirmed they were flying in, and I even made sure we were seen by a nurse!"

"Then you left and brought her straight here?"

"No, uh—" He shifted back his seat like he could get away from me somehow. "We drove to my house while I waited for the boss to call." My eyes burrowed into him and he stuttered, "Butt... but as soon... as soon as he did, we drove straight here. No stops. And I-I made her lie down in the back seat so traffic cameras wouldn't see her."

He'd done relatively well, considering he was out of practice. He'd nearly followed all the steps I had outlined for him oh-so-long ago. I reward him with an, "Excellent," before reaching to the concealed panel beneath my desk. I popped the seal and grabbed one of the many envelopes of cash I kept tucked away, before handing it over to him. He snatched the envelope and pocketed it greedily. While the trap door remained open, I also grabbed the old Nokia cell phone I kept hidden in there. The iPhone on my desk was mostly for appearances. It was the old brick I'm holding that was my real business phone, holding all my real business contacts. I left the phone in my lap. Jack didn't know it existed, and he didn't need to.

I pushed the door shut with my foot so it latched noiselessly before looking back to my renewed business associate. Now that he had his money, he seemed less terrified. He was watching me acutely, and it set my teeth on edge. I was ready to get him out of here and move on to a much more rewarding pastime.

I stood and slapped my palms against the desktop. The sound caught him by surprise and he jolted in his chair. Staring down at him, I pointed to the door behind him and coolly said, "While it's been a pleasure doing business with you again, Jack, I have an important phone call to make. I trust you can show yourself out?"

He rushed from the room. He always was a spineless little coward. His fear would carry him out of my house and into his car just in time for him to piss his cheap khakis on his way down my driveway. Good riddance. I listened to his fading footsteps. Satisfied when I heard the large doors slam behind him, I turned on the ancient phone still cradled on my thigh. Scrolling through the contacts, black against the yellowing screen, I landed on the number I was looking for and hit the call button.

The call connected and his familiar self-important voice answered without waiting for any type of greeting from me. "Daniel!" he exclaimed. "I trust you received my little gift?"

"I did. Thank you, Franklin." If I didn't at least feign gratitude, he'd become even more insufferable. "But it's been so long. What have I done to deserve this?"

He laughed, and it was jackal-like. "I'm shocked Jack didn't tell you! I'm so glad. It would have ruined the surprise."

"Franklin..."

"Well, old friend, four months ago, I planted a seed. And yesterday, it finally grew flowers. I got an interesting call from an employee, one Carl Michaels."

I snarled audibly, and again, he laughed "Oh, I see you remember. Yes, well, I don't much like the man or his ape of a son, either, but he was full of useful information."

"Go on."

"It seems our children have once again found themselves back at Camp Agonde."

I pulled the phone from my ear and opened my mouth in a silent scream. Fuck. I barely kept track of the boy's comings and goings these days, but clearly I should have been. My useless, soft, pussy of a son was more trouble than he was worth. If he weren't my only heir, I'd kill him myself. As it was, all I could do was try to stop Franklin Barrett from doing just that.

"Xavier is well aware of the rules. I assure you, Carl Michaels is wrong. My son would have told me if the girl was there."

"You're so sure of your son's loyalty?"

"No, I'm not that stupid. I'm sure of his weakness, and my son is too weak to lie to me."

"I suppose we'll find out," he answered simply. "But in the meantime, train the girl. I have a buyer lined up."

At the reminder of my new addition waiting for me upstairs, most of the pieces clicked together. All except one. So I asked the only question I had left, "Why now? After all this time?"

And in his typical grandiose fashion he answered, "Well, Daniel, I thought I'd take a page out of your book and teach my daughter a lesson."

Blue Grace
4 months ago

"Are you shitting me, Corbin?!" I howled into the phone. "That's all they're offering?! Tell them to go fuck themselves!"

"Blue, it's a good offer!" he attests meekly. "That's what Luxe Casino paid The Preaching Pistols for their residency."

Anger vibrated through me at our useless agent. "The Pistols are shit. That bitch lead singer couldn't catch a tune if it flew into her mouth. And the Luxe is a shithole. So, once again, Corbin, if you want to keep your job, you will tell them to GO. FUCK. THEMSELVES." And then I hung up. I needed a break. I hated being in this house. A good fuck would really take the edge off, but my only options here were either the help, appealing ten years ago but not so much anymore, or my aging cunt of a wife who's probably passed out upstairs, anyway. Come to think of it, that would mean I could fuck her pussy without having to listen to the sound of her voice. It was slightly appealing, but then I remembered the stash I had tucked away in the studio last time I was here. I hustled out of the kitchen and down the stairs to the basement.

It'd been months since I'd been in this room, but then again, my wife and son were too stupid to ever come down here, so I doubt it's been touched. Landing at the bottom of the stairs, I ignored the actual studio and headed straight to the mixing desk. Dropping my ass in the chair, I ran my hands along the bottom of the sound system until I felt several small bumps. Plastic baggies taped to the bottom and just waiting for me to enjoy. I peeled two of them away from the surface carefully. I'd leave the others for another time. I dropped one bag on the mixer and dumped the other onto the only flat edge, the one that runs along the glass separating this room from the actual studio. I used my pinky finger to shape the white powder into several smile lines and then I sucked the digit into my mouth, savouring the granular feel of the powder on my gums.

Just as I was about to lean in and snort the first line, my phone rang again. I accepted the call and cursed, "Fuck off, Corbin. I already told you. Now go do your goddamn job!"

A chilling voice replies, "It's been a long time since you told me anything, Blue Grace."

"Franklin?" My brain scrambled.

Fuck. Fuck. Fuck. What had I done that Franklin Barrett was calling me? It had been five years since I last heard from the prick. I scraped my memory and came up blank.

He laughed at my silence, and it was a cold and frightening sound.

"Hello, old friend." I was not his friend.

I doubted the man had any friends, but I wasn't about to tell him that, so I answered politely, "Nice to hear from you, Franklin. What can I do for you?"

"I'm looking to renew my charitable contributions for this year. I was thinking of a sizable donation to your wife's foundation for a start. I trust the account information remains the same?"

I swallowed around the lump of fear and shock in my throat. That question only meant one thing. But there was no saying 'no' to Franklin Barrett unless you wanted your life fucking ruined. And I'd rather my next fuck be some tight Vegas pussy and not my new prison roommate, so I gave him the answer he was looking for.

"Yes, sir."

"Excellent," he answered, sounding delighted. "Expect the money come September."

"Delilah will be thrilled. Thank you, Franklin, I had better go tell her—"

"Not so fast, Blue."

I should never have answered this fucking call. I could be eyeballs-deep into my high right now, and instead, this asshole was tugging on ancient puppet strings. I stared at the white lines of powder, barely listening to the demands he was issuing.

"I need you to do something for me. Nothing too taxing. I know you are a busy man," he sneered, condescending and demanding in equal measure. "I just need you to make a phone call..."

There was no choice, of course. Franklin had more than enough ammunition to destroy my slice of paradise. It might have been from years ago, but the evidence he was holding would still do the job. The press would have a fucking field day with what that bastard had on tape. So, I listened as he explained the shit he was about to land me in. The second he was done, he hung up without waiting for any kind of confirmation from me that I was willing to follow his orders. He didn't need it.

I slapped the phone down on the mixer and grabbed the bag of coke again. Fuck making neat lines. Instead, I just dumped it in a pile in front of me. Then, I pulled a bill from my wallet, rolled it into a tight funnel, and snorted as much as I could in one inhale. Once the pile was gone, I moved on to the lines until they were gone, too. What came next would be much more pleasant if I was flying high.

Five minutes later, the drugs were starting to kick in. When they did, I snatched my phone back up and dialled a number I hadn't called in a long time. It rang and rang and as it did, my high peaked. I felt unstoppable. Light. I was floating like a butterfly when someone answered, "Good afternoon, Camp Agonde head office, I'm Riley. How can I help you?"

I drawled, "Good afternoon, Riley. Can I speak to Jack Walker if he's available?"

Time to sting like a goddamned bee.

"Sure! I'll transfer you to his office line," the kid replied cheerfully and put me through.

When it connected, a familiar nasal voice answered, "Jack Walker here, how can I help you?"

"Someone told me you're in urgent need of a Waterfront Director."

"Blue?!" he startled at my statement. His voice shook down the phone line.

"Mmmhmmmm," I confirmed, enjoying the rumble of the sound on my tongue. My jaw twitched side to side as I shaped my next words. "And I've got just the candidate for you, Franklin Barrett approved and all."

"What the fuck?" he gasped.

"Haven't you heard?" I laughed. "We're getting the old gang back together."

"What. The. Fuck," he repeated. His panic felt familiar. I felt the same way, before the drugs, that is.

"The big man's finally sick of looking for his daughter. Wants you to lure her out of hiding, instead," I explained.

There was a beat where neither of us released so much as a breath before he snarled at me, "I have no fucking clue where Antoinette Barrett is!"

"He thought you might say that." I rolled my eyes, ready to be done with this conversation. "Find her, or else. His words, not mine. We're back in business until he gets his daughter back."

"Seriously, Blue. I have no fucking idea how to find that girl." His voice was unnaturally pitched. I could tell he was freaking out, and it was starting to ruin my buzz.

"I don't give a shit. I've done my part by calling your bitch ass. You do yours. You know what will happen if you don't." And maybe because it felt like payback, even though Jack wasn't Frank, I hung up on his weaselly ass ,same as Frank had done to me. Once I had, I swayed my way across the booth on unsteady feet. Words were

swimming across my mind and I needed to get them out. I flung open the studio door. Maybe I'd write some music for the first fucking time in ages. Maybe I'd pass out. Or maybe, I'd just take another bump to help me forget tonight ever happened.

Chapter Thirty-Six

Jack

It had been eight hours since the last kids were picked up by their parents. The thing about running a summer camp was that it could expose the best and worst of families. You learned to separate the faces of the mums who are exhausted and couldn't wait to get rid of their kids for two months from the ones who watched their children's happiness with a joy of their own. You drew invisible lines between the dads, like Carl, who bore down so hard on their boys that the kids looked relieved to leave them behind, and the ones who greeted their parents at pickup with a smile. We, these young adults and I, saw these children as they really were when none of the regular-life shit applied. And it could tell you a hell of a lot.

I stared out across the dining hall, lit up with twinkle lights and candles as it only ever was on this night. It was one of our camp traditions. Just as we'd closed out the summer for the kids this morning, we would do the same as a staff group tonight. True to the tradition, the most senior members of the staff team, including Cole, Brennon, and Xavier had been responsible for serving dinner to their peers as a thank you. The entire senior staff team had been a sombre bunch all day. My eyes followed them each in turn as they moved around the room. And against the backdrop of laughter and affection from the junior staff, their feelings stood in stark contrast. Cole looked like he hated himself. Brennon was as void of emotion as I'd ever seen him, and Xavier looked so determined I figured he might break a tooth. Not to mention the girls. Both Abbi and Michele weren't much better. This night was normally an emotional one, but they both looked close to tears even before the first plates hit the tables.

The meal carried on despite it, followed by a thank-you speech from me and a clustered mix of heartfelt and bullshit goodbyes. Then, one-by-one, the staff loaded themselves into their expensive cars and SUVs, the ones I could have only dreamt of at twenty, and drove away. My Seniors were among the last to leave, watching each other warily as they loaded up their cars. It was late, nearly one a.m. Other than the girls, who exchanged a tight hug, they didn't speak, and not one of them looked happy. I watched them go from the dining hall deck, waving them off with a smile on my face. It wasn't that I relished their misery. I knew Toni's departure weighed on each of them in different ways, just like it weighed on me. But there was no escape for any of us. We'd been saddled with burdens none of us deserved to carry, and yet here we all were.

One mistake and it'd ruin your life. That was what my JV Hockey coach had always said. Unfortunately, youth makes fools of us all, though, so of course, I hadn't listened. And, of course, he was right. My burden was one mistake, made twenty-five years ago, that landed me in front of Franklin Barrett, and I'd been paying for it ever since.

Four months ago, Blue Grace called and reminded me I was still a pawn in Franklin's fucked up games. The joke was on all those assholes, though. Frank, Blue, and Daniel, they all treated me like I was some nobody they could boss around, manipulate, and toss aside when they didn't need me anymore. I might not be into the same fucked up shit that they were, but I could still play the game. And their children would bear the weight of it. What they always seemed to forget was that I spent time, years even, with the children they'd been so quick to neglect, mistreat, and abuse. As kids, they'd come clambering to me for love and affection. And I'd given it to them. It was why they were all still here.

It's also why, back in May, it had taken me all of ten minutes to track down Toni's camper file. The one that contained her mum's old email address. One I prayed was still active. That brief email and a couple of days' patience had paid dividends. Sitting in my inbox was a sweet note from Diane Hillis, formerly Barrett, accompanied by Toni's cell number, and reminiscences about how much Agonde had meant to her young daughter. That lingering affection from her childhood was also, at least partially, the reason she said yes to my offer. I knew their own children better than they did. Five years ago, with the heat of the trial beating down on all of us, but particularly Frank, I'd finally felt like I could crawl out of his evil little spiderweb. Now I knew that had all been a bullshit fantasy. But I wanted out, and I would sell them all to the devil to get there. I didn't like it. I never had. But if it meant using their own kids, and others, like Holly, to make it happen, well, that was just the price of freedom.

Nick Patterson

5 years ago

When my dad hooked me up with an internship during the fall semester of my senior year at West Barrett U, little did I know it would be my ticket to everything I ever wanted.

Frank never told me when exactly he realised we had certain common interests. Working on the executive floor of Barrett Holdings meant I was in and out of his office pretty often, so maybe it was when he caught me holding the framed photo of his pre-teen princess. Or maybe I wasn't as careful with my browser history as I should have been during work hours. Whatever the reason, when Frank Barrett called me into his office on a Tuesday afternoon in March, I assumed I was fucked. Instead, he welcomed me in, and with a shimmer of something like delight in his eyes, introduced me to the other side of the Holdings business, the one that had nothing to do with real estate, and was infinitely more lucrative. And suited my tastes just fine.

"Nick, my boy," he'd said to me from the far side of his big-ass leather desk. "You strike me as someone willing to do what it takes to get what he wants."

From my seat in one of his equally antique club chairs, I quickly answered with a, "Yes, sir," making him smile slyly.

"Good, because I have an offer for you. A job with one of the most profitable arms of the business." He paused deliberately over the words. "And access to all our resources to indulge any of your particular interests." I smiled back at him, the thrill of his offer and all it implied causing tingles to shoot up my spine.

Encouraged by my obvious response, he pressed on, "All of that will be yours come September, provided—" and then came the catch, "Provided you can help me do two things."

"Whatever it is, Mr. Barrett, I'll do it," I supplied.

"Excellent. I never doubted you. What I need, well, you see, son, I need my daughter to disappear, and I need it to look like her mother is responsible."

Darting a quick look at the girl's photo again in its pride of place on the bookshelf to my left, I briefly lamented the loss of such a tasty distraction until he explained, "Oh, I don't mean to kill her." His gaze too had drifted to land on his daughter's image. "I just need to put her somewhere where I can make the best possible use of her."

I shrugged and replied, "Okay, so what do you need me to do?" The answer was what landed me here in the ass-end of nowhere at an elite sports camp for kids. The better part of the last four months had been a fucking misery. Every day, I had to pretend to be some friendly, sensitive, and helpful little shit. Except for the few times that Franklin's wife, Diane, turned up looking to visit her daughter. Then I got to play boytoy. I never let her close enough to see the girl. That wasn't part of Frank's plan. But I did tour her around, show her the inside of the girl's cabin, and my own, too. It put her mind at ease and painted exactly the picture Frank wanted it to. Not that I was interested in her used old body. I found the girls in the senior cabins, with their teasing bodies and their lack of confidence, much more appealing. At fourteen and fifteen, they took one look at my blonde hair and giggled. Unspoiled and eager to please was exactly how I liked them. And in particular, I liked Antoinette Barrett.

All summer long, I'd been priming her with winks and cheeky flirtations that made her blush beautifully. The little bitch wanted me, that much was for sure. The only problem had been getting her away from that fucking fan club of hers. Those three boys were always around. Not today, though.

This afternoon, I'd be fulfilling the second half of my deal with Frank. And if I sampled the merchandise first, well, I considered it part of my payment for a job well done. Hell, the girl was so in love with me she was probably going to beg for it. Yesterday, I held her back after a sailing lesson. Once all the other campers and staff were gone, I'd leaned in and teased her with an almost-kiss before dropping her like a used tissue. And now that she'd had a day to stew on it, she was going to be desperate to redeem herself, to give me what I planned on taking. They always are.

Seated on one of the ropes course installations, a little hammock-like thing, I waited in the otherwise empty adventure park for her to show. When I heard the telltale crunch of feet through the underbrush, I turned to face the direction of the noise and was rewarded for my efforts with a self-conscious blush on Antoinette Barrett's cheeks. Girls my age were such sluts. Whereas Antoinette was all innocence, which was why her crossed arms and shifting eyes didn't faze me. I patted the empty space beside me and she slowly sank into the rope netting, leaving some space between us.

If this was going to work, I needed to put her at ease. It would be better that way. I checked my watch and registered that I had just over thirty minutes for my own fun before Frank's driver, Mikhael, showed up and hauled the girl away. I'd be getting the fuck outta dodge immediately after that. Both of us would be gone long before anyone knew it. From there, Frank promised to make me disappear, to move me overseas to work with his international interests. Thirty minutes was plenty of time, I thought, as I donned my most sheepish smile and mumbled, "Thanks for meeting me, Toni. I... uh..." My meek voice and stuttered words seemed to ease her tension some. I felt the hammock give a little behind me as she eased her back into it.

"I wanted to apologise about yesterday," I said, reaching one arm out to wrap it around her shoulder. Holding her gently, I began to trace my fingertips up her slim arm. The touch of her skin, so soft, nearly made me lose control. But her shoulders stiffened at the connection, so again, I turned back to my shy act. "You, um, you just make me so nervous." Rather than helping, my words just set her hopping to her feet.

"Nick," she practically whispered. "I'm not... um... I don't think I should have come."

"No!" I burst out, causing her to jump in place.

"No, of course, you should have come," I continued more calmly, standing and walking toward her slowly so as not to spook her any further.

"N-n-no, I- I-I don't think I should," her voice wavered as she backed away at the same moment that I reached for her. If she wasn't going to make this easy, I was done wasting my precious time. I would take what I wanted, whether it was offered or not. There was no one to stop me so I yanked on her arm, but as I caught the limb, my sneaker caught on a fucking root and I tripped, sending my body toppling over hers.

Landing in the dirt with Antoinette Barrett pinned beneath me was exactly where I'd wanted to be, anyway. Her heartbeat pounded against my hand as I ran my palm up and over her small breasts. The only pain in the ass was her refusal to submit. The bitch wouldn't stop struggling. Her long legs kicked out continuously at me, and at her sides, her arms grappled unsuccessfully for any kind of purchase on the forest floor. She even rammed her head forward at me. Thank fuck, I managed to turn just in time to avoid getting my nose caved in. Instead, her forehead connected with my jaw, making me bite down painfully on my tongue.

I gripped her hard, lifting her torso and slamming it back to earth quickly. I tasted copper in my mouth. My left hand moved to her throat, squeezing until I felt her windpipe secure against my palm. Her pulse bounced in her neck as I grunted, "Stop struggling," before spitting a mouthful of my blood onto her face. Meanwhile, my other hand skated from her chest down to her shorts. "This could have been so much nicer if you hadn't fucking ruined it!" I shouted. She kicked even harder and screamed when I popped the button open. I clapped my hand from her neck over her mouth, shoving her head down and silencing her, or mostly, in one quick movement.

"Shut up!" I fumed, before taking a second to pin her and catch my breath. While I licked more blood from my lips, I looked down to where her cotton underwear was now exposed and my dick instantly got hard. I felt a rush of blood and adrenaline. Maybe it would be more fun this way. I smiled as her eyes shot to my crotch. She must have felt my reaction, but seeing it made her eyes wide and frightened. I smiled as I leaned forward over her. My mouth was just inches from her sweat-dampened skin, and I could smell dirt and blood on her. Soon I would taste it. Against her flesh, I explained, even as her whole body trembled, "See, I would have given you something nice to remember before sending you back to him." Underneath me, she froze. She was giving in.

"Now, I'll have to send you back to your father looking like a fucking mess. But I'm sure he won't mind, will he, princess?"

Those were my last real words as that little bitch bit down on my hand at the same time as something hard crashed into the side of my skull. My vision blurred. But I didn't have enough time to recover before there was another crack, another hit, and another. So many, so fast, I lost count. I found it hard to speak. After a few minutes, I was only vaguely aware as I was shunted sideways before yet another hit. More and more rained down on me until I couldn't move at all. My hands and legs felt far away. I wanted to move, but couldn't get any reaction from my body, so I just lay there. Soon, the cold set in. My back was damp from the ground and my head was foggy. My last memory was of looking up into the face of a dead-eyed girl and the sound of one final thud before my eyes closed for good.

Acknowledgements

To Adam, for your patience and support always.

To my family and friends, for being supportive and asking the right questions, even when I didn't have any answers.

To Sarah at Tormented Author Services, a giant thank you. You were the first person other than me to read this book, and I've never been so scared to hit send on an email. But your gracious help developing and nurturing this story were beyond what I expected.

To Sarah and the Indie Editorial team, yet another giant thank you, for your patience and expertise in editing and turning my story into a finished work. I am eternally grateful.

About the Author

LA Robbins is Canadian-born but lives in Scotland and her books are the love-child of both places she calls home. A lifelong bookworm, reading everything from Shakespeare to fan fiction (some of which is just as good!), she now writes dark romances in her home office surrounded by her husband, two cats who couldn't care less and a dog who'd really prefer if she stopped writing so much and focused on going for walks instead.

For business enquiries: l.robbinsauthor@gmail.com

To stay up to date with LA's goings on:
Instagram: @larobbinswrites
Threads: @larobbinswrites
TikTok: @larobbins

Printed in Great Britain
by Amazon

58996475R00270